# Books by K.D. Grace

*Single Titles*

The Tutor

The Tutor

ISBN # 978-1-78686-058-3

©Copyright K.D. Grace 2016

Cover Art by Posh Gosh ©Copyright 2016

Interior text design by Claire Siemaszkiewicz

Totally Bound Publishing

Published in 2016 by Totally Bound Publishing, Newland House, The Point, Weaver Road, Lincoln, LN6 3QN, United Kingdom.

# THE TUTOR

K.D. GRACE

# Dedication

This novel is dedicated to Kevin and Victoria Blisse and Kay Jaybee, who were my inspiration for The Tutor — that and a can of pears in heavy syrup. You three are the best.

# Chapter One

"Get out! Get the hell out now! Dillon! Dillon, get this bloody woman out of here!" Lex managed to keep his knees locked and his feet under him until the blasted model, robe slung hurriedly around her, clothes and bag bundled in her arms, was out the door and out of his sight. Then he collapsed in a heap, the floor coming up to meet him with a breath-jarring thud—not that he could breathe anyway, not at the moment at least. The room spun around him like a tilt-a-whirl at an amusement park, and his skin slickened with cold sweat. He knew the fucking drill by now, but it never got any easier and never got any better, not even when he was expecting it, and he sure as hell hadn't been expecting it this time. As he fought back nausea and vertigo and several other little unpleasantries his doctor had slapped labels on so long ago that he couldn't recall their names, he heard his PA passing the horrid model, who was now blubbering as though *she* were the injured party, off to V. Officially, V may have been just the housekeeper, but he and Dillon had long contended she was an alien sent from her distant planet to study Earth and see if there was intelligent life. The Valentine House, they joked, was probably not the ideal place to succeed in her mission. Still, the woman had persevered. They figured it was only because of her alien intellect and a sense of humor that allowed her to handle all the insanity with grace and aplomb.

Which was way more than he could manage at the moment, lying with his cheek plastered against the cool slate tiles of his studio, listening to the rush of footsteps and the woman's nearly hysterical sobs as V—her name was

Vida, but they'd always called her V, calmly led her away to someplace where she could change, have something warm to drink and maybe a bit of whatever Cookie had baked that day. After that, she'd be paid well for her traumatic efforts, politely reminded of the non-disclosure agreement she had signed before she came to model for Lex, and sent on her way. She would not be back.

Another treacherous tilting of the floor and a quick spin of the room had Lex praying to the gods of equilibrium and dignity that he could at least manage to keep his breakfast down. Though dignity was already well gone, he thought. Cautiously, he half opened one eye, and got a quick glimpse of a well-polished pair of loafers before he slammed it shut again and decided there was wisdom in holding his fetal position on the studio floor for just a little bit longer. After all, Dillon had seen him in far worse situations.

"You gonna be all right?" Dillon asked softly.

Lex made some non-committal sound at the back of his throat — about all he could manage at the moment. He heard the brisk *clip, clip* of Dillon's loafers across the slate, then the sound of running water and the footfalls of his return, and when Lex could smell the spicy dark scent of his PA's soap, he risked reaching out for the glass of water he knew the man had set down next to him.

"Anything else?" Dillon asked. "Do you need to throw up?"

"No. I'll be fine," he said, easing himself ever so carefully into a sitting position, still holding onto the floor with one hand and keeping one eye shut. He took a cautious sip of water. "She touched me," he managed after he felt confident the water would stay down.

"I gathered," Dillon said, settling on the floor next to him.

"She came up behind me while I was finishing the sketch. Honestly, I thought she was gone. She was supposed to be gone. Then she — Jesus, Dillon, the next thing I know, she's all over me, and she was cold, so fucking cold." For a second he thought he might change his mind about throwing up after all as, with a hard shudder, he recalled the chill of the woman's bare flesh against him. "And I couldn't get away from her. I couldn't get her to leave me alone, and she was cold, she was just so cold."

"Fuck, bro! I'm so damn sorry," Dillon said. "I was just outside in the hallway. It all happened so fast." The studio door was always kept open and, when Lex worked with a model, someone was always close by. But there had never been an incident before, so protocol had gotten lax.

"I mean what the hell? I swear I didn't do anything to make her think… I mean, I wouldn't. You know I wouldn't."

"I know that, man. I know that. Besides, she knew the rules. They all know the rules before they work with you." He stood and looked around the room until he found the blanket Lex kept handy for models to wrap up in between sketches and on breaks, then laid it on the floor next to him and plopped back down. Lex pulled it around him with a shiver. Even in early summer, the studio was fairly cool and models were warned ahead of time that Lex preferred to work in an unheated space. "There's just something about a vulnerable man that sort of gets the female of the species right here." Dillon tapped his palm against his chest. "Makes 'em want to get all nurturing and rescue-y, you know?"

"I don't look vulnerable. Do I look vulnerable to you? And I don't need nurtured or rescued."

"Trust me," Dillon said, "you don't have to be vulnerable for them to see you that way. And let's face it, there you stand, the long-suffering artist with that mussed hair and just the right amount of stubble, like maybe you just got out of bed, and they start thinking maybe it should be them you just got out of bed with. Hell, bro, I'd be after you myself if I wasn't your best friend." He shrugged. "And if you were a little more versatile in your preferences."

"Too damn bad I'm not, pal. It would sure make my life a whole lot easier."

"Oh, I doubt it," Dillon said with a shake of his head. The

smile on his face darkened. "I seriously doubt it."

Dillon knew about complications in relationships. He knew way more than he ever told, Lex was sure. But at least Dillon could have a relationship.

"Is he all right?" There was a clatter of dishes and silver and V blew into the room with a tray loaded down like it was mealtime. "He didn't throw up, did he?" The two of them always talked about him as though he were their seriously ill patient who had lost all cognitive skills.

"No, he didn't throw up." Lex managed a fair imitation of her voice that earned him a jaundiced look, but nothing else. If he didn't throw up, V fed him. If he did, she waited an hour then fed him. He grudgingly admitted that Dillon and V together knew exactly what he needed and they didn't let him intimidate them out of it.

"Well then, he needs something warming to ground him. Cookie's potato leek soup and a nice cup of chamomile tea is just the ticket," she said, plopping down on the floor next to the two of them.

To his astonishment, she managed not to spill either soup or tea in the process. Once seated, she efficiently poured tea as though they were at the dining room table rather than plunked down on the studio floor discussing his unexpected close encounter with said floor and what should now be done about it.

"I'm not hungry." But he grudgingly spooned up some soup and swallowed it back just to make her leave him alone. He had to admit it tasted pretty damn good, so he had another bite while they went right on talking about him as though he weren't there.

"Well, I can certainly understand why the poor woman thought he needed a little cuddling," V said. "Look at how pale he is. He's the epitome of the suffering artist." She eyeballed the soup then him with a gesture that needed no words, so he shoveled in more soup. "But I really thought Ms. Philips was a keeper. I thought she understood the ground rules and would abide by them. Poor dear was ever so upset when I left her with Cookie. I'm sure she'll never do it again."

"She won't because she won't get the chance," Lex said, this time dropping the spoon back onto the tray with a loud clatter. "I can't run that risk." Besides, he didn't want to try to sketch someone who had seen him so vulnerable, who had seen him…not at his best.

Dillon helped himself to one of the homemade Parmesan bread sticks and spoke around a mouthful. "I'll start looking for someone else. We always get résumés. Most models would kill for an opportunity to work for him." There they went again, speaking around him.

"Don't the two of you have things to do?" he said.

"Not till you finish your soup and drink some of that tea too. It'll help calm you," V replied.

He was their boss. He could force the issue, but they both knew he wouldn't, and he knew that whatever it was they had to do would get done and then some.

"I'll make sure he finishes, V, darling. Why don't you go get on with the accounts? I know you're up to your eyes in it at the moment."

"Well, if you're sure." She shoved her way to her feet with a cracking of joints heartily protesting time spent on the hard floor. "Make sure he doesn't get up until he's ready. And make sure he drinks that tea," she called over her shoulder as she headed for the door. At the last second, she turned and gave him one more look-over, just in case they'd missed something, just in case this time was different than all the other times they'd sat with him until he could function again. Something *was* different, but he wasn't about to tell V that.

When they were both sure that the housekeeper was gone, Dillon turned his eagle eye on Lex. "Well?"

Lex did his best to focus on the last of the soup, but Dillon had been his best friend for years, long before he was his PA, and he didn't miss much.

"You had a naked model with a very nice, very natural

rack rubbing up against your back before you went ballistic on her then hit the floor."

"You're seriously asking me if I got a hard-on from this whole experience?"

"Well, not the whole experience, obviously, but didn't you, you know, feel something before you felt what you usually feel?"

"Not long enough for it to cancel out the old reliable, if that's what you were hoping," Lex said, downing the now tepid tea in a single gulp. He fought back a blush. "Besides, these days it wouldn't matter if I were doing the accounts for V, I'd still be…uncomfortable. It's ridiculous," he said. "If I don't figure out what the fuck my problem is, and soon, I'm going to have repetitive stress syndrome." He flexed the fingers of his right hand. "Can't be all that great for my work either."

Dillon shot a glance back at the door on the outside chance that V might be eavesdropping, which the woman wasn't above doing. Then he scooted a little closer, careful not to make any physical contact, and spoke between barely parted lips. "I might have an idea."

"You might?" Lex shooed the man away from the last breadstick with a snap of the napkin against his wrist, then grabbed it and chomped one end.

"Give me a little time to research it and I'll get back to you," he said, rubbing his wrist as if Lex had actually wounded him. Then he rose to his feet and left him to eat the last of his breadstick in peace.

He knew how Dillon was when he had an idea. He was never sure whether to be excited or terrified. He forced his way to his feet and turned his attention back to the half-finished sketch of Sally Philips now lying on the floor next to the overturned easel among a scatter of other sketches. He had given the whole thing a shove when she'd trapped him between the easel and her half-naked body. Even as he shivered at the thought of her cold touch, he felt a tightening in his jeans.

"Fuck," he whispered under his breath. He wadded the drawing into a ball and tossed it across the room. Truth was, he'd had a hard-on the whole time he was sketching her, but that was often a part of the creative process. He'd read enough to know that creative energy was very closely linked to sexual energy and libido, but under the circumstances, he had very little outlet but a good jerk-off session. Surely Ms. Philips hadn't noticed his chub. He never wore anything that might give away his secret when he was working with a model. Surely she hadn't thought that he was interested. He wasn't. Even if she had been his type, he had given up hopes of anything resembling a relationship or even a quickie with a stranger in an alley a long time ago. He righted the easel and picked up the sketches, organizing them and placing them back in the pad, careful to extract the ones he'd done of Sally Philips. A setback, indeed. They were nearly done. Only a few more sketches and he'd have been ready to begin work on the sculpture for the new women's and children's hospital, but he knew he'd never be able to see sketches of her now without breaking into a cold sweat and feeling slightly nauseated, neither of which was conducive to creative efforts.

# Chapter Two

"*Attention! Kelly Blake, please report to the stockroom. Kelly Blake, report to the stockroom, please.*"

Why the hell would anyone be calling Kelly to the stockroom in Eddie's Supermarket? She hardly ever shopped here. She'd only stopped in to pick up a can of pears in heavy syrup for her friend, Myrna, who was planning some silly treat for her kids from a recipe she'd found in the back of some women's magazine. Myrna was the queen of women's magazines. She read them all and tried everything in them. Most of the time the result was a disaster, but how much harm could she do with a can of pears?

"*Kelly Blake, please report to the stockroom. Kelly Blake, to the stock room, please.*"

She resisted the urge to shout at the speaker that she was coming already. She'd never been called over the loud speaker for anything before, and she blushed hard, hunched her shoulders and hurried through the cereal aisle toward the back. As her name was called yet again, she couldn't help feeling like she was a kid being called to the principal's office for some secret crime — so secret, in fact, that she had no idea what it might be.

The voice sounded oddly familiar, slightly nervous. Well, loud speakers would do that to a person, she supposed. Though it was such an anonymous thing, still having your voice booming out there for the whole world to hear might be almost as intimidating as being the one summoned. Clutching her tin of pears to her chest, Kelly made her way to the back, intrigued by the prospect of seeing just what really was behind the swinging double doors with their metallic sheen and their round windows that made her think of submarines or space ships. Still, the loudspeaker referred to it as the stockroom. That wasn't very glamorous, was it? But then again, who knew what might go on between the rows and rows of canned goods and soft drinks? A murder? Perhaps a clandestine rendezvous? Perhaps it was a time portal, and she was about to step back into the Middle Ages. Maybe it was a wormhole and she'd end up in another dimension or on another planet, or perhaps she'd parked the Subaru in a no-parking zone and the supermarket police were waiting to punish her according to her crime. As she cautiously shoved her way through the double doors, and found herself in a maze of laundry detergent boxes, canned dog food and wooden pallets piled high with shrink-wrapped paper towels, toilet paper and napkins, the one thing she had not expected to find beyond the open back door, where the smokers were all banished when they lit up, was Andy Matthews. He stood shifting nervously from foot to foot under a battered green awning that protected the smokers from sun and rain alike. Andy didn't smoke. Hell, she knew for a fact Andy was just barely old enough to drink legally.

When he looked up and saw her, he reminded her of a frightened rabbit about to make a run for it. In spite of his ripe old age of twenty-one, startled as he was, he could have passed for fifteen, standing there with his face redder than the Eddie's smock he wore, which was at least two sizes too big for him.

"Andy? What's going on? Is everything all right?" she asked.

"I know what you do," he blurted without so much as a greeting. For a moment, she was afraid he was going to hyperventilate. "I mean, besides writing romance. I figured it out," he said, his voice cracking on the last word.

"Oh?" She leaned against the doorframe, wondering whether to murder him and drag the body back into the maze of merchandise, or to turn him over her knee and spank his skinny ass.

"Oh, it's not blackmail or anything," he said, shaking his head so hard that his neck popped. "It's just that..." He bit his lip, and, for a moment, she was afraid he might cry, but that was just the way the shadows fell across his jaw. "Well, I need your help — with a girl."

"I figured it wasn't a guy. Though I have no problem one way or the other," she said, stepping outside onto the cement slab. It startled poor Andy so much that he backed up tight against the metal railing. Perhaps he did think she would do him bodily harm. "What I do have a problem with is being paged over the loudspeaker to come to the back of Eddie's Supermarket. Most of my clients make an appointment with my secretary and she sends them an invoice."

He shook his head. "Oh, I couldn't do that. I..." The blush that had never quite left his cheeks flashed with a vengeance. "An invoice?" His voice cracked again. She knew he was paying for his own education and working several jobs to do it.

"What exactly do you need, Andy?" she asked, glancing down at her watch. She had another client clear across town in two hours. This was supposed to be just a pop-in, pop-out stop.

"There's this girl. I really like her. A lot." He stepped away from the railing, as if speaking of her made him suddenly lose his fear in his enthusiasm for love. "We've had six dates and I want to...you know...but I never have before and I want to know...you know?" The poor guy was going to self-combust if he got any redder. He seemed to have suddenly lost the power of speech. He sputtered twice, gave a couple of fish gasps then nodded, unable to meet her gaze.

"You want to know how to please a girl, and you expect me to give you the lecture and the hand-outs on your fifteen-minute break out behind Eddie's Supermarket, assuming, of course, that no one else decides to take a break and have a smoke."

"They won't," he said breathlessly. He shot a look over Kelly's shoulder back into the bowels of the stockroom, just in case. "I always time my break so I can have the place to myself."

Kelly couldn't help it, with the topic being what it was, she gave his crotch a surreptitious glance, and he reddened still further and tugged his baggy smock down over the telltale areas. "Not for that!" he said. "I… I like to read, and I don't like to have to breathe other people's smoke while I do it."

"Fair enough." Kelly did her own little glance back into the stockroom, then took pity on the guy. God, she was such a sucker. "What have you done so far on those dates?"

Damn! She had hoped that the fact that she'd agreed to help would ease the poor kid's discomfort, but his face went from red to purple and he was suddenly gasping for words. "I, that is we, we, we, we, we kissed. With tongue. She liked that okay. We both did. We liked it a lot." The color in his cheeks softened and the distant look in his eyes told Kelly that he was remembering just how much they had liked it. "And I touched her…" He nodded to Kelly's chest.

"Clothed or skin to skin?" Kelly wondered if the poor guy had asthma as he struggled to breathe.

"Clothed."

"Anything below the waist?"

"I, I, I, I touched her…down there. But only through her jeans." He dropped his gaze and shifted from foot to foot.

"Did she like it?"

If the poor kid could have managed it, Kelly was pretty convinced he'd have disappeared through the ground. "She put my hand down there, then she touched…" He nodded down to where his fist still held the wadded front of the Eddie's smock protectively in front of his crotch.

"Sounds like you were on the right path. Then what happened?"

When he didn't answer, Kelly shoved a hand against her hip and swallowed back the impatient curse just waiting to darken the air between them. "Look, do you want my help or not? Because I have other clients who do."

The realization that she was going to help him lit his face like neon and he dropped his hands to his side, squared his shoulders and met her gaze. "I told her I didn't want to rush. I told her I wanted it to be really good for both of us when we finally did it, then, well, I ran like a scared kid." He shrugged, once again unable to meet her gaze. "I figured she'd never talk to me again. I figured it was over, but then I got this." He shoved his iPhone at Kelly with a text from 'Jenny' that read —

*Last night was the best thing that's ever happened to me. It will be good, Andy. So, so good! Free tomorrow night?*

"That was last night," he managed as she returned his phone. "I have six hours."

"All right." Kelly couldn't help it. She loved a good challenge. She looked down at the can of pears. "I need a can opener and a roll of paper towels, or maybe some wet wipes. This is going to get messy."

He disappeared like a shot into the stockroom and returned way faster than Kelly would have thought possible with all three. On the plastic garden table, she wiped a clean spot with a paper towel, then opened the can of pears. He watched wide-eyed. "Pull up a chair next to mine. As close as you can get." With some effort, she pulled one slippery pear half out of the can and laid it on a wad of paper towels with the open side up, making sure there was just enough of the heavy syrup coating it that it was slick down through the middle. She figured, by that point, the guy would see where she was going with this little exercise, but he only stared at her blankly.

"Have you ever seen a woman's — ?"

"No! Not a real one, I mean only in porn." He shot her

crotch a quick glance, then his face lost all color. For a second, she feared he'd pass out completely.

"Oh, don't worry, I'm not showing you mine, if that's what you're afraid of."

"Oh, I'm sure yours is nice, really cool and all, but Jenny —"

"Jenny's is the one you want to see, and touch. And kiss. I get it." Carefully, she picked up the pear on its cushion of paper towel and, holding it palm up in her left hand, began to stroke the hollow of it with the middle and index finger of her right and, if it were possible, the kid's eyes got even bigger. The way he shifted in the plastic garden chair told her he got it at last. "This is cooler than she'll be when you touch her and not quite as soft and giving as she'll be when you open her with your two fingers. That'll be a little different too. She may be already open and ready for you. If not, you'll have to gently finger your way in between the folds of her flesh to the soft, warm center, and you'll be surprised at just how warm she is." She rubbed her fingers together, now coated generously with the heavy syrup, and he drew a tight breath. "She'll feel less syrupy, more creamy. And when you feel her, when you feel how warm and creamy she is, believe me, you'll want to taste her, just as she'll want to taste you. The taste of a lover, and the scent... Well, put the two together and there's nothing in the world more delicious, more magical. You try it."

She held the pear half palm up, at about the level of a woman's crotch, about in the place she would imagine Andy's Jenny to be if he were kissing and fondling her, then Kelly reached across him and pulled his hand down to the waiting pear half.

"Don't be nervous. Relax. Have fun with it. You're both new to each other and being a little awkward is part of the pleasure of the first time together. Laugh about it, enjoy it, ask her to tell you if you're not sure what she likes. How can you know if she doesn't say? Lovers, good lovers, talk to each other. They're lovers, not mind readers. Now. You touch the pear, like it's Jenny, talk to me, like I'm her. That's it, start from the bottom just like you're opening her folds. That's it, that's good. You might be kissing her, caressing her breasts, she might be stroking your erection. It's okay for you to tell her what you like too, you know? What woman doesn't want to pleasure her man? Or you might want to look at each other's body. The body of your lover is a feast for your eyes."

Andy got the hang of it quickly enough, but it rapidly became clear to Kelly that his imagination was about to get the best of him. "Is that your Coke?" she asked, motioning to the can on the table.

He managed a nod.

"Good. Take a deep breath, take a drink, then take another deep breath. Big lesson, Andy. This is not a foot race. Jenny won't thank you for hurrying things up, unless it's a quickie, then that's another lesson for another time. This is getting to know you, sex. This is discovering your lover's responses to sex. It's not meant to be hurried. Now, give me your hand." She guided it back into the pear and drizzled a bit of juice over his fingers. "Trust me, you want it wet and slick. Now, if the pear were a woman, there would be a little pearl-like node right about…there."

"Her clitoris," he whispered in awe.

"That's right. Wait just a second." Kelly wiped her sticky fingers and fumbled in her purse, until she found the box of Tic Tac Candy. In her awkward effort to shake one free and still hold the pear-half in position, she shook half of them out on the ground before she managed to get one between thumb and forefinger and push it into the soft flesh of the pear-half right at its apex. "Not quite anatomically correct, but closer. Now, use your thumb right there." She guided him to the protruding end of the Tic Tac. He made a little sound at the back of his throat at the contact and began to circle it with his thumb. "Good, that's good."

Suddenly Andy was rocking in his chair. "Jenny," he whispered, as though Kelly were no longer there. "Show me what you like. Show me what you want."

Kelly's pulse accelerated to a gallop as she guided Andy, shifting his thumb just slightly to one side. "Sometimes direct contact is too intense," she instructed.

"What about tongue?" He sounded like he'd been running hard rather than fondling a damn pear-half.

"Never known a woman who didn't like a little tongue on her Tic Tac."

The words were barely out of her mouth before he grabbed her by the wrist and brought hand paper towels, and pear — complete with its Tic Tac clitoris — to his mouth, licking from the bottom end of the pear up through the center and circling the mint before settling his lips around it in a juicy suck and lick of a kiss.

"That's right. That's it. You got it."

"Do you like that, Jenny? Is it good?" he whispered against the pear's slippery opening.

And damn if Kelly wasn't shifting in her seat. Most of the time she talked people through their doubts and problems, most of the time it was more theory and communication than anything else when she tutored people. But this! Well, sometimes object lessons were the best.

In fact, sometimes they might be just a little bit too good. Andy gave a soft grunt and shuddered in his seat, and her phone pinged a message warning her if she were going to make it to her session with the Hammersmiths on time, she needed to leave now.

"Gotta go," she said. "Good luck with Jenny. It'll be fine. You'll see. Oh, and keep the pears." She fled back through the stockroom and left Eddie's Supermarket without any pears in heavy syrup for Myrna's women's mag treat.

# Chapter Three

"Please tell me you haven't been standing there long." Lex sat on the ground, leaning against the trunk of a large oak, his focus on a sculpture of man and a woman in the throes of passion, a tangle of arms and legs, mouths open in their ecstatic moment of release. Contemplating the statue and what he had been fantasizing when he'd created it had led him to his own release, though he hadn't needed much help.

"I saw nothing, and even if I had, I wouldn't tell you. I just assumed you'd be out here. V said you were in the Other Studio, and when you weren't there, I figured you'd be here." The Other Studio was what they had always called the barn at the edge of his private sculpture garden where he worked on nothing but erotic pieces. They were never intended for anyone else's eyes. The art world that so admired his work had no idea that there was another facet to Alexander Valentine's creativity. Masturbation in stone — that was what it was, he supposed — but it did help to create in marble what he knew he couldn't have in the flesh.

"You all right?" Dillon asked.

He nodded, lifting his face to the late afternoon sun. "I'm better now, at least for a little while."

"V said you were down here last night. She figured you must have been dreaming." He came and sat across from Lex, leaning his back against the plinth of the sculpture.

Lex grunted. "The woman has to be an alien. I can't fart without her knowing it and telling you the details."

Dillon nodded. "I'm guessing in the early days I was

abducted and equipped with a device that relays all relevant information about Alexander Valentine's digestive history to the mother ship."

"No doubt by means of an anal probe," Lex commented.

"Those are the best kind."

"You would know, I suppose. Now is there a reason you disturbed me in my masturbatory solitude, or are you just a pervert?"

"Well, I'm not just a pervert," Dillon replied with a little tilt of his head as though he might have had to think about it for a second. "But there is a reason why I sought you out in your pleasure garden. I have two models I think are worth calling in for interviews. Do you want to meet with them or do you trust V and me with their interrogation?"

"Why don't you two do it? I was the one who picked out Sally Philips after what I thought was a very thorough interrogation and you see where that got me."

"Consider it done, bro."

"So? Why are you still here, then? You're disturbing my handiwork."

"Well"—the man stretched long legs out in front of him and folded his arms across his chest—"I actually came out here because of your handiwork."

"You really are a pervert."

Dillon only shrugged and offered a wicked smile. "Nothing slow about you, bro."

"What then?"

He folded his legs under him Indian style and scooted forward. "You remember when I told you I'd do a little research to see if I could maybe find you some help as a preventative for repetitive stress syndrome?"

"Hard to forget," Lex said.

"You know my cousin, Andy?"

"What about him?" Lex had met the kid a couple of times. He knew that he was studying chemistry in Portland State at the moment, putting himself through the program with the aid of a couple scholarships and several part-time jobs.

Lex had offered to help, but the man had wanted to do it himself. He respected that a lot.

"He knows this woman who's a tutor."

"A tutor? What, you mean like for chemistry?"

Dillon chuckled and cocked an eyebrow. "Well, I suppose you might be able to look at it that way, sort of, if you had a good imagination, but no. She's a sex tutor."

"Oh, for fuck's sake." Lex shoved his way to his feet and headed back toward the house. "I don't think a cock doc can help me."

"No, wait," Dillon scrambled to join him. "Hear me out." He caught up and fell into step next to Lex. "It's not like you think. This woman's policy is perfect for you. Apparently when she sees a client, it's strictly no touch."

"No touch? Seriously?"

Dillon nodded and continued. "She doesn't touch anyone and they don't touch her. She arrives clothed, remains clothed and leaves clothed, completely untouched. She doesn't play with her clients, if you know what I mean. She advises and coaches. Very strictly hands off. Andy says the hands-off policy is the woman's number one rule. The way she sees it, people's sex issues won't be solved by her feeling them up."

"And how the hell would Andy know this woman?" Lex asked, slowing his pace as they came into sight of the house. He couldn't help it. He was way more interested than he intended to be.

"He mows her lawn, and her secretary's. Quite by accident, he ended up mowing the lawn of a couple who also happened to be her very satisfied clients, and he started doing a little investigating on his own. Apparently he wanted to be Casanova to some girl he's dating. He was pretty closed-mouthed about it, but... Well, he did think of you."

"Oh, that's thoughtful," Lex grumbled "Glad to know my eternal chub is mentioned in hushed tones on freshly mown lawns all across Portland."

"Oh, don't be a dick. You know Andy would never say anything. He only knows about your situation because he was here once when—"

"When I had a close encounter with the floor. Yes, I remember, but I don't recall that I or anyone else had my cock in their hand when it happened."

"It's not about your cock," Dillon said. "It's about the fact that no one but you can touch said cock."

"And therefore it's about my cock. So what does your cousin think—that I should let this woman advise me while I slap the monkey?" The thought made him very uncomfortable, especially in the region of his crotch, which was quite disturbing. Too disturbing to even contemplate, and yet he found himself asking, "So your cousin's just taking someone's word?"

"Actually my cousin had a little encounter with our sex tutor last week, and apparently it was a rather life-changing experience." Before Lex could ask, Dillon raised his hand. "All I know is that it involved a can of pear halves in heavy syrup out behind Eddie's Supermarket, and, as a result, my awkward virgin of a cousin is suddenly getting laid on a regular basis, and quite well if I'm to believe the lucky bastard."

"A can of pears?"

"I know it's not exactly what you'd expect from a sex therapist, but that's what he told me, with a shit-eating grin that practically split his face."

For a moment, the two men walked in silence, Lex thinking about his midnight rendezvous with the statuary in his private garden. It hadn't been so much sexual release he'd craved as intimacy, and for that there was no real substitute. He figured his raging libido was as much about his isolation as it was about sex, but he didn't see how a sex therapist...er...tutor could help him with that.

"You don't have to meet her in your home. I can call and set up an appointment for you and if she's not okay with meeting you in a hotel room, you can meet her at my apartment. Hell, I stay here most of the time now anyway, so it's free." Before Lex could respond, he added, "Don't worry, bro, I'll check her out very carefully before I set anything up, and I'll double-check with you before we go through with it. Even if you back out at the last minute, I'll just pay the woman. Maybe pay her a little extra for the inconvenience and that'll be that. No skin off anyone's teeth, and no one is any worse for the wear, except maybe your poor aching hand."

"You're an asshole, you know that, Dil?" he said, as both men ascended the stone steps to the patio.

"So I've been told. Look, dude, I'd lend a hand if I could."

"Hell, if you could make it all better, I'd for damn sure let you."

"Shall I give this Kelly Blake a call, then?"

"Let me think about it."

"All right. Just let me know."

* * * *

It was well after midnight when Lex woke wet with sweat, heart racing from a dream he couldn't remember — it wasn't a nightmare. He always remembered the nightmare. It was always the same and it was far too terrifying for him to ever forget, though he wished like hell he could. He shoved his way from under the comforter, knowing sleep would elude him now. He pulled on a pair of training shorts and a ratty hoodie and slipped into the darkened hall barefoot, because he knew only too well how lightly V slept, and fucking Dillon wasn't much better. He wished they didn't worry so much. It wasn't like there was anything they could do, and he functioned just fine — not normal by any stretch of anyone's imagination, but he'd learned to compromise and improvise. He had his routine, and it worked for him. Thankfully he had the entire Valentine fortune to make sure he could compromise and improvise in style, if there was such a thing. And even more thankfully, he had a safety net of people, friends he could rely on to run interference when the shit hit the fan like it had with Sally Philips.

At the back of the house, he made his way through the kitchen, grabbing a couple of Cookie's homemade snickerdoodles from the cookie jar and a bottle of water on his way out. There was a reason they called her Cookie. There was nothing she couldn't do in the kitchen, and she kept them all very well fed. But her specialty was homemade cookies, and snickerdoodles were his favorites. They always turned up in the cookie jar the day after he'd had an incident, and they never lasted long. He considered them just what the doctor ordered. He did all right for himself, he thought, as he bit into one of the little delights, licking cinnamon and sugar off his lips. He managed. He stepped outside to find a heavy moon in the night sky and paused for a moment to look up at the stars before he made his way down to the Other Studio. It was always the Other Studio where he went when he woke in the middle of the night, even if it was the nightmare that disturbed his sleep. The Other Studio was purely escapism from his isolation. It was all erotic sculpture, though some of it bordered more on romance, and it was for his eyes only. His present work was a woman, naked except for an open chemise which exposed her high, firm breasts and the muscles of her belly tightened in arousal. One hand slid between her open legs and the other arm was thrown over her head. He now worked on her face trying to capture the tipping point when all the effort results in that ecstatic moment when there's no turning back. She was his counterpart, he thought, caught in the perpetual need for release that never quite satisfies and unable to figure out why.

He slipped out of the hoodie and began to work on her expression. It was little more than a blank piece of stone at the moment. There was no emotion, no tension, none of the concentration that went with the effort of masturbating oneself to orgasm. As he worked, he recalled his dreams, or at least bits of them. There was a woman. She didn't have a face either, he thought. At least he never saw it. He followed her into the sculpture garden, watched her unseen as she walked among his erotic works, stripping as she went, caressing a marble breast here, a stone cock there, and in between, as she stripped, as she touched and caressed his work, she touched and caressed herself, breasts warm and soft, nipples heavy with arousal, nearly as hard as the stone that turned them both on. And he wanted her. He wanted to trail his fingers along flesh and sinew, warm and giving under his palm. He wanted to curl his fist in her hair and pull her back to him, bruise her mouth with his. He wanted to lift her onto one of the stone plinths of the sculptures she caressed, open her thighs and look at her, touch her down there where it was only ever marble that he touched, down there where he only ever imagined the inner warmth of arousal. And when he had explored her with his eyes, with his hands, with his mouth, then he would take her hard and deep and pour all of what was trapped inside him into her, and she would willingly receive all that he gave.

With a jerk and a groan, he came back from the fantasy, fist tight around his cock, spilling himself onto the partially carved lips and down over the breasts of his creation. Christ, it always felt like it would rip him apart when it happened like this, when the dreams weren't nightmares, but so full of longing that he felt nothing could ever fill the void. When he'd finished coming, he slid down onto the stone cold floor, fumbled his shorts up over his cock and fell asleep.

* * * *

"Here, bro. You look like you could use these." Sunlight shown through the open windows of the studio and Dillon squatted next to him with a cup of coffee in one hand and his hoodie in the other.

"Fuck," he mumbled shoving himself into a sitting position. He grabbed the hoodie and then the coffee, burning his tongue on the first eye-opening sip.

"You're welcome." Dillon sat down on the floor next to him with his own cup in hand. "Another hard night?"

"Fuck you," Lex mumbled into his cup.

"In my dreams, dude, in my dreams."

"A man ought to be able to have a wank in the privacy of his own home without the whole household interfering."

"Shall I take the coffee back?"

Lex clutched the cup to his chest and growled at his friend, who only shrugged and sipped his own brew. They sat for a time in silence, surrounded by the scent of coffee, for which Lex was thankful. He hoped it would overpower the scent of sex, if he could even call what happened to him in these little episodes sex. But the coffee covered up nothing, not to Dillon. Though, bless the man, it was at least an effort to ease any embarrassment he might feel.

"Haven't been able to get hold of either of the two models," Dillon said.

"That's going to set me back."

"I'll sort it shortly."

"I'm sure you will. Thanks."

Through the open door, the two watched a robin in the rose garden battling with a worm.

"You should come and have breakfast. Cookie's making huckleberry pancakes."

Huckleberry pancakes were his favorite and they were always a sign that everyone in the house, including Cookie, knew he'd had a rough night. But then they always knew, didn't they?

"I need a quick shower first," he said.

"Just don't linger or I won't promise there'll be any left." His friend finished his coffee and stood, motioning for Lex to do likewise.

At the kitchen door, Lex stopped and turned to face him. He took a deep breath and threw caution to the wind. "Why don't you make me an appointment with the cock doc? I don't suppose it can hurt. And don't eat all the pancakes."

As he headed through the kitchen, he gave Cookie a wave. She waved a spatula at him and puffed a stray strand of dark hair out of her face.

# Chapter Four

"I would suggest that you start with something a little lower tech." Kelly coughed and waved the thick cloud of baby powder away from her face with the copy of *Hustler* magazine she'd picked up off the bedroom floor. The black latex suit, clearly just out of its plain brown wrapper, looked gray in its heavy patina of powder. It lay crumpled next to a flogger that looked like it could have brought King Kong to his knees. She had to give Clyde and Ina Garrison an A-plus for effort. The couple sat on the edge of the bed wrapped in matching terry robes, also well dusted with baby powder and both looking like they'd just ran a marathon. "Sometimes the kinkiest toys are the ones that cost the least and don't require a case of talcum powder every time you want to play with them. Can we use that?" She motioned to an inflatable doll buried under the pillows and stuffed animals that had clearly been removed from the bed. Mr. G. blushed. Mrs. G. hurried to extricate the doll from the avalanche, a delicate shade of pink crawling up her neck. "It's clean," the woman said. They both nodded. "We've never actually used it," Mrs. G. said, now a bright shade of crimson from throat to scalp.

"Well, you're going to now," Kelly said. She studied the doll that was several inches taller than the petit Mrs. G., though not quite as curvy. From the duffle bag she usually carried with her for these sessions she pulled out a roll of cling film and a pastry box from Jake's Cakes Bakery. The roll of cling film, she handed to Mrs. G. The bakery box, she set on the nightstand along with a roll of paper towels. The Garrisons stood before her like troopers ready to take orders from their captain. She had to smile at that thought. Maybe she'd introduce them to cosplay next time.

"That latex cat suit is neck to ankle, right?"

"And it has a hood too, and a ball gag," Mrs. G. said helpfully.

"All right. I'm guessing that putting it on didn't go so well, am I right?"

The powder-dusted state of the room and the Garrisons was all the answer she needed.

"So, we're going to try low-tech, as I said. Mr. G, you hold the doll, that's it, hold her upright. And Mrs. G, I want you to cover the doll from neck to ankle with the cling film, covering everything you imagine that latex suit would. But I want you to leave exposed the parts you especially want Mr. G to have access to. Can you do that for me?" There was another blush, then an enthusiastic nod as the woman went to work, wrapping the doll, leaving the suspected areas open — the breasts, the crotch — but when the woman got to the knees, she left the back of the them free of cling film. Her husband only stared at her.

"Did you know the backs of your wife's knees were an erogenous zone, Mr. G.?" Kelly asked.

The look on the man's face said he didn't, but the poor guy was preoccupied tugging at his robe, struggling with concealment issues. That was Kelly's cue that it was time to make her exit. "All right, I'm going to love you and leave you with this advice. Play! Make sex fun, not work. Make it an adventure of getting to know each other. In your case, rediscovering each other. Don't be afraid to laugh and make mistakes. Have fun with it. That suit there" — she nodded to the heavily talc-dusted latex — "may figure into that play at some point when you're ready, then have fun with that too. As for the flogger, well, start out with one of those nice soft belts from your robes and double it over." She demonstrated to her round-eyed audience with the removable strap on her duffle bag, giving the stack of pillows a couple of sound thwacks. "Your homework is to be creative and have fun.

What else can you do with cling film, with simple kitchen implements, with food?" She opened the bakery box to reveal two cupcakes, one that looked like a breast, one that looked like a vulva and a very impressive cream-filled éclair that looked like an erect penis. "Suck, lick, touch, feel, nibble, taste, fondle, but remember, the most important thing is to enjoy and have fun." She efficiently re-clipped the strap to the duffle, hefted it and her shoulder bag and nodded her farewell. "I'll let myself out."

She settled in her car for a quick check of messages and emails before she headed home. The Garrisons were her last appointment of a very long day. She seldom had so many back-to-backs, but the moon was full. It had been her discovery that at a full moon, people tended to be more libidinous. She'd been keeping a calendar to track her theory, and it had held true for the year and a half she'd kept a record.

A novelist with a secret life — and what a secret life. Now there was a story in itself, she thought. Mild-mannered, struggling writer by day and sassy, successful sex tutor by night. In fact, her tutoring had become far more lucrative than her moderately successful writing career — so lucrative, in fact, that she found herself in need of a secretary, a secretary she could actually afford to pay. Touch-Able, as she called the business, was the epitome of discretion. In fact, Kelly was always amazed that anyone actually knew she was out there. Though sex and personal relationships were talked about in hushed tones, they *were* talked about, and gossiped about frequently, and word of mouth was most often the best way to spread the news about anything having to do with sex. Kelly had discovered over time that almost everything in any relationship had to do with sex in one way or another and, in one way or another, it usually got discussed with someone. Then, at some point, Touch-Able was mentioned and after that, it was only a matter of time before Myrna's phone rang and someone would bend her ear with a gazillion questions and book a session. When that happened, Kelly set aside her laptop and her work-in-progress, donned her Touch-Able uniform and off she went to the rescue.

She'd just tucked the duffle into the trunk and buckled into her Subaru, ready to head home for the day, when her phone rang. It was Myrna.

"Hey, sweetie, how were the Garrisons?"

"The whole house was covered in talc, but the latex suit is still a virgin," she said with a smile. "Never mind, I don't think the two will be missing the latex much after our little session."

"Pity," Myrna said. "Those suits are expensive," then she added quickly, "or so I hear."

"What's up?"

"I know it's late, hon, but do you have time for one more session, an Alex Valens? Believe it or not, our little lawn boy vouches for him, and he's willing to pay overtime. He's set up to meet you in a very nice suite at The Nines."

"I don't like meeting in expensive hotels, Myrna, you know that. People who can rent an expensive hotel suite for an hour tend to be people who think their little splurge entitles them to do whatever they want."

"I know, sweetie, but the kid all but begged me. Promised it would be okay. He seemed to take it really personally, like it was his brother or something. Besides, he probably feels he owes you after the freebie you gave him. Also talking with this Alex Valens' PA, well, I got the impression that the guy genuinely likes his boss. If you want me to cancel, I will. Obviously I don't want you feeling uncomfortable."

Kelly heaved a sigh and glanced down at her watch. "No, it's okay. I'll go."

"I'll send Tuck over to shadow you. If you're coming from Gresham, he should be there when you arrive." She'd had the money to hire a little muscle too, just in case. Though there had never been an incident in which she'd needed Tucker Swanson to do more than just be there for moral support.

"Fine. I'm on my way, then. I'll see you after."

"I'll have the pizza delivered a little later," Myrna said. "I've got *The Ugly Truth* all queued up and ready to go. A little dose of Gerard Butler will do us both good, girlfriend." Friday night was movie night for the two women, who had no social life, and since Lane and Lana, Myrna's twins, were with their father this weekend, they were going to gorge on rom coms and girlie stuff — the naughtier the better.

"Keep Gerard warm and the beer cold. I'll be there as soon as I finish with Alex Valens. Anything else I should know?"

"His PA'll meet you at the front desk and escort you to the room. Apparently he's as paranoid of you as you are of his boss."

"Well then, maybe I'll have Tuck join me just in case this turns into a tag team event."

\* \* \* \*

"I'm out of my mind," Lex grumbled at Dillon, who had just had room service deliver a bottle of Oregon's best pinot noir, a plate of nibbles and a pot of coffee. There was juice and water in the minibar and the lighting was subdued. "She's the fucking cock doc, not a date or a hooker," he said. Still, he couldn't help feeling like he had come for a blind date or for a clandestine meeting with a prostitute. And a tutor, what the hell was a tutor? If she were Dr. Ruth, at least this adventure would seem a little more legit.

"Doesn't hurt to be hospitable," Dillon said. He checked everything once more before he straightened his jacket and tie and glanced down at his watch. "Right, that's everything in order. Ms. Blake should be here in a few minutes. I'll go down and bring her up."

Lex fought back panic as Dillon pulled the door quietly to behind him. This was such a bad idea. Why the hell had he ever agreed to it? Touch-Able. That was the name of Ms. Blake's business. How could that possibly bode well when he was anything but? And who the hell's advice were they going on but Dillon's nerdy cousin who hadn't even fucked a girl until his little encounter with Ms. Black. Well, at least the kid had gotten laid, which was more than he could say for himself.

He tried to settle on the sofa, flinging an arm across the top in an attempt to look debonair, nonchalant, worldly. And that would last until he opened his mouth and told this woman what he needed her for, until she understood why Dillon was chaperoning them. After that, it would either be doubt or pity. The pity he hated the most. That was why he kept to himself. That was why he kept his private life, or lack thereof, secret. And the doubt wasn't a whole lot better. The last few encounters with women who thought they had the magic touch had been humiliating and extremely unpleasant...for him and for the women. He thought of Sally Philips' goose-fleshed touch and felt slightly queasy.

He stood and paced the room, wondering what the hell he was going to tell this tutor. What exactly *did* he expect her to do for him anyway? Show him a more efficient way to choke the chicken, a way that wouldn't give him carpal tunnel? He moved to look out of the window at the lights of Portland blinking on in the clear summer air. He fought back an insane urge to call Dillon and tell him to cancel, have him tell her that he got called away to a meeting, that he had a heart attack and was on his way to the emergency room. That he died and his body had been taken to the morgue. Christ, how fucked up was he that he'd fantasize about his own demise before he'd entertain the idea of being honest with the bloody cock doc on the outside chance that she might actually be able to help him? Hadn't his father paid a small fortune to find someone who could make his son normal again? Hadn't Lex done the same, even after his father died? Finally he'd gotten tired of the humiliation, tired of the cold knot he got in the pit of his stomach every time he made an appointment for someone else to poke him and prod him and tell him nothing was wrong. He fucking knew nothing was wrong. He was the epitome of health. And yet here he was about to humiliate himself in front of someone else yet again. In a wave of panic, he pulled his iPhone from his pocket and was just about to call Dillon when there was a soft knock. He was too late.

# Chapter Five

"Mr. Valens is waiting for you in the suite. He appreciates you making time for him on such short notice." Alex Valens' very dapper PA gave Kelly a crooked smile, taking in Tuck, who stood slightly behind her. He nodded toward the elevator. "You can bring your bodyguard, though I promise you won't need him. He can keep me company in the lounge."

"You're staying?"

"I guess you could say I'm sort of Mr. Valens' bodyguard." Then he added quickly, "Oh, don't worry, I won't be watching."

"I certainly don't mind you watching if that's what Mr. Valens wants."

Her comment was met with a little chuckle as the elevator doors shut behind them. "My boss and I never had that discussion, Ms. Blake, but I'm certainly up for it if he is. Not much chance of that, though. He is rather shy." The elevator rose with a hydraulic wheeze, and Kelly was well aware she was being studied. In all fairness, she was doing a little studying of her own of this PA, who looked more like he should be the boss, and sounded way too familiar to be just an employee. Was it possible that the two were lovers? Before she could dwell on that thought, the PA spoke.

"There are a few ground rules before I introduce you to Mr. Valens," he said. "Your no-touching policy also happens to be his policy as well. Absolutely no touching, not even a handshake. Under no circumstances are you to touch him. Are we clear?"

"Crystal," she said, suddenly feeling like a child on the

first day of school. Tuck moved in closer to her, and the PA smiled his disarming smile.

"Those rules apply to your bodyguard as well."

She smiled back. "As long as your boss doesn't touch me, I can guarantee that Mr. Swanson here won't touch him."

"Good. Now that we've established the ground rules to everyone's satisfaction, shall we?" The elevator door slid open, and he motioned them into the corridor. About halfway down, he knocked briskly on a door then slid the electronic key into the slot. When the light blinked, he pushed the door open and stepped aside for her and Tuck. "You'll find him in there," he said, nodding to the master suite, then he motioned Tuck to follow him into the lounge.

For a long moment, she stood in the entry hall, gathering herself, finding the whole PA bodyguard lecture slightly disconcerting. She wasn't used to feeling intimidated by her clients before she'd even met them. The fact that this Valens had rented an entire suite at The Nines just for the hour they'd be together didn't help any. But his money was as good as anyone else's and, though she didn't trust the rich and entitled, she had no good reason to say no. Besides, Tuck was in the next room. It would be all right. If she needed to leave in a hurry, well, she would, and that would be that. She took a deep breath and tiptoed down the hallway to the master suite, which was open, then with a soft knock on the doorframe, she stepped inside.

A man, tall and broad of shoulder, stood with his back to her, silhouetted in front of the window overlooking the city.

"Mr. Valens?" she said softly when he didn't turn around. "I'm Kelly Blake."

"Please close the door behind you." His voice was a rough-edged baritone, as though he'd just risen from sleep. A bedroom voice when they hadn't yet begun. She didn't know if that was a good sign or a bad one.

The muscles of her stomach tightened with nerves, but she did what he said, carefully pulling the door to behind her. When she turned back, she found herself the focus of the man's full attention. Though he was still little more than a silhouette in the subdued lighting, she felt as though she were under a microscope.

"Please sit." He motioned her to a wing-backed chair facing a plush blue sofa.

She felt his gaze on her as she sat her duffle bag on the floor and settled in the chair, but he made no effort to move.

She noticed that there was wine, coffee and an assortment of snacks on the coffee table. She smiled and nodded to the small feast. "Are you interested in food play, perhaps, Mr. Valens?"

He startled at the sound of her voice as though she had suddenly regained his attention from where ever else it had been, but, in truth, it hadn't wavered from his studying of her person. Strange that in spite of being the center of his focus, she didn't feel threatened or ogled. "Oh, no. I just wasn't sure what the normal protocol is for a visit from a… sex tutor, and I decided that hospitality is never out of place. Though" — he stepped forward a little, and the lamplight caught his half smile, tinged with mischief — "I have heard that you do interesting things with canned pears. Sadly, those aren't on the room service menu."

She chuckled softly. "Well, I certainly could have brought a can if that's what you wanted."

His laughter was like velvet against her skin, and her forearms rose in goose flesh. "I don't know what I want, exactly." He rubbed a hand over his stubbled chin, then he added, "You're not at all what I expected."

"What exactly did you expect?"

"Someone a little older, sterner," he said.

"Sorry to disappoint."

This time they both laughed. He moved to sit across from her at the end of the sofa and, for the first time, she got a good look at him. His dark hair was mussed, as though he, or someone else, had just run fingers through it. It was in need of a cut, hanging to the collar of a faded denim shirt. He wore jeans that were nearly as faded and a pair lightweight hiking boots. Though the lighting was subdued, she could see the thin scar that began dangerously close to his right eye and curved across his jaw toward his ear, disappearing in his tousled hair. It shown in pale relief against the stubble of several days.

"I didn't say I was disappointed," he said.

"Well, if it's any consolation, you're not exactly what I expected either, not in this place anyway."

He rolled his eyes and gave a little hunch of his shoulders. "I should have met you in Dillon's apartment. We'd have probably both been more comfortable there."

"Your PA?"

He nodded.

"Now, he looks like he belongs here," she said.

"He probably belongs here more than I do, Ms. Blake."

"Kelly, please call me Kelly."

"You do look like a Kelly, much more than you do a... Well you know what I mean."

Both of them laughed nervously as he filled water glasses. As per his PA's warning, she waited until he set the glass on the coffee table in front of her before she reached for it, took a sip then smiled up at him. "Now then, what can I do for you, Mr. Valens?"

Her question seemed to unsettle him. He reached for the water glass, knocked it over, then cursed and looked as though at any second he might bolt.

"It's all right. It's just water. Sit still," she said. "I'll get a towel." She found the bathroom and took her time in returning, giving the man a chance to collect himself. Male ego could be a fragile thing under the best of circumstances, and whatever it was that had driven Alex Valens outside his comfort zone to solicit her services meant this was definitely not the best of times. When she returned, he'd moved from the sofa and once again stood in front of the window, but this time he turned when he heard her.

"Leave it," he said.

She didn't. She knelt on the floor and gave the pristine carpet a brisk rubbing before leaving the towel to absorb the spill, then she returned to her chair.

"It's only water and it only went on the carpet," she said. "I spilled a glass of red wine down the front of an elderly Chinese gentleman's white shirt in Lausanne once, and I wasn't even drunk."

He laughed. They both laughed, and some of the tension left his broad shoulders.

"Oh, sure, I can laugh about it now," she said, "but at the time, I was mortified. It was the poor man's seventy-fifth birthday. He was there with his whole family."

Valens settled tentatively on the arm of the sofa, looking less likely to bolt, but she could see he was still keeping the option open just in case. Sometimes clients took a while to get comfortable, and she expected Alex Valens would need a moment.

"What happened?" he finally asked.

"Turns out the gent didn't speak any English. None of his extended family did either, so I ended up having the waiter translate from English to French to the one teenage granddaughter there who did speak French. "I had him tell them that I would pay for the dry-cleaning, that I would pay for the whole dinner—which I sure as hell couldn't afford—that I would do anything, including becoming his slave, until his next birthday."

"And did he…take you up on any of your generous offers?" he asked, settling back on the sofa, slightly closer to her, but still a safe distance.

"They wouldn't hear of it. Instead, they insisted I join them for their celebration. I didn't understand a word and neither did they, but they were all lovely, and when it came time for cake and the Happy Birthday song, they all insisted I do it in English—solo. In front of the whole restaurant. It was one of the most fun evenings I've ever had." She chuckled. "And that fact alone should tell you that I spend entirely too much time in my own company."

"Now that, I can relate to," he said, offering her a broad, easy smile.

He looked much younger when he smiled so unguardedly. She was betting he didn't do it often.

She refilled his water glass and settled back in her chair. For a long moment, they sat in silence. She had learned long ago that it was best to let the client speak in his own time.

"I need to masturbate a lot," he finally blurted out, then downed all of the water in a single gulp.

"High libido isn't unusual in busy people," she said, "especially if their work is creative."

He nodded. Then there was more silence. This time he fumbled with the bottle of wine. She watched as he opened it and poured himself a glass. He poured her one too, before she could refuse. Then he drank his back in one go. "I mean *a lot*," he said, slapping the glass down on the table with a *thwack* for emphasis. "I'm aroused all the time. If I did it as often as I'm aroused, I'd never get anything else done." He shifted in his seat and folded his hands in his lap as though he were about to say a prayer or just in case she should glance at his crotch. She didn't. A part of what made her good at what she did was that other people's situations never titillated her. They intrigued her. They brought out her sense of empathy. "Do you?" he asked, clearing his throat loudly and pouring himself another glass of wine.

"Do I masturbate a lot?" she asked.

He nodded, as though his head were suddenly loose on his neck.

"I do, yes. But I'm a creative and my job is both stressful and exciting. I need an outlet. It sounds like you do too."

He nodded. This time more thoughtfully. "I... For complicated reasons I'm not in a relationship either, so no help from there," he said. "I'm sure that would make it easier."

"A lot of creatives don't have time for relationships," she said. "Love of their work is their relationship." He hadn't said that he was a creative, but she could tell. She could always recognize another creative person.

When he still said nothing but downed the second glass of wine as quickly as the first, she thought it best to press the issue, just a little bit at least, while he was still sober. "Mr. Valens, what exactly is it that you need? If you're expecting me to advise you to masturbate less, and to give you ways not to, well, I think that's a little premature. I would suggest that perhaps you need to masturbate as much as you do because of your circumstances. That's certainly my case."

"You don't know my circumstances. You can hardly compare your case to mine," he blurted. "You're a lovely woman who could easily have a partner whenever she wanted, hell, you could pick and choose."

She bit back her response, for some strange reason wanting desperately to tell him that he had no idea what her situation was and that he had no right to jump to conclusions. The urge nearly took her breath away. One of the reasons she was so good at what she did was that she could stay neutral, let people tell their stories, let them tell her what they needed in their own time. She took a steadying breath. "I'm not comparing anything with anything, Mr. Valens, and since I don't know your circumstances, I'm generalizing until you give me enough information to make an intelligent suggestion."

"So, *I'm* supposed to tell *you* what to do?" he asked.

"No, but it would help if you told me what you need from me."

He ran a hand through his already mussed hair, and she noticed he was trembling. "If I could get what I need from you, or from anyone else for that matter, I wouldn't be here. Look, this was a mistake. There's nothing you can do. Dillon knows it, you know it, and I know it. I'm really sorry I wasted your time. Dillon!" He shoved his way up from the couch just as his PA and Tuck came into view. "I need to leave. Now."

The PA gave Kelly an accusing glance before turning his attention to his boss.

"Who the hell is he?" Valens asked nodding to Tuck.

"Her bodyguard," the PA replied.

To this, Valens laughed out loud, then shot Kelly a look that suggested he was seeing her for the first time. "If there was any place on earth you don't need him, Ms. Blake, it's here with me."

"What the hell happened?" the PA asked.

"Nothing the fuck happened, what did you think would happen?" Valen's reply was little more than a growl.

"Look, it's your suite," Kelly said, hunching her bag up onto her shoulder and moving past Valens, careful not to touch him. "I'll leave. I'm sorry it didn't work out," she said softly.

Valens nodded, avoiding her gaze, pushing back against the wall of the entryway as far from her as he could get, but not so far that she couldn't see the sheen of sweat on his forehead, the dilation of his pupils and the way he cupped his hands protectively in front of his fly. She looked away, not wanting to know if he had an erection or not, though she was certain if she had looked, that was what she would have seen. Not wanting to distress the man further, she left quickly with Tuck right behind her.

"Do you need a minute?" Dillon shut the door to the room quietly and turned his attention to Lex.

"Christ, Dillon, I'm not quite that out of control."

"Well, our Kelly Blake was rather more pleasant to look at than I'd expected. Maybe I'll take a minute." He rudely adjusted his crotch, and Lex flipped him off.

For a moment, the two stood in silence, then Dillon spoke quietly, sounding a little like Kelly Blake. "What is it you want, Lex?"

"Just take me home. I have work to do, and I'm afraid I had a more intimate encounter with that bottle of pinot noir than I'd planned."

"She got to you, did she?" Dillon opened the door and stood aside for Lex to pass.

43

"For all the good it did."

"Might have done more good than you think," Dillon said. "Though it might have done you even more good if you'd given her half a chance."

"I don't recall asking for your opinion," Lex said.

Dillon only shrugged and pushed his way through the door leading to the stairs. Lex always took the stairs if he had to be in a public building. Elevators were one of his worst nightmares, apt to be empty one minute and *violà*, the doors would open and a whole crowd of people could shove in at any given moment. Why he had suggested that he meet Kelly Blake in a hotel was beyond him. Though he supposed he had hoped that he could impress the woman with his wealth, since he knew he'd fail miserably with his shining example of mental health and his sexual experience and worldliness. Of course, there'd have been no point in seeing the woman at all if he'd have been less neurotic and had even the slightest bit of sexual sophistication. Upon having met Kelly Blake, though, he was pretty sure she was not in the least impressed by wealth and power. That didn't leave him with much to impress her then, did it? And he had to admit he was way more concerned with impressing her after he'd met her than when he had visions of sitting across the room from some elderly auntie cock doc.

It surprised him a little to discover that he actually would have preferred to have met her at his home. That he would have loved to walk with her in the gardens with the wonderful views of the Cascades just as the sun was setting. Then after, he would have entertained her on the veranda over one of Cookie's exquisite dinners. And *then* what? Sent her on her way while he went back to the studio for a good wank?

What the fuck was he thinking? He kept strangers away from his home. In fact, most people had no real idea where Alexander Valentine lived, and even the models who came to him were given the impression that he didn't actually live at Mountain View, that it was only one of his estates. That last part was true, but it was Mountain View he considered home. He seldom visited the other two estates on the West Coast and would sell them outright if they didn't help him keep his real location secret.

Once in the car, he donned his headphones and cranked Rush's *2112 Overture*. This was always Dillon's signal to shut up and give Lex a little space. He knew his friend was dying to hear the details of his meeting with the sex tutor, but he wasn't dying to talk about them. How could it be that he found himself wanting to revisit a situation in which he had been surly, non-communicative, awkward and downright rude, a situation in which nothing had happened? He'd been with the woman maybe twenty minutes of his allotted hour. She made him feel… Well, she didn't *make* him feel anything. Instead she let him struggle to try and figure out what he really *did* feel. And he hadn't liked it one bit. He'd told her nothing, and yet in that nothing, he suspected he'd told her way more than he'd intended to. That was the terrifying thing. No one ever saw into Alexander Valentine's private life. His art was as close as anyone ever got to the man on the inside, and yet this woman… He felt as though he'd sat there exposing himself to her while the whole time she sat there waiting for him to give her permission to look. Now, that did a job on his head. More than likely it was just the wine, he told himself. Once he'd had a few hours in the studio, once he'd settled back into his normal routine, he'd see the whole incident more clearly and more than likely chalk it all up as just one more failed effort to make it all better.

It wasn't until he was home, working away in the studio, that he realized he was calm. He was focused. His cock, which had felt like it was lined with lead when Kelly Blake arrived, now rested comfortably in his athletic shorts, happy for once to be neglected. The surprise of it made him giddy. He threw open the garage doors at the side of his studio and stood looking out at the night sky, breathing in the scent of early summer, still trying to understand what had happened to him at The Nines this evening...or what had not happened to him, as the case might be.

He couldn't say that Kelly Blake had given him a hard-on. He'd already had a good start on one when he'd arrived at the hotel. Neither could he say that the fact that he didn't have one now was an indication that she was unattractive. God knew it wasn't that. So then why was he, for the first time in a very long time, not distracted by his own discomfort? He'd been with the woman twenty minutes, maybe less, and they'd never really gotten past the fact that he masturbated a lot and that she didn't seem to have a problem with that. So what had actually happened in those twenty minutes? Did the woman secretly hypnotize her clients? Was she some kind of witch using magic on him?

Leaving the doors open, he strode across the room to the easel and threw open the sketchpad to a blank page. In a quick, simple line drawing, he sketched her, then he stood twiddling the pencil between his fingers, his mind filling in the details of her. He hadn't been able to see the color of her eyes in the dim light, only that they had been large and alert like a cat's. Her hair had been some non-descript shade of blonde, or brown maybe. He couldn't see that either, but it was long and pulled back in a ponytail. For a second, he lingered on the idea of pulling the tie from that ponytail and letting her thick hair fall around her shoulders. In the sunlight—he'd do that in the sunlight so he could see her true colors. She was slender, athletic of build. He couldn't recall what she'd worn. He couldn't recall a lot. The lighting had been low, and the situation had been stressful. Though he had no real name for what it was that he saw in her, what he did know was that in her essence, she had made him feel more himself than he had in a very long time. That was no small feat. That had him squinting at his drawing, desperate to understand what this woman's magic was. How was it that she could do nothing and it be exactly the right thing to do? How was it that she could be comfortable with his discomfort and wait patiently while he balked and back-pedaled and made things difficult?

That night, he slept the sleep of one who had worked hard and was pleased with his efforts. That night the dreams left him in peace, and, when he woke up in the morning, anxious as he always was to get back to work, the shifting he felt when he stretched and yawned and crawled from beneath the comforter was not the shifting of a hard-on in urgent need of release. Though his cock responded normally to the morning touching and scratching that was routine after a night's sleep, as he stood to shower, as he dressed and went down to breakfast, as he thought of the day ahead of him, it simply let him get on with it.

"You look cheerful today," V said. She had just popped into the kitchen for another cup of coffee. The woman's coffee cup was never empty. Lex had his suspicions that, with all that caffeine, the woman hadn't needed to sleep since the Millennium, but she never got jittery or cranky. He suspected it was because of her alien nature.

"Huckleberry pancakes always make me cheerful," he said. He was demolishing his second stack when Dillon showed up, just as Cookie plopped down a plate in front of him. Mountain View ran like a well-oiled machine, Lex thought, and it had run that way since his father's welcome demise. His father never would have countenanced breakfast in the kitchen with the servants, and Lex couldn't have imagined taking his meals any place else. The kitchen was the heart of Mountain View, and next to his studios, it was his favorite place in the house.

"She's right. You do. And you look well rested too," Dillon said, nabbing a strip of bacon and shoving half of it into his mouth.

Clearly what the man really wanted to know what happened between him and the lovely Ms. Blake last night and why on earth was he in such a good mood when he'd cut the meeting short and run like a scared rabbit. Over the years, he and Dillon had become good at reading each other's brand of subtext.

"I need you to make another appointment with Ms. Blake for me."

Dillon stopped mid-chew. On the far side of the kitchen, there was the clatter of a dropped pan, then silence as Cookie pretended to stir a large pot of something simmering on the stove. The ability to listen to the subtext seemed to be a requirement for working at Mountain View, plus Cookie had super-human hearing. That was just one of her super powers. He and Dillon were convinced that she had a secret life cooking for the Avengers. Her food was the real source of all their super-powers, and when they needed her, she could do scary-assed things to villains with kitchen utensils.

"Okay. When?" Dillon said, wiping his mouth.

"As soon as she can see me."

"Back at The Nines?" he asked. "Or my place?"

"Is the corporate flat free?"

He nodded. "Let me see what I can set up with Ms. Blake first, then we'll make a plan."

# Chapter Six

As she pulled into the deserted underground garage, the racing of Kelly's heart had nothing to do with the fact that hers was the only car there other than a dark blue Audi R8. It had everything to do with the man inside the car. Alex Valens sat slumped in the seat, a pair of Bose headphones nestled down in his ruffled hair and over his ears. His eyes were closed. The rocking of his body and the nodding of his head informed her that whatever he was listening to, he was enjoying the experience. She got out of the car and, for a moment, she stood watching him. Observing the man at his ease, watching him enjoy himself, was like seeing a different person, someone she'd only glimpsed through the haze of tension and nerves he'd wrapped himself in last week. He was a beautiful man, clearly a strong man, and she was glad he'd called her back. She hoped this time he would at least talk to her.

As though he sensed her presence, he opened his eyes, eyes fringed in thick, dark lashes, and offered her a smile that made her insides feel like warm honey. She smiled back, then he glanced around for his minder, but there was no sign of anyone but the two of them. He slid the headphones off and tucked them in the glove box, then he opened the door and unfolded himself, keeping enough personal space not to feel threatened, but not so much that she couldn't see just how tall he was. She was five-ten, and she looked up to him even in her heels.

"Your hair, it's red. Forgive me," he said. "Hotel rooms are never well lit, and last week, well, last week, I preferred it that way. It's just that, in the subdued lighting, I thought you were a blonde."

She absently reached up to stroke her hair and felt a shiver of pleasure as his eyes followed the motion. "Well, it's not proper red, just sort of a weird strawberry blondish." Fuck if she wasn't blushing, and this man was her client, not her date, she reprimanded herself.

"I'm sorry for my bad behavior last week. I was..." He shrugged helplessly as though words had failed him.

"It's all right." She fell into step next to him as he motioned her toward the private elevator. "Often my clients aren't sure how to behave when we first meet. When they see I don't pose a threat, that I really am there to help, they calm down. You're not the first to leave before his hour was up. But you're also not the first to call back for another appointment."

As they entered the elevator, he took one last look at the parking garage. "No bodyguard?"

"Nope. You?"

"I gave him the night off. I don't need him to run interference for me here. I own the place." Then he quickly added, "I hope that's all right."

"I trust you," she said. "And if you pull anything funny, well, I know martial arts, and I fight dirty."

"Somehow that doesn't surprise me."

The elevator glided to a stop and the doors slid aside silently. Kelly found herself in an open-plan apartment with sleek, unobtrusive furniture in neutral tones, all designed to show off the masterpiece of the flat, which was the city and the river just beyond the floor-to-ceiling windows. For a moment, they both admired the view of the sun setting over the river, painting the sky tangerine and peach. "Wow," she said. "Much nicer than the hotel."

He nodded her over to a rounded sofa that curved intimately in an alcove that was also windowed floor to ceiling. Once the niceties were sorted and he'd brought them both a glass of sparkling water, she noticed that he was pushing his limits, sitting as close to her as he dared then backing off just slightly when his pulse began to pound in his temples and his forehead sheened with a patina of perspiration. She started to scoot away, but he raised a hand. "No. Stay where you are. I'm fine. This is how I want it."

"All right." She gave him a moment to gather himself, then she smiled and nodded to her bag. "I brought canned pears, though I would imagine you might want to save those for another day."

"When you touch yourself," he blurted, taking them both by surprise. "What does it feel like? I want to know how it would be to…" He looked down at his hand, which was a tight fist in his lap, and he made a conscious effort to open it, turn it palm up and ease it down next to his thigh until it rested cupped on the sofa between them.

"There's a lot of me to touch, Mr. Valens—"

"Alex." His voice was a forced whisper. "The question I just asked you is a little too personal for you to call me Mr. Valens. Besides, it's—"

"Not your real name, yes, I suspected as much, Alex. Now, as I was saying, there's a lot of me to touch. You watched me touch my hair in the parking garage. It feels soft, sort of cool right now." She smiled as she stroked her hair, and once again his full attention was on the movement of her hand. "I've always thought hair was the most sensual part of a person. The hair on our head, on our faces, on our bodies, it's one of those constant reminders of our connections to our animal cousins. We stroke it for the same reason we stroke a cat's fur. It feels good. I wear mine up most of the time because I have a habit of playing with it." She twisted a strand around her fingers and heard him catch a breath. "It can be distracting."

"It is," he gasped. "Very distracting."

She stopped, pushed her hair back over her shoulder and folded her hands in her lap. "What do you want, Alex? Tell me what you want."

"Your neck," he said. "When you pushed your hair back,

51

there was a trail of goosebumps along your neck, down your throat and over your collar bone. How did that feel?"

She laughed a little breathless grunt. "My nape and my throat, and this area just above my collar bones"—she ran her hand along the path as she described it, feeling another rise of goose bumps—"it's one of my erogenous zones. If someone touches me anywhere there, if I touch myself there, I feel it in a lot of other places."

His gaze dropped to her nipples, then he quickly glanced away.

"It's all right if you look, Alex. Touching my nape and my collar bones makes my nipples hard."

With permission granted, he leaned forward until she could almost feel his breath, studying the path she had described to him and the response of her nipples. Responses further down, he couldn't see, and anyway, she wasn't sure if those were from her touch or from his curious gaze.

"What about you, Alex? What do you feel like?"

He looked down at his open palm. "My hands..." He rubbed the left over the palm of the right in slow circles. "They're calloused from the work I do. V says I should take better care of them. V's my housekeeper," he clarified. "But I like them rough. They remind me of the things I make smooth and there's a contrast, this amazing contrast, when I touch smooth stone or"—he placed a palm against the flat of his belly—"or the more tender parts of my body—my stomach, my inner thighs." He placed both palms in his lap then curled them into relaxed fists and looked up at her. "My cock." If he blushed, the fading light hid it from her, but the rise and fall of his throat as he swallowed could have easily been the shifting of tectonic plates in the unmoving stillness.

"I have callouses," she said, fisting her own hands to mirror his. "From martial arts training. I like the way they feel. They make me feel strong."

"And when you touch your breasts with them?" His voice was little more than a whisper, and this time even the fading light couldn't hide his blush.

"When I touch my breasts with my calloused hands, when I touch myself" — she nodded down to her lap — "that's when I feel strongest, like there are parts of me that can make love to me and protect me and keep me from flying apart into a million little fragments when sometimes I feel like that's a real possibility."

He stood so quickly that she thought perhaps she'd upset him again and that he was going to ask her to leave. "Come with me," he said. "To the kitchen. I want to see you. I can't see you here. That was better last week. It's not better now. I want to see how you touch your hair, how you touch your neck, the way you look when you talk to me."

The kitchen was huge and white. All the surfaces that weren't white marble were stainless.

"Sit there. No, not on the stools, on the countertop." He hurried around the room, turning on more lights from more switches than she had in her whole house. "Get comfortable. Take off your shoes."

She might have been a bit more nervous had she not been drawn into the man's enthusiasm, in such high contrast to the morose brooder she'd been with at the hotel. Once he was certain every light in the kitchen was on and the huge marble worktop was bathed in light, he pulled up one of the stools and sat with his elbows resting on the surface. "Go on, don't dangle your feet." He made a shooing motion with his hands until she pulled her feet and legs onto the cool surface and sat cross-legged, smack dab in the middle of the work space. "That's better. I want to see you. I want to see all of you." He must have caught the look of panic on her face. He backpedaled quickly. "What I mean is that I want to see your face. I... Since I don't have the benefit of physical contact, I've grown more sensitive to people's faces and how they respond to touch. If that makes any sense."

It did.

"What do you want from me, Alex?" It felt strange using

her professional voice when she sat cross-legged and barefoot in the middle of the man's kitchen island, but she had to bring things back on track before she forgot entirely why she was here.

He was quiet so long that she thought she'd lost him again, then he took a deep breath and sat up straight on the stool. "I didn't really know what I wanted when I was with you last week, and that was what frustrated me so. I knew I wanted something from you. I just didn't know what it was."

"And now?"

"I want to know what it would feel like...if I touched you. If I touched any woman," he added quickly before there was another chance for panic.

This time it wasn't panic that overwhelmed her, but the sudden realization that Alex Valens had never touched a woman.

He was right about his ability to read faces. He caught her thoughts almost as though he'd read her mind. "Before you ask me, the answer is yes. I have seen a psychiatrist, numerous psychiatrists, in fact, some of the best in the world. And I've been on multiple types of meds until I got sick of the whole..." He caught his breath and looked around the kitchen, as though he hoped to find the right words on the shelf with the spices. "I'm a creative person, as you said, and my gift depends on me being able to think outside the box, me being able to see things differently, even if I can't...touch anyone or let anyone touch me. Drugs hampered that, and I felt like I couldn't even touch myself when I was taking the meds. And I still couldn't stand to be touched."

"I'm sorry," she said, softly.

"Look, I don't expect you to deal with what a fucked-up mess I am. I realized that what I really want to know is what it feels like, what you feel like, what any woman feels like when she's with a man, or even when she touches herself, and I have no one I would feel comfortable asking without wondering the whole time if they thought that by my asking that I had given them permission to try and fix me. Does that make any sense?"

She had little time to do more than nod before he continued.

"Oh, I've watched enough porn that I get it feels really good. I've read enough erotica to get some picture of how it's supposed to be, but my take on it is always one-sided." He raised his hand and wiggled his fingers as though to demonstrate. "I can't know anything but my own touch. Certainly, I can't feel anything else, so I want you to tell me. I want you to answer my questions. I want you to tell me what I would feel if I touched you, what *you* would feel if I touched you. As for what I would feel if you touched me, well" — he shrugged and offered her a smile that seemed slightly forced — "for that, I'll just have to use my imagination."

She took a deep breath, as though she were about to dive under water. "Okay, well, I'll start with my lips because lovers often start there. I would have made sure they were moist for you before you kissed them, but not so wet as to be off-putting, and you would have done the same. And your first kisses would be tentative, if you're really good, almost like a feather lighting against my mouth softly and repeatedly until I'm breathless for the want of more. Then I would part my lips to give you more surface area so that we could feel each other better." She chuckled softly as she realized they'd both raised their fingers to their mouths. "Then we would both press harder and rub harder. The more surface area we touched the more we'd want and, I think lips swell, not just from the pressure, but in an effort to create that surface area, and when they can swell no more, when I feel like I want to completely take my lover into my mouth, then I would open to him, and there would be a whole new surface area, wet and slick and warm, there would be a whole new motion when our tongues discover each other. I think a kiss reflects what happens in

55

penetrative sex. It's sort of an intimation, if you will." Her gaze locked on him, and, for the first time, she noticed just how blue his eyes were. "A promise of things to come."

"Yes," he whispered. "I've thought of that in my art. I've thought of the interchange we make with mouths and cocks and vaginas." He struggled with the last word.

"It's okay to call it a pussy or a cunt or whatever works for you," she said.

He laughed softly. "How the hell would I know?"

"Well." She stretched out on the countertop and rolled onto her side, resting her head on her hand. "You just have to try them out and see how they fit your mouth."

This time they both laughed. "If they fit my mouth, I wouldn't have to worry about what words I used, would I?"

"Good point," she said.

"Not quite, but getting there fast, thank you."

Again, they both laughed, a strangely relaxed laugh under the bizarre circumstances.

"The thing is," she said, rolling onto her back and staring up at the long rack of copper bottom pans above her head, "words are often as important in sex, and as erotic, as touch. I write in my other life, and I find that while some of my characters get turned on by waxing poetic between the sheets, others get hot by talking dirty."

"How does your cunt feel when some fucker talks dirty to you?" he asked, though not without a hearty blush.

"That would depend on the fucker and the circumstances and how badly I wanted to ride his cock."

"And if it was a fucker whose cock you really wanted to ride, a fucker who was hard and heavy for you? What words would he use, and what response would he elicit?"

"It wouldn't hurt for him to observe aloud what he sees about my body's state of arousal, and how he admires it."

"You mean like how lovely your breasts are when your nipples are so taut that even your areolae are visible through that shirt, which I imagine feels like a caress every time you inhale. You mean like the way your lips are parted and moist. You've not completely shut your mouth for the past five minutes, the way you rock your hips, almost but not quite secretly, and grind your bottom against the countertop. Is that what you mean?"

"Jesus! We shouldn't be doing this." She sat bolt upright on the surface then froze as though someone had hit the pause button. "Alex?"

The man perched on the edge of the counter, just far enough away that she couldn't easily touch him. He had kicked his shoes off and his own nipples peaked to bullet points through his white polo shirt. That would have been enough to hold her attention indefinitely had it not been for the heel of his hand stroking the very obvious, very anxious erection through his jeans.

It was all right. It was fine, she told herself. She'd had more than a few occasions where her job involved watching and coaching someone while they masturbated. This was just her job. That's all.

"It's more obvious with me what I feel," he said, raking her body with a hooded gaze. "And your nipples, well, you could just be cold. Please tell me what you feel when you see me like this, when we talk like this."

She moved to the edge of the counter giving him space, then motioned him onto it, then she opened her legs. "If I weren't wearing trousers, if you could see my panties, you'd know that I'm wet." She nodded to his erection. "You'd know that the thought of what you're doing, the sight of how your body is responding to mine, is making me wetter." She cupped her breasts in turn, through the white blouse. "Every part of me feels heavy, Alex. My breasts feel like my bra can no longer contain them. My nipples ache. And my lips…" She touched her mouth, then, holding his gaze, moved her hand down to rest on the crotch of her trousers. "My lips are swollen, so swollen and slippery and ready to be penetrated." She nodded first to his mouth then to his erection. "Do I want the fucker to give it to me hard and deep in my cunt? What do you think?"

"Oh, God," he managed. Then he stopped talking altogether. His breath came in tight little grunts and gasps as he moved against his hand, holding her in his gaze as surely as if he held her in his embrace, and it was in that instant, the instant she slid her hand down the front of her trousers and into her panties, an action he mirrored, that she knew neither of them would make it out of here intact. She wanted to run, but she didn't. She wanted to take off her clothes and feel his gaze all over her body, but she didn't. She wanted to demand that he strip for her, that he come just for her eyes, but she didn't. She couldn't. She could only cup and grope her breasts until they hurt. She could only stroke herself while she watched him do the same.

The space around them crackled with their energy, and their desperate efforts to breathe were the only sounds beyond the stroke of skin against fabric. In a hungry attempt at relief, they both rocked and bucked, mirror images of each other with one hand down the front of their trousers while the other groped and cupped and tweaked and pinched whatever part of their anatomy it came in contact with. Then breathing stopped, time stopped. Everything around them disappeared until they saw nothing but each other, locked in each other's gazes, more physical than any embrace Kelly had ever felt, and it was enough. Heaven help them, it was enough. He came first by a split second, roaring like a wounded lion, arching back until she feared he'd either break his neck or fall off the counter. But the sight of him so vulnerable in his passion, the fact that even in his release, he kept his eyes on her was all she could handle, and she convulsed against her own hand, convulsed as though she would break apart, never taking her eyes off him, never breaking that connection.

* * * *

When she woke, long toward morning, the kitchen lights

still burned brightly, the room now smelled of sex, the sex that *hadn't* happened, and yet was way more than any sex she'd ever had, the sex that was sadly as close as Alex Valens, or whatever his real name was, was likely to ever get. And she had taken him there. The thought pleased her only until the realization hit her that she had taken their relationship far beyond the professional level. To her surprise, he was stretched out on the wide marble island next to her, but even in sleep, careful not to touch her — and he was deeply asleep. She allowed herself the brief luxury of studying him at his ease. He looked so young. There was no rapid eye movement, so she knew he wasn't dreaming, but when dreams did come, she hoped they'd be good ones. Quietly, she slid off the table and found her shoes and her bag. For another long moment, she stood watching him sleep, feeling gutted, even in the afterglow of the place where they'd taken each other. What she had done was a betrayal of trust and a betrayal of her own professionalism. It was a betrayal of him. They could not, under any circumstances, do this again. She turned and made her way to the elevator. The only way she knew to guarantee she wouldn't do the same with Alex Valens and more was not to see him again.

# Chapter Seven

Kelly woke to the sound of a lawn mower and cursed under her breath. Andy was here. It was his day to mow and do any other yard work that needed to be done. It felt like she'd just gotten to sleep. She opened one eye and peeked at her watch. She actually had just gotten to sleep. Then the night came rushing back to her fast enough and hard enough to take her breath. Oh, she'd been home for hours, but she'd been wide awake because she couldn't put what had happened between her and Alex out of her mind. She hadn't been able to stop berating herself for her breach of protocol. Fuck! It was much more than a breach of protocol. She would have ridden the man like a racehorse if she'd been able to touch him. Thank heaven there was at least that. Thank heaven his situation had prevented her from making things even worse. She had masturbated with her client. She had been intimate with Alex Valens, a man she barely knew, but how well they were acquainted didn't matter. What *was* relevant was that he was her client. She did not have sex with her clients! She did not get personally involved in any way! Okay, so it was only masturbation. Okay, so it was relevant to his situation, but allowing him to see into her personal life, into her desires and needs, her using his arousal to elicit her own – that was not acceptable under any circumstances.

She threw back the covers and made her way to the bathroom to pee, doing her best to convince herself that the rules didn't really apply to her, that her methods were unorthodox and by word of mouth. Lots of people did far shadier things and passed them off as tools to help people sexually, and they weren't even looked at askance. She really tried to convince herself that she'd done nothing wrong. But the rub of it was not that she shouldn't have masturbated with him, if she thought it would help her client, but rather that by the time they were both in the throes of passion, she sure as hell wasn't thinking of Alex Valens as her client. He was a virile man, an exciting man, and goddamn it, in spite of the really crap hand he'd been dealt, he was a damn good lover. Her stomach bottomed as she thought of his eyes locked on her, his breathless requests as to how he wanted her to touch herself and his excited inquiries as to what it felt like when she did. By the time they'd both had their release, she was thinking of him as lots of things, but none of those things was as her client.

"I left without saying goodbye," she whispered to herself in the mirror as she washed her hands. "I didn't even leave him a note as to why I couldn't see him anymore." For a moment, the thought of not seeing Alex Valens again felt like the worst sort of gut punch. The truth was that she had never experienced such raw, honest intimacy in her life, and he had taken her there without so much as touching her. How was that even possible? The man was a mess. Clearly he was seriously haphephobic. He was a disaster, and with her track record with relationships, she wasn't exactly a catch. She might as well have been haphephobic herself. Intimacy issues much? The whole situation, if not nipped in the bud right now, was a disaster waiting to happen, and Alex Valens had enough serious shit to deal with without her complicating his life further. And no matter what, she couldn't pretend that he was just a client, not now. Not after what had happened between them.

The lawn mower growled loudly just below the bathroom window as Andy worried the high grass close to the house into submission. Damn it, she wished he'd go away. She had to think. She needed to talk to Myrna. Fuck, she needed to talk to Myrna right now. She had to know that Kelly could accept no more appointments from Mr. Valens, and the man being who he was, he'd probably already had his PA call.

She stumbled into the bedroom and punched in Myrna's number. Her friend would have been up for hours with the two kiddos who ran on a sugar high whether they'd had any or not.

"What?" came the curt answer. "Lane, stop using my curling iron on the dog," her friend yelled away from the speaker. "Sorry, hon, what's up?"

"I need you to make excuses if Mr. Valens' PA calls to make an appointment. I can't see him again."

"Jesus, hon, did he hurt you? Damn, I knew you should have taken Tuck with you. Private executive apartments have disaster written all over them. I'll cancel his appointment right away."

Kelly did a mental head desk. "He's already called?"

"Several hours ago, actually. What the hell did he do to you, sweetie?"

"Mom's cussing! Mom's gotta put money in the Language Box," Lana called in the background.

"Go outside and play, you little heathens." Myrna hissed. "Right now! I'm talking grown-up stuff with your auntie, now, move! Go bug Andy. I hear him out there."

Kelly heard scrambling and a shriek, then more scrambling, and the sound of the mower got louder then softer again. She waited until Myrna half-whispered, "Sweetie, what the fuck happened? I'll cancel that bastard right now and I'll be over in one second."

Kelly disconnected and dug through the stack of clothes over the back of the captain's chair for her baggy sweats and a tank top. By the time she was dressed, Myrna was already making coffee in the kitchen. God, she wondered what she'd do without the woman.

On the table, there was a pastry box from Jake's Cakes and the room smelled of French roast. The noise from the mower had receded to Myrna's back yard, every once in a while accompanied by the sound of Myrna's not-too-subtle brood pestering Andy, who never seemed to mind.

Myrna nodded to the table and nabbed a stack of napkins for the cheese Danish. "What did he do to you, sweetie?" she asked. She settled in across from Kelly and patted her hand in a motherly fashion that would have made Kelly laugh if she hadn't actually needed to be mothered, or at the very least big-sistered, at that moment.

"He didn't do anything to me. That's the problem, Myrna. It's what I did to him."

The screech of the chair legs on the kitchen tiles overpowered the gurgle of the coffee maker as Myrna scooted closer for the skinny. "What did you do to him, hon?"

Over coffee and two cheese Danishes each, Kelly told her friend the gory details and Myrna listened with a wide-eyed look of titillation that suggested to Kelly that she might not quite get the gravity of the situation.

"Fucking hell," Myrna half-whispered when the story was finished, then shot a quick look over her shoulder to make sure her kids hadn't caught her in a violation of the Kieran family language code. If they knew the half of it, the woman would be buying pizzas for her two and all the kids in the neighborhood every day for a year. Kelly often marveled at her friend's capacity to speak G-rated language around the twins, their friends and their mothers, but cuss like a sailor when it suited her. She very seldom mixed languages and even this morning, it was only because she was worried about her friend.

"Frankly, I don't see what the problem is." Myrna spoke around a mouthful of chocolate chip muffin. "You're both consenting adults. I mean, you work with consenting adults, and you set the rules. And to be honest, sweetie, I can't see that you've broken them." She raised a hand before Kelly could argue. "Oh, I canceled your meeting with the very sensual Mr. Valens, but if I'd known the situation before I'd done so, I'd have tried to make you reconsider."

"I wouldn't. I won't. I can't!"

"Can't what, Auntie Kell?" A tornado in the form of the Kieran twins burst through the door with Andy right behind them. Lana, the oldest of the two by four minutes, never missed anything. Fortunately she was instantly distracted by the remaining pastries, as was her brother. Myrna ordered them to take only one each, and not to get their dirty fingers all over the rest, and to save some for Andy.

Andy, who was used to the drill, elbowed his way in and grabbed a bear claw, then helped himself to a cup and some coffee. They all had a routine. Andy mowed both their lawns, then he had a coffee break at whichever house the scent of coffee was coming from while the two women informed him of any other yard work or basic handyman jobs they wanted him to do for the morning.

"Can't what, Auntie Kell? Can't what?" Though Lana was easily distracted, she never forgot.

"I can't keep the two of you in milk," Kelly said. She grabbed two glasses from the cupboard and filled them from the gallon of milk she kept on hand just for the twins, who could have easily been an advert for the dairy industry.

"Now take your donuts and go out on the patio, you two, so we can talk without having to scream over you."

Lane stuck his donut in his mouth and grabbed another one before ducking under his mother's arm and heading out onto the patio.

"I noticed you're starting to get aphids on the roses again, Ms. K.," Andy said, looking after the twins as they pushed and shoved their way out of the door. "I'll take care of them. I brought the sprayer." Andy Matthews might have looked like a kid, but he was a chemistry genius and had come up with some really effective organic and non-toxic treatments for ordinary garden pests.

"Well, aren't you just on the ball today, Mr. Matthews," Myrna said. "Kelly, do men glow, because I do believe our lovely lawn boy is glowing?"

"It's going really well with Jenny," he said around a blush

that was almost neon. The discrete 'I owe you majorly' nod wasn't actually necessary because Myrna knew the whole story. Myrna knew almost everything, even when she wasn't supposed to.

"You're the one who's responsible for sending Alex Valens our way, right?" Myrna was never subtle.

The blank look on Andy's face was the first, and probably only, hint of coy Kelly had ever seen with the guy. "Oh, Alex. Right?" Then she remembered Alex Valens was not the man's real name, so the kid was not coy at all, just not quite sure what lies had been told.

Myrna's phone played a loud piano riff that sounded like it belonged in a strip club. She checked the screen and pushed away from the table. "It's Terry. Fingers crossed it's good news." She slipped out onto the patio with the kiddos, leaving Kelly to instruct Andy on weeding the front beds and dead-heading the geraniums in the planters, information to which he was clearly only half-listening.

"Thank you," he said. "For the pears." This time his smile was as big as his blush.

"I'm guessing you got the results you'd hoped for."

"Way more than I'd hoped for, Ms. B. Way more. I don't know how I can ever repay you."

"Well, for starters, you can remember my death threat. I asked you not to say anything."

The blush was back with a vengeance. "I know, and I'm sorry, but I didn't think you'd mind under the circumstances. Le…er…Mr. Valens is such a nice man, and his situation is not his fault. I just thought maybe you could help him. That's all."

"I know, Andy. Never mind. You're just too nice for your own good. I understand that. But it doesn't mean the threat doesn't still stand. I think a dead body under Ms. K.'s roses would never be found. Plus I hear corpses are great fertilizer."

"Well, that is true if you take into account the basic components of the human body. When it decomposes—"

"Damn! Damn, damn, damn!" Thankfully Myrna's curses, spoken with feeling, but not loudly enough for the little darlings to hear, interrupted the decomposition expose, and none too soon, either.

"What? What is it? Is Terry all right?" Kelly asked. Terry was Myrna's ex. They got along like a house afire ever since their divorce. The man worked in PR, and he had managed some juicy concert and theatre tickets for his ex and her friend in the time Kelly had known them, but this wasn't one of those times.

"He's fine. But he says even with his promise of his first born" — she nodded her head out to the patio where an argument on who was stronger, the Hulk or Iron Man, was well and truly in progress — "he still couldn't get us tickets to Alexander Valentine's exhibition. Damn, I was so sure he could swing it."

"I know, sweetie" — Kelly patted her friend's arm — "but we both knew that it was a long shot. I hear that there'll be a virtual exhibition on his website the next day. That'll have to do, I'm afraid."

"The sculptor, Alexander Valentine?" Andy asked.

"Is there any other?" Myrna said. "Half of the exhibition is new work, work that no one has seen before."

"And no one will see again once they end up in the gardens and foyers of the rich bastards who can afford them," Kelly said.

"But the money's for a good cause," Andy added quickly. "I've been on Le — er…Alexander Valentine's website, and I've read in *The Oregonian* all about the new women's and children's hospital. It'll be amazing. Why not let those who can afford it foot the bill?"

"No argument there," Kelly said, "but they shouldn't be the only ones allowed to appreciate Alexander Valentine's genius. That's all. I mean would it have hurt to leave the exhibition up for a few days and open to the general public? I bet Valentine wouldn't appreciate the fact that his work's going to be just one more way of shutting out the ordinary people, the people the hospital is supposed to benefit."

"No, he wouldn't appreciate that at all," Andy said, then he added quickly, "Or at least I don't think he would, based on...you know...what I've read about him...you know. So you're really big fans? Both of you?"

"Hell yeah," Myrna said. Her fan girl alter ego obviously didn't care about the Kieran rules on language.

Kelly nodded enthusiastic agreement.

"There has to be some way to get tickets." Andy spoke as though he were trying to solve a chemistry problem. He got that look in his eyes he often did when his thoughts were somewhere else — the nerd look, Myrna called it. Then he heaved a sigh and swallowed back the last of his coffee, nabbing another bear claw for sustenance. "I'll get right on those aphids and the weeding." He slipped out of the door, oblivious to their thank yous and goodbyes — definitely the nerd look.

Outside the door, once Andy was out of noise range of the Kieran twins, he pulled his iPhone out of his pocket and punched in his cousin's number. "'Sup?" he said, when Dillon picked up. "You sound like someone just ran over your dog."

"Not a good time, dude," Dillon said. Whatever he was doing on the other end of the line, he was clearly distracted. "Not a good time."

"Oh sorry, cuz. This won't take but a minute."

"Make it quick, then."

"It's just that you know the woman I told you about, the tutor with the canned pears? You know, Kelly Blake?"

"What about her?" Andy had been accused of being obtuse from time to time, but even he could tell that he had his cousin's complete attention at the mention of Kelly Blake.

"Can you nab a couple tickets to Lex's big charity exhibition? I owe her majorly and it turns out both she and her secretary are huge fans."

"Oh, are they now?" Dillon said.

"Yes, well, and while you're at it, you might want to mention to Lex, though I don't know if he can do anything about it or even if he already knows, but that the exhibition is only for one night, and only the rich and entitled will have access. I can't imagine him being happy about that. Kelly Blake's secretary's ex is doing the PR for the event, and even he couldn't get his hands on tickets for them, and well, I work for both of them, as you know, and I really, really owe Ms. B., I mean if it wasn't for her—"

"A big fan?" Andy could tell his cousin was taking notes.

"That's right. Big fans. Really disappointed that they couldn't get tickets too. I bet Lex has no idea, does he? I mean, I know he stays as far away from these things as he can, what with all the rubbing shoulders and all, but really, he should at least know what's going on, don't you think?"

"Yes, Andrew, I most definitely think Lex should take more of an interest in what's going on." Dillon always called him Andrew when he had something up his sleeve. "I'll see that these two ladies get tickets and I'll discuss the arrangement with Lex. Don't you worry, cuz, I think you might just have taken a huge step toward paying off your debt. Thanks, Andrew. Oh and, cuz, might be good if you didn't let them know that the tickets are due to your generosity. I have a plan in mind, and well, you know Lex's circumstances. I think I might be able to work out something from this, something really good for him too."

"Sure. No worries." Andy liked Lex a lot, and his situation really sucked. He'd said it to his cousin, and he'd say it again, if anyone could help Lex Valentine, it was Kelly Blake.

"Thanks, cuz," Dillon said. "You've just made my day a whole lot better."

He disconnected, and Andy smiled at just how happy Ms. B. and Ms. K. would be when they found out they had tickets to the big event.

# Chapter Eight

"I wouldn't go in there if I were you," V said, shaking her head. "I can't guarantee you'll come out alive."

"I think I might just have something that'll calm the angry beast," Dillon said.

"You'd better, because if he kills you, I don't do corpse cleanup."

"Go away, Dillon, and the two of you stop talking about me like I'm not here," Lex growled without looking up from his efforts at making short work of a sketchpad.

"Oh, you don't want me to go away, bro. I'm here to spread tidings of good cheer."

The man made no response, but sat on the floor hunched over a sketchpad in the middle of a growing array of drawings, most of them looking like the things one might find in a deeply disturbing graphic novel or a nightmare—best forgotten as soon as possible. Even if the sketches made his skin crawl, Dillon knew that Lex's drawing of his demons was one of the few truly therapeutic tools the man had taken away from myriad encounters with shrinks he'd seen through the years. Christ, if he ever got this Kelly Blake alone, he'd shake her teeth out for doing this to Lex.

Oh, he'd seen the official email from Ms. Blake apologizing for 'unprofessional behavior,' whatever the hell that meant, and stating that last night's meeting had convinced her that she was not the right fit for Mr. Valens' needs. The right fit? What the fuck was that supposed to mean? At the moment, Lex was completely non-communicative about whatever the hell happened. In fact, the man hadn't spoken more than a dozen words since he'd returned home in the wee hours, and most of those would have scorched the hair off a porcupine. Oh, no matter how much he wished he could lay the blame at Kelly Blake's feet, he couldn't. How the fuck was she supposed to know? He should have warned her about Lex before he got the two of them together. He should have vetted her better. He was the one who had talked Lex into seeing the woman in the first place, and yet, there was something about the two of them together that had made him ridiculously hopeful. He couldn't just give up. Whatever it was that Kelly Blake had done last night, whatever it was that had happened between the two of them, it was the closest to a normal fucked-up relationship between a man and a woman Lex had ever been, and Dillon wasn't quite ready to admit failure yet—especially not after his little phone convo with his cousin.

He shoved aside drawings that were mostly teeth and claws and faceless phantoms with skeletal hands and sat down next to Lex. "I need two tickets for the Valentine exhibition next Saturday."

Lex gave a one-shouldered shrug and continued to sketch. "So get two tickets. Hell, get a dozen, I don't give a fuck."

"While your generosity astounds me, I only need two. I need them for Kelly Blake and her secretary, who are huge fans of Alexander Valentine and terribly disappointed that the tickets are all taken by a bunch of rich bastards, who'll be the only ones getting to see the exhibition."

"What?" Lex laid down his pencil and looked up at Dillon. "I don't have anything to do with any of that, and whoever set up the exhibition like that needs his ass kicked, but—"

"But if you did, if you made sure that these two lovely ladies had tickets and that the exhibition was held over for someone other than the wealthy to see and enjoy, well..."

"Well, what?"

In spite of his efforts to look uninterested, Dillon knew he had Lex's full attention.

"Once Kelly Blake's at the exhibition, softened up a bit by expensive champagne and your sculptures, which my cousin assures me she adores, I'll take her aside and talk to her. I'm sure we can sort something out. I can be very persuasive, you know. I'd be willing to bet the two of you'll be meeting regularly within a week."

"She likes my work?" Lex asked, running a charcoal-smudged finger down the chiseled cheekbone of a ghoul in a black robe.

"She loves your work. She hates that no one gets to see it."

"I didn't know," he said. "Get the PR team on the horn and change it. Do whatever it takes. The clinic is for everyone. The exhibition should be too."

"I thought you'd feel that way," Dillon said. "And the tickets?"

"Get them to Ms. Blake, with Alexander Valentine's complements."

"Good. Perfect," Dillon said, pulling out his iPhone to make a few notes. "I'll send a courier today. That'll give them time to go shopping, have their hair done, maybe throw in a spa day for good measure." When Lex looked at him like he was speaking Chinese, he said, "It's a black-tie event, bro, a gala evening, a perfect opportunity to put on the ritz."

"Of course," Lex said. "I don't get out much. I forget these things."

For a moment, the two men sat in silence, Lex lost in thought that Dillon hoped didn't have to do with the demons he now drew. At last he spoke. "Look, Lex, I'll sort everything. And the night of the exhibition, I'll take the lovely Ms. Blake aside and make her see reason. Hell, when I finish, she'll want to be your own private tutor, I promise. I won't come home until I can bring good news."

"No," Lex said. The charcoal pencil snapped between his fingers with a sharp pop.

"No? No, what?"

"I'll talk to her myself." Lex's pulse hammered against his temple as though it would explode, and suddenly Dillon's pulse wasn't much slower.

"Look, maybe I can con her into coming back here to meet you, or wheedle her friend into it, you know, manipulating her in a tag team sort of way, but I can't guarantee that, Lex, short of tying the woman up and kidnapping her, I can't guarantee she'll want to see you even when she knows who you are. Though, I suppose I could arrange it so that she doesn't know until she gets here, but that would mean bringing someone else in to play your PA to persuade her, I mean she knows me already."

"No. There'll be no more subterfuge, at least not where Kelly's concerned. That's how we got into this mess to begin with. I'll go to the exhibition and I'll talk with her in person."

If Dillon hadn't already been sitting down, he might have fallen down from the shock of that little bomb. "Jesus, Lex, are you out of your mind? I mean look at you. Even talking about it you've gone white as a sheet and you're shaking like a leaf. How can you possibly go to an event like that? You have no idea what it's like. When I say it's rubbing shoulders with the rich and famous, I mean it, Lex. I *mean* it."

The man braced himself against the floor with both palms, as though he were afraid it might give beneath him. "Well then, we'll just have to figure out a way, because I'm going to my own exhibition, and I'm going to talk to Kelly Blake in person." He closed his eyes, and, for a moment, Dillon was afraid Lex would pass out. Then he pushed his way to his feet, and wiped his smudged hands on his shorts. "Anyway, it's about time I found out what happens to my work after it leaves the studio, isn't it? It's about time I took a little responsibility." On unsteady legs, he made his way carefully toward the studio door, then he turned and forced a desperate smile. "I mean, surely there must be a way to manage it, Dillon. There has to be."

Dillon took a deep breath, stood up and came to his side. "We'll find a way, bro. We'll find a way." And if the woman meant that much to him, he would, even if it killed him. As he followed Lex into the hallway, he texted V.

*Gonna need serious help on this one, dear lady. Meet me in the day room in 30. D*

# Chapter Nine

The glitz and glam of an exclusive exhibition at the Hendricks Gallery intimidated Kelly only for the few seconds it took her to ensconce herself in front of the first sculpture, called simply 'Horse and Rider'. After that, it no longer mattered that several US senators, two daytime TV gurus, a couple of movie stars, Portland and Seattle's wealthiest and everyone who was anyone in the art community was at the exhibition. They were all background noise. She had half a dozen coffee-table books full of photos of Alexander Valentine's sculptures and, unlike most coffee-table books, they were dog-eared and ratty-looking from use. She couldn't count the number of times the mysterious sculptor's work had inspired her writing. In fact, Tom Angleton, the main character of her latest work in progress, was an artist patterned after her fantasies of what Alexander Valentine must be like. Of course, for all she knew, he might be a surly prick. But the fact that he stayed completely out of public view and that no one knew where he lived or where his studio was made the man all the more intriguing. That he had donated so much of his work for an auction to benefit the much-needed women and children's hospital surely said a lot about the man. And it didn't hurt that when he'd found out his work was being shown for only one night and only to the rich and entitled, he'd thrown a fit, placed a very strongly-worded editorial in *The Oregonian* about art being for everyone, and forced Hendricks Gallery to open its doors for two weeks following the auction for people to view the work for free with an opportunity to donate to the cause as they saw fit.

Of course, if she wasn't convinced that the man was somewhere between a god and a saint before, she certainly was after the tickets arrived. They were delivered by a dapper courier, who stood at attention as though he were awaiting a military inspection. Then there was the note. It was handwritten on embossed stationary from the desk of Alexander Valentine.

*Dear Ms. Blake,*
*Please accept these tickets to my exhibition at the Hendricks Gallery as a token of my esteem and respect from one artist to another.*
*Lex*

Lex! That was how he had signed it. Who knew that his friends called him Lex? She would have figured Al, Alex, Zander, but Lex. She liked it. It was different. She liked it especially because he'd felt her enough of a comrade in creativity to refer to himself as such.

*Dear Mr. Valentine,*

She couldn't bring herself to call him Lex, and after all, he had offered her the politeness of allowing for her professionalism.

*I'm deeply touched by your kind consideration. As one artist to another, I thank you for your unexpected and welcome esteem. As a squeeing fan girl, however, I jump up and down and squeal 'thank you' for the tickets. And from both the fellow artist and the fun girl, thank you for your work, which inspires me daily.*
*Kelly*

She'd always fancied that, though she'd never actually met the man, she somehow knew him through his work, and the magically appearing tickets made that sense of connection feel even deeper. The thing that she loved most about his work was that all of it, every piece, practically begged to be touched — to be fondled, even. She stood in front of the 'Horse and Rider' that greeted guests in the grand foyer of the Hendricks Gallery. It was well placed, she thought. The horse's withers practically quivered to be stroked, as did the tight calf muscles of the woman riding it. There was a declaration of unspoken oneness between the saddleless, bridleless horse and the rider who grasped him between her muscular thighs as though he were somehow a part of her. The look on both of their faces was wild ecstasy that made Kelly think of sex, but something more than sex. It made her think of a connection that brought horse and rider into the realm of the other, realms in which neither would belong without the consent and the aid of the other. As she contemplated the sensuality of the sculpture, she found herself thinking about Alex Valens. She wondered if he were able to physically connect with animals. Perhaps if Alex might find healing aboard the broad back of a spirited horse or in stroking the sleek, warm fur of a sleeping cat. In her mind's eye, she couldn't keep from having that discussion with him, couldn't keep from imagining what it would be like to share the exhibition with him, to be able to bring him here alone, to have the whole gallery to themselves, so that he would feel safe, so that he would be completely at his ease. She couldn't keep herself from fantasizing about what it would be like to share something with him so sensual that the stone itself almost lived and breathed. It was easy for her to imagine Alex Valens touching, stroking, caressing, while she watched him and imagined that it was her he was touching.

Her stomach bottomed as she thought of that night, of walking out while he slept, of desperately wanting to touch him in his sleep, steal a moment of flesh on flesh, to know what he felt like. The worst part of it all was that she had ruined it, had ruined any hope they might have had for... For what? He was her client. She was his tutor. It was her job to facilitate healing, to help people become more comfortable with their own sexuality, and she'd blown it so badly it hurt to even remember. But then again, she could never really be sure if the pain she felt below her breastbone was from feeling sorry that she'd done what she'd done or feeling sorry she hadn't done more. At any rate, it was a moot point now, wasn't it? She had cancelled their next meeting and said she couldn't see him anymore. He had sent back a stiff, formal and very vague apology. And that had been that. In the time that had passed, every day when she asked Myrna for her messages, she hoped against hope that Alex Valens' PA would have asked again if maybe they could try one more time. And she would have said yes, if he had. Even though she was pretty sure she shouldn't. But in the end, she'd done the right thing and it was better this way. It really was.

"You are not going to believe this in a million years." Myrna grabbed her by the arm and pulled her away from the Horse and Rider as one of the Hendricks artists in residence began to give a running commentary on the sculpture for several couples clustered around her.

"What?" she asked. Half listening to the biography of Alexander Valentine the artist was sharing, Kelly wondered how much of it was fact and how much of it was conjecture, considering that no one actually knew much about him other than that his work was genius.

"He's actually going to be here."

"Who's going to be here?"

"Him!" She nodded to the sculpture. "I just talked to Terry and he says Alexander Valentine has shocked everyone by, just out of the clear blue, deciding to make an appearance. Can you believe it? We're actually going to meet the man in person, maybe even get a chance to talk to him and shake his hand." She fanned herself with the program. "Oh, honey, I'm so glad we went shopping. If I never get to wear this dress again, at least I'll have fond memories of the night I met Alexander Valentine looking like a million bucks." It was true, the woman looked like a porcelain doll in the antique peach number that could have come straight from a party in Downton Abbey. For a moment, Kelly was glad that she'd had her friend to help her pick out the deep red dress that she would have completely ignored if Myrna hadn't insisted she try it on. She didn't shop, in fact she hated shopping, but this was Alexander Valentine, and though, for all she knew, he could be old and fat and bald, any genius who could create such moving work deserved high homage from a fan girl in a red dress.

* * * *

"Look, Lex, it's okay if you change your mind. It's not too late. I can make your excuses and, I promise, I won't let the lovely Ms. Blake off the premises before I speak to her."

Lex came out of the bathroom a little unsteady on his feet and dropped onto the loveseat next to the picture window. "I just went in there for a piss, Dil, not to puke. Do you mind?"

Dillon had commandeered the director's office for the evening, and she'd been only too happy to give it over when she'd found out Alexander Valentine was going to make an appearance. He'd hired a team of six bodyguards dressed like guests to surround Lex's person without getting too close. He'd stacked the decks with people who knew the situation working on the wait staff, on the gallery's security staff, even the maintenance staff, and everyone who worked there from the director down to the lowliest janitor had been warned on pain of death not to touch Alexander Valentine. No! Matter! What! He'd even wrangled Lex's personal physician into being there just in case. Jesus, he hoped it didn't come to that, but it was a base he had to cover—certainly one Lex wouldn't be happy about. He'd made sure there was a getaway car waiting at every possible exit. He'd equipped himself with every kind of sedative and calmative he thought he might get down Lex's throat in case of an emergency, though usually Lex couldn't swallow anything in his attacks, and he refused to take anything before. He was reassured that the doctor would be equipped with needles and injections and more immediate solutions to any possible incidents. Dillon had even tucked a couple of airsick bags away in the inside pocket of his jacket. He honestly didn't know what else he could do. Fuck, this was such a bad, bad idea, and yet here they were. Here they fucking were!

So far, Lex had managed to keep his dinner down, what little of it Cookie had cajoled him to eat and, though he had the complexion of cottage cheese at the moment, he wasn't hyperventilating and he wasn't throwing up. He was calm and focused.

"Is she there?" he asked, keeping his gaze on the few notes he'd written down for the little welcome the director had asked him to give. He didn't mind speaking in front of people, he said, though Dillon didn't know how he'd know that when he'd never done it before.

"Oh, she's there, all right. She's wearing a heart's blood red dress, and when she stands next to the white marble of your sculptures, well let's just say she's breathtaking. And Lex, the woman is totally — I mean totally — focused on your work."

"Heart's blood." A blush crawled up Lex's cheeks, lending some much-needed color. "I like that."

"She's very excited that you're going to be there."

"She might change her mind when she sees me," he said. "Especially if I throw up on her shoes."

"Well, just don't throw up on her dress, because it really is stunning."

The two men sat in silence for a moment, and though Lex pretended to be focused on his notes, Dillon knew that he wasn't. Dillon knew that he was focused on getting through this night so he could get to Kelly Blake. What the fuck had the woman done to make the man go all love-sick stalker, to make him willing to do what had to be the most terrifying thing imaginable for a person who was as haphephobic as Lex was?

Dillon had been able to get no details from the man, only that he kept saying it was all his fault. Since then, there had been lots of brooding and solitude, even more than usual, and not much sleep, even less than usual. Dillon had offered to go and speak with Ms. Blake in person, but Lex had absolutely forbidden it, and he had forbidden any of the rest of his staff to talk to her either, as if Dillon might involve V or Cookie or Duncan the gardener in his plans to get to the bottom of the situation. As it turned out, the very informative call from Andy about Ms. Blake's love of Alexander Valentine's sculpture and her desire to see the exhibition of his work had made an all-out intervention unnecessary. Though, as he sat there looking at Lex's chalk-pale face, his tux pockets stuffed with airsick bags and the troops standing by, he wondered if an intervention might have been easier. They were definitely in uncharted waters where Kelly Blake was concerned. Dillon didn't know whether to be encouraged or to start researching psychologists just in case things went south.

"Lex, you do realize that once you've done this, you've crossed the Rubicon. There'll be no turning back. The place is crawling with press and paparazzi and your face, which has remained secret up until now, will be splashed all over the media."

Lex only nodded and wiped sweaty palms on his trousers.

"It's not too late to back out, you know?"

"I know." His voice was little more than a whisper. "I know, but I'm not backing out. Not this time." He returned his attention to his notecards, his hands trembling just slightly.

There was a soft knock on the door and the director stuck her head in. "Mr. Valentine, everything is set up. We're ready for you." She offered a reassuring smile and stepped aside as Lex came to his feet with way more confidence and aplomb than Dillon knew he felt. But that was okay, as long as Dillon was the only one who knew. He gave his friend a nod and a smile and said a silent prayer to every god he could think of who might have something to do with getting a clinically haphephobic man through a night in a crowded gallery with several hundred fans who would love nothing more than to shake his hand or rub up against him. And all of this he did in hopes of talking to a woman.

# Chapter Ten

Kelly was studying a sculpture of a child asleep in her mother's arms—one of three works at the exhibition that were the results of preliminary studies Alexander Valentine had done for the sculpture that would grace the foyer of the women and children's hospital—when the *ping! ping! ping!* against the side of a champagne flute brought the buzz of polite conversation to a halt. There was a soft hum followed by a loud pop and crackle over the sound system, then the director, Candice Holland's, voice filled the room, breathless with excitement.

"May I have your attention, please. It's my pleasure to extend all of you Hendricks Gallery's warmest welcome to what is, without a doubt, our highlight of the year—the Valentine exhibition and auction for the benefit of the Cascadia Hospital for Women and Children. It's even more my pleasure to welcome you now that you've all opened your checkbooks so generously. A little reminder that the silent auction for the pieces marked will go on all week, and let me just say, the money is pouring in."

There was a round of enthusiastic applause, which the woman patiently waited for before she continued. "When we were approached by Mr. Valentine's people, we were both elated by the offer and astounded by the sheer generosity of the man to donate so much of his exquisite work for such a good cause. I can tell by the buzz and the energy in this room tonight that everyone here is as excited as I am. But never mind the energy. Never mind the excitement. Let's talk cold, hard cash, shall we?" There was an even bigger round of applause, and when the room quieted once again,

Ms. Holland looked down at the small piece of paper she held in her hand. "Remember, half of the art on exhibit here tonight is being sold in the silent auction. That should excite you all terribly, when you hear that tonight, we've raised over five million dollars, the Horse and Rider in the grand foyer alone going for a cool three quarters of a million."

The resulting applause was thunderous, and Kelly was elated to know that it had been her favorite sculpture that had brought the most.

Kelly had moved into the main exhibition hall where she could see the woman standing at a wooden podium on a small stage that had been set for guests of honor, but at the moment, Ms. Holland was the only one on the stage. Kelly missed what the woman said next in her eager glance around to see if she could pick out the elusive Alexander Valentine. As the crowd pushed closer to the stage, phones poised at the ready to get the first ever glimpses and photos of the artist, she knew they were doing exactly the same.

In the crowding of the stage, however, Kelly couldn't keep from noticing that the area to the left of the platform had been cleared by plain clothes security all the way back to the side entrance. Kelly's uncle owned a security company, and she'd spent lots of time with him and his daughter when she was younger. She knew how to recognize plain clothes security, though in this case it couldn't have been more obvious. What the hell was going on? She returned her attention to the rambling Ms. Holland, who was saying how excited everyone at Hendricks was to be the gallery in which Alexander Valentine would make his first public appearance.

Then she rattled on about the man's illustrious career and how excited they all were that the exhibition would be held over for the public for two weeks because, as Mr. Valentine had said, art should be for everyone.

"Get on with it, already," Myrna whispered as she moved to stand next to Kelly.

It was then that Kelly noticed Dillon Mathews, Alex

Valens' PA, standing at the door to the left of the stage, and the niggle of a suspicion rose in her chest and made her pulse jump. She grabbed Myrna's arm. "What the hell's he doing here?"

Before Myrna could comment, Candice Holland cut to the chase and welcomed Alexander Valentine. Dillon Matthews then pushed the door to the left of the stage open and stood back as none other than Alex Valens, dressed in a black tux that looked like it was made for him, broad shoulders squared, face the epitome of calm, walked into the room to a thunderous round of applause.

"I'm stupid," Kelly said, taking a step forward on legs that no longer felt quite like they were connected with the floor, feeling like all the air in the room had been sucked out of that side exit when Alex Valens, AKA Alexander Valentine, walked through it. "I'm so fucking stupid. How could I be so damn stupid?"

She took another step forward with Myrna at her elbow, hissing in her ear, "Stupid? What's stupid? Why the hell are you stupid?"

"Alex Valens is Alexander Valentine."

"Are you serious? You can't be serious. You're serious. Holy shit!"

She received a glare and a shush from the rotund woman in front of them, who looked like she was dressed in a tapestry, then the entire room fell silent except for the snap, snap, snapping of cameras and smart phones, which, Alex...Alexander...er...Lex took calmly, standing for a moment in what could only be considered a pose, as though he were born to it. For a second, Kelly wondered if the man had been lying to her about his haphephobia, but the left side of the stage remained clear and Candice Holland had been very careful not to touch him when he stepped onto the stage. There hadn't been so much as a handshake. A sudden knot in Kelly's stomach tightened to a fist and, for a second, she couldn't breathe. Dear God, what the hell was the man doing here? She took another step forward then froze like a deer in headlights as he looked right at her, offered a sincere smile and cleared his throat to speak.

When the door opened, when Lex heard the applause, saw Dillon's reassuring but worried smile, it was all much easier than he expected it to be. His legs worked just fine. They didn't shake and he didn't fall over his feet. There was no cold sweat, no butterflies other than the usual that accompanied a public speaking experience. But then it shouldn't surprise him too much, not really. For him, there was only one person in the room, only one that mattered anyway, and he was a man on a mission that had nothing to do with the wonderful new women and children's hospital the auction would help build, no matter how much he believed in the work. He would make things right with Kelly Blake tonight or know the reason why not. As for humiliating himself in front of so many people, well yes, that was a very distinct possibility. The logistics of keeping hands off his person were staggering, he was sure, and yet Dillon had managed it. He knew that his friend was worried, and he would be, too, if he wasn't so focused. As he climbed the stairs to the stage, cameras and smart phones flashed. He'd been expecting that. It was all right. Let them take photos, he was a bit of an anomaly after all, and he would gladly pose for the guests if it would get him a chance to be with Kelly.

When he reached the podium, he stood quietly for a few moments, smiling out at the audience, letting them have their photo op as he looked out over crowded space, taking them all in with his warmest smile — at least that was how it must have appeared to them — but the truth was his smile was for one person only, the woman he'd fantasized about seeing again every day since he woke up in the middle of the marble kitchen island to find her gone. A red dress, Dillon had said. Heart's blood red, he'd called it. His pulse raced at the thought. In truth, there were a good few women in red dresses, but not heart's blood red, not the color he pictured suiting Kelly Blake like no other he could imagine. The snapping of cameras had died back to only a few, and now the crowd leaned forward to hear what the great Alexander Valentine had to say to them. Fuck, if only they knew. And just when things might have gotten awkward if he didn't say something, he spotted her toward the back in the grand entryway, behind the Horse and Rider looming white against the red, like a vision, like a dream. Dillon had been so right. She was breathtaking. She was flanked by the woman he assumed to be her secretary, who looked nearly as surprised as she did. He wished like hell she was closer so he could be certain if the look on her face was shock, or surprise, or confusion. At least it didn't appear to be anger. But she really was a little far from the stage for him to be sure of what was going through her beautiful head. They could iron all that out later. She was here. That was the main thing. He took a deep breath, feeling suddenly, completely happy — something he could never remember feeling before. He let that sink in for the tiniest of seconds, then he began to speak.

Kelly hadn't realized she was holding her breath until he began to speak, then she gulped air as though in doing so she could take in his words.

"You'll have to excuse me in my awkwardness," he said, still holding her gaze. "I don't get out much."

To that, the crowd responded with an appreciative chuckle.

He continued. "As you can imagine, I'm quite outside my comfort zone at the moment, but sometimes there are very good reasons to push the boundaries that we're used to. Sometimes there are very good reasons to take the risk, to throw caution to the wind and just do what needs to be done." He didn't take his eyes off her as he spoke, a favor she blatantly returned. She always looked people in the eyes when they spoke to her, and she was certain he was speaking to her. She was certain his message was for her.

She was surprised to find that there was not so much as a tremor in his voice, though he most definitely looked pale, and Dillon had moved to the foot of the steps, watching him with hawk eyes. Dear God, what a risk the man was taking! He was either very brave or very stupid, and she knew he wasn't the latter.

"It's very easy for those of us who were raised to privilege to go through our lives with blinders on, to spend our days in our own little well-protected worlds, insulated by our good fortune while we remain totally unaware of the plight of those around us who haven't had such good fortune, who have had struggles we can't even imagine. But being privileged doesn't mean we're not members of the world community, and it doesn't absolve us of our responsibility toward the rest of that community. No one knows better than I that privilege doesn't protect any of us from tragedy, from pain, from loss. In this, there is no separating ourselves from the rest of humanity. In this, our need for comfort, for community, for hope, for solace is just as raw, just as aching. We're here tonight to remember that we all face our humanity together, from the moment of our birth to the instant of our death. That being the case, we're also here because all of us have come, in our own personal ways, perhaps through our own tragedies, to realize that with our privilege comes responsibility, and I'm happy to see so many here taking that responsibility seriously."

Kelly was certain the whole crowd leaned forward in an effort to get closer to Alexander Valentine. The irony of their desire to be close and his desire to keep a safe distance was not lost on her. He nodded at one of the sculptures to his left, another of the clinic preliminaries, a heavily pregnant woman cradling her belly in an embrace not unlike the way she might hold the child once it was born. The look on her face was concentration, tenderness, excitement and hope. "The hand that rocks the cradle rules the world," he said. "Too often we forget that. Too often we forget that the welfare of women is the welfare of our children. The welfare of our children is the welfare of every single one of us. And the welfare of every single one of us is both our inheritance and our legacy." He paused to catch his breath, ran his teeth over his bottom lip, and the look on his face darkened. "My own good mother died tragically a long time ago, and I'm a lesser man for her absence. Hers is an absence I feel in ways that are still being revealed to me every day of my life. This event, this auction, was conceived in her honor, and I hope that each of you will think of your own mothers and daughters and sons as the Cascadia Women and Children's Hospital becomes a reality. It will be your legacy to those who birth the next generation. Let that next generation be birthed in safety and good health."

The applause was thunderous, and everything went smoothly until Alexander Valentine chose an alternate route for his planned exit of the building, the one that would take him right through the middle of the crowd and straight to her.

# Chapter Eleven

It was not his finest moment, nor was it a well thought out decision. Lex wasn't used to dealing with crowd control, since he tended to avoid them like the plague. But if he left the stage via the planned route, Kelly Blake could simply turn and leave by any number of other exits open to her. If she did that, then the whole evening, the long days and nights of angsting and planning, would have been for nothing. She would know the truth of his identity and still she could walk away and, fucking hell, he might be a lot of things, but he wasn't a stalker. So he chose the direct route, took the steps down the front of the stage, feeling the connection between the two of them so powerfully that it was like they were reeling each other in, and to his delight, she was moving forward, moving toward him.

For a moment, he didn't notice anything else. For a moment, everything seemed just fine, the plan was working. She would give him a chance to plead his case. For a moment, his eyes remained locked on hers. He had some vague awareness of Dillon and several of the bodyguards he'd hired scrambling to create a wedge in front of him and almost literally pushing people aside, then he lost sight of her, then a camera flashed in his face, a TV camera pressed in, and he was jostled by the shoving of several other people wielding cameras and microphones.

"What the hell are you doing?'" Dillon gasped, elbowing a large man with a Dictaphone out of the way. "I had a plan. You knew I had a plan. Get out of his way, give the man some room," he barked at a woman wielding a large camera.

"Can you tell us what it's like to be at such an exciting event after so long in seclusion?" It was a woman who spoke this time, and she thrust another Dictaphone under his nose. Damn it! She was close enough that her breath was hot on his face and, for a terrifying moment, he thought he'd pass out.

"Crowded," he managed breathlessly. To the woman's credit, she backed off, but the press was now shoving forward closer and closer to Lex. He felt a brush against the sleeve of his jacket and suddenly there was no air for him to breathe. His shirt clung to his body, now bathed in icy sweat, and his stomach threatened projectile vomiting if he didn't get out of this place fast. Not that that had ever actually happened, but for a brief second, *The Exorcist* flashed through his head, and he would have laughed had he not been so terrified of what might happen if he actually did open his mouth.

More of the security guards had cued in on what was happening and began to push and elbow their way through the middle of the crowd from the left where the space was cleared, which meant that there was no place for people to go but to press back and right into Lex's exit path. "Please let me pass," he managed between barely parted lips. The guests yielded politely, the press and the paparazzi, not so much. The push and the shove of the bodyguards that had worked in Lex's favor at the beginning now became detrimental, being forced back dangerously close to the man's body.

Candice Holland's voice boomed over the sound system. "Please back off, folks. Please give Mr. Valentine room. Give the man some air." But the press ignored her pleas.

Where the hell was Kelly? The floor suddenly felt like the rocking of a ship, and he swallowed back bile. He stumbled and righted himself only a split second before ending up in the arms of a hefty woman in a dress that looked like a tapestry. Black spots danced before his vision, and he forced himself forward. He was not going to pass out. He was not!

He couldn't humiliate himself until he got to Kelly. How much farther could it be, if she was moving toward him and he was moving toward her, surely he was almost there. But what if she'd seen the mess he'd caused and decided to leave him to it? Kelly Blake wouldn't do that, whatever she was, she understood his struggles. She wouldn't leave him to his own devices without giving him the satisfaction of hearing him out. Black spots were now bouncing about with the rocking of the floor and the roiling of his stomach, and, just when he thought it couldn't get any worse, the horrid woman from Talk About Town Radio elbowed her way between two security guards and stopped progress in its tracks.

"Please let me through."
Kelly heard the desperate plea in his voice.
But the press ignored it.
"Jesus Christ! What the hell are they doing? What the hell are they doing?" Myrna gasped. "Sonovabitch, isn't that Gale Ann Spaulding from Talk About Town? Oh God, he so doesn't need to deal with that bitch."
Sure enough, Talk About Town radio's diva, Gale Ann Spaulding, dressed in white like a vitriol-spewing angel, elbowed her way in close and shoved a Dictaphone in Alexander Valentine's now chalk-white face. Abrasive didn't begin to describe the woman, and even those who loathed her — pretty much anyone who occasionally used their brain for thinking — couldn't avoid the woman's influence as Talk About Town had billboards of her deceptively pretty face with its blinding, eat-your-heart-while-it's-still-beating smile plastered all over the city. Talk About Town wasn't known for its forward-thinking, intelligent journalism, and Gale Ann Spaulding fit right in. She had used her show as a platform to claw her way to the top of bad radio way more by sensationalism than journalism. She ignored his pleas to let him pass.
"Mr. Valentine, could you please tell us just exactly what

procedures will be performed at this women and children's hospital your work is helping to build?"

"Oh, she did not just say that," Myrna growled. "She fucking did not just say *that!*"

"I'm an artist, not a doctor, but if you were listening earlier, Dr. Forsythe addressed that subject," he replied in a voice that was visibly shaking. "Now, please let me pass."

"Take that, you bitch!" Myrna said, one hand clenched in a tight fist while the other was in danger of snapping the stem of the champagne flute she held.

Several cameras flashed, and Alexander Valentine blinked and stumbled, and the woman pressed forward. "Do you mean to tell me you're willing to offer work you've clearly spent thousands of man hours on to a cause you don't fully understand?"

"Get out of my way, Ms. Spaulding," he said between gritted teeth and stumbled again to a visible gasp of the other guests, several of whom, not clearly understanding the situation, were pressing forward to offer the distressed man a hand. All the while, Candice Holland kept pleading over the mic for everyone to back off and let Mr. Valentine pass. But the reporters, in particular Gale Ann Spaulding, clearly didn't think that plea applied to them.

"He's not going to make it. He's doing to pass out," Myrna gasped.

"The hell he is," Kelly grabbed two glasses of champagne from the tray of a waiter who watched the commotion with wide eyes, then thought better of it and traded them in for two glasses of red wine, which were larger. "Help me," she said to Myrna. The woman was nothing if not perceptive and took one of the glasses from her, then grabbed the arm of her equally perceptive ex. Following the lead of the two women, he grabbed a half-empty magnum of champagne away from a server.

While Lex swayed on his feet, the tenacious Gale Ann Spaulding went into rant mode about taxpayers' money used for unnecessary procedures, the Dictaphone now in her face, since it really was all about her and she didn't want her adoring audience to miss a single golden word she uttered. She was just about to lay a hand on Lex's lapel in an effort to stop his progress when it was shower time. It took Lex a moment to figure out what happened, as he felt a couple of droplets against his face like it had just started to rain in the gallery. Then the horrible woman let out a high-pitched squeal and stepped back, but not in time to prevent a serious drenching in red wine. It was surreal, really. If he hadn't been afraid he'd pass out or throw up, Lex might have enjoyed it as the woman let out a barrage of expletives in a total *Carrie* moment — minus the pig's blood and the bad things happening to good people and burning the place down.

But then things turned decidedly *Aliens* when Kelly and her secretary pushed their way front and center, empty glasses clenched in their fists, and Lex could have sworn Kelly said something along the lines of 'Get away from him, you bitch.' Then Dillon caught on to what was happening, as everyone pressing in close to Lex's person got showered in expensive champagne, complements of a man who seemed to be in cahoots with Kelly's secretary.

"Get him out of here," Dillon yelled to Kelly. "There's a limo waiting out front."

Lex just barely heard the exchange over the ringing in his ears.

Kelly's secretary, and the man with her, elbowed and shoved. Several of the other guests had gotten the idea and showered the paparazzi in a veritable downpour of expensive alcoholic beverages with special attention paid to Gale Ann Spaulding, who was still ranting something about tax payers' money, then she spotted Kelly, but somehow that didn't matter, because Kelly's full attention was on Lex. That was all that mattered to him as she motioned him toward the exit. He was vaguely aware of Dillon leaping onto the stage, introducing himself loudly as Lex's PA and saying he would happily answer any questions. Then there was another shower of champagne and Lex and Kelly had the break they needed.

It was all like instant replay when Lex was able to actually think about what had happened in those few minutes. When it was happening, when he was in the midst of it, sure he was going to die, even as he knew he wouldn't, even as he knew it was just the phobia, all he could manage was to stay on his feet and not throw up. He kept his eyes on the woman in the heart's blood dress, focusing on her only, following her like a beacon as she cajoled and encouraged him breathlessly toward the front exit, toward the waiting limo, toward relief. All this she did without ever once touching him. Out front, the driver was at the ready. He hurried them both inside, slammed the door and sped away. Only then did she start yelling at Lex.

# Chapter Twelve

"Why did you do that? Why the hell did you do that? That woman's insane, and the crowd, they don't know. They were sympathetic, but they have no idea. You could have ended up passed out on the floor. Christ, you could have ended up in the hospital."

"At least I waited until after the auction," he mumbled.

"Er… Well, that's good, I guess," she said, then she added quickly, "This isn't funny. You're reckless." She fumbled in the mini bar until she found a bottle of water, which she opened and handed to him. He shook his head.

"Not yet. I need to…just be still." His complexion had gone gray with a tinge of green around the gills. She looked about desperately then grabbed the silver ice bucket and offered it to him—just in case.

He nodded slightly, but said nothing, only laid his head back against the seat and scrunched his eyes shut tightly, ice bucket balanced in a suicide grip on one knee.

If he were anyone else, she would have grabbed one of the cloth napkins, wet it in the cold water and wiped his sweating forehead and, God knew, she wanted to touch him, to hold his head if he threw up, to do something, anything to ease his distress. Instead, she sat silently, because that was what she wanted when she felt nauseated—for people to shut the fuck up and leave her alone.

Apparently that wasn't exactly the case with him. "Why did you leave without saying goodbye?" he managed, then swallowed hard a couple of times.

"What do you mean, why? You know why." She jammed her feet hard against the floorboards to keep her knees steady. It was bad enough one of them shaking like a leaf, she thought. "What happened... It was—"

"Unprofessional. Yes, I know. Your secretary's goddamned email said as much. But you could have least—" He was suddenly shallow-breathing, lowering his head between his knees.

"Fuck! Are you going to pass out? Please don't pass out. How the hell will I know what to do if you pass out?"

"I'm not going to fucking... Oh, God."

"Do you need the bucket? Some water? What do you need?"

"I need my dignity back," he said, bent double like he was talking to the floorboards. "It's humiliating enough to be in this position, let alone having the woman I masturbated with watch."

"Shh!" She glanced back through the open privacy window. "Shall I roll down the windows so you can shout it to all of Portland, maybe? And anyway, goddamn it, you brought it on yourself. Clearly Dillon had everything planned out carefully for you. All you had to do was follow his instructions and then—"

"And then I saw you," he said to the floorboard. "I wasn't going to run the risk...fuck." He reached again for the bucket.

She couldn't help it, her own stomach did a little pirouette. "Try to breathe deeply," she said. "Let it roll over you."

"Please shut up for a minute," he half-whispered.

Had he really put himself through what had to have been his worst nightmare because he wanted to see her? Idiot! Her—not him! She was an idiot for not giving him the closure he needed. Fuck! She'd worked as a tutor for almost four years now. She knew how important closure was. She knew it, and yet, in her embarrassment at her unprofessional behavior, she had denied him that essential element. She sat with her eyes down, trying to give the man as much privacy as she could under the circumstances. She felt like a total asshole. She wondered what to say, wondered how the hell she could ever make up to him for what she'd put him through. When his breathing eased, she glanced up. He was still pale, but at least the green and gray were fading, and his gaze was locked on her.

"What?" she asked. A blush crawled up her cheeks for some reason she couldn't name.

"Dillon was right," he said, offering her the first relaxed smile she'd seen since they'd left the gallery.

"About what?"

"The dress. He said it was the color of heart's blood and that it suited you." He shrugged. "I have no idea how he knows what color heart's blood is, though I've long suspected him of being some kind of practitioner of magic, possibly even a dabbler in the dark arts, but only for a good cause, of course."

"Of course," she said.

"But he was right about the dress suiting you. When I looked out across the room before I gave my little speech, you were like a beacon. You were all I could see."

She tugged at the fitted bodice and sat up a little straighter. "Myrna helped me pick it out. She said it was my color."

He leaned back against the seat, still studying her. "It looks soft."

"It is." She struggled not to squirm under the intensity of his gaze. "Do you want to touch it?" she asked, blushing at the look of surprise on his face. "Well, you don't have to touch me to touch the fabric, do you?" She shifted slightly to one side and tugged at the tail of the dress where the fabric was split high up her left thigh. With a bit more shifting and wriggling, all the while with him watching wide-eyed, she held the length of the dress from the split out to him. "Is that enough?"

He nodded, his breathing suddenly faster and his pulse beating hard against his throat. He was breathing faster, and she was holding her breath. He reached out and took the hem of the dress into his hand, and she let go, both of them sighing in unison.

"That's wonderful," he said. "It must feel like you're constantly being caressed every time you move."

"That's really why I chose it—the way it feels." She ran a finger over the fabric of the bodice, feeling her nipples peak beneath it. "I love soft things against my skin."

"Me too," he said. Holding her gaze, he lifted the fabric, brushed it over the stubble of his cheek then brought it to his lips and pressed a kiss into its folds. She wasn't sure, but she thought she might have moaned.

* * * *

"Is that woman his girlfriend?" One of the reporters asked Dillon, who was now standing at the podium answering questions about Lex. The driver had just texted that that he and Kelly Blake were in the limo en route back to Mountain View. He couldn't help it, the thought of the lovely Kelly Blake offering the man comfort gave him a warm fuzzy. Damn, he was such a soppy romantic.

And, truth be told, he was a bit of a schemer too. Though Dillon hadn't planned it, he certainly didn't try to correct himself when the words just popped right out of his mouth. "She's his fiancée." The crowd erupted in chaos over which he could hear an occasional clinking of glasses from a far less sedate group than the one that had arrived at the Hendricks several hours ago. After the little wine shower had loosened everyone up, they were ready to party, and he'd just given them one more excuse. Hell, he figured surely he could run interference with the press long enough for the idea to sink in and take root. Really, what harm could it do? The man had put himself at risk of humiliation and possibly even hospitalization to be with Kelly Blake, for fuck's sake. And she...well, she had more than acquitted herself very nicely, indeed, with the risk of her own humiliation and, considering the vitriol Ms. Spaulding was spewing after the pinot noir bath, he reckoned she had risked life and limb as well. And no doubt the story the bitch would tell on Talk About Town tomorrow would not flatter Ms. Blake overmuch, though he was pretty sure she'd made more than a few fans tonight for her heroic efforts. He liked her. He liked her a lot. She was good for Lex, and Lex needed something…someone good in his life. That being the case, Dillon was willing to go out on a limb and take a chance. "They're just newly engaged, actually, as of tonight. Mr. Valentine wanted to ask her on this special occasion." The crowed oohed and awwed their approval, and Dillon figured he was on a roll, or at least he was until he saw Kelly's secretary making wide-eyed fish gasps from the back, then he took another chance.

"Look, I'm not the expert on my boss's lovely new fiancée, but her secretary certainly is." He motioned Myrna to the stage, noting that the PR guy for the event, the man who was also her ex, if his research served him right, was pushing her front and center with a reassuring smile.

As she mounted the stage, giving him something related to the evil eye, he leaned in to kiss her cheek like they were old friends. "I saw the way you helped her. I know you think exactly what I do about the two of them. Help me out here?"

The smile on her face went from strained to genuine, a look he'd seen before on women who couldn't resist the urge to make matches wherever the opportunity presented itself and even sometimes when it didn't. Oh, he was so right about this.

Myrna moved to the microphone and nodded. "Ms. Blake is a writer, a novelist, in fact. She writes the Sarah Cassidy novels among others, under the name of Gina Alan."

With the amount of press shoving Dictaphones and cameras their way, Dillon figured that should boost book sales considerably. The woman was really good at her job.

Once she'd let that soak in, she continued. "I've had the pleasure of working for her for the past four years now, and the privilege of considering her my friend for longer still. Though this engagement may be sudden, it's most definitely welcomed by all who know the happy couple."

Oh, she really was good, he thought.

"She threw wine on me," Gale Ann Spaulding moaned. There was an undercurrent from the audience more than hinting that she bloody well deserved it.

"Mr. Valentine isn't comfortable around crowds, Ms. Spaulding," Myrna said with enough syrup in her voice to give the whole room diabetes. "Ms. Holland did ask multiple times for everyone to step back and give the man some breathing room." Her smile was all sweetness and light, but Dillon was pretty sure she would happily rip the woman's head off with her bare hands and stuff it up her ass given half a chance.

Myrna continued. "The two have kept their plans secret because they both value their privacy and they hope very much you'll understand that and give them the space they need to build a relationship that will result in more great work from both of them."

Dillon had to resist the urge to cheer, but the crowd did not, and when the reporters rushed to speak all at once, Myrna raised a hand. "No more questions tonight. Just enjoy the rest of the evening and the lovely art." Then she turned and walked off the stage with Dillon's hand under her elbow.

"Is she going to kill you?" he whispered without moving his lips.

"Probably, and will you be joining me in death, Mr. Matthews?"

"More than likely."

At the bottom of the steps as the two moved toward the east exit, which was still relatively free of people, she handed him her card. "I'll call her in the morning, and I'll expect a full account from you as well."

He resisted the urge to salute.

* * * *

"I think we're being followed," Kelly said, glancing out of the back window.

"Wouldn't be surprised. There were three limos and two cars waiting to pick me up if I needed a quick getaway."

"A good plan," she replied. "Possibly the only part of your plan that was good."

"That's what Dil said."

"You should have listened to him, you look terrible."

"I've been worse," he said, and the boyish smile slipped from his lips. "Much worse. Thanks to you and your friend, that Spaulding woman only grazed my lapel with a fingernail long enough to disembowel a mammoth." He shivered.

At Kelly's suggestion, Lex now lay in the seat across from her, eyes closed, still stroking the hem of her dress. Though he'd managed to keep down the few sips of water he'd had, and didn't seem to be in any real danger, he wasn't quite recovered enough to fully engage.

"Thank you," he said, his lips curling in a smile, "for rescuing me from that harridan."

"It was my pleasure." She studied his face while she could, while he had his eyes closed. "I'm normally not for wasting good Oregon Pinot Noir, but, seriously, it was a Kodak moment."

"It was that. Wish I'd have been able to enjoy it a little better." He laughed softly, then moaned and sucked in a tight breath.

"Still nauseated?"

He shook his head. "It's just that the seat keeps spinning beneath me."

"That sounds more like you're drunk," she said. "Put one foot on the floorboard, that's supposed to help."

He followed her advice.

This time, she did douse a napkin in cool water, then she laid it on the seat next to him. "You can put it on your forehead, or your neck is better still, at least it is for me."

He did as she said and she was rewarded with a sigh.

"That's nice. Thank you, Kelly."

"I don't know what to call you," she said. "Jesus, I don't know anything after everything that has happened. I've just been sitting here yelling at Alexander Valentine and before that I…" She shoved a hand to her forehead and her face burned with heat. "Oh God, I can't believe what I did before that."

"Lex," he said, offering her a smile that was warm enough to make her insides tremble. "Please call me Lex, and I'm glad you know the truth."

They sat in silence for a long moment, the headlights of passing cars having a strobe light effect on the dark interior.

"I don't know what to say to you," she half-whispered. "Not after everything that's happened between us."

"Say you won't stop being my tutor." There was another flash of a smile. "Look how much I've improved since you've started seeing me. I'm now able to go to crowded parties and make an utter fool of myself."

"Just like everyone else then, are we?" she said with a chuckle.

He shook his head. "I do it with a lot more drama."

"I can't argue that point. You stole the show."

"Will you, then? Keep being my tutor?"

"I'll think about it."

# Chapter Thirteen

"You feeling better?" she asked, when the smile came back to his face, even though he kept his eyes closed.

"Much, thank you. In fact, I'm feeling downright smug."

"And why's that?"

"Well…" He opened his eyes and sat up, taking the water she offered him, still holding to the hem of her dress in one hand. "I only wanted to talk to you, to try to make things right. I wasn't even sure you'd listen to me, but I actually got you to come home with me. Dillon would say I have the moves."

"I would have. Listened, I mean." Then she added, trying not to sound angry or hurt, "You could have told me who you are, you know?"

"And would that have changed how you treated me? I just wanted your help. Granted, it could have been that you didn't know who the hell Alexander Valentine was. A lot of people don't, but as it turned out, I was right to keep it from you." Before she could comment further, he continued. "Look, there's a lot about me and about my family you don't know, and there are a lot of things the people who work for me and live with me have learned not to mention, not to refer to. If you feel you need to know, I'll tell you what I can, what I'm able. If you'll be my tutor again."

"We didn't get very far," she said.

"You have no idea how far we got, how excited I was to be able to interact with another person…in that way."

"I…took advantage."

"No, you didn't. You did exactly what I needed, and if I'd have felt for one minute that you were out of line, I'd have

103

sent you packing."

Before she could argue with him, the limo stopped in front of a house the size of the shopping mall in the town where she'd grown up, but much more elegant. "Wow!" she managed "Are you roommates with Bruce Wayne or is this Xavier's School for the Gifted?"

"It's actually the Valentine School for the Neurotic," he said. Then he added, "Although my cook does moonlight as chef for the Avengers from time to time."

"Nice! I had no idea art paid so well," she said.

"I do all right for myself," he said, "but this place, I inherited from my bastard of a father, who married my mother for it."

"As one does," she said in a really bad *Pride and Prejudice* accent.

He laughed. "Indeed."

The door to the limo burst open before the driver was even out of the vehicle, and a woman, who might have passed for Mrs. Danvers, stuck her head in. But the minute she opened her mouth, it was clear she would have been no use to Daphne du Maurier where villainous household staff was concerned. "Are you all right, Alexander? Dillon called ahead to tell me what happened. I'm so terribly sorry. Can you walk? Do you need to sit a minute? Did you throw up?"

"Yes, no and no, in that order," he said, shooing her aside so he could get out. "This is Kelly Blake." He nodded in her direction.

She got out of the other side and scurried around to help him, though in truth there was little she could do but cheer him on, and Mrs. Danvers' not-so-evil twin seemed to be doing a great job of that.

"Dillon told me that too. Ms. Blake, it's such a pleasure," she said, grabbing Kelly's hand, which was safe to touch, and giving it a hearty shake. "Welcome to Mountain View. I'm V. Now hurry on in, both of you, but not too fast, Alexander, I don't want you having a relapse. Cookie's made your favorite Irish stew with carrot cake for dessert. Those schmooze-y kinds of events are exhausting under the best of circumstances, and these circumstances must have been pretty harrowing. You'll be starving by now, I'd imagine."

"Cookie? She the one who cooks for the Avengers?"

"Only part-time," V said, without missing a beat. "When Alexander can spare her. Oh, I'm sure that Nick Fury guy would love nothing better than to hire her away, but she likes it at Mountain View because it's so much more peaceful. She's a cook, not a super hero, at least that's what she tells everyone." She moved ahead of the two, opening doors and straightening knickknacks that didn't need straightening. "We so seldom get company, Ms. Blake, what with Alexander's condition and his work and all, so we're all in a bit of a dither."

"Please, it's Kelly," she said to the woman.

"I hope you don't mind that we all eat in the kitchen. I've told Alexander ad nauseum that it's not right for the master of the house to eat with the servants, but well, you know artists are a quirky lot, Ms. Blake...er, Kelly."

"Yes they are, V, and the kitchen suits me just fine," Lex said.

Kelly had to rush to keep up with the woman, and Lex was right on her heels, seeming completely recovered from the incident at the gallery.

"Dillon will be along shortly. He was dealing with the press when he texted me. What was it he called it? Oh yes, playing spin doctor for the diva." She raised a hand. "And, Alexander, you watch your language. He was only teasing. He's just glad you're all right, as are we all. Come along now, we don't want to keep Cookie waiting."

They took the straight path through the enormous house then made a sharp left down a corridor that was a little narrower and a little less opulent than the grand entry hall. Kelly had been so busy taking in all the marble and oak that she nearly ran into V, as she stopped in the middle of an enormous entrance through which she could view a kitchen that was bigger than her whole house. The floor was dark green tile polished to a mirrored shine and the wall a stuccoed terracotta that would not have been out of place in the Southwest somewhere. "Alexander's mother had the kitchen designed herself. She loved to cook, even though his father frowned on it."

"Enough of the family history," Lex said. "Let the poor woman eat." He nodded her into a room that made her mouth water with the scent of fresh stew and spicy carrot cake. She inhaled and closed her eyes with a moan.

At the battered trestle table in the middle of the floor, a tiny Hispanic woman who would have had to stand on tiptoe to reach five feet ladled the succulent stew into two bowls. A third place was set, no doubt for Dillon when he arrived. The woman offered her a bright smile and a nod then motioned them to the table with a stream of Spanish that Lex seemed to understand completely. Whatever it was the woman said made him blush heartily. "Speak English, Cookie, so our guest can understand you."

"It's a pleasure," the woman said in English that was as good as her Spanish and completely without accent.

"You see why Nick Fury wants to hire her away from me, besides her fantastic cooking skills, the woman's a polyglot," he said, pulling out a chair for Kelly.

She figured to do so was really pushing the envelope for him, based on the wide-eyed stares of the two women.

"*Dios mio*," Cookie whispered, crossing herself.

Lex rolled his eyes and shooed her away. "Go on, you two, leave us to eat in peace while you listen at the pantry door."

There was another stream of what sounded like possibly Russian from V and the little cook responded in kind. Kelly heard her name and Lex's mentioned before the two pushed their way through the door.

"It's pretty clear they adore you," she said.

A faint blush crawled up his cheeks, which were now

flushed with health. "They know I let them get away with anything as long as they feed me, keep my house halfway clean and leave me to my work." He motioned to the stew. "Please, eat, I'm starving, and you must be too. Save room for carrot cake. It's one of Cookie's specialties."

The first few bites were eaten without conversation, in the presence of groans and sighs that always accompany good food, but it didn't take long for Kelly to realize that Lex was watching her over his raised spoon.

"What?" she said, suddenly self-conscious as she covered her mouth with her napkin.

"It's just, I was wondering what it would be like to be able to take you to a restaurant and maybe dancing. Do you like to dance?"

"I don't know how," she said.

He laughed. "Neither do I." Then he was suddenly serious. "I was learning, actually when I...before..." He looked around as though he were searching for words. "And anyway at that age I hated it because I had to dance with girls, but my mother said that one day I'd be glad that I knew how." The smile returned again. "Dillon said I could still learn. All I need is an inflatable doll, but well, with my situation being what it is, no self-respecting inflatable would be caught dead around me."

They both laughed, and that was how Dillon found them, laughing over the last of their stew. "Dear lady, I thank you for getting my young charge home safely," he said with a chivalrous bow. "He can be rather ill-behaved at times," to which Lex responded with a raised middle finger.

"It was my pleasure," she said.

Cookie brought Dillon's stew and V buzzed in long enough to greet the man.

"Your secretary is a keeper," Dillon said, "and she's got great aim with a glass of wine. The wine baptism of Gale Ann Spaulding will be talked about around dinner tables and in back alley bars for many years to come." He shoveled in a mouthful of stew, winced as he burnt his tongue and continued. "The party heated up after you two got things started, and those tight-assed philanthropists and rich moneybags let their hair down and loosened up."

"You're talking about us, you know, bro?" Lex said.

"Shh! Don't tell her." Dillon nodded to Kelly. "Maybe she'll like us anyway."

When Cookie delivered carrot cake, Dillon grabbed up his and made his excuses. "V," he called as the woman passed in the hall, "I need to discuss something with you when you have a few minutes." Then he turned back to the table. "Kelly, it might be wise for you to stay here tonight. After our little exhibition at the exhibition, the press was pretty rabid. Oh, not in a bad way, but now that they know who you are, well... I wouldn't expect any problems, but you're here and it's a long way back into town. V will have a room made up for you."

"It's already been done," V replied from her listening post in the doorway, large travel mug of coffee clutched in one hand, small iPad in the other. She turned her attention to Kelly. "When Dillon alerted me to the situation, well, with it being late and the circumstances being what they were, I thought your staying might be a prudent choice."

Kelly looked from Lex to Dillon to V and back again. "I... to tell you the truth I hadn't thought about anything other than getting Lex away from the crowd and that horrid woman."

"And that horrid woman will make sure you pay for it." Dillon waved his hand dismissively. "Not a big deal, I'm sure a word from Alexander Valentine's people will make her look like the idiot she is, but the thing is, the rest of the press saw a woman coming to the rescue of her man, a man who's already their hero." Lex made a derisive sound, which Dillon ignored. "A man that, you must remember, they were all seeing for the first time. Everybody's a closest romantic, and the two of you leaving in a limo together, well, need I say more?"

Kelly felt the muscles in her stomach tighten. "What did

you tell them?"

Dillon held her gaze. "What did you want me to tell them, Ms. Blake, that you were Alexander Valentine's sex tutor? It seemed prudent at the time, and your secretary agreed, to let the idea slide that the two of you were an item. The rich and famous have dalliances all the time. They usually don't last long. You'll be the talk of the town for a few days, a week tops, which can do neither of you any harm, probably sell you a boat load of books and get Lex a few more commissions he doesn't have time to do. Gale Ann Spaulding will sling mud at your name, which will sell even more books, and get more commissions for Lex, then it'll all blow over. No harm done." He looked from Lex to her. "Whatever happens between the two of you, well, that's between the two of you. Fair?"

"All right," Kelly said, noticing that Lex was keeping his eyes on the remains of his cake. "I suppose I can stay here for the night. I don't have anything with me, though."

"Don't worry," V said, moving to refill her travel mug for at least the third time since Kelly's arrival. "I've taken care of everything. I put you in the Meadowlark suite. Alexander, perhaps you could show her and help her settle in while I speak with Dillon?"

Kelly didn't miss the sharp look that Lex gave his housekeeper, which only lasted long enough to dissolve into a blush that was little more than a flash of color. "Of course," he replied, swallowing the last bite of his cake without chewing. "I'd like to get out of this monkey suit and take a shower."

"I wouldn't mind a shower too." Suddenly Kelly found the expectant eyes of everyone in the room on the two of them. "If that's okay." Fuck, she sounded like a little kid asking for an extra piece of candy.

"I'll take you up, then," Lex said.

Almost before Kelly knew what was happening, he had pushed back his chair and moved to pull hers out.

There was a little gasp from Cookie, and something

whispered under Dillon's breath that she couldn't hear, but clearly she and Lex were the center of attention.

"What?" Lex said, giving everyone a jaundiced eye. "I do know how to behave around women, even if I don't entertain them very often."

"Like never," Dillon said with a bit of a tease in his voice.

Lex flipped him off again, and his PA chuckled.

"Doesn't anyone around here have anything to do?" Lex said over his shoulder as he nodded Kelly out of the kitchen.

# Chapter Fourteen

Dillon waited until he was certain the two were gone. Then he followed V into her office, but not before he nabbed a second piece of cake. He figured he'd need it for courage. "You put her in the Meadowlark suite?" he asked as she shut the door behind them and turned to face him. "You're as subtle as a train wreck. You might as well just have put her right in his bed. It's big enough for both of them."

The woman shrugged. "He didn't complain, did he?"

"I didn't say it was a bad idea. I just said it wasn't very subtle."

"Not much in this house is subtle, and I see no reason to break with a long-standing tradition. Now tell me what happened." She nodded Dillon to the small loveseat that took up a good chunk of the tiny room, then parked herself in the captain's chair behind her desk.

Between hefty bites of cake, he told her the events of the evening in as much detail as possible, not because he didn't want to cut to the chase, but because V was an interrogator extraordinaire—no doubt a part of her training for alien infiltration. By the time he'd gotten to what he really needed to talk to her about, she had consumed another travel mug of black coffee without so much as flinching. That had to be the alien bladder. He was about to piss himself from just watching her drink.

"The thing is, V, I may have put a little too much spin on tonight's titillating adventure when I addressed the press, and I just want you to be prepared for it."

"Oh?" She scooted forward and leaned over her desk like she was the principal about to decide if her student needed to be punished or not.

"Well, as I told Kelly, you can imagine how it looked — her coming to Lex's rescue, the near cat fight — I mean, she literally called Spaulding a bitch. Of course, after that the press was primed and ready for it. Before I even addressed them, they were making the two into a couple. It's the romance thing. They wanted it. They all wanted it. Well, except for Gale Ann Spaulding, of course, who wanted blood."

"Dillon, what did you do?"

"Well… When one particularly romantic woman in the press asked me if our lovely Ms. Blake was Lex's girlfriend…"

"You said yes. I know. I got that."

"More like I said the charming Ms. B was Lex's fiancée."

"You what?"

For a second, Dillon thought the woman was going to catapult over the desk.

"Oh, don't act so shocked. You're the one who put her in the Meadowlark suite."

"Yes, but I didn't announce it to the press."

"Her secretary went along with it," he said, stuffing the last bite of cake in his mouth.

"Whose? Ms. Blake's? You can't be serious."

"Oh, I am, very serious. She stood right up there next to me and lied. In fact, she's damn good at it. Makes you wonder, doesn't it?"

"It certainly does," she said.

"Oh, come on, like you wouldn't have done the same thing, V! We talked about this. We agreed that we'd both do what we had to in order to be sure Lex had at least a chance with Kelly Blake. I mean, seriously, you saw them together. And if you'd been there, if you'd seen how she fought for him, how she led him out of the gallery, so careful not to touch him. And the chemistry between the two of them, well, it was all but sizzling from the moment they met." He leaned forward in his seat and glanced at the door, as if he feared someone might overhear him. "And didn't you see the way he pulled out her chair for her? Okay, so he didn't actually touch her, but that's a hundred times closer than you'd have gotten him without a major attack before, and you know it. Admit it, V, she's good for him. *Really* good for him."

V moved around the desk and sat on the edge in front of him, folding her arms across her chest. "But how are we going to convince Ms. Blake that he's good for her? I mean we know him. We're all used to his neuroses and his quirks and foibles, but she has no idea."

"And that's why you put her in the Meadowlark suite?"

This time the woman offered a twitch of a smile. "You said it yourself, everyone's a romantic, but you've really upped the stakes here, Dillon. How do you suggest we deal with it, because you know neither of them is going to be happy when they find out what you and this secretary leaked to the press."

He stood and came to sit next to her, one ass cheek hanging off the edge of the desk. "That's why I had to up the stakes still further."

She tap, tap, tapped her fingers on the blotter, the way she always did when she was scheming. "And just how did you do that?"

"Very simple, really. I accidentally let one of the reporters, one I know who has very good ears for news, overhear me saying that the couple were heading over to Kelly's place for the night." He stood and began to pace in front of the desk, empty cake plate still in hand. "Unless I'm sadly mistaken about that lust for the sensational and that instinct for romance, Ms. Blake's lawn will be full of reporters tomorrow morning ready to camp out until they get a glimpse of the lovely couple."

V responded with a chuckle only slightly this side of devious. "And all the time, they'll be safely tucked away at Mountain View."

He nodded enthusiastically nearly dropping his fork.

"Exactly! No one else has even a clue where Alexander Valentine hangs his hat. That still hasn't changed just because he's made a public appearance, has it?"

"So then, basically, our Kelly Blake is stuck here with Alexander until the heat cools at her place, right?"

Dillon nodded. "That's the plan. We'll make it so they really and truly are stuck in each other's space, then maybe the door between the Meadowlark suite and the Sunrise suite will be opened forever."

For a moment, V sat in silence, toying with the lid of her empty travel mug. Then she began slowly nodding, as though a great idea was being born. "He did pull her chair out for her."

"He did. Yes."

"She did come to his rescue."

"Yup. She did that."

"I can see progress, real progress, and made in a very short time," V said. "There's certainly chemistry between the two. Plus, Ms. Blake is nice. I really like her. She suits him."

"Lex's chances for happiness, for any kind of a relationship, are slim at best. That's the worst tragedy of his situation. If there's an opportunity, even a slight one for some healing, for some genuine affection, maybe even for something more, then I think it's worth the risk, V. Don't you?"

\* \* \* \*

"Kell, honey, are you all right?" Myrna sounded breathless on the phone, like she'd been running. "I've been worried sick about you."

"Not worried enough to call and check in, though." Kelly sat in the middle of the big bed, sheet pulled up over her breasts. Unable to sleep, she had decided to call Myrna. "What's going on? Are you all right? Are the kids okay?"

"Kids are fine, we're all fine. Kids are great. They're with their Grandma Pearl for the weekend, and I would have called, but Dillon Matthews phoned to assure me you were fine, so I figured you'd be…you know, busy."

"Oh." Kelly waited for it, like she did with her clients, waiting for the person to speak in their own time, but that tactic seldom worked with Myrna. "You're okay, though? Dillon said you helped him face down the press."

"Yeah, right! I did, me and Terry. It was good. It's all good. No worries."

Kelly knew Myrna well enough to know when she was hiding something, but she also knew that it would be impossible to pry it out of her over the phone. A proper interrogation of Myrna Kieran required time, chocolate and lots of wine. The woman had the alcohol tolerance of a gorilla…though, come to think of it, Kelly doubted gorillas drank much alcohol.

"Listen, Myrna, I'm staying here for the night at Lex's place. Dillon seemed to think it would be better, and it is late."

"Right, okay, fine. Dillon did mention that to me. Listen, I have to go, sweetie. Call me in the morning?"

The phone went dead, leaving Kelly to frown at her lighted screen. Something was definitely going on. She'd expected Myrna to give her the third degree over whisking Alexander Valentine himself away right from under everyone's noses. She'd expected to be asked details about the man, what he was like, what his place was like, what they did while she was with him. Oh, those questions would come, Kelly was sure of it, but in the meantime, something was definitely going on with her best friend.

From her seat in the middle of the bed, she could just make out the pale blue glow from the iMac in the study where she'd made a futile attempt to write. Yes, the suite actually had its own study with a library she'd like to make love to — one book at a time. Not tonight, though, nothing creative would happen tonight when her mind was so preoccupied with the enigmatic Lex Valentine sleeping in the suite next door…or not.

At first, she thought Lex was talking to someone. The two suites were joined by double French doors separating her from him by just thin panes of glass. They were covered with antique Belgian lace, which meant that the person on the other side was visible, but not in detail. That way-too-intimate arrangement was mitigated by the fact that the suites were connected between the two lounges rather than the bedrooms. Lounge, study, bathtub bigger than the local swimming pool...the Meadowlark suite even sported a fucking mini gym complete with an elliptical tucked away in an alcove near the balcony that guaranteed a workout with a view. Even in the dark, the discreet night lighting showcased the lush garden that would have been right at home in Renaissance Italy.

Lex had seemed embarrassed when he'd showed her the suite. At first, she thought that might be because he didn't like to flaunt his wealth, until he explained that the Meadowlark suite was joined to his own Sunrise Suite. The two suites had belonged to his parents, he said, both wanting their own space, and not really very affectionate toward each other. The French doors ensured that the occasional conjugal visits, or lack thereof, were private. "Anyway," he'd said, avoiding her gaze, "my mother seldom stayed here, though, in truth, I think she would liked to have lived here, but my father wouldn't have it. The forest all around belongs to the Valentine Estate. My father used Mountain View more as a hunting lodge. He was a trophy hunter. If it walked or flew or breathed, he wanted to know what it felt like to kill it." He caught his breath and tried to laugh. "Obviously, his trophies were the first things to go after he died. He brought his wealthy buddies and their women here several times a year.

"And then, when I...when I could no longer tolerate polite company or any other kind, he sent me here. For healing, he said, but the truth was he wanted to keep my embarrassing condition from becoming public knowledge. When he died, I chose to make the place my home, I had it gutted and redone to my tastes and to suit my needs as an artist. I don't know why I kept the two suites joined. At the time, I had some idea about switching back and forth between them. There was a period around the time of my father's death when I couldn't stand to sleep in the same room two nights in a row. But that all changed once I redid the place. I don't know why.

"Putting you here was V's scheming, I'm sure. I'm sorry. If you're uncomfortable, I can have you moved to another suite."

She had reassured him she was fine where she was, though, in truth, the arrangement did make her a little nervous, as it clearly had him. Not so much because he was so close, but because sleeping, for her, was such a private thing, and knowing how close they were sleeping made her situation with Lex Valentine feel way more intimate than she was prepared for under the circumstances.

"I promise I'll keep my hands off you," he'd said. Then he had offered that little tease of a smile that always made her feel like her insides had melted to warm toffee. There had been a nervous shuffling of feet and a twitter of laughter as they'd said their awkward goodnights at the door.

She shoved her way from the bed and moved on tiptoe to stand next to the French doors, holding her breath. Listening. Perhaps he was talking to Dillon. But there was only one voice – Lex Valentine's voice – and it was becoming more and more distressed by the second.

"Please move, please move, please move," the words became a breathless mantra. It was then that Kelly realized he was dreaming, and it didn't seem to be a good one, either. Perhaps he was dreaming about the press of people at the gallery. It could have been nothing less than terrifying for a haphephobic of his magnitude. "No! No! *No! No! No!*" His voice was filled with such fear that the fine hairs on the back of her neck stood and goosebumps rose over her arms. "No, no, no, no! Please move. You have to move. *You have to move!*" The last words were little less than the primal cry of absolute terror, and Kelly leaped away from the door with a cry of her own. Then there was silence.

She held her breath, pulse hammering against her temples. What the hell should she do? Was there someone she could call, someone who could help? Should she help? It was then that she saw a light go on, several lights. In fact, if the brightness were any indication, the man had turned on every light in his suite. She stepped around the corner into the bedroom and once again held her breath. A minute passed, maybe two, then there was scrambling around the room, the sound of something heavy crashing to the floor and a muffled curse. Another minute, and she thought she heard the toilet flush. Her heart ached to go to him. Knowing that he had put himself at such a risk tonight because of her brought on a wave of guilt. His distress had left her chilled and trembling, a sudden reminder of her nakedness. She fumbled for an oversized blue hoodie she'd found hanging on a peg by the balcony door and had been wearing in lieu of a bathrobe. The sleeves fell to her fingertips and it hung halfway to her knees. She fancied it smelled like Lex — evergreen and dark forest with a hint of high desert and ozone — but then it was probably just her imagination working overtime in an unfamiliar place, in a situation that was…well, bizarre to say the least.

There was some quiet moving about in Lex's rooms, then she heard the door to his suite open and close. She strained to hear footfalls in the hall, and, for a second, she thought he might be coming to her. In truth, there might have been a pause in front of her door, but then the footsteps retreated, moving with purpose down the hallway. She listened, barely breathing, as they receded and were finally swallowed up by the silence of the huge house. Still uneasy, and even less able to sleep than she had been before, she moved back toward the study thinking to make another attempt at writing. It was then that movement in her peripheral vision caught her attention. Clutching the hoodie tightly across her breasts, she moved on silent feet to the open balcony, wondering if perhaps a deer or some other wildlife was moving about the garden, but instead, it was Lex who stood in the moonlight. She couldn't blame him at all for wanting to be outside on a glorious night like this. She could think of no better way to clear the remnants of an unwanted dream than a moonlight walk.

He lingered near a tinkling fountain with Diana of the Hunt at the center. It wasn't his work, she was sure. It was classical, but it was old and weathered, and though she was not a critic, the workmanship was not nearly as fine as his. She just barely managed to step back out of view when he turned, and his gaze rose to the balcony on which she'd been standing. With her heart hammering against her ribs, she stood watching him watch. Surely he couldn't see her, and even if he could, well, he had to suspect that his nightmare had woken her. He would be concerned, she figured. At last, he turned and hurried through the garden, down a stone path that led to a non-descript outbuilding that was barely more than a shadow near the tall evergreens. As he opened the door and flipped on a light switch, her stomach cratered, and she stepped back onto the balcony, suddenly forgetting her efforts to stay hidden. The place was flooded with illumination and her angle was just right that she glimpsed a large open space. He left the door standing wide, a melon slice of light brightening the flagstone courtyard that surrounded the building just enough that she could see several lumps of unshaped stone and several more in varying stages of completion. She was looking at Alexander Valentine's studio! She had spent hours poring over the photos of his sculptures in her battered coffee-table books, and now she had the chance to see the man himself in action. Her breath caught in her chest as she recalled the Horse and Rider, as she recalled her plan to stay at Hendricks Gallery until the security guards chased her out, so she could linger and study and enjoy Alexander Valentine's genius just a few minutes longer. Okay, so that plan had gotten seriously kyboshed, but how could any person in their right mind resist the urge to watch Alexander Valentine create?

# Chapter Fifteen

She slipped into the pair of yoga pants V had laid out for her, zipped up the hoodie and was out the door of the Meadowlark suite before she had time to ponder her choice. With no shoes but the nosebleed heels Myrna had convinced her to pay a small fortune for, she went barefoot to save her feet, making no sound on the marble and wood as she descended the steps and found the French doors that led into the garden standing open. The path was well lit and, no doubt, well travelled in the wee hours. She did her best work in the middle of the night. Why should Lex be any different, especially if he were troubled by dreams? Sometimes bad dreams could be just the thing for unleashing creativity, as though it had been frightened to the surface by the horrors of the dream world. Certainly the creative process had been a way of purging her night terrors, of finding her way back to her center when she got lost.

As she neared the open door, she slowed her pace, listening for the sound of chisel on stone, but she heard nothing other than the call of an owl from the forest beyond the lit garden. Quietly, carefully, she eased forward and peeked inside. The first sight of him left her breathless — an artist at work, her hero at work, a hero she had seen at his most vulnerable. In the vulnerability of his phobia, in the darkness of his nightmares, the hero had been transformed to a man and, God, she liked him even better for the transformation. His work was suddenly all the more powerful for the weakness, for the pain and fear from which it was born and for the staggering isolation from whence it was created.

On closer observation, the studio wasn't as well-lit as she'd thought. He sat on a wooden stool in a pool of light coming from a free-standing, crook-necked lamp, like he was the focus of the sun, like everything beyond the bright circle was just peripheral. Her view of him was in profile, him perched in front of an easel sketching away. The hoodie he wore was identical to the one that now rested warm against her bare skin. He wore loose-fitting running shorts, and his feet were as bare as her own. The space was silent except for the quiet night sounds filtering through the back of the studio, which was a giant open garage door. His broad shoulders blocked out his efforts on the easel, and she found herself less interested in what he sketched than in the movement of his body while he sketched. She wished like hell he'd lose the hoodie. The thought of the man's naked back, muscles bunching and relaxing while he drew nearly drove her to her knees. The power to transfer what was in the creative mind through the body and out into a medium the world beyond could see and appreciate was a power that she often thought about as a writer, but her medium of transfer, her way of bringing what was in her head to the world at large, was much more abstract. This man created a literal representation of his inner world. That thought made her heart race and, for a moment, her own art seemed woefully inadequate to the task.

It was as he shrugged out of the hoodie that the view of his naked back—and it was naked beneath—became secondary to the view of the sketch on the pad. She must have let out a little gasp of surprise, because he startled and turned to face her, dropping the charcoal, which shattered on the floor. The color in his cheeks rose in the incredible contrast of dark hair and pale skin, and he moved toward her, eyes wide with question.

"I'm sorry. I didn't mean to..." She nodded to the fractured charcoal on the floor, then she moved into the room as though she were sleepwalking, eyes locked on the half-finished sketched which was disturbingly like looking into a mirror.

"I hope it's all right. I… I should have asked." His voice was little more than the breathless beating of his heart in his throat as he followed her gaze. "It's just that I kept thinking about the way you looked when you came for me at the gallery."

Though that was a discussion to be had, all thought of the gallery, all thought of anything that had been in her head just seconds before fled – power of speech not far behind, as she took in, for the first time, the man. The underside of his right arm and the area of flesh along the ribs beneath was a pale puckering of scars that rippled down over his hip and disappeared into his shorts, reappearing under the bottom on the outside of his thigh and stopping just above the knee. The room reeled around her and her vision blurred. There was no way she could have hidden her reaction, even if she had wanted to, and no way she could have ignored what she saw. Whatever it was that was between them, it had always been honest, and the man stood before her in nothing but his shorts and his marred, tortured skin.

"What happened?" She forced the words up through her constricted throat.

The blush on his cheeks deepened, but he didn't flinch at her gaze, nor her question. He made no effort to move, no effort to cover himself again. Instead, he stood there tall and unmoving. "A car accident. A long time ago. Burns." His breathing was fast and shallow as he knelt to pick up the broken charcoal. "I couldn't get my shirt off due to other injuries. It doesn't hurt." He glanced up at her and offered a genuine smile. "I have full range of movement, muscles, tendons, everything. I just don't wear my Speedo in public anymore." He stood and deposited the charcoal on the edge of the easel, then he wiped his hands on his shorts.

"I'm terribly sorry about the Speedo," she managed with a little hiccup of a sob.

"I know, right? Completely ruined my chances at the

beach."

"Oh, I don't know. Lots of women like scars."

When he only stood there looking a little lost, she wondered if she'd said the wrong thing. Then he offered her a tentative smile. "That's what Dillon keeps telling me. Scars are a chick magnet, he says." He motioned her on in and nodded to a small kitchenette off to one side. "Aware of my distress and my rather challenging night at the gallery, Cookie, living valiantly up to her name, has made chocolate chip peanut butter cookies and stuffed the jar there full of them. They're a bit like Reese's Peanut Butter Cups on steroids. I've already massacred at least a half a dozen. Help yourself while you still can. There's water and soft drinks in the fridge." He nodded to a low-slung leather armchair off to one side and perched once more in front of the drawing of her, then he added quickly, "It is all right if I sketch you?"

"Of course." She nabbed a cookie and came to stand behind him while he drew, but when his efforts on the curve of her cheek slowed then stopped, she stepped back. "I'm sorry, am I making you uncomfortable?" she managed around a mouthful of cookie.

He shook his head. "It's not that. It's just that, well as lovely as you looked in that dress at the exhibition, stunning actually, it wasn't the real you. It was all show for the event and for this nebulous Alexander Valentine you were expecting to meet." He waved the piece of charcoal in the air dismissively. "Black-tie affairs are no less masked ball just because you can see people's faces."

"True," she said, plopping down in the chair. "My feet may never forgive me for those damn shoes."

"You're real now." He chuckled softly and looked down at the charcoal gripped delicately in his fingers. "Everyone's a bit more real in the darkest hours of the night. And a lot more vulnerable." He shuddered.

"Nightmares, you mean?"

He nodded, but then made a dismissive grunt. "I don't

sleep much."

"Dreams about what happened at the gallery?" She asked, slumping in the chair so that her feet hung over one arm and her shoulder rested low on the other.

"Oh, no." He offered a flirty smile that surprised her. "If I'd been dreaming about that, the dreams would have been far from nightmares."

She felt his words like a caress, and a tingle ran down her body as though her skin were bathed in the expensive champagne from the gallery's party. "Then I'm sorry that you weren't dreaming about the gallery."

"Me too," he said, then he flipped the sketchpad to a blank page. "Is it all right if I sketch you? Like you are now, I mean."

She nodded to the collection of female nudes tacked to a corkboard along one wall. "As long as I don't have to take my clothes off."

This time his smile was positively wicked. "If you take off your clothes, woman, I won't be able to concentrate on sketching at all, and I'm not really in the mood to discuss my self-abuse problems right at the moment."

She laughed and shook her hair back over her shoulders. "Self-abuse, oh pa-lease." She shifted again to get more comfortable and the hoodie slipped down off her shoulder, leaving her neck and clavicle and the swell of one braless breast exposed.

"Leave it," he said, when she started to zip the offending garment a little higher. "I want to sketch your erogenous zones." And fuck if it didn't feel like he had just touched her there on the nape of her neck and traced a calloused finger over her collar bone and down onto the top of her breast. He chuckled knowingly at the trail of rising gooseflesh along the path she had just imagined his hand following. "Did you feel that? My sketching you there?"

"You have eyes," came her breathless reply. Then she caught a little breath and shivered. "Jesus, how do you do that?"

"There's a connection between what I see and what I sketch. It's a brain thing. That's why people who are paralyzed from the neck down can still draw even without the use of their hands. But I think there's a much bigger connection than simply exceptional hand-eye coordination. I think it's the ability to translate into physical form what we perceive and how it affects us. I've read your books, Kelly. You do the same thing, only your vision is all internal, but it's no less magic when you elicit the feeling you want in your reader."

She shivered again and her nipples hardened. "I've never made a reader feel this."

"Oh, I imagine you have," he said. The look on his face was something beyond concentration, something very much like Kelly had seen in the eyes of lovers in good romantic films when they made love.

"It's a substitute for touch," she managed in a breathless gasp.

"Of course it's a substitute for touch," he said. "It's the connection to the flesh that I'm no longer capable of having in the real world. It's tactile voyeurism. It's everything I can't experience, but dream about." He huffed out a little breath. "When I'm not having nightmares, that is."

"Jesus, that's... That's uncanny." She was suddenly struggling not to squirm in the chair. "Do you do this with all your models?"

"God, no! Of course not. I don't know them. They don't know me. I..." He stopped sketching for a second and looked around the room, as though searching for the right words, and Kelly felt the disconnect as surely as if he'd been caressing her breast then stopped. "I have no intimacy with them. When I sketch models for a given commission for which I have a deadline, I sketch them...I don't know... once removed. It's not personal. It's a job. They do theirs, and I do mine, and it's as if we're all working with a barrier between us. Please don't take this the wrong way, but I don't feel that with you." He began to sketch again, and she leaned back and closed her eyes as the champagne-bubble feeling returned in force. She might have moaned. Just a little. And he might have done the same in return.

"You know what you said about self-abuse," she finally managed, struggling to breathe.

He only grunted in reply, his hand moving at speed over the sketchpad, which he didn't look at. His eyes remained locked on her.

"Well, what happened at the apartment when we were together…"

"There's a connection, Kelly. That's all I know. I know you aren't the kind to take advantage. I knew that from what Dillon's nephew had said. You gave me the first true intimacy I've had since the accident. Does that sound like taking advantage to you?" He laid the charcoal down on the easel and began to stroke the sketch with his ring finger, blending and shading, and she practically came out of the chair, the response of his touch was so strong. Her nearness to orgasm was startling and a little bit frightening.

"Are you fucking feeling this?" she gasped. "How can this be? How can I feel what you're doing on that sketchpad?"

"Of course I'm feeling it. How could I look at you, at your response, and not?"

"Jesus, Lex. Jesus!" His eyes were on her but his finger still stroked the paper on the easel. "If you don't stop…"

"Do you want me to stop?" His voice cracked with the last word. From where she sat, she couldn't tell if he had a hard-on, and though his voice was as tight and breathless as her own, he clearly wasn't touching himself. One of his hands gripped the edge of the sketch pad and with the other, he made strokes and circles on the paper, blending, shading, evening out the tone. She knew that, of course she knew that, so why the hell did it feel like what he was doing to a simple charcoal drawing, he was doing to her body?

"Of course I don't want you to stop," she gasped, shifting against the phantom sensation of what she imagined his fingers were doing to the sketch of her. "Oh… Oh, God! I definitely don't want you to stop!"

The room dissolved in the sound of heavy breathing and moans and grunts, some hers, some his, all blended together. In the beginning, she might have been posing on the chair, but the situation had devolved to the point that she could not have held still if her life depended on it, and there was no other word for what she was now doing in the chair but writhing.

From behind the easel, Lex stood and gave the stool a hard shove, knocking it over with loud *ka-thunk* on the floor that resulted in a throaty curse. He mantled the sketch of her like a hawk over its prey. When she could focus through the growing fog of arousal, she saw that he once again sketched with the charcoal, his hand moving with a motion not unlike how she would want him to stroke her right now with her so close. How she had fantasized about him stroking her since that night in the apartment, even though she tried not to. And she couldn't keep from wondering if he were stroking the drawing there, right where she needed it. His other hand still rendered and smoothed and shaded and moved across her body, until the only thought she could hold in her head was the thought of his hands drawing her, drawing her, drawing her ever closer until she could stand it no longer, then she arched her back. With a startled cry, she dragged a breath into her lungs as though it were her last. She tumbled out of the chair, hitting the floor hard with her ass, bruising an elbow and thumping her head on the stone tiles as she convulsed and shivered, and the world dissolved into pinpoints of light behind her tightly clenched eyes.

She heard the deep-chested groan, followed by a hard thump from behind the easel and, when she opened her eyes again, he was on his knees beneath it, one hand cupped to the front of his shorts, the other braced against the floor as though he feared gravity would disappear and it would toss him into the void. His eyes were wide, darkened with lust and with, quite likely, the same look of shock mirrored in her own. His bare chest heaved and shuddered over and over again. Kelly couldn't stop watching him, couldn't take her eyes of the quiver of muscle, the sheen of perspiration, the clench of charcoal-dusted fists and, for an instant, she wished like hell that *she* could draw *him*.

# Chapter Sixteen

They sat on the floor with the overhead light turned off. The moon set below the trees and a mother-of-pearl dawn had taken its place. The cookie jar sat defiled and nearly empty between them, along with two bottles of water.

He nodded to the easel now sitting in shadows. "You saw the sketch." Then he asked in a voice not unlike that of a shy boy, "Do you like it?"

"Of course I like it. It's beautiful," she said, covering her mouth to prevent a spray of cookie crumbs. "You make it look like I have the moonlight inside me. I...well, I don't photograph well, and I'm actually a bit camera shy."

"I'm not a camera," he said, "and I can't imagine any photo of you being less than breathtaking."

"Oh, it's flattery now, is it?"

"Not flattery. Just the truth." He raised his face to the anemic morning light so that his features were bathed in shades of silver and gray that made her think of his sculptures. "Afraid if it's flattery you want, you'll have to see Dillon. He's the resident spin doctor."

"And damn good at it, if what my secretary says is any indication. But he's more than that, isn't he?" She shifted on the floor and pressed her back up against the wall. "In fact, everyone I've met in this house is way more than just your staff."

*"I grew up with Dillon. He's been my best friend for as long as I can remember. We went to school together until I couldn't anymore."* He shrugged and looked away. *"He's the only one who never minded that I suddenly became the crazy kid who couldn't stand to be touched. I mean, of course he minded. The two of us*

used to devise schemes designed to help me get over it. None of them worked. The ones I was brave enough to let him try on me always ended… Well, you saw how it ends. His father was way more of a father to me than mine was, and mine was happy to let him be. I was almost seventeen when my father died. Zack Matthews was my guardian until I came of age, and he was my closest financial advisor. Still is, actually. His son, well, his son is my hands and often my heart. He has a law degree. Graduated top of his class. That makes him a very good advisor and very good at seeing implications that Alexander Valentine might miss because he's too tunnel-visioned with his work. V and Cookie, along with Duncan, the gardener, well, they came with the house. I can't imagine life without them."

As though talking about him was a summons, Dillon suddenly appeared at the door, knocking softly before he stepped inside. He was dressed in jeans and a yellow polo shirt, freshly shaved and showered. Kelly didn't miss the lines in his forehead as he sought out his friend, nor the way they disappeared when he saw the two of them together. He offered his usual genial smile. "V said she heard you cry out in the night. She sent me in case triage was necessary, but I see it's not. Nice sketch," he said nodding to the drawing of Kelly. He squatted next to them and grabbed a cookie, but she was pretty sure it was less about the cookie than it was a chance to inspect Lex for damage from the dream world and from the adventure at the gallery. Lex ignored him, but she could see the slight tinge of color in his cheeks. This was a routine he was used to, she could tell, but not one he wanted to share with a stranger, no matter how intimate they'd been. She looked away to give the two a little privacy and noticed that the tops of the trees were now haloed in gold as the day arrived in earnest.

"Cookie's making huckleberry pancakes whenever you're ready, and, frankly, I wish you'd hurry up, I'm starving and she's making me wait for it."

"You're in for a treat, Kelly. Cookie's huckleberry

pancakes are the best," Lex said, brushing crumbs from his lap as he stood. Dillon offered her his hand and helped her to her feet, but then moved out of the way so that Lex could walk next to her, choosing the distance that was most comfortable. Then he fell into step on Kelly's other side.

"Did you sleep well?" he asked.

"Of course she didn't," Lex answered. "And frankly I don't know how V figured she would with me next door in the banshee bed. I doubt the poor woman got a wink."

Dillon looked from one of them to the other and raised a blond eyebrow. "She doesn't look any worse for the wear and neither do you, but do me a favor and try to look a little hard done by when you see Cookie so she won't feel she's wasted good pancakes."

Lex flipped him off.

Just before they got to the kitchen, V hurried to join them and pulled Dillon aside. Whatever the topic of their whispered discussion was, neither of them seemed very happy about it.

\* \* \* \*

"Wake up, sleepyhead." Myrna felt a warm kiss on her cheek and caught a mouthwatering whiff of freshly brewed French Roast. "Coffee's served, and we have the whole day without the little demons." She opened one eye and looked up at her ex's broad smile. He offered her a steaming mug from his perch on the edge of the bed, where he sat totally starkers, his junk clearly happy to see her. And the past night came rushing back. Holy shit, she had fucked her ex! Not only had she fucked her ex, but she had fucked him repeatedly! And it had been fucking good! Way better than it had been when they were married.

She pushed her way up to sit against the headboard. Realizing that she was as starkers as he, she tugged the sheet up over her breasts and nodded to his cock. "You'd better do something with that thing before someone loses an eye."

He offered her a wicked smile. "Care to assist me before or after coffee?" This time he dropped a kiss on her mouth, one with plenty of tongue in all the right places, and by the time he pulled back she was seriously considering just how badly she needed her caffeine fix.

A knock on the back door caused them both to jump and dribble coffee on the comforter. "Oh, hell," she managed, grabbing a handful of Kleenex to wipe up the spill. "It's Saturday. That'll be Andy here to do the grass. He never knocks. Why the hell is he knocking today? He knows what to do. Talk about the epitome of poor timing."

Terry took the cup from her and set it on the nightstand, then gave her breasts a good groping. "Ignore him, and he'll go away."

But Andy was nothing if not persistent, and, after the third rousing knock, she cursed profoundly, shoved into her robe, and stomped to the back door. She threw it open about the give the kid a piece of her mind, took one look at him and pulled him inside. "What the hell happened to you?"

There were grass stains on both his knees. His hair was standing on end. His shirt was covered in dirt and he had a skinned elbow. "I had to climb the fence in the alley to get here. Did you know Lex and Ms. B. are engaged?"

"What?" Both Terry and Myrna said at the same time.

"Where the hell did you hear that?" Myrna asked.

Andy nodded to the front of the house. "There are reporters and cameras all over Ms. B.'s front lawn. I don't know how I'm going to mow it, and when they saw me, they practically attacked me, asking if I knew Kelly Blake and if I knew anything about her engagement with Alexander Valentine." His eyes were wide. "They were rabid. I barely escaped over the fence into Mrs. Hanson's rose garden. Then she set that yappy little dog on me, and I fell, then I made it into the alley and... I didn't know where else to turn." Then he realized his poor timing, and color rose to his cheeks as he looked from Myrna in her disheveled robe to Terry in his boxers and back again. The kid might have been new to the world of morning nookie, but he wasn't stupid. There was no time for apologies, though. The shit was about to hit the fan.

"Oh, fuck!" Myrna raced to the front room, with Terry and Andy right on her heels, and peeked out the drawn curtain. "I'm a dead woman. She's absolutely gonna fucking kill me." Andy was right. There was a lawn party going on outside Kelly's front door and all the guests were reporters and paparazzi. "She is *so* going to kill me."

"She's not going to kill you," Terry said, making his way into the den where the television was. He turned it on and, for a long moment, he stood shaking his head as they watched the incoming reports. "I think you might be right," he said at last. "I'll do what I can to prevent your untimely demise, darling, but I'm only human."

Andy and Myrna flanked him as the three watched the news channel run footage of last night's gala event at the Hendricks. A young reporter in a dark pencil skirt spoke sincerely into the microphone. "Though there's no denying the gala exhibition and auction of renowned sculptor, Alexander Valentine, was a huge success, raising millions of dollars for the Cascadia Women and Children's Hospital, the real star of the show was Alexander Valentine himself making his first ever public appearance." There was a cut to a clip of Alexander Valentine speaking to the awed crowd voiced over by the reporter who talked her audience through Valentine's efforts to get through the crowd to the mysterious woman in red, through his being accosted by Gale Ann Spaulding and the resulting wine bath that had allowed him to pass to his fiancée, who helped him escape to a waiting limo that whisked the couple away into the night. Then the feed cut back to the reporter. "The money's been pouring in since last night's news with many people donating to the hospital as an engagement gift for the happy couple. After the two left, Alexander Valentine's PA and his fiancée's secretary gave a statement breaking the happy news."

Dillon Matthews took the podium then invited Myrna to join him, and she waltzed right on up there and opened her big fat mouth in a bald-face lie right in front of the press, the motherfucking press!

She watched in horror as her television image said, "Though this engagement may be sudden, it's most definitely welcomed by all who know the happy couple."

"You look great, Ms. K.," Andy said cheerfully.

All Myrna could say was, "She is going to fucking *kill* me."

# Chapter Seventeen

*"Though this engagement may be sudden, it's most definitely welcomed by all who know the happy couple."*

"I'm going to fucking kill her!" Kelly had gone back to the Meadowlark suite to change clothes for breakfast, having been told that she would find something that fit her in the closet. The closet was full of lovely possibilities, the closet was great. The news when she turned it on, not so much.

She had just shoved her way into a brand new pair of black jeans that fit like a glove when suddenly she found herself watching Dillon Mathews on the big screen, announcing her engagement to Alexander Valentine to a cheering crowd. She stumbled back against the bedstead and grabbed for the remote to turn up the volume. "I'm gonna kill him," she'd growled. "What the hell was he thinking?" Then it hit her, surely he wouldn't make such a statement without Lex's consent? A chill ran down her spine. Was she trapped? Was Lex Valentine a haphephobic madman who had stalked his prey and when the moment was right reeled her, completely unaware of what was happening, into his lair? Jesus! Surely not! Surely he wouldn't do that. She was a good judge of character. She always had been. She couldn't possibly make such a stupid mistake. But then there were the free tickets that came with the great Alexander Valentine's complements, and there was the limo he'd sent to pick them up.

She was about to begin plotting her escape when who should mount the stage right next to Dillon 'the liar' Matthews but her best friend, Myrna 'the traitor' fucking Kieran! "How could you? How could you do this to me,

Judas! Brutus! Benedict Arnold!" she growled at the image of her friend, then lobbed the half drank bottle of water at the enormous television, using every expletive she knew and some she'd only just made up. Then she grabbed her cell phone and punched up Myrna's number so hard that she broke two nails.

"What the hell have you done?" she yelled into the phone the second Myrna picked up, not giving her a chance to respond. "Dillon fucking Matthews said that it was a good idea to tell the press that I was Lex's girlfriend, for spin purposes, since he couldn't tell them what I really do. He didn't say anything about telling them I was his bloody fiancée! How could you do this? What the hell were you thinking?"

"I was thinking that the two of you are good together," came the mousy little voice that was so not Myrna Kieran.

"Good together? Good together! I've seen the man a whopping three times. Once he ran out, once I ran out and the third we both fucking ran out."

"Dillon said—"

"I know what Dillon said. The whole goddamned world knows what Dillon said, and what you said! The engagement is off! Spin *that*. Now get your ass out here, and pick me up," then she added as an afterthought, "and bring me some clothes. I'll send you the address. Oh, fuck! I don't even know the address! Do you have any idea the position you've put me in?"

"I have the address," her friend said softly. "Dillon gave it to me when he called me last night. I'll be there as soon as I can."

* * * *

"I'm going to fucking kill you," Lex shouted at Dillon. "Jesus, do you have any idea what Kelly's going to think now? I already look enough like a stalker as it is. I was just beginning to get her to trust me, just beginning to make her consider that just possibly I wasn't quite the nutter that I appear to be, then you go and pull a stupid-assed stunt like this and remove all doubt."

Dillon took the ass-chewing he had completely expected to get and waited quietly until Lex stopped ranting to take a breath, then he said, "She doesn't think you're a nutter. She never thought that, and she won't blame you. I'll make sure of it. That's part of the reason I involved her secretary."

"So you've put their friendship at risk with your little scheme too, have you? Did it ever occur that Myrna Kieran is more than just Kelly's secretary, and you've convinced her to betray that trust between them? Dillon, how could you do this? What the hell were you thinking?"

Dillon looked down at his hands folded on his desk as though he were about to say a prayer, and he certainly would have if he'd thought it might help. True, he had expected this, but that didn't make it any easier. "What I was thinking," he replied, taking in a shaky breath, "is that you risked a helluva lot to be with this woman, to see her again. What I was thinking is that she didn't hesitate for a moment in coming to your rescue, not one moment. What I was thinking is that she's good for you, you're good for each other."

Lex brought the flat of his hand down hard on the desktop, and the papers and other detritus rustled around it. "That's not your decision to make. It's hers…Kelly's and mine. And now you two, Mr. and Mrs. Fix-it, have taken whatever might have happened naturally out of our hands." He turned and left the office, slamming the door hard enough behind him to make Dillon jump.

\* \* \* \*

Kelly struggled her way back into the red dress and grabbed up what few belongings she had. The anger had given way to sadness. Lex, Alexander Valentine had been her hero. She really, really liked the man. How could he

138

possibly pull a stunt like this? She forced herself not to think of last night's intimacy. Surely that couldn't have been a lie. Then she moved into the study and began searching through the Internet news. *Alexander Valentine a Nut Case and His Fiancée a Hooligan*. That was the headline for the Talk About Town podcast. Well, that came as no surprise. The local stations, though, were all filled with joyous felicitations for the happy couples' imminent nuptials. Apparently some marketing savvy person had already set up a fund to which people could donate to the women and children's hospital as an engagement gift. Damn it! How was she ever going to undo this tangle? In the midst of all the hoopla was an interview with a prominent psychologist who was an expert on haphephobia, which he said was clearly the condition from which the unfortunate Alexander Valentine suffered. To prove his point, the network ran slow mos and replays of Lex at different times in the evening — usually the times when he was the most vulnerable. The whole damn thing made her chest ache. Surely it couldn't have all been some ploy for publicity.

She shut off the computer, shoved her cell phone into her clutch and walked to the door like the room behind her was on fire. She stomped down the stairs in the worse-for-wear red dress, barefoot and carrying the suicide heels. She planned just to wait in the entryway next to the door for Myrna the Traitor, but then she heard raised voices in the kitchen and decided there was a better use for her time.

As she rounded the corner, Dillon was just coming out of his office right behind Lex. "Lex, wait, listen to me," he was saying. Cookie had just stepped in from the kitchen, spatula in hand, and V came to the door of her office to see what all the commotion was about. All eyes were suddenly on Kelly.

"Shit!" Both men said in unison.

"You!" Kelly said in a voice that was loud enough to raise the dead. "You!" She approached Dillon Matthews at speed, stopped dead in front of him and slapped him as hard as she could, nearly knocking the unsuspecting man off his feet. When he'd steadied himself, eyes watering and cheek bearing a bright red likeness of her handprint, she spoke. "That was for you, you sonovabitch. And this—" She slapped his other cheek just as hard, doing her best to hide the fact that it hurt her damn near as much as it hurt him. "Well, you're Alexander Valentine's PA, so you see to it that he gets whatever the hands-off equivalent of that is. And you!" She turned her fury on Lex." You, I would kill if I could touch you!"

"Kelly, Lex—"

"You shut up! I'm not talking to you," she cut Dillon off at the pass. "You're the PA, not the brains behind the operation. How could I have been so stupid? How could I have not seen this? Why?"

"Kelly, I—" She turned on Dillon and slapped him again. "Fucking hell," he grunted.

"I told you I wasn't talking to you. I'm talking to your slime bag, rat bastard sleaze bucket of a boss who…" She turned her attention to back to Lex. "What was it you wanted from me? An apology for walking out on you the last time we were together? Well, you already had that. But you had to go and complicate things further by…" She gave a couple of fish gasps in an effort to find words. "I trusted you, Lex. I fucking trusted you. Here I thought we had connected, and all this is just a goddamned publicity stunt?"

Lex, who had stood silently through her whole rant exploded. "A publicity stunt? Seriously? You think I need to use someone no one has ever heard of for publicity? What about you? It was your secretary who made sure everyone knew that you were a writer and exactly what you wrote."

"You bastard, you, you, you, you!" This time when words failed her, she grabbed an apple out of the fruit bowl on the breakfast table and lobbed it at him. Her aim was true and it hit him in the chest with a hard *ka-thunk*, then rolled across the floor to stop at V's feet.

"You hit me! You fucking hit me!" Lex said, hand resting

against his chest as though he'd been shot. He looked around the room wide-eyed and fierce then grabbed the half-eaten pineapple muffin from V's hand and tossed it like a pitcher for the pros, hitting her right between the eyes.

Cookie uttered a little cry and crossed herself. V shot Dillon a concerned glance, but the man only shook his head before Kelly grabbed up a glass of cranberry juice from the table and tossed it in Lex's face. V didn't snigger, but Dillon did, so she lobbed a shoe at him, which hit him on the temple and bounced off. "Bloody hell, woman, you've got an arm on you," he said.

"Shut up, Dillon!" Lex had grabbed a kitchen towel to wipe his face. Then he turned it on Kelly, flicking it at her with a loud snap that nabbed her in the middle of the stomach.

"You sonovabitch" — she threw several apricots and a plum in fast succession — "I don't need your help to sell my books." A banana hit him on the top of the head and bounced off as he snapped her again with the towel — this time on the ass. "I didn't need it before —" For emphasis, she fast-pitched a nectarine and a rapid-fire barrage of Thompson seedless grapes, targeting everything from the man's forehead to his crotch as he did a little dance to avoid them. "And I don't need it now, and in case you've forgotten, you invited me to your goddamned exhibition!"

He grabbed a glass of water and gave her a drenching. She responded with more grapes.

"Lex didn't know! Kelly, Lex had no idea!"

There was another barrage of grapes and Cookie yelped and barely saved the basket of muffins from Lex before he settled on three slices of bread and a poppy seed roll, the last hitting her on her left tit and bouncing off.

By that time Dillon fucking Matthews was flat-out laughing. She was just about to give him another good slapping when she froze. "What the hell did you say?"

"I said, that Lex had nothing to do with what Myrna and I told the press last night, and I instigated the whole thing.

She would have never done it without my putting her in a very awkward situation."

Kelly stood, with one hand in the depleted fruit basket and another suicide gripping her bag, suddenly feeling very silly. "Well why didn't you tell me? Why the hell didn't somebody tell me?"

"I was rather enjoying you and Lex's version of angry sex."

This time it was Lex who picked up a carafe of tomato juice from the table and up-ended the whole thing over the man's head. But not before Kelly realized the obvious, Lex was hard and she was wet in places far removed from her dripping head. They stood at the center of the ransacked kitchen, both blushing hard, both making furtive glances for tell-tale signs of the heat they were each feeling. "I'm sorry, Lex," she said. "As for you—" She glared at Dillon, who, dripping tomato juice, raised his hand to block just in case she slapped him again. "Your imminent, very bloody, death may no longer be a given, but you'd do well to remember that it's still in the realm of serious possibilities."

Into the chaos, Kelly's phone rang. "What!" she said when she saw it was Myrna.

"Hi, hon." She immediately recognized Myrna's 'things-not-going-to-plan' voice. "I couldn't get to your house without dealing with a mass of reporters, so I had a shower and made coffee. When I got finished the reporters were all gone. I went to your house to get you some clothes, just like you said, and… Well, maybe you'd better turn on the TV, because I don't think I'm going to get to you without major problems."

Just then there was a knock at the back door and the gardener let himself in, shifting from foot to foot and looking rather worse for the wear. "I'm sorry, Cookie, but I think Mr. Valentine needs to know that I had a terrible time getting through the gate this morning. Cameras and television vans everywhere. Best no one leaves if they don't have to."

V had just switched on the television, and Kelly recognized a good number of the same reporters from the exhibition standing outside the gates to Mountain View.

The reporter in the dark pencil skirt, looking less fresh than she had when she stood in front of Kelly's house, but at least as excited, updated her enthralled audience. "If you live in a cave, you might have missed the unexpected twists and turns of Hendricks Gallery's gala charity auction of renowned and reclusive sculptor, Alexander Valentine's work, which he generously donated for the Cascadia Women and Children's Hospital. Mr. Valentine surprised all in attendance by making his first ever public appearance. The evening very nearly ended in disaster, though, as the haphephobic artist was crowded by fans, only to be rescued by the mysterious woman in red, who is no longer a mystery. In fact, she's quite familiar to Alexander Valentine, as novelist Kelly Blake, is soon to be the future Mrs. Valentine."

"So we *were* being followed last night," Kelly said.

The reporter continued. "The little adventure which was highlighted by Ms. Blake's dramatic rescue of her fiancé from the crowd and their escape via Valentine's limo, has created as many questions as it has answered. How did the couple meet? Does their work inspire each other? Where does Alexander Valentine stay? Is the future Mrs. Valentine able to touch her fiancé or are there…issues?"

"Fuck." Lex, his face suddenly crimson, reached for the remote and switched the television off just as the woman was informing everyone that at least the mystery of Alexander Valentine's lair had been solved and that the reporters had it on good authority that the happy couple were in residence at Mountain View. "Fuck," he said again. He tossed the remote on the ruined breakfast table and shoved his way past the gardener and out of the house through the biggest veg patch Kelly had ever seen.

"Fuck," she cursed her agreement. She lobbed her remaining shoe at the tomato juice-dripping Dillon

Matthews. Then she turned to the gardener. "Can you dig a grave on the grounds somewhere for me?" She shot Dillon another glare then looked down at her phone, where Myrna was still on hold. "Make it a double." Then she headed back upstairs to the Meadowlark suite for a much-needed shower.

# Chapter Eighteen

Gale Ann Spaulding sat back in her chair and looked over the notes for her show, which would begin in exactly fifteen minutes. She had one of Talk About Town's researchers digging up all she could about that bitch, Kelly Blake, and surely there must be more available on Alexander Valentine somewhere. Anyone that the public loved as much as they loved him had to have secrets and, now that she had a face to go with the name, now that the man himself had opened Pandora's Box, she intended to take full advantage. In the meantime, she could get several more shows' worth of mileage off her harrowing experience at the Hendricks Gallery last night. This was her Saturday noon show, People Talk. She really didn't have to do much but give a bit of a rant about that horrid woman and plant a few questions about what Valentine and his fans were actually supporting at this shady new hospital and let people talk. It was a good gossip session with like-minded people. Well, they thought she was like-minded, anyway. Truth was, she only gave a fuck about what her listeners thought because they boosted her ratings. Still, she was more than a little intrigued by Valentine and his fiancée. People that seemed too good to be true usually were, and nothing made for good talk radio like uncovering people's shit.

Her phone buzzed a text. It was from Talk About Town's reporter out at Valentine's Mountain View residence, saying that the gardener had just fought his way through the gates, but there had been no sightings.

She texted back that she didn't give a fuck. Text her if there was something to report. Though she secretly hoped the couple wouldn't make an appearance until she got out there, but she couldn't do that until her show was over. She set aside her notes and picked up her Dictaphone, playing back the little snippet from Kelly Blake's lawn boy. Andy Matthews, his name was. Where had she heard that name before? Andy Matthews.

*"Ms. B.'s not here this morning."* He called her Ms. B, wasn't that sweet? *"That's really unusual. I don't know where she is."*

"You might not know where she is," Gale Ann whispered, "but you know way more than you're telling, Andy, darling." She played the Dictaphone recording again. One of the neighbors had happily given her Andy's name. Said he'd been mowing lawns and doing yard work for Blake and her secretary, who lived next door and, though the secretary was clearly home, the curtains remained closed and no one answered the doorbell. She did see a man peek out of the front window at one point. He looked like Terry Kieran, the gallery's PR and marketing person. That could be interesting. What was he doing there so early in the morning?

Gale Ann's job was to find angles that would rouse public debate — more like rouse public ire, actually — which was way more fun to rouse. She wrote a note on her pages for the day.

*Man in house, Terry Kieran? Myrna Kieran single mother. Bad influence? Wait a minute, same last name, maybe her ex?*

But it was the lawn boy she couldn't shake. She recognized him from somewhere or she'd heard the name. In any case, she had a feeling he saw a lot more and knew a lot more than he let on. Cleaners and gardeners and such often did. She picked up the phone and dialed her researcher. "Madeline?" She glanced down at her watch. "This Andy Matthews, why does his name sound familiar?"

"Same last name as Valentine's PA, for one thing, I suppose," Madeline said, "but he also dates my cousin,

Jenny Fallon. Though I doubt you've heard me mention them together. Jenny's studying journalism."

She thanked her researcher and hung up. Dating Madeline's cousin, the journalism major, was he? Well, that was one more avenue to explore. And she hadn't thought about him having the same last name as Valentine's PA. But then lots of people had the same last name. Connections with connections were what this business was all about. Still, she was certain she knew Andy Matthews from somewhere else. She looked down at her watch again and headed for the studio. She'd figure it out. She always did. But first she had some mud to sling.

* * * *

Life always looked a little brighter after a shower. Kelly was relieved to know that Lex wasn't involved in the media subterfuge. That he'd gone to such a huge effort to get her to the auction and to meet her there, to the point that he had braved his first public appearance ever and, in doing so, revealed his debilitating phobia in a very public, very humiliating way, well, she wasn't sure how she felt about that. A part of her was very flattered. Another part of her was scared. Really scared. It wasn't so much that she feared he was stalking her as it was she feared the fact that she enjoyed being with him so much, and the chemistry was — her stomach cratered and her pulse raced when she thought of what had happened in the kitchen. If they had been alone and if he'd been anyone else, they'd have ended up fucking each other's brains out in the middle of the kitchen table. Angry sex — Dillon hadn't been wrong about that. The scary thing was that angry sex was happening right before everyone's eyes, and no one had known it. If Dillon hadn't interrupted with the truth, she would have orgasmed, and she was pretty sure Lex would have as well. Hell, they didn't even have to touch each other to be intimate.

She sat in front of the iMac, trying to take notes on the

situation. She always took notes about her clients, because it helped her know what was actually happening, which was quite often not what it appeared on the surface. It also gave her ideas as to ways she might guide them to a more satisfying sex life. Truth was, she was too keyed up to actually take notes, too much of Lex Valentine was still coursing through her veins. Then, as she often did when she was stuck with her writing, she opened a file for another project she was working on. It just happened to be her romance with Tom Angleton, who was now more than ever just a pseudonym for Alexander Valentine. Before she knew it, Tom Angleton and Sharon Hastings were in his studio together, and he was sketching her, and she felt each stroke of the charcoal as though he were touching her body. In her head, she could already picture an angry food fight in the kitchen. She was busily tap-tapping away on the keyboard when there was a knock on the door. She quickly closed the document in a wave of guilt and answered.

To her surprise, it was V with a loaded tray. She offered a bright smile, taking in the black jeans and red pullover Kelly now wore. "Caitlin did well for you, I see. She's our personal shopper here at Mountain View. As I'm sure you've guessed, we don't get out much." Before Kelly could respond, she nodded down to the tray. "Since most of breakfast ended up on the floor and the kitchen walls. And on the men of the house," she added with a chuckle, "Cookie thought you might like something that would actually end up doing your body some good."

"I'm sorry about the breakfast and the kitchen." Kelly stepped aside and motioned her in. "I'm usually a better behaved guest. I hope Cookie wasn't too upset."

"On the contrary, Cookie enjoyed every minute of it, as did I. We haven't had this much excitement at Mountain View since the fawn of a white-tail deer wandered into Lex's studio and refused to leave." She sat the tray down on the small dining table in front of the balcony and uncovered a mouthwatering array of breakfast treats from a ham and cheese omelet to the much raved about huckleberry pancakes. In addition, there was an assortment of fruits, breakfast breads, a bowl of oatmeal and a large pot of coffee. "She wasn't sure what you'd like, and since it's almost lunch time, she opted for brunch. Hope that's okay."

"It's perfect." And right on cue, Kelly's stomach rumbled. "There's enough food for an army, though," she said, sitting down and spreading a napkin over her lap. "Care to join me?"

"Well, perhaps for some coffee." The woman sought out an extra cup from the kitchenette and poured for them both, then seated herself across from Kelly, who dug in voraciously.

For a long moment, V let her eat in silence, a half-smile curling her lips. It was the kind that was always the prelude to serious conversation. At last she spoke, looking down into her coffee cup. "You know, Dillon meant well."

"He doesn't do things by halves, does he?" Kelly forked up a mouthful of pancake that was only just this side of orgasmic, and the sudden thought of feeding them to Lex nearly took her breath away.

"Never has," V replied. "Neither of them ever has. They've had each other's back since they were in pre-school. Instant friendship. They were both way too intense for most children their age."

"Is this your version of the 'boys will be boys' lecture?" Kelly asked.

"No. It isn't that. You have every right to be angry, furious even, and I suppose you could sue if you wanted to. I'm sure Lex would settle. You *are* the wronged party."

"Jesus," Kelly whispered, pushing her plate aside, "I don't want Lex's money, and I'm sure as hell not going to sue, but..." She ran a hand through her hair, struggling to find words. "Jesus!"

V reached across the table and pushed the plate gently back in front of her. "Finish your breakfast, dear. I didn't think for a moment that you wanted Lex's money. I think that you feel hurt and betrayed and you don't trust the other feelings you have when you're with the man."

"What I feel is really not your business," Kelly said, her shoulders tensing like iron.

"It is, actually, Ms. Blake, Kelly. Every one of us in this house has lived in the presence of Lex's pain, has done what we could to ease his loneliness and his isolation. There are no new employees at Mountain View because every one of us here loves working for the man, loves that in his quirky, awkward way, he treats all of us as though we're people, and we matter. That also means that every one of us would do anything for him. Anything." She shrugged. "Dillon just got a bit carried away, that's all, and you should ask yourself, do you think your friend, Myrna..." She raised a hand to wave away Kelly's protest at bringing up Myrna. "Of course, I know she's your friend more than your secretary. That's obvious just from her few minutes on stage with Dillon. You should ask yourself if you think your friend would have stood up in front of those cameras and said what she said if she hadn't seen something good when the two of you are together. You know as well as I do the woman would have ripped Dillon's throat out right in front of reporters, cameras and all, if she'd thought for one second what he said would damage you in any way." V sat in silence for a few moments, then drained her coffee. "All I'm saying is please don't throw out the baby with the bathwater. Your apparent willingness to do just that is what forced Lex to go public in the first place."

"Oh, so now it's my fault?" The minute she said it, Kelly felt like a naughty child trying to shove the blame off onto someone else.

"It's no one's fault, dear. It's not about blame. I'm just telling you how it is. I'm just asking you to think before you do anything rash." With that, the woman stood and nodded. "Enjoy your breakfast. Someone will be up to collect the tray and make up your room at your convenience."

Kelly finished her breakfast and settled at the iMac in an effort to write down and sort through more of the insane events of the past—could it actually have been less than twenty-four hours? It felt like a lifetime. Once again, she found herself opening the Heart of Stone document and was surprised to find that, with a little twisting and tweaking, those events seemed to fit right in nicely with Tom and Sharon's story. In fact, she found that her characters were practically leaping off the page and taking shape with a clarity she'd not managed in a long time. It was the ringing of her phone that brought her back from Tom and Sharon's world with a startled gasp.

"Hi, sweetie." Kelly could tell by the sound of her friend's voice that she had assumed the repentant bestie mode. And really, what were friends for if not to forgive each other for being assholes every once in a while? "Is this a good time?" she asked when Kelly didn't respond immediately.

"It's fine. It's okay, yes."

There was another long pause. Kelly waited for it, and this time she held out.

"I'm sorry, Kelly. I'm so, so sorry that I let Dillon Matthews lead me astray last night, but he's right, you know? You really need to sort things out with Alex…er… Mr. Valentine…er, Lex. Hell, I don't know what to call him anymore."

"I was in his limo with him on the way to his house, Myrna. Don't you think an engagement announcement was a just a tad bit premature?"

"Possibly, but you do understand why I did it, why we did it, don't you, hon?"

Kelly rolled her eyes. "This is what happens when Team Lex and Team Kelly both decide to take matters into their own hands. Yes, I get it, Myrna. And Lex's team is just as rabid for his happiness as you are for mine. Trouble is, that can lead to major interference. I nearly brained Lex with… Well, just about everything I could get my hands on from the breakfast table, and Dillon too, until Dillon set me straight that Lex had no more idea of what was happening than I did."

Myrna laughed. "Wish I'd have seen that."

Kelly chuckled back. "Oh, if you'd been here, you'd have been on the receiving end of my pitching arm as well, you know?" There was a long pause on the other end of the phone, and Kelly's stomach was just beginning to tighten with the oh-God-what-now knot when her friend spoke, all humor gone from her voice.

"You should take him up on his offer, Kell. Be his tutor. Dillon tells me you're good for him, and you're out there anyway. I've obviously had to cancel all your other appointments, so you might as well be earning some money while you spend time in the lap of luxury with the sexiest man on the planet. Christ! Who knew he was so gorgeous?"

It would have been the kind of girl talk that Kelly and Myrna would have stayed up late with over a bottle of wine and some seriously decadent chocolate if not for one small consideration. "He's gorgeous, and he's untouchable," Kelly said, feeling for some reason as though stating the obvious was a betrayal of Lex's trust, a betrayal of something he'd held secret until last night.

"But you can change that. From what Dillon told me this morning, you're already changing that."

"What the fuck? Are the two of you comparing notes?"

"No, I just called because I was worried, and I knew you were too angry to talk to me."

"You got that right," Kelly said, moving to stand on the balcony and look out over the massive back garden that hugged Mountain View. "And I'm not a psychologist. I'm way out of my depth here. I mean, the man is amazing, and he's kind and he's funny, but never mind all that for a second. I'm taking on a role I'm not at all qualified for, and I sure as hell can't live up to everyone hoping that I can make Alexander Valentine whole again. That's not a responsibility I can carry. I mean, what if I do something wrong? What if I inadvertently make matters worse? Hell,

Myrna, he came to the exhibition last night because I *did* something wrong, something stupid. I didn't give him closure. I just walked out. Do you have any idea what a total disaster that could have been?" Kelly's skin crawled at the thought. "He could have been seriously hurt and the damage could have been… Jesus, Myrna, I shudder to think!" She was now pacing the balcony in rant mode. "And the damage I did anyway — the man's secret is out there in the public realm. Have you seen the slo-mo footage they're flashing all over the television? I mean, fuck. The press keeps showing him at his most vulnerable, in a situation to which he should have never been exposed. Have you seen the horrible Tweets? And now there's a crowd at his gate, waiting like vultures. I may have already done irreparable damage, and with the press and the fake engagement, and with the loss of his guarded privacy, the damage I've done may be just beginning."

"Oh, for fuck's sake, Kelly, now you're just being melodramatic," Myrna said. "Does the man seem any worse for the wear? Dillon told me that he's never seen his boss happier. I can't see how anything but good could come from you being there, from you being his tutor. I mean, you have to be there anyway, Kell. You might as well make it good for both of you. You've always found his work inspiring and you've always wanted to meet him. It's a win-win, hon. Don't go sabotaging yourself when this could be the best thing that ever happened to both of you."

There was another long pause. "Kell? Are you all right?"

Kelly nodded and remembered that Myrna couldn't see her. "I'm fine, yes. It's just… You're right, of course. I… I'll talk to him once we're off the phone."

"Good. That's great. You're doing the right thing, hon. I know you are and my instincts are never wrong. Kell? You still there? You sure you're okay?"

It took her a moment to realize that she'd not responded, even though she was still gripping the phone to her ear. She gulped a huge breath of the oxygen that suddenly seemed sparse around her. She couldn't help but feel that she'd just been given her friend's blessing to jump off the Empire State Building, and she was excited because it was exactly the thing she had wanted — needed — to hear. "Fine. I'm fine," she answered breathlessly. "I've gotta go, Myrna. I'll talk to you later."

# Chapter Nineteen

It had been a lively show in which everything about Valentine and Blake was called into question, from their sexual persuasions to their terrorist affiliations. Granted that last was a real stretch, and the man who'd called it in was a bit of a nut case anyway, but he was always a good conversation starter. Quite pleased with her efforts, Gale Ann Spaulding left the station with her computer bag slung over one shoulder and the ruined dress from last night's fiasco at the gallery in its garment bag over the other. There was a cleaner near Eddie's Supermarket that was supposedly the best at getting out wine stains. She'd give it a try. No biggie one way or another. The dress was a part of her substantial wardrobe allowance. A white dress covered in red wine was pretty much a write-off. But the dress had cost a bomb, and she really liked it.

She figured she'd pop into Eddie's Supermarket and kill two birds with one stone. There was no coffee in the house and no food either. The lack of food bothered her less as she seldom ate at home anyway and never cooked. She pulled the car into the shared parking lot at Eddie's and dropped off the dress. She had left the cleaners, pleased that the woman behind the counter felt certain they could get the stains out. In the supermarket, she grabbed a basket, pausing to check her phone to see what the media was saying about the happy couple. Definitely not what she was saying, and there was no news from Carl out at Mountain View. She would grab something to eat, go home and have a shower, then head out to Mountain View and switch him out. It was her story and she had the wine-stained dress to prove it.

She was not about to let some amateur take the credit when Valentine and Blake did decide to show themselves. She'd just slipped the phone back in her bag when she looked up a split second before running into Andy Matthews, who was wearing a bright red Eddie's smock.

"Ms. Spaulding," he said, blushing ear to ear. "I didn't know you shopped here."

She offered him her brightest smile. "Mr. Matthews, I didn't know you worked here." She extended her hand and, when he shook it, he blushed even harder.

"I just stock shelves. Paying for university," he said. "Studying chemistry," he added, shuffling from foot to foot.

"Well, good for you." She leaned over to fondle a tomato she had no intention of buying just to make sure he saw her most excellent cleavage. "So you work two jobs, do you? I swear it gets harder and harder for anyone to get an education these days."

"I know, but I don't want a loan. I don't want to graduate already in debt."

"A very wise man," she said. "It's people like you who make this country great, never expecting a handout, never expecting privilege, and it's nice of Ms. Blake and her secretary to help you in your efforts."

"They're good folks, and they pay well."

"They pay well, do they? Both her *and* her secretary?" She leaned over to fondle a cucumber. "So Ms. Blake is quite successful as a novelist, then, is she? Not an easy business to make it in, writing fiction."

The resulting blush was way out of proportion to a simple question about an employer, and Gale Ann's news sense tingled.

"I…" The kid squirmed. "Well, she's really good at it. Writing novels, I mean. She writes lots and they're good." God, the kid was so transparent.

She stepped closer. The guy was easily tall enough to look down her blouse and she was happy to let him if it would keep him off balance enough that something might just slip.

"What? Does our Ms. Blake moonlight too? Is that how she and Alexander Valentine met?"

The blush was swallowed up by panic. The kid glanced at his watch and looked around him, as if he were expecting wild beasts to come out from behind the produce counters and devour him any minute. "Look, it was lovely talking to you, Ms. Spaulding, but my boss will kill me if she catches me standing around." With that, he bolted like his jeans were on fire.

As he disappeared through the swinging double doors at the back, she pulled her phone out of her bag again and texted her researcher.

*Madeline, check to see if Kelly Blake supplements her income by moonlighting and, if so, doing what?*

She returned the phone and picked up her coffee, delighted when two women in the frozen foods aisle recognized her. Before she left with her groceries, she decided that she would treat herself to one of Eddie's famous Gourmet Box Lunches for the stakeout, and a very expensive Cabernet… That was for later, of course. She picked up several bottles of Diet Pepsi to go with her meal and made her way to the checkout. *My, my, my, but things are getting interesting.* She was really looking forward to her first views of what was clearly the palatial residence of the elusive and apparently very phobic Alexander Valentine. She was still kicking herself for not putting two and two together with the phobia thing — haphephobia, that was what the psychologist had called it. A phobia was just a short walk away from the nut house in Talk About Town's book, and she was already getting good mileage out of that one. Some of the Tweets practically had her wetting herself.

*How are they going to do it when they can't touch?*

*Is foreplay a game of scrabble – she is a writer.*

*Perhaps she just writes their sex scenes.*

People could be so snarky, and Gale Ann Spaulding could snark with the best. That's why they paid her the big bucks.

* * * *

After her talk with Myrna, Kelly went looking for Lex. When he wasn't in his studio, she asked Cookie, who knelt in the enormous vegetable patch, filling a basket with succulent young carrots. The woman wiped her hands on her apron and pointed toward the woods that bordered Mountain View in the back. "He's probably in his private sculpture garden," she said. "He goes there when he needs to think. It's off limits to everyone but him, though." Even as the woman warned her of the no-go zone, she jerked her head spastically toward the path leading that way. Then she turned back to her work, as though she'd seen nothing, said nothing.

Fucking hell! Was everyone at Mountain View secretly complicit with Dillon's scheming? For a moment she stood unmoving, tempted to go back to the house and wait for Lex's return, but how could she not want to see Alexander Valentine's private, off-limits sculpture garden? What was in it? His favorite works? Works he couldn't bear to part with? Perhaps it was more to do with the space he'd chosen to set the sculptures. The grounds and natural surroundings of Mountain View were exquisite, after all. A perfect place to be inspired and lost in one's thoughts.

As she moved into the shade of the woodland, the path all but disappeared in the thicket, and she was beginning to wonder if she'd missed a turn somewhere when the trees gave way to a small meadow, barely more than a grassy spot nestled beneath the evergreens, but the space was filled with sculptures so lifelike that in the play of light and shadow through the branches, Kelly could have almost believed that there was a secret garden party going on in this secluded place. As she stepped into the sunlight, however, she realized instantly that the tableau before her was no garden party. It was nothing less than a wild orgy sculpted in stone. The work was quintessential Valentine, detailed down to the trailing of goosebumps, the press of fingertips against breasts, the purse of lips against flesh and, in that detail, the stone itself seemed to live and breathe and have its own inner warmth. It was especially true in the heat of midday. The sun had warmed the curve of the muscular male shoulder that she slid her finger cautiously over, almost as though she feared she'd startle him with her touch. His partner in stone lay sprawled in front of him on the rumpled folds of a blanket mussed by their romp. Her legs were parted wide in invitation, and the details of her readiness were as obvious as his own as she reached out to guide him home, her face an anxious study in desire that could no longer be denied, a look that he returned. Every muscle of the two lovers was stretched tight, bulging and ready, desperate for the act of joining. So perfect was their connection, so intense their intimacy that Kelly found it hard not to look away with that sense of embarrassment one feels when someone else's private moment has been inadvertently invaded. But the act sculpted in stone welcomed the voyeur, and the fact that the sculptures were life size meant they also welcomed the touch and caress of an outsider drawn into their intimacy.

With her heart hammering, she traced the shape of the man's shoulder and down the curve of his back to the wonderfully straight angles of muscle and bone at the hip, the joining point to the pelvic girdle, the point so uniquely and deliciously masculine that a woman couldn't keep her hands from wandering there when she caressed a lover. That the marble was warm to the touch made the caress startling, like skin against skin, and her stomach clenched as she thought of Lex caressing that warmth, of him thinking exactly the same thing, of him creating these works of intimacy and putting them here for that very reason, so he could feel the warmth of skin on skin.

The creation of such a work was extended foreplay, was a relationship based entirely on touch and caress and teasing out from the stone the intimate acts hidden within. Was it any wonder that the man was a sculptor? Was it any wonder that he was brilliant? She knew too well the connectedness artists feel to their work. She felt it with her writing at times when the story flowed, at times when the bottom fell out of what she had created and she found herself in a whole new place, deeper, more personal, a place that allowed her far more intimacy with her characters than she would have been bold enough to expect. But her work was not her only intimacy. It was not the only touch she could have if she craved it. Work in isolation, even work one loved as much as she loved hers, would have to be raised to a completely different level to make up, even a little bit, for the loss of intimacy. The whole glade was full of the man's efforts to make up for that loss.

"What are you doing here?" The voice behind her made her yelp and jump. She fell back against the sculpture's bare buttocks and her hand slipped in her efforts to regain balance, ending up on the man's aroused goodies.

She turned to find Lex in a ratty T-shirt and shorts, standing in front of her with his arms folded across his chest. His efforts not to smile belied the harsh reprimand in his voice.

"Looking for you," she managed.

"Got a little sidetracked en route, did we?" He nodded to her hand on the sculpture's cock, and she jerked it away and blushed heartily. "This garden is not open to the public."

She folded her arms across her chest, mirroring his stance. "I'm not the public, and frankly, if you want me to tutor you, well, this is a great place to get on with it, because clearly it's therapy for you."

He raised an eyebrow and shifted, and she noticed that he was barefoot and covered in fine dust. In one hand, he held a chisel. "Clearly, it's porn for me." He came to her side and defiantly stroked the woman's breast, not taking his eyes off her. "Interactive porn."

"It's just as well then, because I quite often assign my clients to watch porn." Just as defiantly, she curled her fingers around the man's erection, and Lex's gaze followed her hand, his breath catching in his chest. "This will make my job a whole lot easier, and way more interesting than film porn."

"So you're willing?" He blushed hard and dragged his gaze back to her face. "To be my tutor, I mean."

"I'm willing, yes. It seems I'm stuck here for the time being, so we might as well make the best of it." She turned away from his overpowering gaze and moved on to the next sculpture, in which the couple was in the act, the woman seated on the man's lap, his lips lowered to her nipple with her fingers curled in his hair, holding him to her breast. Lex followed her as she strolled among the erotic statuary. "It's pretty clear to me that I can't...that we can't interact the way I normally would with my clients. I don't know how I feel about that, Lex." She turned suddenly to face him, and he nearly ran into her, stepping back as though he'd narrowly escaped falling off a cliff. His breath accelerated, as though he'd just done something physical, his pulse beating a rapid staccato in his temples. In response, she scrambled to put a safe space between them, noting to herself that she had to be careful not to put him in such a dangerous position if they were to work together. She'd never worked with a haphephobic before, and even though her policy was strictly hands-off with her clients, she never thought about the number of times there was a handshake at the door or a hug of thanks or just a touch of encouragement. She would have to rethink her client interaction entirely where Lex was concerned. "I'm sorry," she said, as he leaned against the plinth to gather himself.

"It's all right." He straightened to meet her gaze. "I take some getting used to, and the truth is, I feel comfortable being a little closer to you. It's no big deal."

"Well, actually, it is a big deal," she said, feeling her own pulse accelerate at his comment. "It's a huge deal for you to be able to move beyond your comfort zone, and when those boundaries change, it's natural that there'll be times when you'll overstep them and that won't be comfortable."

He smiled at her and nodded her on to the next sculpture. "You're talking like a tutor now."

"But we both know I haven't been behaving like a tutor." This time she was careful to keep him always in her peripheral vision.

He moved ahead of her on light feet and turned to face her. "You're behaving like the tutor I need you to be. That's the important thing."

She could see the excitement in his eyes and, for a second, he looked around as though searching for something. Then he motioned her to a series of female nudes all without partners, all in differing poses. He came to one that stood much as Kelly had been standing, legs slightly spread, feet firmly planted on the ground and arms relaxed at her side. He moved in close to her and took her gently by the shoulders, and Kelly felt her heart bounce as he stroked the statue's bare arms.

"Don't you see, Kelly, how exciting it is for me to suddenly have a connection? And how confusing it is, how disappointing to have that connection yanked away?" He ran an open palm up the woman's shoulder and neck, and Kelly felt the trail of goosebumps rising along her nape as he cupped the sculpture's cheek. "I'm not a stalker. Surely you can see that. I couldn't just let go. I need to know, Kelly, I need to know where this will lead. You have to understand that. And I'll admit" — he skimmed the hairline with an index finger — "your response intrigues me almost as much as my own. It must intrigue you too." He turned back to her, and her knees nearly gave with the intensity of the connection he could elicit through simply touching a piece of stone. "Don't you want to know what will happen?"

"Of course I do," she said, looking around until she found a male sculpture curled next to a sleeping woman in a spoon position. She sat on the plinth beside him and gently stroked his arm, and the sudden catch in Lex's breath was almost a gasp. "That's why I'm still here." She ran her hand down to rest on the statue's flank, and Lex sighed. "I just don't like being lied to, and I don't like being manipulated." She turned back to him. "But you're not responsible for Dillon and Myrna's bad behavior. That being the case, like it or not, I'm here now as your fiancée until the interest blows over and the press finds something else to titillate. So let's make the best of it."

The smile he offered her made it very clear how he felt about that arrangement.

# Chapter Twenty

"I reserve the right to walk away if things get uncomfortable," Kelly said, pacing the floor in a drawing room somewhere deep in the bowels of Mountain View Cottage. She had insisted that when she was being his tutor, they meet somewhere outside their two suites on neutral ground.

Lex sat on the sofa, watching her pace with just the hint of a smile on his face. "I walked out. I don't see why you shouldn't have the same options. Hold it." He cocked his head and squinted as though he were suddenly deep in thought. "Come to think of it, you walked out, too. So see, you've already exercised the right you've reserved."

"Yeah, well, I still reserve it. You, however..." She turned to face him. "I would prefer you not walking out if you're uncomfortable, but that you tell me you are, and I'll back off and we can talk about it."

"I want to know why you're uncomfortable too, Kelly."

"That's not part of the deal," she said.

"Well, it should be." He leaned forward on the sofa. "Look, I'm a socially awkward, frighteningly oblivious basket case. How the hell am I supposed to know what I've done if you don't tell me?"

She settled on the other end of the sofa and turned to face him. "I didn't mean that I wouldn't tell you what made me uncomfortable. I meant that there could possibly be times when we might both need a break."

"You mean like last night in the studio? This afternoon in the sculpture garden?"

"Look, do you want me to do this or not, because if you

164

don't, then I can have V sneak me out with the dirty linens in the back of the laundry van."

He offered a quirk of a smile. "We don't have a laundry service. It gets done on site."

"Whatever." She waved a dismissive hand. "That's not the point."

"The point is that you're uncomfortable with the situation. I get that. I'm not terribly comfortable myself, but I know that you can help me, so I'll abide by your rules. Just tell me what you want me to do. But I do have one request."

As though it had all been timed out, there was a knock on the door, and Dillon stepped in with a small grocery bag. "I won't be long, Kelly. I just have something I need to tell you." He sat the bag on the coffee table and settled into the Queen Anne chair.

Kelly braced herself. So far, the big announcements Dillon had made did not bode well for her.

"Andy Matthews is my cousin," he said.

"Oh?"

"He's the one who told me about your tutoring business and I passed the word on to Lex."

The muscles in Kelly's neck tightened. "I should have killed him and buried him in the garden when I had the chance. He wasn't supposed to tell."

"He just wanted to help. He admires Lex a great deal. Since he was a kid, he's looked up to him and has been sympathetic, and frankly as shy as he is, he could identify with Lex's situation in a lot of ways. I figured he'd become a monk or something, he was that uncomfortable around girls. But then he started dating Jenny Fallon and…well, he was a nervous wreck when she wanted to…to take the relationship to the next level. I tried to help him out, you know advise him—older cousin and all—but I guess he thought that because the last person I dated was a guy, I might not know anything about women. Anyway, he comes back a week later swaggering like Casanova, smiling ear to ear. It was pretty obvious he'd gotten seriously laid."

Dillon chuckled the way men did when a brother had just joined the League of Frequent Fuckers, as Myrna called it. "Of course I teased him mercilessly, as any good cousin would. Then he told me about his little encounter with you in Eddie's Supermarket." He stood and pulled a can of pears in heavy syrup and a can opener from the bag and sat them down rather ceremoniously on the coffee table.

Just then there was another knock and V stepped in with several towels, a roll of paper towels and packet of Wet Wipes. Kelly found herself blushing hard.

"The kid cornered me," she said. "I had to improvise." She looked at the three who were all looking back at her expectantly. "Well, I was just going to tell him to fuck off. I mean, the guy mows my lawn every Saturday and eats half a box of doughnuts from Jake's Cakes at my kitchen table. But then he just looked so desperate. I was in a hurry, I had a can of pears I'd picked up for Myrna. She has this thing she does for the twins, making pears look like little mice. She uses peanut halves for the ears and Red Hots for eyes, and those little skinny licorice whips – you know the ones I mean – she uses them for the tails."

Dillon chuckled. "I'll have Cookie be sure and get the recipe. Lex loves canned pears."

"I do," Lex said with a serious nod. "Though I'm not keen on Red Hots."

"She could probably use raisins," V said. "You love raisins or chocolate chips. That would be nice. Hershey's Kisses would be even better," she added. Both men nodded thoughtfully. During this enlightening conversation, V spread the table with a towel and placed all of the other items on it with the precision of a surgical nurse. Then she opened the can of pears and dumped them into a bowl that looked like it might well have come from the formal dining service. Just when Kelly was beginning to wonder if she and Lex were going to have an audience, V sat the extra towels on the end table and rubbed her hands together in a 'mission-accomplished' gesture that would have made

Kelly laugh under different circumstances. "Alexander, be sure to put down towels on the sofa before you get started."

"Oh, for heaven sakes, V, I'm not going to piss on the furniture, if that's what you're afraid of."

She gave him the evil eye. Then she motioned Dillon to follow her and turned on her heels toward the door, which was barely closed behind them before Lex stiffened on the sofa, his whole body tense as though he sat at full attention.

"Was this your idea or Dillon's?" Kelly asked, hoping to relax him.

"It was mine, after Andy told Dillon and he told me. I thought it was something that I…" The muscles along his jaw looked as though they were made out of iron, and a fine blush crawled up his neck, tinting his ears bright pink. "I've never touched a woman…in that way." He forced a laugh. "Obviously. I've…" The blush deepened, and he avoided her gaze. "I've put lube on some of the sculptures, you know, down there, but I… Well it isn't the same."

"The pears won't be either," she said. Her heart suddenly ached at the physical isolation this man endured on a daily basis, and it wasn't just her heart that ached, she felt his lack deep in her core. It had been easier with Andy. She had been almost flippant with him. She was sorry for that now. She spread one of the towels on the Queen Anne chair across from him and settled herself onto it so they were facing each other. "The texture will be different and with the pear there'll be less give." She dipped her fingers in the bowl and rubbed the heavy juice between her index finger and her thumb. "If you touch a woman, she'll be much warmer." She gave him a conspiratorial smile. "You'll be amazed at how warm and how soft she'll be down there when she's ready to be touched. With Andy, this" — she nodded down to the pears — "was improvisation. This was the best I could do under the circumstances, but a woman, well, a woman feels like nothing you've ever touched before."

He was no longer avoiding her gaze. His eyes were locked on her, and he was struggling to keep them on her face, she knew that. She understood the urge for him to drop his eyes to the place of which she spoke, the place with which she was so intimate, the place that couldn't help but respond to the topic, to the situation, to the strange intimacy they had shared almost since the moment they'd met. "You can look, if you want." She opened her legs so that he could see the place in between clothed in black denim, completely disguised and yet so very obvious. "And I'll look at you too." She nodded down to his own jeans straining to contain him already. "It's what men and women are naturally inclined to do when there's sexual attraction."

With her heart hammering in her throat, she took one of the pear halves into the cupped palm of her left hand, then she brought it down between her spread thighs, feeling the juice of it run over her fingers and drip onto the towel as she spread her legs a little farther and held her palm to mimic the position of her vulva. "Touch it like a woman would touch it, and you'll always get it right." She dragged her index and middle finger up from the bottom of the pear to the center and felt her own body respond in empathy. "The pear has no folds, no secret valleys, no swollen flesh to be teased open, so you'll have to use your imagination with that."

Lex gave a little moan, soft and deep in his chest, as he shifted to make himself more comfortable. "I know the anatomy," he said. "I've watched porn and I've studied drawings. I know how it *looks* like it might feel. I know the response it elicits." He flicked his tongue nervously over his upper lip. "Of course that's just acting, isn't it?"

"Porn is about fantasy, about voyeurism, and it doesn't matter if it's real if it gets you off. But when it is real" — she spread her index and middle fingers up the sides of the pear's central opening — "if you're good, if you're sensitive, you'll feel the spasms of your lover's orgasm, even see them if you're using your tongue, and you can feel them gripping at your cock when you're inside her. If you're paying attention.

"The clitoris." She laughed softly. "Well, with Andy, I used a Tic Tac, but he's a chemistry major. He likes charts and graphs and periodic tables. You're an artist, you live in your imagination, so you don't need a Tic Tac. Some women like the thumb stroking and circling while the other fingers work inside. Some women like to use their fingers." She demonstrated on the pear, and Lex groaned. "It's always best to ask and be sure."

"What do you like?" His words were a labored rasp against the back of his throat, and Kelly found herself stunned by the question, and way more aroused than she wanted to be. He shouldn't have asked. She shouldn't have answered. But she did.

"I like it this way." She shifted her hips and opened a little further so he could see her thrust and scissor, circle and probe technique, and her body responded with the tight grip and release of muscle memory.

"Jesus," he whispered, moving forward on the sofa and leaning closer for a better look. "And when someone uses their tongue?"

She caught her breath in a giddy laugh. "Afraid I can't tell you what I do since, sadly, I'm not that flexible."

"But you can tell me what you like." His voice had gone rough.

"I like the flat of the tongue to part me and then probe me, circle my clit then add a little lip action and kiss and suck." She closed her eyes, finding it difficult to meet his gaze when she spoke about something so intimate, so secret. Come to think of it, she'd never had a man actually ask her how she liked it. The few who had given a rat's ass about her pleasure had been happy enough to let her order them about, but never quite got the hang of it.

It was the loud schussing sound that caused her to open her eyes. Lex had moved the coffee table out of the way, paying no attention to the slosh of pear juice all over the towel V had spread. His eyes were locked on Kelly as he fished out his own pear half and fell to his knees in front of her. When she realized what the man was about to do, she dropped the pear she'd been holding with a little gasp of surprise and scooted as far back in the chair as she could. He knelt low, holding the pear in the cup of his hand, as she had, placing it against the edge of the chair between her legs! She gave a little yelp and scrambled back in the chair still further, spreading her thighs over the rise of the chair arms to keep from touching him. He moved forward, the back of his hand so close to her crotch that she could feel the heat of it, and he lowered himself still further until his hair nearly brushed the insides of her thighs. Then, still looking up at her from his position on the floor, he began at the bottom of the open pear half and ran his tongue flat and undulating all the way up, flicking in just slightly in a little circle at the top end before he closed his lips around the apex and she could hear the slurp and suck of the sweet syrup.

"Oh! Lex! Ah!" And then she went non-verbal, holding her breath, tightening muscles deep inside her body, the only muscles she dared to move if she were to keep from touching him. She raised both arms and fisted her hands around the back of the chair to keep from curling them in his hair. Her thighs trembled from her efforts to keep her legs on the chair arms and not throw them over his shoulders for leverage. She didn't move. She didn't breathe as he licked and nuzzled and suckled until pear juice ran down his chin and onto his T-shirt, until his face was damp and sticky, until his forehead was sheened with perspiration, and still he held her gaze as though they were locked together in each other's orbit, neither able to move without the other's consent.

"Oh God, I'm gonna come." She barely managed a warning when his own convulsion brought him dangerously near her body. He had stopped breathing, she was sure of it. She practically climbed the back of the chair to keep from touching him as he lost control. Then with a tremendous gasp of oxygen, he straightened, let the pear fall from his hand onto the aubusson carpet and looked up at her.

"I'm going to pass out." And he did.

"Are you all right?"

He came to curled in a fetal position on the drawing room carpet with half a pear lying next to him. When his vision cleared a little more, he saw that Kelly sat cross-legged next to him, offering him a bottle of water, then it all came back to him, and he smiled up at her, careful not to move his head just yet. "Never better," he managed.

"You passed out," she said.

He couldn't help noticing she looked pretty damned pale.

"I did," he managed, then he added quickly, "but don't worry. It was worth it, I promise."

Her eyes were huge and fever bright in the fading light of the room, and her hand shook when she reached to push a strand of hair back behind her ear. She said nothing, only gave him an owl-like blink and, for a moment, he thought she was going to cry.

"Please don't worry, Kelly." He wished desperately he could take her in his arms and comfort her. "It's my fault for getting too close, but I couldn't help myself. I didn't mean to frighten you. I just… I just wanted to feel as much as I could."

She nodded her understanding and caught her breath, her eyes still locked on him as though she feared he might suddenly explode. "If you're sure."

"I'm very sure." There was another tense silence under her watchful eye, which he found he really didn't mind at all. He was feeling rather cocky in spite of his close communion with the floor. He smacked his lips. His face was sticky and so were his hands. "So, how was I?" he asked with a little chuckle.

She gave a hiccup of a laugh. "Well, all I can say is that is one very happy pear half." God, she had a beautiful smile. He loved it when she smiled.

"And you?" he said. "How are you?"

"I'm not the one who hit the floor, though I might have if I'd not been pushed back in the chair as far as I could get to keep from touching you." She took a deep breath. "I wasn't expecting that."

"Neither was I." He closed his eyes to keep the room from spinning, but realized even as he did so that he might not be able to wipe the smile off his face until sometime next week.

"Nothing like that has ever happened to me," she managed. Her voice was still breathless, and even over the heavy scent of pears and his own musky release, he thought he could smell her scent, earthy like the woodland floor after a summer rain.

"That goes without saying for me," he said. He risked pushing himself into a sitting position and leaned back against the sofa, studying her, cheeks flushed now that she knew he was okay, nipples peaked through the red pullover. "Can I ask you a question?"

"Of course."

"If I'd have done that to you, would you have come?"

"You did do that to me, and I did come." Her eyes were suddenly serious, and for a moment, he feared she would bolt, but then she smiled. "I have no idea how you did it. From the very beginning at the gallery last night, I kept wondering if you're very brave or just reckless. I think the jury might still be out."

He felt lightheaded again and lowered himself back onto the floor. "It's all right," he said in response to her look of alarm. "I just had a moment to think about what happened, and as for your observations, well, I'm not sure, either." When the room stopped spinning, he opened his eyes and looked up at her glorious smile, which he returned in kind. "What I do know is that was the best sex I've ever had."

# Chapter Twenty-One

Gale Ann Spaulding had just come off another kick-ass show chock-full of speculation and rants about Alexander Valentine and his little girlfriend. It was ridiculously petty of her, but she hated it that the woman's novels were suddenly jumping off the shelves. She hadn't read one, but went out of her way to make sure the people who talked to her on the show didn't like them. They were rubbish, full of filth and porn, one commenter had said. Tawdry dribble, another had commented. She'd left that comment off, disappointed that the caller hadn't known the difference between drivel and dribble, but then her business dealt in the lowest common denominators, in people who would much rather take hearsay as gospel than actually bother to do the research. That made her job easier too. However, it didn't mean she could rest on her laurels. A tiny bit of research, just the right bit of research presented in just the right way could go a long way with an audience like hers, and her instinct kept telling her that little Ms. Blake was keeping secrets, big, fat juicy secrets. Her run-in with Andy Matthews at Eddie's Supermarket had piqued her interest majorly. No on reacted the way that boy did unless they were hiding something, something pertaining to Ms. Pert Ass. He was still her best lead. Gale Ann's stakeout at Mountain View had turned up nothing. No one had gone in and no one had come out. Her sources told her that at Kelly Blake's house, nothing had changed, and the woman's secretary was terrifyingly protective of her friend. No one was brave enough to tackle her, especially since they figured it would take nothing less than torture of the highest magnitude to get her to tell them anything. Still, an intrepid few reporters hung out on her front lawn just in case. But she was through hanging out anywhere waiting for something to happen. She was sure that the result of shoving a Dictaphone in either of the major players' faces would be no more satisfying than it had been the last time—though she had gotten a good amount of mileage from that little incident. She checked her email to find that her researcher, at her request, had set up a meeting with Jenny, her cousin, the journalism major, the one who was dating Andy Matthews. They would meet for drinks at Clyde Common—her treat. Nothing softened up a poor college student better than drinks with a celeb and a pricey place. If this Jenny had any idea what Andy was hiding, she'd lubricate it out of her with a few Cosmos. It worked every time. She was great at being a girl's best friend when she had to be.

* * * *

Andy groaned and slapped at his phone in an awkward one-handed stretch as the alarm went off. Jenny half mumbled a protest in an attempt to make him lie still. She had one leg thrown over his belly and an arm over his chest with her face buried in the hollow of his neck. He stretched harder, knocking the phone off onto the floor, and grunted a curse. "Jenny, honey, I've got to get up. I've got a chem lab in half an hour." He liked that they'd already fallen into the habit of calling each other pet names, and he liked that once a week, sometimes more, she stayed over. Though in all honesty, they seldom got much sleep when she did. They were always ravenous for each other. He smiled to himself as she gave him a sloppy kiss on the shoulder and rolled over, barely breaking the surface of sleep in her efforts. His cock hardened at the fleeting glimpse of a pink nipple in the gray morning light as she did so. But it was chemistry lab and he couldn't afford to miss it for another romp between her glorious thighs. He could risk a little kiss, though.

He shut off the alarm and pulled down the comforter just enough to nuzzle her breast and give her a teasing suck. She gave a little kitten growl and reached for him, but he only grabbed her hand and kissed her fingertips. "Gotta go, love. Stay as long as you like." He headed for the bathroom, thinking bromides to keep his cock from taking over all higher brain functions. He peed then hopped into the steam of the shower, smiling at the fact they'd barely got dinner eaten before they were all over each other. No matter what happened from now on for the rest of his life, he would always consider Kelly Blake a saint. She had given him confidence he would have never had, and in such a simple, unobtrusive way. She was a goddess. He wished he could afford to pay her, he really did. As he got out of the shower to the smell of coffee drifting in from the kitchen, he didn't think he could have smiled harder if he tried. Jenny was waiting for him in the kitchen with his travel mug filled and ready to go along with a croissant tucked in a napkin, warm from the microwave.

"It was amazing last night," she said, when he pulled her into his arms, not missing the fact that she was wrapped in his pajama top. "You were amazing."

"No, *you* were amazing," he said, nipping her ear and releasing her to her own coffee. For a long moment, they stood smiling stupidly at each other, and the she gave him that little pout that said she was about to ask an important question and she wasn't sure how he'd respond. "What?" he said. They hadn't been together long enough for any of his responses to be negative, nor for any of her questions to be troublesome.

"My birthday's next week," she waved her hand dismissively. "You already know that and it's not a hint, really. It's just that I got a birthday card from my Aunt Phyllis yesterday and she always sends money, a lot of money."

"Ooh, nice to have an aunt like that," he said.

"Yeah, well, I was going to spend it on a spa weekend for me and my best friend Sherry, you know, surprise her. But that was before." She blushed prettily and reached to straighten his collar. "Anyway, I was just wondering, since your little impromptu session with Kelly Blake had such fabulous results, maybe I could forget the spa weekend and we could, you know"—she made a very suggestive nod down at his crotch—"go for a little tutoring sesh together and see what comes up."

"Seriously? That's what you want to do with your birthday money? Wow! Honey, it's a great idea! I mean, great minds, right? I was just thinking that I wish there was a way without me offering up our first born to pay for a few more sessions with Kelly Blake." Oh, she liked the mention of a firstborn, he could see it in her smile. So did he, actually.

"Well, this will save our offspring from such a clandestine exchange and"—she sucked in an excited breath and rolled her eyes—"and completely eliminate any possibility of sleep for the two of us in the foreseeable future."

"And a sacrifice well worth the making, I'd say." He glanced at his watch and grabbed his keys. "Gotta go."

She followed him to the door. "The money's already in the bank. You just make the arrangements and I'll make myself available."

"Oh," Andy said, stopping in his tracks. "There might be a small problem, though I'm sure it's only temporary, and besides that, my cousin, Dillon, can handle the situation for us, I'm sure."

"Problem?"

"Well, actually it's not really a problem. You see, Kelly Blake has just recently become engaged, and you'll never believe to whom." He didn't give her the chance to guess. "Alexander Valentine."

"Oh, my God!" she said. "I do remember hearing something about that on the news, but I didn't make the connection that it was your Kelly Blake. Wow! It's been all over the TV, actually, and who knew he was so hot? Not as hot as you, though," she added quickly.

"Well, my cousin, Dillon, works for Lex Valentine and it seems that at the moment, with the press hounding the two of them and all, they're holed up at Lex's fortress. Now that would be amazing if Kelly could meet us there," he said. "Anyway, my point is that at the moment they're under siege by the press, but hopefully that'll pass soon enough, and anyway, we have plenty of time, don't we? Christ! Speaking of time, I gotta go. Dinner tomorrow night?" he said, pulling the door open and giving her a sloppy kiss that was more of a miss.

"Sure, though I might be a few minutes late. I'm meeting my cousin Madeline over at Clyde Common for cocktails. She's bringing some friend from work she thinks I ought to meet. Good for my career, she said. But if I know you're here waiting for me, I'm sure I'll be motivated to speed things along and limit the intake of alcohol so I'll be ready for the evening's entertainment." She flashed him a naked breast, and blew him a kiss as he rushed out of the door contemplating what other food items Kelly Blake might use for her tutorials besides canned pears.

# Chapter Twenty-Two

It always started with the chattering of teeth. It always started soft, not frightening at all. It reminded him of castanets in a spastic fandango, but he always knew it wasn't castanets. It was never castanets, though every time, even when he knew what was coming, he prayed that this time he'd be wrong, that this time he really would be dreaming about some fandango dancer with castanets that sounded like teeth chattering, just like in the cartoons. But it was never like the cartoons. It was nothing like the cartoons. The chatter of teeth was the only sound he heard. It was like the only sound his ears could register for so long, so very long, and all that eternity he had nothing to do, there was nothing he could do but lie there aware only of the icy burning of his side and the constant, endless castanets of chattering teeth as he waited for it. Then she spoke to him, her voice so strange in its effort to convince him everything would be all right. She believed it, maybe, but he'd been in this place long enough to know better. Still, he never had the heart to tell her. "Lie still, darling, just lie still. You're injured. Someone will come for us soon. Lie still now and I'll keep you warm." She said that over and over through chattering teeth. Then the heaviness came upon him. At first, it was warm and pleasant, and he welcomed it. He wished she would stop talking, stop chattering and let him sleep. He was tired and cold and his teeth were chattering too, but he no longer felt the horrible pain in his side. All that was left was the smell of fire, burnt out and chilling on the wind. There had been wind, horrible, howling wind, but he hadn't noticed it over the chattering of teeth. As the weight got heavier, the howling of the wind grew then the nightmare began. The nightmare always began when there was no more chattering teeth, when the *castanets stopped, letting the howling wind in, and the weight pressed against him harder and harder and colder and colder. He screamed. Of course, he screamed. She said someone would come for them, but how could anyone know they were even here, and where was here? They were somewhere in the snow and ice, and the weight on top of him, it kept getting heavier and he couldn't breathe. He screamed again and again, until the weight became so heavy that he couldn't scream anymore. He couldn't breathe anymore. All that was left was the consciousness of cold, dark weight that got heavier and heavier and he couldn't move, he couldn't move. He couldn't move!*

\* \* \* \*

It was the wild animal cry from the Sunrise suite that woke Kelly with a start. She sat up straight in the middle of the big bed, heart pounding. For a second, she didn't know where she was. For another, she didn't know what was going on, then another cry brought everything back to her. She was at Mountain View in the Meadowlark suite. She was tutoring Lex Valentine and he was having nightmares in the next room. She grabbed for the thick terry robe and threw it on over the tank and panties she'd fallen asleep in. In the time it took her to do that and orient herself, there was a loud thump in the next room and a gasp, followed by the opening and shutting of a door then footfalls in the hall. She tiptoed to the balcony and waited. Sure enough, Lex fled across the back garden as though he were being chased. He wore nothing but a pair of shorts, the scar along his side catching the moonlight like a pale stretch of ribbon snaking along his ribs, curving around his hip and low over his abdomen. A deep-throated moan that crescendoed and rose to a keening made gooseflesh rise along her spine. Dear God, the man was still asleep! Dillon and V and everyone at Mountain View knew of Lex's nightmares and how best to cope with them. Surely she couldn't have been the only one to hear his distress, but it was a risk she wasn't willing to take. The decision was made in a split second, and she was out of her room, racing down the stairs into the garden. She'd expected him to turn toward his studio, but instead, he headed into the woods, into the sculpture garden. Heading into the woods and still asleep, he could seriously injure himself.

"Lex. Lex!" she hissed, speeding up to catch him. She wasn't sure it was wise to wake him. Hell, she didn't know what to do, so she sped up further, ignoring the odd pebble digging into her bare feet and the slap-slap of the dew-drenched grass against her calves.

She lost him for a moment as he ducked through the thicket and disappeared into the sculpture garden. She shoved and fought her way through behind him, raising her arm to keep the branches from smacking her in the face. The sculptures gleamed silver in the heavy moon and the light breeze made them appear to inhale and exhale and sigh. She shivered and tried not to think of ghosts and demon spirits. There was no sign of Lex among the sculptures she had seen when she was with him yesterday afternoon, but it was easy to see that there was a trail of sculptures disappearing into the woods along a curving path. The deeper into the trees she stumbled, however, the harder it was to see. The thrum of her pulse and the heavy drag of her breath drowned out all other sounds, and sweat trickled down her spine, cooling in the night breeze as she fought her way into the darkness, one hand stretched out before her, eyes open wide in an effort to let in as much light as possible.

When the same wounded animal cry pierced the air, making the fine hairs on the back of her neck rise, she stumbled forward on the uneven ground, ignoring the smack of branches and the gouge of pebbles. "Lex!" she called. Surely he'd hear her crashing through the thicket like a bull moose. "Lex!" But there was still no response. She shoved aside the branches of an oak and, to her relief, caught sight of him in the moonlight.

Her relief was short lived, though, when he dropped to his knees, held his head in his hand and cried out, "Don't go, don't go, don't go!" Then he shoved to his feet again and stumbled forward with way more speed than she would have thought possible under the circumstances, which were heart-stopping in themselves — him clearly still fast asleep and unaware that he was crashing through the woods in the dark in nothing but his shorts. She shoved through the undergrowth after him, all the horrible things that could befall a sleepwalker flashing through her head as she lost sight of him again.

With both of them stumbling through the trees, how could she possibly tell his thrashing about from her own? She stopped dead, holding her breath until it felt like her lungs would explode. Then she heard him just ahead of her, just beyond a couple of tall pine trees. She rushed forward, then the noise stopped.

She found him in a clearing obscured by several large rhododendrons. At first, she thought it was some sort of sarcophagus he knelt in front of, then she saw that it was, instead, a sculpture of a woman sleeping on a bed. She lay curled on her side, head resting in the crook of her elbow. The pose was so relaxed, so real that Kelly half expected to see her chest rising and falling in the moon glow filtering through the trees, the movement of light and shadow through the branches, adding to the illusion. At last, he came to his feet, his back turned to her.

"Lex," she whispered. But he still didn't hear her. He still slept. He bent over the woman and ran a finger along her cheek and down over the curve of her spine. Then he leaned forward and kissed her very softly on the mouth, as though he were afraid he might wake her. The sigh that escaped his lips was more of a sob. Then he climbed onto the stone bed next to her and curled his body around her like she was the love of his heart and he would now sleep with her in his arms. Kelly fought back her own sob at the sight of him. Once he had settled, taking pains to mold his body to fit the sculpture, seeing to her comfort before his, he gave a softer, more contented sigh, and, within seconds, his breathing slowed and he relaxed to restful, deep sleep.

Kelly approached on tiptoes, half fearing she'd wake him, half wishing she would. It wasn't cold out. It was a clear summer night, but it was Oregon, the foothills of the Cascades. It wasn't warm either. There was a rise of gooseflesh over his arm and down his flank. She was pretty sure it was no longer brought on by night terrors.

"Lex," she said aloud, reaching out and almost touching him before she remembered not to. But then he was asleep. What could it hurt, to feel the rise and fall of him against her hand, to trace the scars, to smooth his hair? Though he couldn't endure touch when he was awake, perhaps if he was already sleeping soundly it might ease him, comfort him on some deep, unconscious level. Intrigued by the idea, she reached out, but he shifted slightly and moaned in his sleep and she pulled back as though she had almost touched fire. It was an uninvited betrayal, no matter how sound her reasoning, and she stepped back out of temptation.

She had no way of knowing how long she stood watching him. Finally, she moved to sit on the other side of the woman, but as the night crawled on around her, she began to nod off as well. He had done this before, she was sure of it. He would be okay or someone else would have followed him out. Surely there had been a plan put into place to keep him safe, to make sure he didn't harm himself when the night terrors came upon him, and even though the sculpture garden was his private place, she had no doubt that both Dillon and V were familiar with every sculpture, every little nook and hiding place that the sleep-walking Lex might get to. Perhaps there were even guards who kept watch at night just in case. They wouldn't leave him vulnerable. They wouldn't! And still she couldn't go. She looked toward the house longingly, though in truth, she wasn't sure she could find her way back in the night if she wanted to. Then she made a decision. She crawled up on the stone bed on the other side of the woman and did her best to settle, but seeing a goose-fleshed shoulder out of her peripheral vision, she heaved a sigh, slipped out of the oversized robe and spread it awkwardly over all three of them. There was just barely enough to cover her shoulders and, if she pulled her knees up under the stretchy tank top, she could scrunch into a fetal position and cover almost all exposed body parts. Once she got as comfortable as she possibly could under the circumstances, she closed her eyes and listened to the quiet in and out of his breath, wishing that she could take the woman's place, wishing that he could find comfort in her flesh instead of having to seek it out in cold, hard stone. She would never sleep, keeping watch as she was. Probably V and Dillon would laugh at her in the morning, but it didn't matter. She couldn't leave him vulnerable. That was her last thought before she drifted off.

* * * *

Her first thought as her consciousness rose to that level that wasn't quite awake but was no longer sleep, either, was that someone was watching her. Her second thought was that she was cold and she ached all over. She opened her eyes to find Lex standing over her. He offered her a drowsy smile. "Coffee will be ready by now and something warm to eat." He offered her the robe in his outstretched hand. "You must be freezing. I know I am." He held her gaze. "Though not as cold as I sometimes am."

She took the robe from him, careful to touch only the fabric, and slipped into it, mumbling incoherent appreciation between shivers.

"Thank you," he said.

She mumbled something in return and followed him back to the house.

# Chapter Twenty-Three

"Day two of the siege and still no relief in sight," Cookie said as the two came into the kitchen looking worse for the wear. "Get in here, both of you, and at least get a cup of coffee and a piece of toast and warm up. I'll have the eggs ready soon." She turned her attention to Kelly. "Eggs Benedict, because I'm running out of huckleberries until this year's are ready."

"She picks her own from a patch out in the woods that she somehow manages to share peacefully with the bears," Lex said, as he grabbed a hoodie from the peg near the door. Kelly suspected that there were probably hoodies and extra clothes all over the house and his studios for the man, and maybe even strategically placed in the woods and about the grounds too. She wondered how they coped with his night peregrinations in the dead of winter.

"The bears wouldn't dare interfere," Dillon said, coming into the room and giving the two a quick look to assess the situation. He had the good grace not to comment. Cookie poured him coffee and mumbled something that sure as hell sounded like Arabic.

"You do speak English, don't you?" Kelly asked jokingly.

"Better than they do," the woman said, nodding to the two men. "And breakfast will be late if I don't break some eggs."

They all watched her return to the kitchen.

"Where'd she learn to speak all those languages?" Kelly asked.

"Her father was a spy," Lex said.

Dillon added, "If we tell you who he worked for, we'd

have to kill you."

V buzzed through for another cup of coffee. "Bad night?" she said, clearly not expecting an answer.

"Could have been worse." Lex flashed Kelly a hint of a smile above his coffee cup, and she felt warmth that didn't come from a hot beverage.

The eggs were beautiful, as everything Cookie made was, and Kelly was stuffed to the gills and about to head to her suite for a shower when Dillon spoke up.

"Look, Lex, I really hate to press the issue, but you have to make a decision about the models. You have a deadline and I've rescheduled their interviews multiple times."

"Damn it!" Lex glanced down at the watch he wasn't wearing. "I'm just swamped. Can't we make it next week?"

"You're always swamped, and this project is important, so buck up. I've already said that if you don't want to see them and you trust V and me, we'll do the interviews. We know what to look for."

"I don't want another damn model. It's too risky. There has to be another way."

"You've worked with lots of models and you never had a problem before, Alexander," V said. "It was purely a fluke. The odds of it happening again are very slim and you know it."

He shivered and chuffed his arms as though he were suddenly cold. "Well, I don't like the risk. It was a horrible experience."

"What happened?" Kelly asked.

When both V and Dillon deferred to Lex, he blushed heartily and told Kelly in terse, jerky sentences the story of Sally Philips.

She shivered for him, seeing the acceleration of his pulse and the loss of color in his cheeks just from the telling. She couldn't help thinking of what it had been like for him at the gallery. "Can't blame you for being gun shy."

"Gun shy or not," Dillon said, "the man's a sculptor, and while he has a great imagination, he still needs a muse."

He looked Kelly up and down. "You interested? You're already here and you definitely have the kind of look Lex is needing."

"I'm no model, and I'm not about to get starkers for the whole damn world to see."

"You wouldn't have to take your clothes off," Lex said. "Dil's right, you're just exactly the type I've been looking for. I've found most of the models the agency sends are too thin and it's not easy to find one with real breasts these days." The blush was back with a vengeance. "Er, I mean... I didn't mean to imply that yours are... Well, I've never actually seen yours, have I?"

"You're just digging yourself a deeper hole, bro," Dillon said with a chuckle.

"You modeled for me the other night," Lex said. He blushed still harder, and so did she as they both recalled where that had led.

"That's because I didn't have to get my clothes off," she replied into her coffee cup, avoiding the interested gazes of everyone else at the table.

"You won't. I promise I can manage just fine if you'll just do it for me."

"Please, Kelly," Dillon said. "Save us all the horror of model interviews."

"You are already here," V added. "It would help you pass the time."

"I'll think about it," Kelly said. She couldn't imagine how Lex would manage to get any real work done if their last little modeling experiment was any indication, but she wasn't about to bring that up in mixed company. "Right now, if you'll excuse me, I need a shower." More than that, she needed not to be the center of attention when the topic was something neither she nor Lex could think about without blushing.

She was halfway up the stairs when Lex caught up to her.

"Thanks for last night," he said softly. "I'm sorry I woke you."

"It's all right. I enjoy a good camp out now and then."

"Seriously, though, you didn't have to stay. But it was nice waking up next to you." He shrugged. "Well, as next to you as I could get, anyway."

"It was nice," she replied, and she meant it in spite of the crook in her neck. "I just wish the circumstances leading up to it could have been a little more pleasant for you."

"I wish that too." He turned to face her as they reached the Meadowlark suite. "For both of us." He left her by her door, but at his suite, he turned back to her. "Can we have another session?"

"Of course we can. Whenever you're ready." She might have managed to use her professional voice with him, but the cratering of her stomach as she thought about their last session was definitely not standard operating procedure.

She asked V about the safety issues of Lex's night wanderings when the woman brought her fresh towels — a job that Kelly was pretty sure wasn't hers — and a fresh pot of coffee, the truth being revealed in the sharing thereof that V wanted to know what had happened last night. Later, Dillon stopped in for the same reason. His excuse was to update her on the press at the gate — nothing she didn't already strongly suspect. Both V and Dillon assured her that Lex was never truly alone, but they gave the man his space as much as they could, understanding how difficult it was for him to have to pull people into his situation when there was nothing anyone could really do. Most of the time, if they didn't need to intervene, they left him to deal with it in his own way. But they reassured her there was always someone watching out for him, though it had clearly pleased them that Kelly had taken matters into her own hands.

* * * *

It had been a shit day from the get-go. The show hadn't been one of Gale Ann Spaulding's best. She should have seen the portents when the heel broke on her very favorite pair of shoes, leaving her to limp into the studio, looking silly in front of the secretaries and the sound technician and serving to put her off balance in other aspects as well. She had stumbled over her own tongue at the beginning of the cast—more than once before she hit her stride—only to have her program for the day fall flat. She had decided to do a show on the overinflated value of the artsy fartsy in Portland when the money could have been spent for something else—though that something was pretty nebulous. She had hoped to tie it all back to Alexander Valentine's grandiose gesture to help pay for a glorified family planning clinic, but her audience hadn't quite known what to do with it, and no real coherent discussion had resulted. Though it had been a decent enough program, it definitely wouldn't go down as one of her most controversial, or one of her most memorable.

She was counting on drinks with Madeline's cousin to open up some interesting new insights into Kelly Blake, but, at the last minute, the girl had canceled because of an impromptu interview she'd been chasing with a city councilman for the university newspaper. Apparently Jenny Fallon was good. She'd had several freelance pieces taken by local magazines and newspapers, and people, some important people, actually knew who she was, so drinks got rescheduled, and Gale Ann was faced with the prospect of drinking alone at a place it was best to be seen with someone who mattered, or an early evening in her apartment surfing the web. Neither was her idea of a good time.

She stumbled into her flat, tossed her bag onto the dining room table and the ruined shoes in the trash. Clearly, her cleaner hadn't come today. Her breakfast dishes were still in the sink and last night's wine glass still on the corner of her desk. What the hell did she pay the woman for? It was late and she was hungry. She'd expected to come home to a clean house. Surely that wasn't too much to ask. She booted the iMac on her desk with a vengeful punch of her index finger, set the deli salad and the Diet Coke next to it and went in search of a clean fork.

She returned to find her email page up with a message from Madeline marked urgent. Shoving a bite of salad into her mouth, she opened the email, which simply read—

*I thought you might find these very interesting.—M.*

That was an understatement! Suddenly Gale Ann Spaulding forgot all about her bad day.

The first thing on the page of a long list of links was an old one from *The Oregonian*. When she opened it, the headline read *Ellen Valentine-Vance Killed in Freak Auto Accident. 10-Year-Old Son Badly Injured.*

Madeleine was an absolute genius! Gale Ann scrolled through the pages from her researcher. While there was still no real dirt on Kelly Blake, if she couldn't get some serious mileage off this new revelation about Alexander Valentine, then she wasn't much of a journalist, was she? Why had she not seen this? Why had no one seen this? Seriously, could it be more obvious? She finished her salad and drink then made and consumed a pot of coffee, all the while taking notes and reading through the links Madeline had sent her as the secrets of Alexander Valentine unfolded right before her eyes. By midnight, she had called her producer and there was a plan in the works for a program that would, at the very least, get her the national recognition she deserved, and very possibly a Pulitzer.

"Oh, I am going to get some serious mileage off this," Gale Ann said. In her head, she was already planning a shopping spree after the revelation of who Alexander Valentine really was. She had her eyes on a nice new silver Audi R8, fully loaded. She was due it. She deserved it, and she would deserve it even more when her show got national syndication, and really, as this story unfolded, it was just a matter of time, wasn't it?

# Chapter Twenty-Four

"Lex wonders if you would meet him in his studio now?" It was Dillon who delivered his boss's request, a request the PA made in person rather than calling or sending an email. That somehow made the whole prospect seem more formal, more like a date and, though that was the last thing she needed for it to seem like, Kelly couldn't help the dance of butterflies in her stomach, even as she cursed herself for getting so excited about something that should have been just her job. But then she no longer truly believed that any more than Lex or anyone else at Mountain View did.

The studio was drenched in midday sun when she stepped inside. The sight of Lex, naked to the waist in a pair of gray sweat pants that hung low around his waist, nearly took her breath away. He worked on a piece of granite only slightly shorter than he was. She stood watching, with him lost in his work, completely unaware of her presence. It was almost as though he were literally releasing a woman from the stone with the intimation of long flowing locks, the shape of a breast and a hip, the curve of one buttock and the hint of an arm raised overhead. Watching him in his own creative process made her heart beat faster, made her stomach bottom. Whatever happened when Lex Valentine worked was way more than the man, way more than the art. Somehow the channeling of all his pain, all his isolation, all his fears and doubts into the beauty of his work kept him safe, kept him from flying apart into the brokenness that was all of humanity in one way or another. But that brokenness had been his close companion. It had shaped his life for a very long time. A writing teacher had once told her that the most powerful writing came from the places the writer most feared to go, the places of pain, the places of suffering. As she watched Lex create, she was pretty sure the same applied.

Then he caught sight of her in his peripheral vision, and the concentration was transformed into warmth as he turned to greet her with a smile, and she felt everything inside her soften and tremble, feeling ridiculously pleased that the sight of her could make him happy.

"You came," he said, as though he'd thought she might not.

"I told you I would." For a second, they stood looking at each other smiling, until she remembered that this was work. She was here to tutor Lex.

He came back to himself at the same moment, as though he'd just woken from a dream — but this time it was a good dream. He gave a little shake of his shoulders and took a deep breath. "I wondered if you would walk with me in the sculpture garden?" He added quickly, "You said that it would be a good tool for our sessions."

"I did, yes. Of course, I will."

He reached for one of the ever-present hoodies and slipped it on. She followed him through the door and let him lead the way through the thicket and into the sculpture garden. Once they were there, she looked around then led him to the sculptures of the women without partners. "I'm assuming that you created these so that you could interact with them as you would a woman." She'd not meant it to sound callous, but feared that it might have when he flinched.

"Pretty pathetic, I know, but it was the best I could do under the circumstances." Then he offered an embarrassed little laugh and shuffled from foot to foot. "Inflatables just aren't substantial enough."

"I shouldn't think so," she said, "and I don't think it's pathetic at all. I think it's a powerful effort toward healing. Creativity is the path through the minefield of our own fears and neuroses. It's not a cure. I don't mean to imply that it is, but it makes the journey a little more bearable and, at the end of the day, you have something to show for it."

"You sound like you're speaking from experience," he said.

"Of course, I am. My neurotic fearful self is exactly the reason I write." She nodded to the sculptures of couples. "In those, I would imagine, you were placing yourself in the role of the males."

His blush was visible and his nod just barely. She stepped as close as she dared forcing him to look up at her. "The men, they're all the same, bodily, but the women are all different."

"I..." He cleared his throat. "I... They're—the men, that is—they're self-portraits." The blush was back with vengeance.

"You're...fit," she said, feeling the tug low in her belly. "Really fit."

This time he laughed. "I can interact with one body and one body only. That being the case, I'd like it to be in good shape. I'd like for it to feel good to my touch. Besides," he added, with another unnecessary clearing of the throat, "the working out has always been one of the best ways to cope with my situation, you know, to let off a little steam, get rid of some...stress. I find that after I've had an incident, and I've recovered enough to be functional, I have a lot of anger and frustration to work out. Sometimes that manifests... you know...sexually. Working out is an alternative to... Well, it's an effort to prevent repetitive stress syndrome." They both chuckled at that, and he added, "It helps."

For a little while, they stood in silence surrounded by the female nudes. She could tell he was struggling to put what was on his mind into words. She gave him time to think about it, to try to formulate what it was he wanted from their session. He'd interacted with her through the sculpture so well yesterday, but today, he seemed at a loss.

"Lex," she said at last. "Tell me what you want."

"I want to make love to you," he blurted out.

The sheer hunger in his words left her weak-kneed, but he gave her no chance to reply. "I want to make love to you, Kelly, and I don't care if it's therapy or not, I want to find a way that we can be together."

In spite of everything, all the arguments she'd had with herself, in spite of all the reasons she shouldn't want the same thing, she did. She desperately did. She made one last valiant effort at being professional. "Lex, I… We shouldn't… My job is —"

"I don't care what your job is. I stopped caring about that a long time ago."

"You don't mean that. You can't."

"Don't tell me what I mean," he snapped. "I know exactly what I mean, and you can't tell me that your job is what you're thinking about either when we're together. Besides, how can you know what will heal me when no one else does? None of the most expensive doctors and shrinks in the world did. I understand if you feel uncomfortable with my wanting to make love to you, but that doesn't make my desire wrong, and it doesn't make me want you any less. And it doesn't mean that my healing can't come from just being with you."

The space around them was silent except for the accelerated rush of their breathing. Then he moved to one of the sculptures and stood in front of it, making the motion of pushing the hair away from the face, of cupping the cheek, of moving in with a feather brush of his lips against the stone mouth, and it was insane, but Kelly felt it. They both did. In a state that she could only describe as under his power, she moved to stand behind the sculpture he caressed, so close that her body pressed against it, so close that one slip of his hand and it would be her that he caressed. It was risky, it was more than risky, it was terrifying and yet in the adrenaline rush of knowing that his hand might slip and touch her, knowing that they were separated by nothing but a slab of marble, she felt arousal prickle along her body, and, in spite of her best efforts to hold still, she found herself rocking and undulating against the stone.

He kissed along the exposed nape of the sculpture and across its collarbone, and Kelly uttered a little cry. She threw back her head and moved her fingers along the rise of gooseflesh on her neck and shoulder. With eyes locked on her, he kissed the throat, one hand falling to cup a breast, then he straightened, struggling to breathe, holding her in a ravenous gaze, as though he waited for her to catch up before he trailed kisses along the statue's breastbone. He licked and caressed and fondled his way down over the swell of her breast and around an erect nipple before he pulled it into his mouth with a purse of his lips and a tight hollowing of his cheeks, all the while keeping his gaze locked on Kelly.

Any other time she might have been embarrassed by the little kitten whimpers and the deep-chested moans she couldn't hold back, but she was lost in Lex's touch, totally lost in what he could do without so much as laying a hand on her.

"It's not fair," she gasped. "I can't respond to you like this. I can't make love to you back." Pulling away from the female sculpture, she glanced around the garden until she found what she was looking for. It was the sculpture combination she'd fallen against the first time she'd found him here – the man leaning over his woman, who lay spread before him waiting to be mounted. There was enough room between the two nudes for her to wriggle and squirm until she all but sat on the woman's lap, but the woman was irrelevant, the woman was a vague representation of all femininity, all of what Lex had wanted but couldn't have. The man, however, represented Lex, always Lex, created in stone by Lex, and it was Lex she wanted. She moved to one side to keep clear of the stone phallus until she was ready for it. She positioned herself so that her body curved upward around one well-muscled thigh, her dress riding up over her hips until she knew Lex could see her panties and no doubt the shape of her through them. Her desire to hide her body from him disappeared with her lust. She wrapped her legs around the male's thigh and her arms around his neck to pull herself up the length of his body, trailing kisses from the spot just above his hip bone up along the scars that would have snaked over his ribs — those Lex had chosen not to represent in the sculptures. His wide-eyed stare and his open-mouthed gasp told her, however, that he knew. He understood fully what she had just done, and he shivered as he lay a hand against the bulge that tented his sweat pants.

In efforts to climb onto the marble bed, the male's thigh was raised in such a way that Kelly could ride it, shift and undulate against it, never forgetting as she did so that the sculpture was a self-portrait of the man she wanted so desperately to touch. She pulled herself up until she could kiss him on the mouth, then she began a slow descent of sloppy wet tongue kisses down over his jaw and throat, onto his hard pectoral muscles and the stiffened little points of his nipples. Lex gave a soft grunt of a curse as she did so and came to stand behind the sculpture's female counterpart, thumbing her heavy nipples, cupping her breasts and caressing down the length of her body until he slipped one hand between her thighs and stroked her much as he had the half pear.

"Oh God, Lex, you're killing me," Kelly gasped as he thumbed the hard nib of the sculpture's clitoris, which he had taken care to expose. With the other hand, he tugged urgently at the elastic of his waistband, with a squirm and a grind, shoving them down to expose his erection.

"Don't," she gasped, as he turned his attention to stroking himself. "That's for me. I want to look at it."

His face reddened briefly, then he threw back his shoulders and stood defiantly, fists clenched at his sides, a little moan escaping his throat as she slid her hand down onto his stone counterpart. As she began to stroke the length of it, his moan became a strangled curse.

"Do you want to see me too, Lex, shall I show you what I look like, what I feel like when I touch myself?"

He only managed another moan.

"Then ask for it. Tell me what you want. Tell me what you want from me, Lex."

"I want to see you," he blurted. "I want you to take off your panties so I can look."

She let go of the stone cock and, with some awkward maneuvering, was just about out of her panties when he added, "And your breasts. I want to see your breasts too."

"Greedy bastard," she said with a little chuckle as she tugged the dress up over her head, unhooked the designer bra and let it fall, all the while he took her in with devouring eyes and nodded his approval, which made her far more pleased than she figured it should have.

"Show me how you touch yourself," he said.

"We're making love not masturbating, remember?" Then she shocked even herself by taking the sculpture's erection into her mouth, deep into her mouth.

"Jesus Christ in Heaven," came the barely breathed response, and when she raised her gaze to him again, he stood pressing his thumb hard to the underside of his cock to keep from coming.

She pulled away, leaving a trail of saliva. "I want you inside me," she gasped, struggling to catch her breath.

"Oh, God." He sounded like he would suffocate. "Not there. Not like that. Come with me."

She half-scrambled, half-fell off the sculpture, struggling to keep up, as he motioned her to a bed-like plinth on which Lex's counterpart lay on his back, erection pointing skyward. A woman straddled his face, clearly preparing to return the favor in a classic sixty-nine, but not quite there yet. Lex's eyes shown with expectation, and Kelly's heart leaped with the audacity, the shear cheekiness of what she was about to do as she crawled onto the plinth, first taking Lex's cock into her mouth to get him ready for her — she had

196

stopped thinking about the sculptures as anything other than surrogates for Lex. In truth, preparation wasn't really necessary, she knew how wet she was, she knew how much her body wanted Lex, at least as much as his clearly wanted hers. He now mounted the bed himself and straddled the male, leaning back against the breasts of the woman, who was quite well endowed. Kelly wondered if she was someone who had modeled for him or only someone who had come from his imagination. It didn't matter. At the moment, she had his full attention, and as she positioned herself, squatting over Lex's stone erection, he fisted and stroked his flesh-and-blood counterpart and shifted against the torso of the sculpture, sounding as though he were hyperventilating, and she sure as hell didn't sound much better.

"Are you sure?" he managed through barely parted lips. "Kelly, are you sure?"

She answered by holding his gaze, shifting her hips slightly backward and easing herself down onto the stone phallus. And suddenly it was as though Lex were inside her. She lost all shyness and all shame as her body took control then completely lost it again, as she thrust and shoved and rode the stone representation of Lex, who sat scant inches away stroking and tugging as though there was no tomorrow.

Grunts and groans dissolved into breathless tight silence as they both approached climax, joints popped, muscles strained and pulses hammered.

"I have to come," Lex gasped at last.

He started to dismount, but she shook her head and cupped her breasts. "Come here, Lex, come on my body, then I'll be able to feel you, to feel your passion."

Totally focused on the cupping and kneading of her offered breasts, with only a few more strokes, he convulsed and the pearlescent wet of his release exploded hot against her cool skin. She gave a little yelp of surprise at the feel of it, the velvety slickness of it on her body, one last thrust onto the stone cock, and she was consumed by her own convulsions, rubbing and stroking his semen against her flesh, holding his gaze as he held hers. "There, you see, Lex?" she said, licking the last of his release from her fingers. "Now you've touched me and I've touched you, and it was amazing." And it was. It was like no sex she'd ever had. In truth, she had never experienced anything so intimate. But what he did next raised the experience to a whole new level. "I want to taste you too," he said, motioning her to dismount. Then he leaned over, forcing her to shove back onto the male's thighs as he took the stone phallus into his mouth, licking and sucking the taste of her from it while she could do nothing but tremble with aftershocks. At last he pulled away, wiping his mouth on the back of his hand. "You don't taste anything like a pear," he said with a smile his face was just barely big enough to contain.

# Chapter Twenty-Five

"I'm starving," Lex said. He shoved himself off the edge of the plinth where the two of them had lain, crowded on either side of the man, who was occupied with the woman sitting on his face. "I think Cookie has some leftover rice pudding in the fridge. That might stave off starvation for a little while."

Kelly enjoyed the view of his very fine backside as he bent to pick up his sweat bottoms, and her insides gave a little jerk of excitement when she realized that he was commando. She'd been in no condition to think about that when he'd removed them. As he watched her slip into her panties, he gave the face-sitting woman's breasts a buss with just a flick of tongue and smiled, right proud of himself when Kelly pulled a heavy breath, but when she stroked the male's erection and held his gaze defiantly, he literally growled at her. "Keep that up, woman, and the rice pudding will have to wait." While they'd lain next to each other on the plinth, neither of them had spoken about what had just happened, no doubt both too stunned to say much, but as they made their back to the house, Lex glanced over at her. "Are you all right?"

She smiled. "I was about to ask you the same thing."

"Well? Are you?"

"If you mean am I okay with what just happened, well, I'm not sure. If you mean am I going to bolt because of it, no."

"Well, that's good." He pushed his way through the last of the thicket and out on to the main flagstone path. For a little while, they walked lost in their thoughts, then Lex spoke again. "Was it…?"

"Was it what?" she asked.

"Was it good?" There was a slight hint of a twitch along his jawbone, and he avoided her gaze.

"You know it was," she replied. "It was amazing."

"I don't know," he said. "How could I? I… Well, I never made love to a woman before, and we did make love, didn't we?" He glanced up at her, but this time he didn't look away.

"Oh, we definitely did do that, Lex. We made love, and it was truly amazing."

Her answer was rewarded with another of his stunning smiles.

When they pushed their way into the kitchen, which was silent except for the sound of Cookie doing something in the pantry. Otherwise, the place was deserted. Lex raided the refrigerator, bringing out two bowls covered with cling film and two bottles of water, which he stuffed into the pockets of his hoodie along with two spoons that were considerably larger than dessertspoons. His table-waiting skills might have left a bit to be desired, but his enthusiasm more than made up for the lack as he laid everything out then sat down across from her, offering a wicked smile. "I have fantasies about eating rice pudding off your body." He laughed softly. "Do you like that idea or did your pulse just jump because you're anticipating another of Cookie's culinary triumphs?" He was toying with her now, but before she could respond, he continued, "After I've licked my rice pudding off of every luscious curve and swell and arch of you, of course then I'd reciprocate by letting you eat yours off my" — he nodded down to his lap — "well, you get the picture."

"Oh, I get the picture all right, in 3D Technicolor." Then she leaned across the table into his hungry gaze. "That gives me an idea."

When he glanced nervously over his shoulder to where Cookie was still rooting in the pantry, she quickly added,

"Oh, don't worry. It's nothing unfit for general viewing. But it might be just the ticket to push the envelope a bit, if you're willing."

"What do you have in mind?" he said, laying down his spoon and wiping nervous palms on his sweats.

"Just this." She filled her spoon with a generous helping of rice pudding and offered it to him across the table.

For a long moment, he sat staring at her then at the spoon, as if she were offering him worms to eat. His pulse bounced against his throat, and the color had leached from his face.

"You don't have to if it's more than you can handle, but I won't be touching you. It'll just be the spoon and the food. Feeding each other is one of the age-old ways of connecting with a lover." She nodded to the tempting spoonful and smiled encouragingly.

He took a deep breath, as though he was about to dive under water, then he leaned as far as he could across the table. One last gasp for courage, and he took the offered pudding into his mouth, breathing like he'd just run a mile. His first response was a startled grunt, but it was followed immediately by a soft moan and the fluttering of eyelids as the taste of the delectable treat hit his palate. "It's good," he managed. He spooned up a heaping helping and returned the favor, trembling just enough that he left a trail of pudding across the table, and the better part of what remained ended up on her chin and in her cleavage, but what did get to her mouth, she made an appreciative show of enjoying thoroughly with a flick of her tongue and a deep-chested sigh of pleasure.

"That wasn't so bad, was it?" she said, dabbing at the tops of her breasts with a swipe of her finger then popping the salvaged dessert into her mouth while he looked on wide-eyed.

He answered by leaning forward, pointing to his open mouth, and she shoved home another spoonful. The feeding frenzy was accomplished with childish giggles and teasing sloppiness. Lex was a different man when he was relaxed, when he laughed and joked, and Kelly would be the first to admit, he was a man whose company she enjoyed immensely. They made quick work of the pudding and made a half-assed effort to clean up after themselves, snapping each other with kitchen towels and wash cloths and chasing each other around the table, while being careful that no one actually caught anyone. Kelly's cell phone rang amid the laughter and teasing. She'd forgotten she'd stuffed it in the pocket of the sundress, and she figured she was damn lucky she hadn't lost it in the woods someplace. It was Myrna. She spoke without greeting.

"You need to turn on the radio to Talk About Town now." Her voice was breathless and louder than usual, almost hysterical. Lex moved close enough that he could hear, though that wasn't difficult in the once again quiet kitchen.

"Myrna, calm down, and tell me what's going on," Kelly managed before Myrna did just that, though certainly not calmly.

"Gale Ann Spaulding is talking about Lex, and if what she's saying is true... Kelly, do you know if what she's saying is true, because if it is, Christ! If it is, holy shit!" Before Myrna could finish the string of expletives, Lex reached for the radio on the credenza and tuned in Talk About Town, catching the vinegar and honey voice of Gale Ann Spaulding mid-rant.

"Alexander Valentine. Oh, that's not his real name but, as I said at the beginning of today's show, all shall be revealed. Of course, a lot of artsy-fartsy people use pseudonyms. We already know that Valentine's little fiancée does. One has to wonder how often a pseudonym is just to cover up work one is too embarrassed to sign one's name to, but that's a topic for another time."

"Stupid woman," Lex said under his breath.

"Once I've told all, you'll understand that Alexander Valentine, poor crazy Alexander Valentine, had other reasons for hiding his true identity."

"Rubbish!" V rushed in from her office and reached to

shut off the radio. Her face was nearly as white as the marble of Lex's sculptures.

"Turn it off, V! Turn that bitch off." Dillon rushed into the room with Cookie right on his tail and stopped in his tracks when he saw Lex and Kelly standing in the middle of the kitchen. "It's just trash talk, Lex. Turn it off and forget about it."

"No!" Lex raised a hand. "Leave it."

"Everyone has secrets," Gale Ann Spaulding was saying, "and most of us are happy to respect other people's secrets as none of our business."

V muttered something that had to do with places where Gale Ann Spaulding could stuff her secrets and, once again, Lex growled a warning as she made another attempt to shut it off.

"The job of the press has always been to expose those secrets when they involve anything that affects the welfare of the public. While Alexander Valentine kept to himself, while he lived a secluded life and made an honest, if rather overpaid living—"

"She would know about being overpaid," Dillon interjected.

"—the press left the man to his work," Spaulding continued. "But Valentine forfeited his right to secrets Saturday night when he chose to move once again into the realm of public figures and celebrities." There was a slight pause and a rattling of paper, which was, no doubt for dramatic effect. Then Spaulding read without preamble, "Ellen Valentine-Vance Killed in Freak Auto Accident. 10-Year-Old Son Critically Injured."

Lex moved back to the table and dropped into a chair as though he could no longer stand.

"This is a headline from *The Oregonian* from twenty-five years ago," Spaulding said. "No doubt some of my esteemed listeners will remember that evening well. It was quite a blow to Portland's movers and shakers, and much more of a blow to one little boy, who, as it turns out, wasn't supposed to be with his mother in the first place that night, but I'm getting ahead of myself with our story here."

"With our story? With our fucking story?" Dillon cursed.

Lex shushed him as the woman went on, her voice dripping smugness.

"On that cold February night, socialite and philanthropist Ellen Valentine-Vance picked up her son after his fencing lesson, a job that would have normally fallen to one of the family's chauffeurs and, for reasons unknown, headed over Mount Hood in a pending blizzard, where she met an untimely death when the car she was driving spun out of control on US 26 near the Mount Hood Summit. The car careened off an embankment just out of view of passing traffic. The visibility, I'm told by those who remember that night, was pretty much non-existent, as any of you will know who've ever been caught out on Hood in bad weather. By the time the wrecked car was discovered, Ellen Valentine-Vance was dead. Her ten-year-old son, and only child, Alden Valentine-Vance II, was taken from the wreckage in critical condition and, on the way to the hospital, he lapsed into a coma, where he remained for six long weeks. Again, I emphasize, he was the only child and heir to the Valentine fortune. Yes, my dear listeners, you heard me right, it was the Valentine fortune the boy was heir to, not the Vance fortune because there was no Vance fortune, but I digress.

"Police reports say that the car hit an icy spot and rolled down an embankment where it was just far enough out of site to go unnoticed. The child was found outside the car unconscious, badly burned and suffering from hypothermia. Later reports would surface of possible foul play, of possible tampering with the car, of, well you know how people love their conspiracy theories."

"Takes one to know one," Cookie said.

"Six weeks later, when the poor child came out of the coma, the world had changed almost beyond recognition. He regained consciousness only to find his mother dead and his father already engaged to another woman. "'I'm elated. My son who was lost has returned to me,' Vance was quoted as saying—a quote from the Bible story of the prodigal son. Vance told the press that he would now have his son sent to a private facility where he would receive the rehabilitation he needed. No doubt Vance expected to have his son back and to resume a normal life as soon as he had recovered enough to be released, but sadly that was not to be.

"Talk About Town did some research, thinking it rather suspicious that there was no evidence of young Alden Vance II after his eleventh birthday—not so much as a graduation announcement—and certainly if the boy had died, there would have been at least a mention of it in the news after the scandal and speculation over his mother's death. But there was nothing. Not a word written anywhere after the boy's eleventh birthday. What we, at Talk About Town, discovered, will shock you. While Alden Vance the First died six years after that tragic accident from a heart attack, Talk About Town discovered that Vance's jilted fiancée, Josephine Beasley—and, make no mistake, dear listeners, she was jilted—is very much alive and well and was more than willing to talk. Here's what she told this reporter."

A recording of a woman with a nasal east coast accent followed, and Kelly didn't miss the way Lex flinched at the sound of her voice. "Believe me, all was never happy in paradise after young Alden's return home. I thought at the time that he resented me taking his mother's place, or at least that's the way a young boy might have seen it. But you see, Alden, his father, and I were together a long time before Ellen's death. I was his mistress. I gave him what Ellen refused him, a loving relationship."

"Wicked fiend of a bitch," V interjected.

"She wasn't the problem, and you know it," Dillon replied.

They all turned their attention back to the radio.

"Oh, Alden tried to keep it from his son, but the child was

very perceptive. Nevertheless, he was still a child and he didn't understand adult relationships, adult needs."

This time Lex had to tell everyone to shut up as protests rose in the kitchen to a fevered pitch.

"Almost immediately after he returned home, the child began passing out and having some kind of fits or seizures when I, or anyone else, touched him. Oh, at first Alden thought it was the boy's way of getting back at him for me, and he punished him for it, which only made matters worse, until he actually had to have the child taken by ambulance to a private hospital. We thought he was going to die. We really did."

There was a sigh that was supposed to be sympathetic, Kelly figured, but they all knew better.

"After that," the recording said, "his father took him to the best doctors, the best specialists, the best psychiatrists money could buy, but the child's mental health continued to deteriorate until Alden was forced to hospitalize him then later institutionalized him for a time, where he was diagnosed with severe haphephobia. As you can imagine, the stress on our relationship was tremendous, and I found out that there was another woman, a nurse at the facility where Alden junior was being treated, and when I tried to force the issue, well, he ended the relationship. Then I went back home to Maryland. I didn't keep track of what happened to the child."

"For my esteemed listeners who haven't yet connected the dots," Spaulding's voice cut in, "haphephobia is fear of being touched, fear of human contact. While Ms. Beasley may not know what happened after she left, we at Talk About Town know very well after looking into the matter." She gave a satisfied little sigh. "After it became clear that the boy was not improving, and that he was not capable of interacting with people under normal circumstances, Vance had his son moved to some unknown location for his own protection. There were people who claimed to have seen him at his father's hunting lodge, which just happened to be Mountain View, by the way, but most people just assumed he'd been institutionalized and eventually gone insane. No one was much interested. When Vance died six years later, the Valentine estate was sold off to some mysterious holding company, and that was the end of it, or so everyone thought."

Kelly had dropped into a chair at the table next to Lex, who sat as still as the marble sculptures in his garden, shoulders stiff, mouth set in a tight, straight line, staring into the empty space in front of him. She wished desperately she could touch him, take his hand and offer him some support, but the best that she could do was sit there beside him while they all listened to the venomous delight in Gale Ann Spaulding's voice as she finished her little expose for her adoring audience.

"One has to wonder when the inmates are running the asylum, what other secrets are being withheld from the public." She paused to let that pithy little statement sink in, making sure her slower listeners got the asylum reference, then she continued, a hint of well-practiced sadness in her voice. "Oh, I'm sympathetic for poor young Alden, of course I am. But if Alden Vance II plans to enter the public domain in such a dramatic way as he most certainly did Saturday night, as he came to us all, deceived us all as Alexander Valentine, then he can expect the press and the public to take an interest. The public won't tolerate being lied to, and they have the right to know who their heroes really are and what they represent. That goes double for the gold-digging harridans who shove their way into the lives of the mentally unstable and take advantage for their own personal gain." Then in her best 'I represent the interests of the people' voice, she opened the show for callers.

As Spaulding's loony fans began their rabid call-in, Dillon switched off the radio, plunging the room into stunned silence. It took Kelly a second to realize all eyes were on her. Lex stood, gaze locked on her, shoulders squared, jaw set like it was cast in iron. He nodded toward the radio.

"Do you have a problem with this?" His voice was little more than a whisper, but in the silent room it was loud in its defiance.

"Don't be ridiculous!" She returned his look with defiance of her own. "Did you seriously think that I would?"

His shoulders relaxed and the tension drained from him like water. The collective sigh of relief in the room was audible. "No. I didn't," he said. On the table, he moved his hand so close to Kelly's that there was another audible sigh in the room and her pulse jumped as though her heart were trying to escape her chest, not helped at all by the smile that suddenly split his face.

Then Dillon cleared his throat with a loud 'eh-hem'. "While Kelly might not care about your deep, dark past, the public will." He suddenly had everyone's attention.

"What do you suggest? You're the spin doctor."

"There's nothing to spin," Dillon replied. "Public sympathy will be on your side if you act fast. Clearly you weren't trying to deceive anyone. Your efforts have always been self-preservation and peace. The audience is a sympathetic one, and will be more so if you come forward and tell your side of the story."

V offered her agreement. "You need to speak to the press, Alexander." She nodded out of the window. "You've got a captive audience right outside the gate."

Lex paled visibly and his breath came in shallow gasps. But before he could protest, Dillon continued.

"You're on your home turf. There are far fewer variables than there were the other night at the gallery. We could pull this off with you still inside the gate if that'll make it easier for you. We can make sure that no one touches you. But we need to act fast."

"All right." Lex stood and straightened his hoodie. "You go tell them that I'm planning a press conference in…" He looked down at his watch. "Maybe thirty minutes. I need a shower."

"Make it forty-five minutes," V said. "For this, you need

your fiancée beside you, and while Ms. Blake is a stunning woman, it's best that we make the most of her features for the press."

"Are you okay with that?" Lex asked, holding her gaze.

"I am." She was more than okay with it, she realized, and the smile that Lex offered her in return made her even more okay with it. "I'm all yours, V." She stood and followed the woman upstairs.

# Chapter Twenty-Six

V had worked her magic with a sedate but stunning mauve jacket and skirt, minimal makeup and an unobtrusive pearl necklace with matching earrings. She had scooped Kelly's hair into a sleek chignon with just a few tendrils of curls free around her face to make the look a bit more romantic. They were both admiring the finished product in front of the full-length mirror when there was a soft knock on the French doors between the two suites. Lex stepped inside, timidly at first, having not been in the suite since Kelly had taken up residence there. But when he saw her, his face brightened with approval.

"V does good work," she said, warmth crawling up her cheeks.

"You made V's work ridiculously easy, I'm sure," he said. He nodded his thanks to his housekeeper and dismissed her with an unspoken message that he wanted Kelly to himself for a few minutes.

"You all right?" Kelly asked.

"Better now that you know." He looked around the room and gave a helpless shrug. "Kelly, I wasn't trying to hide anything from you. It's just that, well, that part of my life I like to forget, and after my father died, I was given the chance to live another life, a different life, one that worked for me. I let Alden Vance die and, with Dillon's help, and the help of his father, Alexander Valentine was born. That holding company that bought up all of Valentine's assets, well, that was the Matthews family, and it was nothing but a transfer of assets for my protection and for my peace of mind. Alden Vance II was never who I was. I was always

Alexander Valentine, even before I knew it."

"It's all right, Lex. You did what you had to, like we all do," she said. "I know the man you've become. That's enough for me."

He smiled as though he were smiling to himself. "I wish I could kiss you for that. The man that I've become seldom gets the notice of a beautiful, intelligent woman."

She laughed softly. "Flattery will not get you laid, Alexander Valentine."

For a moment, they both stood smiling at each other like a couple of Cheshire cats, then he moved to the credenza near the mirror and set a velvet box down on top of it. "The press is nothing if not perceptive. Since you're my fiancée, I thought it might be wise for there to be some concrete evidence." He nodded to the box.

She opened it with trembling fingers, finding that it was a struggle to remind herself their engagement wasn't real, none of it was real.

"My grandmother, Clarissa Valentine, loved sapphires," he said in response to the catch of her breath. "She actually wasn't much for baubles, as she called them, but she made an exception for sapphires, and this ring was one my grandfather gave her on their twenty-fifth wedding anniversary. I thought it would serve as an engagement ring that the press could ooh and ah over. If you're okay with it, that is."

"I think if I try real hard, I might be able to be okay with that," she said, taking the sapphire from the box and slipping it onto the ring finger of her left hand. The sight of it there and what it represented made her a little unsteady on her feet and giddy all over.

"It fits," he said. His smile had that possessive edge to it that she could easily imagine a groom might have for his future bride.

She liked it that he looked at her that way.

A knock on the door made them both jump. "It's time," Dillon said.

Dillon's candy-apple-red Jeep with the top off was his version of the Pope Mobile, he joked. It would be better than addressing the press from inside the gate. "I've instructed everyone to step back. I've warned them again that the haphephobia is real and that while you're happy to talk with them, you'd rather not throw up on them."

"Jesus, you didn't say that?" Lex said. "Tell me you didn't say that."

Dillon shot him a wicked little grin. "You may be the great Alexander Valentine, and they may all love you, but they still don't want to be puked on."

"I hate you so bad," Lex growled.

"Don't you just," came the reply. "Don't you just."

The drive to the gate took a full ten minutes with Dillon taking his time, giving Lex a chance to prepare himself. Kelly sat at his side, wishing desperately she could hold his hand for reassurance. Instead, she smiled every time he shot her a glance, which was often, actually. She liked that. She liked that she could offer him at least that much.

As they approached the gate, Dillon spoke with authority. "Once the gates open and the press steps back, Lex will get out and move to stand in front of the Jeep, if you're okay with that, bro. If not, speak from the Jeep. Believe me, the press won't mind, and Kelly, I just need you to follow his lead. If he gets out, you get out. Stand by his side. There'll be questions for you, you know?"

"I know," Kelly said. "I'm okay with that."

"I'll try to direct as much of the interaction to Lex as I can. The fewer lies we have to tell, the better."

She found it jarring, the reference to lies. Christ, how could it be that she could so completely allow herself to fit into the fabrication they were creating? And yet she did. It felt good to be by Lex's side. It felt good to wear his grandmother's ring, to think of it as her engagement ring, but it wasn't, was it? It was all just a part of the ruse she'd allowed herself to be dragged into. Without warning, a vision of Lex standing naked in the sculpture garden in the throes of passion, passion that belonged to her, the feel of his heat against her breasts, flashed through her head and she caught her breath in a little gasp. She thought it was a little gasp, at least, but it was enough to cause Lex to turn to her, a look of concern on his face, and then he saw, or he must have somehow intuited, where her mind had gone. He glanced down at her breasts then at her lap and his lips curled in a lazy smile. "Can't keep your mind off sex for five minutes, can you, Ms. Blake?"

Thoughts of lies or deception or past secrets vanished in the warmth of that smile as he leaned just close enough to be almost in the danger zone and said between barely parted lips. "If you give me a hard-on before I have to speak in front of a gazillion rabid reporters, I'll make you pay for it."

"Ooh, I'm shivering in my Louis Vuittons," she whispered back.

"What? Is everything all right?" Dillon said from the front with a quick glance over the seat.

"Fine," Lex said, his gaze still locked on Kelly. "Everything is just fine."

Then they were at the gates, which opened as if by magic, and reporters parted like the Red Sea as the Jeep moved through and came to a halt. "You good to get out?" Dillon asked, but Lex already had his door open.

Kelly followed his lead. As he moved to stand in front of the Jeep in a flurry of snapping shutters and words mumbled into Dictaphones, everyone stepped back politely and gave him space.

When they were all settled and he had given them a fair amount of time to take photos and get microphone levels for those who were there with television, he spoke with an ease Kelly could have never imagined under the circumstances.

"As you all know by now, thanks to the intrepid reporting of Gale Ann Spaulding, I was born Alden Vance II. You also know the details of my past, thanks to Ms. Spaulding, and if you've done your research, which I figure you all have, then you no doubt now know a lot more than what Ms. Spaulding was able to fit into a thirty-minute broadcast. The facts are all on the Internet. There's neither been an effort to hide them nor to get rid of them. If any of you had asked me about my past, I'd not have lied to you. And, as you all saw from Saturday night's unexpected drama, I have very good reasons for keeping to myself. Alden Vance II was a tragic character. He was a victim of circumstances beyond his control. There's nothing new or unique in that. It's an old story. None of us come through tragedy without being changed. Sometimes those changes are good, sometimes not so much.

"In my case those changes were good, very good." To this statement, the crowd erupted in surprised murmurs. "I was destined from my birth to take over Valentine Industries, to run my mother's company, to be my father's legacy. No one on this planet was less suited or had less desire to do that than Alden Vance II." He shrugged. "But what do ten-year-old boys know of the world and what they'll be facing, of what it means to take on a role they weren't made for and never wanted? When I was ten, I never doubted my future. When I woke up in that hospital to discover my mother dead, my body scarred and myself incapable of touching another person or allowing another person to touch me, I doubted everything. Everything."

A deathly silence fell over the press and they leaned forward, their faces filled with empathy.

"What I didn't doubt was that in art I found comfort, healing. What I didn't doubt was that the creative process, the channeling of all that was inside me, all that I didn't understand into my art, would keep me sane. What I also didn't doubt was that no matter what transpired after I woke up from the coma, Alden Vance II died in that car crash along with his mother. It was Alexander Valentine who arose from the hospital bed and walked away," he offered a twitch of a smile. "Of course, it took me a few years to understand that.

"Ms. Spaulding called me mentally unstable. Perhaps that's true. We artists have a reputation for mental instability, but I would like it to be known that I was most definitely in my right mind when I agreed to support the funding for the Cascadia Womens and Children's Hospital with the work of my hands, that I was most definitely in my right mind when I chose to attend the gallery auction Saturday night and move for the first time since Alexander Valentine was born, into the public eye, and I was beyond a doubt in my right mind when I chose to ask my lovely lady, Kelly Blake, to be my wife."

To Kelly's surprise, she found her throat tightening with emotion and she blinked back tears. Without thinking, she laid her left hand against her chest, and there was an instant wave of shutter snapping before she realized she had inadvertently flashed the ring, which made Dillon smile like the cat that got the cream as the crowd broke into an impromptu round of applause.

When the press quieted again, Lex continued. "I don't remember what happened the night my mother died. I remember her picking me up after my lesson. I remember her telling me we were going to the house in Bend for the weekend. I remember that the weather was bad when we ascended the pass." He shook his head. "And then I woke up in the hospital. That's all. When my father died unexpectedly, my guardian had the sense and the compassion to listen when I told him what I wanted, what I needed. What I needed was not to be Alden Vance II. What I needed was to be left alone to heal and to try and figure out who it was that survived that wreckage. Two years later, I sold my first sculpture and Alexander Valentine was born.

"I never meant to deceive. I never meant to cause drama. For me, the two are separate lives. For me, healing has come from looking forward, looking to the future and not dwelling on the past, over which I had no power. I hope you can forgive me for any unintended subterfuge and that you'll allow me, along with my fiancée, the peace and privacy we need to continue that journey forward. Now then, if you have questions, I'll do my best to answer them."

"Mr. Valentine," came the response from the reporter for one of the cable television stations, "since you're engaged and looking forward to the future, is it fair for us to assume that you are...finding some effective treatment for your phobia?"

Lex shot Kelly a mischievous smile. "If you're asking if the love of a good woman is the cure for what ails me, then I have to say absolutely. However," he added, raising his voice above the resulting cheers, "healing takes time and patience, and I'm looking forward to a very long, very happy convalescence." This time he made no effort to stop the cheering. He just gave Kelly a look that was at least as physical as any embrace she'd ever had, physical enough to leave her breathless and giddy like the future bride she was pretending to be.

"Carl Freeman, Talk About Town Radio," the man introduced himself. Clearly, he was lower in the pecking order than Spaulding and had been sent here to hold down the fort just in case. Spaulding would be truly pissed when she discovered that the man got an interview, Kelly thought. "What about you, Ms. Blake?" the reporter asked. "How are you finding a relationship in which intimacy is impossible?"

She bit her tongue to keep from commenting on the man's ignorance, then saw out of the corner of her eye, Lex was quietly laughing. She bit the inside of her cheek to keep from doing the same. "I can assure you whole-heartedly, Mr. Freeman, there are lots of other wonderful ways to be intimate that don't involve physical touch."

The press caught the ribald undertones and there were a few wolf-whistles and good-natured cat-calls. Lex just smiled and shot her a steamy glance.

"Will the public be seeing more of you in the future?" The reporter from *The Oregonian* asked.

"That depends on how willing the public is to back off

and give me breathing room so I won't throw up on their shoes," Lex replied, to which the crowd laughed.

"As you said, Mr. Valentine, we've all done our research after Ms. Spaulding's story broke," a short reporter in the front row with a Cleopatra hair cut began, "and I would like to address the so-called conspiracy theories concerning your mother's accident. It became clear to me, as I read through the files, that it's quite possible there was foul play involved. If I'm aware of it, I'm sure you are too. Have you followed up on any of these leads?"

The tension rose in Lex's shoulders, and Kelly was close enough to hear the sharp intake of breath, but he didn't stumble, nor did he allow any emotion into his voice. In fact, he seemed quite distant when he answered the reporter. "I was ten at the time, and fairly precocious, so once I recovered enough to understand what had happened to my mother, of course, I heard the rumors. My father tried to keep the investigation from me, but he couldn't. I had allies, friends who didn't treat me like an ignorant child, but took my concerns seriously." Kelly didn't miss the brief glance at Dillon. "But by the time I was healed enough to question and seek out answers, I had other problems to deal with, as Ms. Spaulding so helpfully informed you. And also by that time, nearly six months had passed since the accident.

"Later, Alexander Valentine investigated the theories, in fact, I still have an investigator trying to discover if there's any truth in those theories, but as you can imagine, after this much time, it's a cold case if there even is a case. Nevertheless, I owe it to my mother to make sure the truth is found out if things happened differently than what the police reports say."

"Were you the reason your father broke up with Josephine Beasley?" someone asked.

"Not directly, though I'm sure my situation was a strain on their relationship. It was unlikely that my father would have ever married Josephine Beasley or anyone else, for that matter. My mother had made sure the family fortune would pass to her children. I discovered much later that my father had several illegitimate children. I don't like to speak ill of the dead, but Alden Vance was a philanderer and anyone who knew him will tell you that. His son knew it almost before he knew how to read." There was a loud mumbling among the crowd, and Lex waited until they quieted. "My father had no access to the fortune. He apparently didn't know this until after my mother's death. I'm told that he was to be allowed to live on the properties, to have a substantial stipend and to keep his share of interest from the stocks my mother had given to him as a wedding present. The truth was, other than those bequeathals, he had nothing to offer any woman who didn't marry him for love.

"I never meant to keep secrets," Lex said, looking out over the crowd. "My father kept me secluded when my haphephobia was diagnosed, for my own safety and protection. After the accident, I could no longer be the son he wanted me to be, so it was better that way, for him and for me. I'm not a mystery at all. I'm just a man who's better off in the privacy of his own home. I encourage you to keep researching the subject of my mother's death, if you want to delve deeper. The more eyes on the case, the better the chances of the truth being uncovered, even if it's nothing more than what the police report says. But I ask that you go home to your lives and leave my fiancée and me to ours. In the future, I'll do my best to keep the public in the loop as necessary, but I would really like to have my space back to myself, if you don't mind."

There was a murmur among the reporters and a few nods of agreement. Kelly figured they'd be glad to get home as well.

"Just one more question," Dillon intervened. "Then I hope you'll all find that the mystery of Alexander Valentine is well enough solved so that you can go home to your families."

"Mr. Valentine," a reporter from the back began, "have you and Ms. Blake set a date for the wedding yet?"

"We haven't, but it can't be soon enough for me." Lex offered Kelly such a bright smile that once again she found herself forgetting there would be no wedding and that as soon as everything settled, there would be only a staged break-up and they would both go their separate ways. That made her feel much sadder than it should have. But then Alexander Valentine totally took her mind off the break-up by doing the unthinkable and taking her hand. The crowd gasped, Dillon nearly had a heart attack, and she whispered between her teeth. "What the hell are you doing?"

"I'm holding my fiancée's hand, what the hell does it look like I'm doing?" He stumbled only slightly and reached for the side of the Jeep to support himself. But Kelly could hear his efforts to breathe and see the sweat breaking on his forehead as the color left his face.

"Jesus! Jesus H. Christ!" Kelly whispered. "Don't you dare pass out on me. Don't you dare!"

Dillon had the door open and ready for them, and still Lex wouldn't release Kelly's hand, nodding her in ahead of him then all but falling onto the seat.

"You're gonna regret this," Dillon said as he all but spun gravel turning the Jeep around and heading back through the open gate.

"No, I'm not," Lex managed between clenched teeth. He swallowed hard and screwed his eyes shut. Fortunately, the road back to Mountain View was well paved, but it didn't matter.

"Lex, let go! Lex let go of my hand, damn it." But he didn't. He held tight, damn near tight enough to crush bone. By the time they rounded the corner into the stand of evergreen that made Mountain View invisible from the road, his face was gray and covered with sweat. Kelly was assaulting him with a fine mix of pleading and cursing when Dillon stopped the Jeep and sat quietly while Lex managed his exit with way more dignity than Kelly would have thought possible, before he stumbled into the rhododendron thicket, dropped onto his knees and vomited.

"Jesus Christ, why the hell did he do that?" Kelly reached for the door to go to him.

"Stay put," Dillon ordered. "He doesn't need your help to puke, and if you can't understand why he did what he did, then you're not nearly as bright as I gave you credit for."

Suddenly Kelly found herself close to tears. She did understand. She understood exactly why he did it. Some things were just worth the cost. She looked down at her clenched fist, still tingling from his suicide grip on it. Lex Valentine had touched her and she had been so fucking concerned that she had missed the moment, a moment he'd wanted to share with her.

"It's all right," Dillon said, as though he completely understood what she felt. "He's all right. In fact, I wager he's more than all right, or will be as soon as he's finished puking." He handed her a bottle of water. "For him. He'll need it when he's ready."

It seemed like an eternity before he stood, wiped his mouth on the back of his hand and made his way on shaky legs back to the Jeep. He took the bottle of water, rinsed his mouth and settled himself in the seat next to Kelly.

"All right now?" she asked, still fighting the urge to sob for him.

He offered her a broad smile. "Never better." Then he closed his eyes and laid his head back against the seat for the rest of the trip home.

# Chapter Twenty-Seven

"The bastard! The bloody fucking bastard!" Gale Ann Spaulding threw her bottle of Diet Coke against the door that Carl Freeman had just shut behind him not two seconds before. How the hell was she supposed to know that Alexander fucking Valentine would call her bluff and have a fucking press conference? She should have been there. The scoop should have been hers! She was the one who had done all the work, all the research to set the whole thing in motion. And Carl fucking Freeman didn't even ask anything worth asking. "How are you finding a relationship in which intimacy is impossible?" she quoted him in a mocking tone. What the hell kind of question was that? A man question, that was what it was, always wanting to know about screwing.

She paced the floor in front of her desk, giving the Coke bottle, which had rolled into her path, a hard kick that did nothing for her pedicure or her feet in her open-toed Kurt Geigers. Freeman was an amateur, just an amateur! He got lucky that was all, and now he was getting the credit.

And if that wasn't bad enough, the ever so forthcoming Alexander fucking Valentine and his bitch had made her look stupid again. She'd broken the story, she'd put it out there, she'd done the work, and now this! She paced a couple more times then grabbed her cigarettes from her bag and shoved the window open. Sitting with one ass cheek on the sill and her head out, she lit up. She really was trying to cut back, but Jesus, it was so hard when things were so stressful. This should have been an award-winning story. This should have been her ticket to national syndication.

Instead, Carl fucking Freeman would get the credit for the actual interview. Carl fucking Freeman who wanted to know nothing more than how the two of them could be together and not fuck. Of course, everyone wanted to know that. It was the burning question for a man who couldn't touch anyone, but still, it was the big moment, it was a major break-through. There must have been something better, anything better. She would have certainly thought of something better. She wouldn't have let the bastard and his bitch of a fiancée off nearly so easily.

She finished the cigarette, flipped the butt onto the pavement below, then came back into the room to listen to a copy of the interview that Freeman had given her for her call-in show. Freeman had the personality of a wet rag. He might have been there for the press conference, but she was the one who could take what he'd recorded, pick it apart, and find the juicy tidbits that would titillate her call-in audience. She was the one they wanted to hear it from, not Carl Fucking Freeman.

As she listened to Kelly Blake's response to the intimacy question, like some fifty-dollar hooker ready to jump the man, she Googled Blake's pen name, Gina Alan, for the thousandth time. There were lots of links leading to her website, a blog and to numerous other pages including her author pages on Amazon. The woman was not only prolific but well-respected in the writing community, in spite of being only moderately successful. That gave her an idea. She Googled how much money the average writer made and whistled through her teeth. Holy fuck, not even a frugal person living on the street could manage on what the average writer made. But clearly Gina Alan was above average. Her books were well reviewed by numerous readers. She had won several awards and several of her novels had been on local and regional bestseller lists. She picked up the phone and dialed Madeline, who answered immediately.

"Is there any way you can find out how much Kelly Blake,

AKA Gina Alan, makes off her novel sales?"

"I can find out how much a good mid-range author might make, if that'll help. Otherwise, I don't have the authority to look into the finances of a private citizen."

"That'll do. As soon as you can," Gale Ann ordered and hung up, tapping a freshly manicured nail on the top of her desk while she glared at the monitor. She pulled up the images from the articles done by reporters hanging out on Blake's lawn the day after the gallery incident. Then she pulled up Google Earth. The house was a really nice house in a good neighborhood. It wasn't your typical starter home for a single woman with a single income trying to get onto the property ladder. She drove a Subaru, albeit a nice one. There was nothing out of the ordinary for a person in the decent middle-income bracket. But then Kelly Blake didn't really strike her as someone who would be ostentatious or showy with her wealth, if she had any. And really, how much fucking space did someone need to write a novel? She grabbed up the Diet Coke bottle at her feet and took a sip, then made a face. It was tepid. She screwed the lid back on, tossed it back onto the floor and continued perusing the links to Gina Alan. How the hell did a nobody like Kelly Blake meet Valentine, she wondered. It wasn't like he was a social butterfly, and as good as Kelly Blake had looked at the gallery the other night, there were no social butterflies in her neighborhood either, so the chances of the two of them running into each other at a bar on a Saturday night were slim to nothing, and seriously, she couldn't imagine that Alexander Valentine would be a huge fan of romance novels. But then again, maybe a man who couldn't have an intimate relationship of his own would find the happily ever afters of a good roll in the hay bodice ripper just what the doctor ordered. The thing was that for the past twenty-five years, the man had lived as a recluse. No one knew what had gone on during that time. She wrote that down. That was a possible angle for the call-in show. For that matter, in spite of her impressive résumé of novels, Kelly Blake had not exactly been in the limelight either. The bottom line was that something just didn't add up. If she could find it, she would have the key to getting syndication, she was sure of it.

Madeline called back. "Just sent you over some links and a couple of typical novel contracts. Of course those would be different for Nora Roberts or J.K. Rowling or someone like that. But for the average novelist, the contracts are pretty standard, though there's some negotiating room, which an agent would know about. I suppose I could talk to an agent if you'd like."

"Thanks. I'll think about it," Gale Anne said.

"Oh, by the way," Madeline added. "My cousin, Jenny, is free tomorrow evening if you'd like to talk to her."

"Oh, right. That's good. That's great. I'd love to meet her for cocktails like we'd planned, say same time same place."

"Great. I'll set it up for you."

The line went dead and Gale Ann pulled up the links Madeline had sent her. Maybe she could get something from Andy's girlfriend. She was sure there had to be some dirt, some hidden secret. She planned to uncover it, and serve it up with a nice, fat, raised middle finger to Kelly fucking Blake.

\* \* \* \*

Once Lex had recovered from his first-ever experience of holding hands with a girl, there was no denying the atmosphere of celebration that Mountain View exuded. There were freshly baked snickerdoodles in the cookie jar and there was an absolute feast for dinner with roast chicken, fresh garden veg and Cookie's famous white chocolate raspberry crème brûlée — the recipe that got her invited to cook for the Avengers, Lex informed Kelly. Not only was the man completely recovered, but he couldn't seem to wipe the smile off his face, and neither could anyone else, including her.

"I still can't believe you actually held her hand," V said with a smile that would have been right at home on the face of any proud mother. "The next thing you know, it'll be dancing lessons. Maybe for the wedding," she said, nodding down to the ring, which Lex had insisted Kelly wear for the duration of their engagement.

"Yup, V, you would have been proud of your little boy," Dillon said. "He did real good."

After dinner there was dancing. V and Dillon were both light on their feet, and Lex informed Kelly that while he could do nothing more than line dance, and that only if the other dancers didn't get too close, he loved to watch. So they sat side-by side, not quite touching, but much closer than Kelly could ever remember him being to her and watched Dillon and V do first a lovely Viennese waltz then a wicked rendition of the Charleston.

"It must have been hard for you, having the past dug up like that," she said when he walked her to the Meadowlark suite later. In spite of his excitement, he was clearly exhausted and had let her talk him into going to bed like a normal person and getting some rest. She convinced him that he could work in the studio when he woke up. He'd have more energy that way. He'd agreed without much persuasion.

"It would have been horrible if you hadn't been there," he said. "A shrink I had for a while — one of the better ones, actually — said that sometimes one of the most helpful things is just to have someone witness for you, you know, witness your pain, validate that something has happened to you and that you're trying to cope with it. I felt like you were my witness today. I felt like you validated me." Then he added quickly, "I'm sorry about the whole holding your hand and throwing up thing."

"I'm not," she said. "I'm sorry about the throwing up, but I loved the holding your hand thing."

He shifted from foot to foot, suddenly too shy to meet her gaze. "I'm dying to try it again, only sometime when it's less stressful, sometime when we can maybe work up to it, you know, like start with a pinkie touch." He wiggled his little finger at her.

"I think that's a great idea, Lex."

There was another silence. It was the silence into which usually a dating couple would have fit in a goodnight kiss, and Kelly was pretty sure Lex wanted that almost as much as she did. At last, he raised two fingers to his lips and kissed them, then turned them toward her, and she blew him an air kiss in return. "Good night, Kelly. I look forward to the time when that'll be for real."

* * * *

At first, the sound was far off, and he hoped against hope that it would be something else, anything else. He really thought perhaps today had been a breakthrough, that maybe tonight he'd sleep peacefully. The chattering of teeth sounded like castanets, just like always, and just like always, he tried desperately to get out of the dream before it set upon him, he tried desperately to wake up. He needed Kelly. Where was Kelly? He tried to call out to her, but no sound came, nothing came from his mouth but an effort to breathe that collapsed in on itself like the ground giving way in an earthquake, like a wave folding over itself before it ceased to be a wave. The chattering of teeth grew louder and louder. His own teeth chattered. He couldn't remember ever being so cold, so cold that he forgot about the burning, forgot about the pain, so cold that there was nothing in the world but cold. Still, she kept saying it would be all right. She said it over and over again. And her teeth chattered, and his teeth chattered, and they were both so cold. The blood that had been warm on his face had cooled and he feared it had frozen, and the dream was awash in the cold copper scent of it. He tried to breathe through his mouth so he wouldn't have to smell it, but when the chattering stopped and the crushing weight got heavier and heavier, he forgot about the scent, all he thought about was breath, all the while he fought back panic, telling himself it would be okay, telling himself someone would find them. She wouldn't lie to him. She would never lie to him. It would be all right. But breath…breath becomes the center of the universe, the most important thing, the only thing the mind can conceive of when you can't get enough, when each breath you take is less and less helpful than the last. Then the chants began, mantras of desperation, endless repetitions of the only words he could remember, the only ones that mattered in his frozen shrunken universe. "Please move, please move, please move. You have to move, please move! Please move! You have to move!" And the weight got heavier, and he was in a tomb—he knew he was. He had to be. There was no light, there was no space, there was no air, and it was cold, so terribly cold, and the weight was relentless. Surely it was the weight of the earth above him, heaped onto his grave. But he wasn't dead. He wasn't dead. He wasn't dead!

Kelly, he needed Kelly, he had to have Kelly, but how could Kelly find him in this dark, cold place. Kelly didn't even know where he was or who he was or how he was. If she did, how could she care about him, how could she understand him, how could she love him? Oh God, he wanted her to love him. He wanted her to lift the weight off him and take him into her warmth. But he couldn't breathe. He couldn't breathe. He couldn't get out from under the crushing weight. "Get off me, get off me, get off me," the mantra began, the one that always brought the final desperation. "Get off me, get off me, Get! Off! Me!"

"Lex! Lex, I'm here. Lex wake up!"

He came to as though he had been drowning, gasping for air, shouting like a banshee, bursting upright in a bed that was shaking like there really was an earthquake.

"Lex! Wake up. I'm here. I'm right here. It's all right."

He woke in danger of hyperventilating to find himself tangled in sheets that were soaked with the cold sweat of nightmares. Kelly was shaking his bed with all of her strength and calling out for him to wake up. She stopped abruptly when he erupted from the blankets. Stumbling back to keep from touching him, she tripped over the discarded comforter and fell onto the floor, landing with a muffled cry.

"Jesus! Kelly, are you all right?"

"You were dreaming."

"I didn't hurt you, did I?"

"Are you okay? You cried out, and I was worried."

They were suddenly talking over each other in breathless gasps and hissing whispers as if his wild jungle shrieks hadn't been enough to wake the whole household and half of Multnomah County.

"I'm fine, don't worry," she said, pulling herself up off the floor. "Sit."

He did as she said, realizing that he was lucky his legs had held him upright long enough to at least stand and make sure she was okay.

She disappeared into the bathroom and returned shortly with a towel and a glass of water, both of which she sat on the nightstand next to him then waited patiently while he drank back the water in thirsty gulps then toweled off the sweat now chilling on his body.

"I'm sure the dream has come up in your therapy."

"Every single time." He finished the water and set the glass aside. "It's obviously about the accident. In it, my mother keeps telling me it'll be all right, that someone will find us and everything will be fine. But I don't remember any of what happened, as I said to the press. Oh, I've written it all down in detail ad nauseum. To have to drag it all into the waking world is almost as unpleasant as the dream itself. All the therapists seemed to think that if I could understand the dream, if I could just remember what happened that night, that I'd be able to finally get past it and the phobia would go away. That's why I often end up working in the studio afterward. I always hope maybe something will come to the surface when my mind is elsewhere. But so far, nothing has changed."

She sat next to him close enough to be comforting, but not so close that he felt his space threatened. "Do you want to tell me about it?"

He found that, strangely enough, he did. He told her everything, all that he could remember in as much detail as he could manage. She brought him more water and handed him his robe when he began to shiver, all the while listening with no comment.

When he'd finished, when he could think of nothing else, they sat for a long moment in companionable silence, then she said, "What about when you sleepwalk, are you dreaming then as well?"

He nodded. "In those dreams, I somehow get out of the car, but I don't know how. In those dreams, I'm chasing after someone, trying to catch up with someone who was just there, just a few seconds ago. Whoever it is, they're always gone before I can talk to them, before I can get them to help me find my way back home."

"And you end up sleeping in the sculpture garden."

He nodded again. "Always by the same sculpture, always either curled around her or down in her arms."

"Do you think she represents your mother?"

He shook his head. "In the dreams, the sleepwalking dreams, I always know my mother's already dead. I always know that something inside me is broken, that I've lost something more than just my mother, something I may never get back." He shrugged. "I suspect the sculpture represents the human touch, the intimacy I've lost, but that's just sort of a Jungian bog standard guess, you know? Only *you* understand what your dreams are trying to tell you, that's what the therapists all said."

For a long moment, they sat in silence again, both wrapped in matching terry robes, both looking slightly worse for the wear. He was okay with that. He could have sat there with her all night, but she broke the spell. "Lex, you're exhausted. Do you think you could try to get some more sleep?"

"Stay with me." The words were out before he could stop them. "If you stay with me, I can sleep."

She stood and looked back at his bed and, for a dreadful moment, he thought she was going to say no. "All right then, but your bed's a train wreck. Why don't you come to mine? It's virtually undreamed in tonight. Besides, I only allow good dreams in my bed." She nodded to the open French doors and gave him an encouraging smile.

Back in the Meadowlark suite, she went to work on their sleeping arrangements, putting a barrier of pillows down the middle between them. It was a huge bed, just like his, so there was still lots of room. "There are enough cushions and pillows and throws for a herd of elephants to have a slumber party," she said. "I don't move much when I sleep, but this will make sure that I don't accidentally touch you or you me." She pulled back the covers and nodded to the space. "Get comfy and I'll tuck you in." He did as she asked, wishing desperately that they could lose the pillow barrier and that he could take her in his arms and hold her all night and wake up with her still pressed against him. The thought made his chest ache with longing, but that she was here, that she was next to him, sleeping close, that would do. That was so much better than anything he'd ever been able to imagine for himself.

When she was settled in on the other side of the pillow barrier, he couldn't keep from smiling. She was in his bed. Well, technically it was his bed, wasn't it? She wore his engagement ring, and she did! She still wore it. She hadn't taken it off. At least for the moment he could almost imagine the two of them as a normal couple climbing into their bed together after a hard day, lying close to each other before they both drifted off to sleep. What must that feel like? Would he ever know? If he ever did, at this moment he couldn't imagine anyone he'd rather share his bed with than Kelly Blake. And just before he drifted off to sleep, he remembered that she had found him, she had followed him and come searching for him, both the other night in the sculpture garden and tonight. She had rescued him from the dream world and she hadn't been repulsed by his neediness. She had stayed with him.

* * * *

Kelly woke with a pillow tossed carelessly over her face and a heavy warm weight on her body. It was only when she moved slightly in an effort to dislodge whatever it was that she realized the heavy weight was Lex Valentine. She froze, heart somersaulting in her chest, right exactly where his head rested, dark hair tickling her chin. All around them she could see nothing but mounds of pillows, but there were none between them. There was nothing between them. He lay with his head between her breasts, his breath warm and humid against one, while he cupped the other in a calloused palm. One well-muscled leg was thrown over her body just above her hip, which his morning erection prodded enthusiastically. What the hell should she do? If he woke up like this, he would pass out or throw up or both. At the very least, he would have a panic attack, but she hadn't moved. He had found his way to her in his sleep, and he clung to her like he would a lover. Like he would a lover! That thought focused her enough that she made an effort to relax. It was human contact. The cost, from what she had seen yesterday — at least between the two of them — the cost was worth paying. His unconscious had known exactly what he needed, what he desired. So why not let his unconscious take care of the need he couldn't yet take care of consciously? Did she think that he would be able to at some point? She desperately wanted to believe that, and she wanted to be there when it happened. She wanted to be the one he took consciously into his arms.

His thumb brushed her nipple and she battled to hold still in the bed as it stiffened and rose against his stroking.

The satin hardness of his erection surged where it pressed between her hip and his body, and he began to shift and slide against her. She swallowed back a moan, feeling the rush of heat down low where her legs were spread. Had she slept that way, or was it an unconscious response to the nearness of him and his obvious need for her? She couldn't help it, she wriggled slightly beneath him until she was a little more open and the rhythmic clench and release, clench and release, of her pelvic muscles mirrored his slide and shift, slide and shift. He squirmed and moaned, and she froze, for a moment fearing he was waking up and once again at a loss as to what she should do to make it easier for him. But instead of waking up, he shifted more fully onto her until he was almost, but on quite on top of her. His cock pressed up against the inside of her thigh, and still he shifted and slid and moaned softly and, God help her, she found herself wriggling and grinding in an effort to get more fully beneath his body, in an effort to get him inside her. Jesus, she wanted him inside her! She wanted him inside her like she'd never wanted anything. He curled his fingers around her breast, kneading in rhythm to his shifting, in rhythm to the undulation of her hips. Then he took his hand away, and she all but cried out in her frustration, catching herself just before there was any sound other than a heavy intake of breath. But there was very little time to dwell on the absence of his hand as he moved splayed fingers down the flat of her belly and wriggled his way into the top of her panties, where he rested his hand only for a moment on her pubic curls and she arched against it, effectively willing him to seek out the place where she needed to be touched. And thank fuck, he did! He found that place, and memories of the slippery pear half flashed through her head as he carefully but urgently fingered her open and began to stroke and probe.

This was insane. He was asleep. She absolutely had to wake him before it was too late. If he woke up like this, he'd be embarrassed as well as panicked. If he woke up like this, he would think she was taking advantage, which she was. Then he found her clitoris, and she held her breath and dug her heels into the mattress to keep from moving as he circled her—first with his thumb and then with two fingers slick with her own lust. Then he found her rhythm and he thrust and scissored, circled and probed, exactly as she had told him she liked it, as she had demonstrated on the pear.

There was nothing she could do but let him touch her, let the feel of him wash over her in waves, the incredible sensation of being caressed so intimately by Lex Valentine. Her haze of arousal was sharply punctuated by his moans and grunts, not the sounds of distress, but the sounds of a man about to ejaculate. Though her own shifting and rocking had become almost entirely internal, she was there with him, right on the edge as he stroked and touched and tweaked. Christ, how could anything feel better than this? He stopped breathing. His whole body was one tightly clenched muscle, the shifting and sliding had become outright thrusting, and the moans and grunts had escalated to guttural growls. At some point, she didn't know when it had happened, she grabbed onto the headboard to keep back the overpowering urge to touch him, to take him by the wrist and hold his hand down where she needed it, to grab him by the cock and stroke him until he came, or even better, to guide his erection down between her legs where she wanted him most of all. But before there was time to think about it, he grunted, then grunted again, and she felt the warm wetness of his release against her thigh. That was enough to send her over the edge. Try though she might, she couldn't lie still, and Lex woke up.

"Kelly? Fuck!" His words were followed by a hard thud and a barely swallowed string of curses as he rolled off onto the floor.

"Christ, Lex, are you all right? Are you okay? I'm sorry, I didn't know what to do. I should have woken you up."

"You did wake me up," he managed between gasps for

breath. "Christ, woman, no one has ever woken me up like that before." He groaned and rolled onto his side.

"Are you okay?"

"Never better," he said with a soft laugh that sounded somewhat painful. "I'll be even better still if I can get the room to stop spinning." For a long moment, there was no sound but the sound of his breathing. She wasn't breathing at all, though she desperately needed to. She was too busy trying to listen to him, to make sure he was okay.

At last he spoke. "Did I just...? Did we just?"

She couldn't help the giddy little laugh. "Your fingers aren't sticky from fondling canned pears, big boy, and I'm gonna need clean sheets."

He brought his fingers to his lips, then flicked his tongue over them and moaned. "I thought it was a dream. The best dream ever, and the next thing I know I wake up in your arms and we're both...coming."

"Are you okay?" she asked again. "Do you think you can hold down some water?"

"Worth a try," he said. Then he chuckled rather smugly. "Sex is thirsty work."

She padded to the bathroom and, in a repeat performance of last night, only in better circumstances, she brought water and a towel, both of which she set on the floor in easy reach. The she seated herself beside him. "Didn't you have boxers on when you crawled into my bed last night?" she said, brazenly admiring his nakedness.

"It must have been one helluva dream," he commented, still lying on the floor with his eyes closed, but the smile splitting his face suggested that he would probably recover quite nicely.

There was a soft knock on the door and V called quietly. "There's coffee and breakfast on the tray when you're ready for it."

"Thanks," they both called out, then laughed behind their hands like children caught in the act.

"If I've had a bad night, if I've not left my room by

breakfast time, Cookie sends a tray up. But everyone around here knows even when I take a piss, so it's no surprise that the breakfast treats came to your door this morning." He managed a sitting position, but then quickly lay back down, assuring her that he'd be just fine. Sometimes it just took a while, and after all, all of the blood was probably still in his cock.

By the time she'd retrieved the tray and poured them both coffee, he was sitting leaned against the bed, the sheet pulled off around his shoulders and over his lap. "Last night was one of the worst nightmares I've had in a long time," he said. "Followed by one of the best dreams and an even better reality."

"You scared the liver out of me, waking up to find you all but on top of me. I didn't know what to do, how to wake you without causing an attack, then, well things just got too hot for me to care too much if you had an attack or not."

"Imagine my surprise to wake up with my hand in your panties and both of us coming." He smiled over his coffee cup. "A good way to wake up."

It was amazing to Kelly that Lex's staff always knew exactly what to do and when. The tray was full of fresh fruits, cold meats and cheeses and homemade breakfast breads and spreads. There was nothing that could get cold, nothing that couldn't wait if Lex had woken up nauseated or too shaken to eat. There was nothing that couldn't wait if Lex had gone back to bed and slept until noon.

They grazed on the breakfast treats in silence for a little while, then Lex said, "I feel like something is about to change, Kelly. I feel it in my dreams, and I feel it when I'm awake too. I feel like whatever was before, it won't be for much longer." He shook his head. "I don't know if maybe it's just me and wishful thinking, though the truth of it is, I'm scared witless as much as I am excited. My life's been the same for so long. After my father died and I was suddenly free to live without being terrorized or shamed, I ordered my world in a way that I could live in it and be as comfortable as possible under the circumstances. I had Dillon's father, Zack, to help me with that. He and Dillon are still my best allies. It's been like that. I've surrounded myself with a few people I could trust, a few people I was comfortable confiding in, and I had my work. I've always been prolific and that kept me from dwelling too much on what I was missing. They say you don't miss what you've never had. That's not true at all. I've never had a relationship. I couldn't. Hell, I'm still a virgin." He blushed heartily at that bold statement. "You have to be able to touch someone to make love to them, and I could never get close enough to anyone without passing out or throwing up. Not much of a turn-on. But now that we've gotten this close, Kelly, I can't go back to the way things were before. I just can't. I have to know what it's like. I have to find some way to restore contact. Will you help me?"

"You know I will," she said, swallowing around the sudden tightness in her throat.

"I know the press is gone, and hopefully the pressure is off, but I'd like it if you'd stay here at Mountain View at least for a little while longer." He nodded down to the ring on her finger. "I like the way that looks on you."

"I'll have to make a trip home today or tomorrow. There are things I have to take care of, things that have been left undone and, as much as I love having V's personal shopper filling up that closet with expensive clothes, I do have some things of my own that I miss, and I'd like to catch up with Myrna, you know, have a little time with my bestie."

"Of course," he said, pouring them both another cup of coffee. "It was never my intention to hold you prisoner in my home, but I have to be honest, I like having you here, and so does everyone else." He moved dangerously close to her and her heart skipped a beat when he offered her a bright smile. "Will you model for me today? I need to get on with the commissions for Cascadia Hospital and I've got some really wonderful ideas, but they all involve a new model, one that looks an awful lot like you."

"I'll give it a try, but if I don't like it, all bets are off. Deal?"

"Deal."

# Chapter Twenty-Eight

"She went to him, you know? Woke him from his nightmare. After that, well, they slept in her room last night." V was giving Cookie the morning low-down on Lex and Kelly when Dillon entered the kitchen. "And sleep's not all they did, Greta assured me after she changed the sheets."

"Jesus, V! Too much information," Dillon said. He grabbed a chocolate peanut butter brownie hot off the rack before Cookie could slap his hand away. "Seriously? They were...?" He shoved his finger in and out of the circled thumb and index of the other hand, brownie hanging precariously from his mouth.

V gave a quick glance over her shoulder to make sure the subjects of the conversation hadn't miraculously appeared at the kitchen door. "Well, I know they can't touch each other yet, and the poor boy did lose his lunch after holding her hand yesterday, but it's pretty obvious they're getting on with it, and I say, let 'em. They'll work this out together in their own way, and you mark my words, she'll be wearing that ring for real before very long. And where is she now, but down at the studio modeling for him? How can he not be inspired by the woman he loves?" Just in case Dillon might protest, she gave a dismissive wave of her hand. "Don't think I don't know love in someone's eyes when I see it. Trust me, they both have that look. It won't be long now."

Dillon's cell phone rang and, when he saw that it was Myrna, he grabbed another cookie and exited to the kitchen garden so the women could gossip, though to be honest, he would have to bug them for the details — them and Greta — a little later. And to be equally honest, he shared V's enthusiasm. He hoped with all his heart that she was right, that they were all right, and that Lex could finally find the happiness he deserved. He said a silent prayer to any god who might be listening that Lex not get hurt. He couldn't even imagine the devastation the man would face after having his hopes raised so high. He turned his attention back to Myrna and got an earful.

"Lana, get your muddy shoes off the sofa!" were her first words. "Dillon?"

"Yes?"

"Take that basketball outside, Lane! Now!" Myrna shouted away from the receiver, then returned her attention to back him. "Don't ever have children, Dillon, just don't. Trust me, it only ends in tears and premature insanity."

"What are they doing home? Isn't it a school day?"

"Parent-teacher conferences. Already had mine and now I've got to entertain the little heathens for the rest of the day." He knew for a fact that Myrna was the kind of mother most kids dreamed of having, and her kids knew that too. Nonetheless, her kids had a reputation for being…creative and energetic in all their endeavors.

"Bad reports?"

"Oh, no! Good reports, at least grade wise. That's the problem, they're too damn smart for their own good."

"Language, Mom," a girl's voice taunted from the background.

"Damn's not an actual swear word, sweetheart. It doesn't really count."

"Oh, yes it does. You said it does, and if it doesn't then what about shit? That's just a bodily function, and what about fu — ?"

"Honey, I'm on the phone. We'll have this discussion later. Go play basketball with your brother."

"What can I do for you, Myrna?" Dillon asked, holding back a chuckle at the interaction between mother and children.

"I saw the press conference, and that rock Kelly was wearing — pretty damned impressive."

"The press thought so too."

"Never mind that. It's all true then, that Alexander Valentine was Alden Vance the Second."

"*Was* being the operative word, but yes, all true."

There was a momentary silence. "Wow! Who knew?"

"Now everyone does," Dillon replied. "And personally, I think Lex will be the better for the honesty. There are some demons you just have to face."

"You know I have a million questions, and most of them are none of my business and the answers are not yours to tell, but this whole situation heavily involves my best friend, and that is my business. How's Kelly?"

"You haven't talked to her?" he said, trying to take an inconspicuous bite of his brownie.

"I'm asking you because you'll give me an unbiased opinion."

"Lady, I'm the one who got us into this mess to begin with. You don't seriously think I'm unbiased, do you?"

"When I say unbiased I mean…well, how are…things… you know, things between them? They certainly looked happy enough at the press conference, and Kelly, well, bless her heart, she's never been a very good actress."

"They slept together last night." Okay, he shouldn't have done it. He knew he was being as gossipy as he accused V and Cookie of being, but he just couldn't help himself.

There was a war whoop that nearly deafened his right ear, then a breathless, "Get out of town! Are you serious? I mean can he…? You know… I thought…"

"Myrna, Myrna, Myrna, surely you're old enough and experienced enough to know that there's more than one way to feed the cat cream."

She giggled. "Feed the cat cream! Oh, I see what you did there, Mr. Matthews."

"To answer your question, no, he still can't get skin to

skin with her, but my nephew, Andy, wasn't kidding about the woman being amazing. He's come so far. I mean, you saw that he actually held her hand at the press conference and we got halfway back to the house before he had to stop the Jeep and... Well, my point is it's three steps forward and only a half a step back, and this is a man who's been dealing with this horrible affliction for twenty-five years."

"Jesus! That's wonderful! That's fucking fantastic, but..."

"But?"

"I just don't want Kelly getting hurt, that's all. I mean you and I both know how we manipulated to get the two of them together, and even before I knew who Alex Valens actually was, I thought she was crazy for not sticking with the man. But it's, well, maybe I'm not the one to judge, since I couldn't make my own marriage work, but Kell's not good with relationships. Okay, that's not fair either. She just doesn't have them. She had... Well, she has issues of her own, and while I can see the wisdom in her being cautious, she's not her mother, and she's not likely to end up with someone like her father either. Certainly Lex is not like that."

"Jesus, Myrna, what are you trying to tell me here?"

There was a long pause on the other end of the phone then a deep breath that sounded like a windstorm. "It's not really mine to tell, but after yesterday's little incident and with that awful bitch, Spaulding, out for blood, I think you need to know. Lex might have defused the situation yesterday, but that'll only make the woman more rabid, you know that."

Dillon carefully shut the door and with it, the sound of V and Cookie talking in the background. Then he moved out toward the far end of the vegetable patch where he could talk without the risk of being overheard. "Okay, sing," he said and, out of instinct, he braced for impact.

* * * *

Gale Ann Spaulding had the distinct impression that Jenny Fallon didn't agree with her politics or her point of view, but that didn't take away the awe of being in the presence of celebrity and, really, politics and points of view, they were only what they needed to be to get her what she wanted. She could play the hometown girl and bestie easily enough, and after a bit of girl talk, a few laughs and a couple of Cosmos, she'd have the chick eating out of her hand.

The girl was cute, she really was, and she had some serious potential, so Gale Ann was happy to talk to her about the business, about what it was like to be a local media personality, about what she found hardest, about what she enjoyed most, tips for breaking into the market — that sort of thing. It was all just the standard spiel that she'd give any newbie, all done with lots of eye contact, lots of use of the kid's name and lots of making her feel she was important.

When she was certain that little miss Jenny was softened up enough, she offered a sad little sigh and a shake of her head. "The hardest part about this business, at least at my level, is that I don't have time for a relationship." That got the girl's full attention. She had yet to meet a university student, especially a girl, who didn't want to talk about relationships when it came right down to it. "Oh, it could be that I just don't manage my time well enough, but the truth is, there just isn't a whole lot of it left to manage at the end of the day. I suppose I could look online, but even that takes more time and energy than I can manage. What about you, Jenny? Do you have a boyfriend?"

The girl gave her a huge smile and a cute little blush. "I do, as a matter of fact."

"Is he also studying journalism?"

"Chemistry, actually, and he's very good at it."

"Oh, I love a good nerd. From what I hear" — she leaned across the table and offered her best chick's-night-out smile — "forget the jocks." She looked around as though she didn't want anyone overhearing. "Go for the nerds if you want someone who's really good in bed."

The girl blushed harder and nearly choked on her Cosmo, and they both laughed.

"Can I take that to mean that it's true, then?" she asked, toying with the olive in her martini, then she added, "Oh, I've heard that some of them are slow starters, you know, so focused on their studies that they're oblivious to anything else, including the women who find them hot. But when they do start, they can go all night long and right on into the morning."

This time the girl gave an enthusiastic nod. "You have no idea."

"What—that he was a slow starter or that he can go all night?"

"Both," Jenny said. She finished off her Cosmo and leaned over the table, eyes bright with puppy love. "In the beginning, when we started dating, he kept telling me he'd feel better if we knew each other a little more before we… you know. He didn't want to take advantage, he said."

"Oh, that's so sweet! The world needs more men like that." Gale Ann nodded her hearty approval.

"Well, yes, but then after a while, I was beginning to think that maybe he didn't want to be with me. I mean, I really didn't understand. We had so much in common. We enjoyed each other's company. He was so easy to be with and such an interesting person. Well, I sort of forced the issue," she said. She ran a finger around the rim of the fresh Cosmo glass the waiter had just delivered, complements of Gale Ann, who knew well enough to keep them coming.

She had a deal with the bartender, while her prey was slowly getting plastered on Cosmos, the martinis she'd been ordering were just water. The man was used to her methods and she made sure he got a good tip for it.

"I mean, a girl has needs," Jenny said, and they both giggled and sipped.

"Anyway, he arrived at our next date more than ready to perform, and all I can say, is holy crap, was he worth the wait!"

"Seriously?" Gale Ann leaned close, hoping for more details.

"I was sore for three days. Just in time to do it all again." This time they both laughed

"You go, girl!" Gale Ann high-fived her and ordered another round.

"No, please, I've had enough," the girl said for the third time.

"Oh, come on," Gale Ann cajoled, "we're celebrating here, and didn't you say you took the Metro?"

"Well, actually, Andy's picking me up after. He doesn't like me out late all by myself."

"Aw, isn't that sweet," she said. "Make a girl jealous, will you? Cosmos followed by hot sex."

Jenny blushed. "Well, I am staying over at his place tonight, and it's not far from here. Easy for him to pick me up."

"So, weren't you surprised that after this little reluctant innocent act of your boyfriend's that he was so good in bed?"

"I was, actually, and he was…innocent, I mean. That's why he was shy. And here's him thinking that I was all experienced." She shrugged. "I guess we all sort of want people to think that about us. Jeez," she said, "I'm sorry, I sound like a stupid teenager. It's just that Andy really is amazing, and I'm so lucky to have him."

"Yes you are, sweetie, and don't you dare be embarrassed. I know how I come across all hard-nosed on the radio and all, but that's just an act. I'm a romantic at heart, a total softie when it comes to love and, honestly, I really do adore hearing people's stories. I suppose it's a vicarious way to enjoy what I don't have." She made sure to look ever so slightly sad and just a tad bit embarrassed. Her excellent acting skills and enough Cosmos won out every time, and she could tell Jenny Fallon was just about to let her in on a little secret.

"Well, as it turns out, my boy had sought a little advice

from an expert."

"Oh?"

"There's this woman. He mows her lawn actually, well, she works as a tutor."

"You mean like chemistry?"

She leaned closer. "I mean like sex."

The girl took another sip of her Cosmo, gave a slight glance around the room to make sure no one could overhear, and Gale Ann had her. But more importantly, Gale Ann had that vicious bitch, Kelly Blake.

* * * *

It wasn't until the Cosmos turned evil and her pounding head began to clear as she threw them up in Andy's toilet, him gently rubbing her back while she made a complete fool of herself that Jenny Fallon realized just what she'd done. "Oh, Andy," she said, wiping her mouth on the piece of toilet paper he handed her and flushing the commode with a shaky hand. "I made a really, really horrible mistake."

"I'd say you did," he said with a very soft chuckle. "Like about six too many Cosmos. Those things are deadly."

And the thought of Cosmos set her puking again. When at last she thought it was safe to stand and make her way to the bed with Andy's arm supportively around her waist, she began to cry. "Oh, Andy, you're gonna hate me. You're never gonna want to see me again after I tell you what I did. It was Gale Ann Spaulding. I didn't know it was Gale Ann Spaulding. My cousin, Madeline, works with her, and when she told me there was someone I might want to meet who was a journalist, I didn't think. Then Gale Ann was there, and I was too embarrassed to just walk out, and she was so nice, and she kept buying me Cosmos" — she shivered at the very word — "and I kept drinking them. Then we started talking about guys, and I got to talking about you and how good it was with us and…" She buried her face in the pillow and sobbed.

For a moment, Andy was deathly quiet. She thought maybe he'd left the room until she felt his weight settle on the bed beside her. When she opened her eyes and looked up at him, he was pale as a ghost. "You told her. About Kelly, you told her about Kelly."

"I'm sorry, Andy. I'm so, so sorry." She started sobbing again and made a valiant effort to get out of the bed, sure he'd want her gone now after what she'd done, surprised when he gently eased her back onto the pillow, took her hand to his lips and kissed it.

"Gale Ann Spaulding's been looking for dirt on Kelly and Lex ever since Kelly drenched her in red wine at the exhibition last Saturday. Didn't you see Lex's press conference last night?"

She snuffled and shook her head, which was a big mistake. "I had an interview out in Sandy."

"She uncovered the details of Lex's past and thought it would be nice to splash them all over the airwaves."

"Lex's past?"

As briefly as he could manage such an incredible story, he told her about Alexander Valentine really being Alden Vance the Second. That only made her sob worse. Poor Lex. And now he'd found Kelly, and she'd messed it all up for them.

"Anyway, Lex is no dummy. He called her bluff and countered with a press conference out at his place, which Spaulding wasn't present for. That really pissed her off, so now she's taking it out on Kelly."

"Oh God, Andy! I didn't know. I didn't know, I'm so, so sorry."

"It's all right," he said, handing her a couple of tissues and gently pushing her hair away from her face. "Don't cry, sweetheart. We'll sort this. The woman's a viper. You didn't know." After a long moment, he kissed her on the forehead and stood. "I'll call Kelly and warn her. You get some rest." He squared his shoulders and left the room like a man walking to his own hanging, and Jenny buried her face in the pillow and cried.

A short time later, he came back with a bottle of water and handed it to her. "Drink this. You won't feel so bad in the morning if you're not dehydrated."

She sat up, blew her nose and drank a couple of sips. "What did she say?"

"She's not answering her phone. That's not like her."

# Chapter Twenty-Nine

Kelly lay quietly for a long time in the early morning light, peeking over the tops of the pillows, watching Lex sleep. He was naked. So was she. The modeling session had devolved into mutual masturbation, and yet the work the man had done was exquisite. Each stroke of charcoal against paper was like a caress, his passion shown through the sketches. In truth, she couldn't wait to see what the work looked like in stone. She'd meant to go home, sleep in her own bed, regroup and come back after she'd had a chance to think and prepare herself, but then Cookie had fixed chicken enchiladas for dinner with her own special version of *tres leches* cake, and it was such a family affair that she had to stay. She loved being around Cookie and V and Dillon. She especially loved that they loved Lex and cared for him as though he really was family. And the next thing she knew, it was bedtime, and Lex was inviting her to his bed, which Greta had already made up with its pillow boundary down the middle — easily removed if the need arose.

Slowly, they'd undressed for each other, and they'd showered together. Lex's shower was bigger than most car washes and with twin hand-held showerheads, they could actually bathe each other, and caress and stimulate each other with the massage setting. It was late when they finally made it to the bed, and not without several more hot masturbation sessions. "Show me how you like it," he would say. "Tell me what you want. If I could touch you, I'd…" And the list was endlessly delicious. She was the writer. Word play was her specialty, but his haphephobia had made him a master of dirty talk and innuendo. She was sure at least once she came just from him telling her what he would do with his mouth if he could.

It was early morning when they'd finally drifted off. He'd not dreamed, but she had. Beautiful, explicit dreams of him doing exactly what he said he'd like to do to her, of him pulling her into his arms, of him sleeping pressed against her body. She woke with an ache and a longing that only settled and eased a bit as she peeked over the mound of pillows and saw him there sleeping peacefully, dark lashes resting against smooth cheeks, lips slightly parted. The blanket had fallen to his waist, giving her an exquisite view of his chest, which rose and fell with the deep, even breathing of sleep. His chest was hairless, nipples peaked dark pink in the morning chill. One arm was flung above his head, the other thrown over the mound of pillows dangerously close to her belly. She had to fight the urge to move closer until it actually touched her. God, how she wanted his touch, just a little touch, just the tips of his fingers.

As though he'd heard her thoughts, he opened his eyes, stretched and offered her a sleepy smile. Before she could ask if he slept well and how he felt, he left her speechless. "I'm going to touch you now, Kelly, only a little, because I just have to. I can't help myself."

"Okay." She managed, her heart thundering so loudly in her ears that she could hardly hear. She lay dead still, holding her breath as he tossed the pillows out from between them and rolled onto his side, resting his head on one arm. Then with the very tip of his index finger, he skimmed her cheek. They both caught their breaths in a self-conscious whisper of a laugh, as he reeled in a strand of her hair, curled it around his knuckles and brought it to his lips.

"I never imagined it could be like this," he said, watching her as though he'd never seen anything so wonderful and, God, she loved it when he looked at her that way. "I don't know what I imagined. I guess I didn't imagine anything really, because I thought…" A pained look crossed his face, a look that in its loneliness made her ache inside and, without thinking, she reached out and returned the gesture, just skimming his cheekbone with her fingertip. His pulse jumped, and his breath caught with a low moan.

"Kelly," he whispered.

She could hear his heartbeat in her name.

"Your touch has to be the most wonderful sensation ever. I dream about your touch. It's your touch that guides me through the nightmares. It's your touch waiting for me when the nightmares end that keeps me going. I never imagined anything could terrify me so and yet at the same time feel so much like my own breath, like my own heartbeat, like I just came back to myself after a long absence."

He frowned down at her. "Why are you crying? Kelly, please, don't cry." With the tip of his finger, he brushed away the tears and, even as his pulse raced and he gasped for breath, his face split into a broad smile that she returned in kind. He was making progress. He really was, and that she had played some part in that journey made her outrageously happy.

He sighed and stretched, then sat on the edge of the bed and found his shorts. "We should make an appearance at breakfast, I suppose." He raked her with a mischievous glance. "People talk, you know. Especially around this house, and the fact that we're sleeping together has given them all something to talk about."

"Well, I for one, am glad to have provided entertainment for the locals," she said. "It gives me purpose." When she stood and moved past him toward the bathroom, he grabbed up his T-shirt and snapped her on the bottom with it. She flipped him off.

"Bring it on!" he called after her.

When the limo pulled around to the front to take her back to her house, she was surprised to find Lex sitting rather smugly in the back seat waiting for her.

"Don't you have work to do?" she asked.

"I am working." He pulled a sketchpad from the pocket on the side of the door. "You are my model, after all. Besides, it gives us a few more minutes together."

She climbed in next to him. "You make it sound like I'm going to Outer Mongolia or something. It's just Gresham, and only to pick up a few things and make sure wild heathens haven't invaded and taken over, or Myrna's kids, whichever comes first."

"Then you'll be back in time for bed?"

"I wouldn't miss it," she said, feeling her stomach bottom with thoughts of just what that might mean.

The journey back to her place was taken up with him sketching and her enjoying the fact that his full attention was on her. Before they knew it, the driver was opening the door for her. "Wait!" Lex said. As she turned back to see what he wanted, he released his seatbelt, darted forward and kissed her. It was awkward and fleeting and punctuated with a moan that might have been pleasure, might have been panic, and her response was full of a good deal of both too.

"You're insane," she said, when he sat back, pale and wobbly in the seat, and redid his belt with unsteady hands. Then she did something equally insane. She leaned in and returned the kiss, careful to touch only his lips. Catching him completely by surprise and open-mouthed, she gave him a quick, but decisive flick of her tongue and pulled back, giving him his space. "I hope that doesn't make you throw up, but I felt it was maybe worth the risk."

"Oh God, yes." He sounded like he'd just run a marathon.

"Good. Now go home and get back to work."

"Kelly," he called after her just before the driver shut the door. "Hurry back home."

Back home! Christ, it actually felt that way, she thought, as she waved her goodbye and turned to find Myrna and the two wildlings plowing down the steps to meet her open-armed.

"I hope you've got time for coffee. I've got goodies from Jake's Cakes waiting on the table," Myrna said, lifting her off the ground in a bear hug. "I want to know details, woman, details and lots of them. I've got a bit of news of my own, too," she said, "and no, I didn't win the lottery and I'm not fu—er...I'm not doing Sam Heughan, though God knows I'm willing."

"Doing what to Sam Heughan, Mom?" Lana asked. Lane and Lana bounced around Kelly like a couple of super balls on sugar and caffeine, and she realized just how much she'd missed her friend and her family.

"I've been trying to call you for the past two hours, hon. What's going on?" Myrna said, taking her hand and guiding her back toward the house.

"Oh, shi—oot!" Kelly said, taking quick note of the two younger Kierans darting around her. "I forgot to charge my phone, what with one thing and another. Lex kindly provided a charger, but I just forgot."

"I bet you did," Myrna said, giving her an accusatory smile.

"I haven't been needing it much lately, to be honest with you. It was kind of nice to lay it aside for a while."

"You'll probably have a gazillion reporters calling trying to get comments from you after Lex's press conference," Myrna said. "And I can't even imagine what your inbox is going to look like."

"I hadn't even thought about that," Kelly said. "Now bring on the donuts and coffee. I'm starving."

\* \* \* \*

Gale Anne Spaulding sat parked across the street from Kelly Blake's house. She had taken a chance that the woman would be there now that the press had left Mountain View. She would surely come back home at some point. As far as everyone knew, she didn't actually live with Valentine, but then no one had really known anything until Valentine's PA had dropped the bomb at Hendricks Gallery the other night. She made an executive decision not to break the news that the very drunk Jenny Fallon had shared just yet. She really wanted to confront Blake with her discoveries, and with the little tidbit of information, she'd been able to dig up on Blake's mother, well, the confrontation should absolutely guarantee her national syndication. She was delighted to find that her gamble had paid off. Blake's Subaru was in the drive and the curtains were open. Occasionally, she would see movement within. Her neighbor, Myrna *Whatzit* and her two rug rats were home as well. The rug rats did make her a bit nervous. Kids were always unpredictable. It was best to keep them out of the equation, if at all possible. Still, they were playing in the backyard and, because she was the only journalist who knew about Blake's secret life, it should be a quick in and out before anyone was the wiser, and tonight's show would be explosive to say the least.

She sipped at her Diet Coke and yawned. With the excitement of knowing what was about to happen, she hadn't slept much, and she'd kept Madeline up half the night, but they'd found the dirt on Kelly Blake's mother. Like mother like daughter, Gale Ann thought. She had been very careful to hide the fact that she'd used Madeline's cousin to get the skinny on Blake. She'd simply told her that she'd found out nothing of interest about Andy Matthews, but she was pretty sure once the shit hit that fan, she'd have to find another researcher. With her clout, it would be easy enough to get Madeline fired if she caused problems. And really, it was her job to do research. It was work. Nothing more.

The door of Kelly Blake's house opened, and the woman stopped right at the threshold. Gale Ann couldn't help shrinking down in the seat just a little bit, fearing that Blake had seen her, but then she saw the woman snap her fingers as though she had forgotten something and turn back, shutting the door behind her. It was all right. Everything would be just fine. It wouldn't be long now. For the dozenth time, Gale Ann tested her Dictaphone to make sure the batteries were fresh and it was ready to roll. This was her big moment. She didn't want to miss it.

* * * *

Kelly dug through the detritus in the drawer of her bedside table until she found the unopened package of condoms. *Hope springs eternal,* she thought, and, in her mind, she was already trying to figure a way that she and Lex could have penetrative sex with minimal touch. They were both creative people. She reckoned with a little patience and imagination, they were ready to manage it now. She touched her lips and recalled the fleeting feel of his against hers, the surprised gasp, and the taste of him as she returned the kiss with just a touch of tongue. God, she wanted to give him so much more. She wanted to give him everything. He deserved it. They both did. Perhaps he had his own stash of condoms, because hope did spring eternal. If it didn't, he would have never gotten in contact with her and they would have never met. She couldn't imagine Lex Valentine not being a part of her life now, and she was anxious to get back to Mountain View, anxious to get back to him.

She had already stayed longer than she'd planned. But she and Myrna had needed a good catch-up. She was surprised and delighted to discover that Myrna was sleeping with Terry again. They weren't just sleeping together, but they were actually dating, all romantic and sweet like teenagers. She was happy for them. They'd married too young, that was all, and they'd both had some growing up to do. Terry, bless him, he'd never been an absent father. His kids adored him. He provided and he spent quality time with them. It was no wonder they were both so smart and so well-adjusted.

She grabbed up her shoulder bag and pulled the suitcase to the door, where she gave one more look around to make sure everything was in order, everything shut down and turned off and that she wasn't forgetting anything. Her mind was on the condoms in her bag and how she and Lex might put them to good use as she pulled the door to behind her, heard the lock click, and found herself face to face with Gale Ann Spaulding, who shoved a Dictaphone at her.

"Talk About Town has it on good authority, Ms. Blake, that you do a little moonlighting in addition to your writing career. Care to comment on that?"

Kelly's heart fell to her stomach and, in spite of her best efforts at a poker face, she could feel heat rising in her cheeks. "No," she said, and tried to push past, but Gale Ann stepped in front of her, blocking her way unless she wanted to wade through the planters of geraniums Andy had just deadheaded—Andy, who was now a dead man.

"You don't care to comment on the fact that you moonlight as a sex worker, just like your mother."

"A sex worker? Seriously?" That was the only thing she could manage as the wave of shock rolled over her. Just then Myrna and her brood stepped out to tell her goodbye. Lana was toying with her new iPhone, the one her mother had promised she could take photos of Auntie Kell with before she left. The kid was turning out to be a damn good photographer.

"Yes, a sex worker," Gale Ann said, doing a little dance in front of Kelly that kept her from escaping. "Hooker, prostitute, whore, if you'd prefer another word. Does Alexander Valentine know? Or did he hire you for your services? Is it *Pretty Woman* with no nookie?"

"Mom, that nasty woman just called Auntie Kell a prostitute. She's not," Lane said. "Hey, you," he called, heading across the lawn in spite of his mother's efforts to stop him. "My aunt is not a prostitute and you're trespassing. You leave her alone." And the next thing Kelly knew, the kid had stepped right in the middle of the geraniums, all but vaulting them to stand at her side. "She's not a prostitute. She helps people. You take that back." Lane grabbed for the Dictaphone, but Spaulding pulled it away just in time.

Clearly taken aback by the arrival of the cavalry, the woman gave a quick glance around, but didn't lose focus.

"It's all right, Lane," Kelly said, taking the boy by the hand. From the corner of her eye, she saw Lana standing just out of the line of sight, iPhone raised, recording everything.

"Look, son," Spaulding said, doing her level best and failing miserably at sounding parental. "There are things little boys your age don't understand. This is adult talk. Go on back to your mother now."

"I know what a prostitute is, lady, and I also know what slander is. I'm not stupid." Lane folded his arms across his chest and held his ground.

"You may not be, boy, but Kelly Blake most definitely is a sex worker, and so was her mother before her." Spaulding spoke into the Dictaphone, doing her best to keep control of the situation. On the neighboring lawns, people had gathered to watch, whispering among themselves. "Like mother like daughter, isn't that true, Ms. Blake? Isn't it true that you've followed in your mother's footsteps and you've either deceived Alexander Valentine into giving you that rock you're wearing there, or he's paying for your services. Either way, the apple doesn't fall far from the tree, does it? Like mother like daughter?"

This time, when she shoved the Dictaphone back into Kelly's face, Kelly snapped, grabbed the device away and found herself in a scary calm place as she spoke decisively and clearly. "No, Ms. Spaulding. Sadly I'm not like my mother. I wish that I were. With all of my heart I wish I could live up to her example. Yes, it's true, my mother worked as a prostitute for six months when I was a little girl. She did it to put food on the table after my father overdrew the checking account, took the car and ran off with another woman. We lost the house. We lost everything. She left me with my grandmother at nights while she worked. I only know this because she told me later." When the fish-gasping Gale Ann Spaulding tried to get her Dictaphone back, Lane stepped in front of her. "But if you'd done your research instead of looking for what crap you could dig up, you would have discovered that my mother went on to put herself through medical school. She worked in thoracic surgery in a hospital in one of the poorer parts of New York City until she joined Doctors without Borders five years ago. Two years ago, Ms. Spaulding, Elizabeth Katherine Blake was killed in a border skirmish in Afghanistan. So yes, my mother worked as a prostitute. My friend there would have done the same if her children were at risk." She nodded to Myrna, who laid a hand on Lana's shoulders and gave an enthusiastic nod. All the while, the girl busily recorded every word. "I'll bet you any of my neighbors here would have done the same for their children. But you're right, I suppose technically you could say that I'm a sex worker. I'm a tutor. I talk people through sexual issues, I listen, I advise, I encourage. That's what I do when I'm not writing. If I was secretive about it, well, there are a lot of people who depend upon my discretion. Clearly no concern of yours unless it gets you the attention you crave. As for Alexander Valentine, he knows full well what I do. Now, does that give you enough dirt for your radio show? Can I go now?" She shoved the Dictaphone back at the gaping Spaulding, grabbed her bag and moved like a sleepwalker to her car, wanting desperately to make a run for it, but needing to maintain control. The crowd that had gathered in the street and in her driveway parted as she backed the car out and drove away. But instead of turning toward Lex and Mountain View, she left a message for Myrna and headed out Highway 26 toward Mount Hood. She needed some time. She needed to think, and she couldn't bear the thought of facing Lex with all this shit storm until she'd had time to sort it out.

# Chapter Thirty

"Have you heard anything from her?" Lex Valentine spoke without preamble when Myrna opened her front door. He was dressed in walking gear and scuffed hiking boots.

"Not yet." She did her best not to sound as worried as she felt. Adding her worry to his wouldn't help. "She said she just needed time to think." Myrna stepped aside and nodded him in, careful not to brush against him. "Her mother's cabin isn't far. She said—"

"I know what she said. You told me what she said, but she's not back yet, and she should be, and she's not answering her phone, and she'd call if she was going to be late, surely she would."

"She promised me she'd charge her phone before she left here," Myrna said. "But with everything on her mind, she might have forgotten."

Lex moved inside like he was walking in a daze and took in the kitchen table where Andy sat with his girlfriend, who was crying softly. Apparently, she had been the one who spilled the beans. Terry sat across from them. He'd come as soon as he'd heard. He'd helped Lana get her video of Gale Ann Spaulding's ill-fated attempt at an interview on YouTube, where everyone could see what that vicious bitch had done, and it was now trending on Twitter.

When Andy saw who it was, he stood and came to greet Lex. He reminded Myrna of one of the twins when they were about to be punished. "I'm so sorry, Lex. I tried to get hold of Kelly. It wasn't Jenny's fault, that Spaulding woman got her drunk. She deceived her."

"It *was* my fault," Jenny said, coming to join Andy. "There's no one to blame but me, Mr. Valentine, and I'm so, so sorry. I'll do anything, anything you need me to do."

"I just need to find her," Lex said. "I just need to let her know that it doesn't matter. Dear God, surely she knows that."

"Of course she knows that," Terry said, joining them and offering a nod in lieu of a handshake. "Kelly wouldn't do anything stupid."

"I know that. I do, but she must have been so upset, and she's not back yet, and she's out there alone." Lex gave both Myrna and Terry a desperate look.

"Bringing up her mother like Spaulding did, that's still very raw with her," Myrna said. "She's… Well, she's never really processed it all, and I'm sure she just wanted to have time to think before she came back to Mountain View. I mean, she insisted that I let you know." That was what was worrying, she thought. Not only was Kelly always on time, but she was usually five minutes early.

"I thought you could give me directions to her cabin," Lex said. "I can't just do nothing. I need to go to her."

"Not alone, you don't," Myrna said, taking Terry's arm.

"She's right. We both know the place. We've both been up there and used it as a getaway with the kids several times. It'll be dusk when we get there and the weather's changing. With any luck, we'll meet her coming down and we'll have all worried over nothing. But no matter what, you're not going alone."

"Jenny and Andy have already agreed to stay with the twins," Myrna said. "Let us help."

As Myrna gathered the rucksack she had packed and put on her hiking boots, Lex turned his attention to her kids. "Lana, Lane?"

They both looked up at him from where they sat on the sofa with their iPads checking weather reports and monitoring responses to Lana's video.

"Thank you, both of you. Kelly's lucky to have a niece

259

and a nephew like you two."

Lane bit his lip and blushed, giving a little nod. Lana gave him a thumbs-up and a smile that trembled a little bit around the edges. "Just find Auntie Kell, please."

* * * *

*"Mom, that nasty woman just called Auntie Kell a prostitute… My aunt is not a prostitute and you're trespassing. You leave her alone."*

Gale Ann Spaulding wished like hell she could look away from the YouTube video that the Kieran kid had posted, but even if her boss wasn't glaring down at it from where he stood just behind her chair, the thing had gone viral. The whole damn world had seen it by now. So she sat stiff-backed, eyes forward, hands clenched in her lap as she watched herself shove the Dictaphone in Kelly Blake's face and say, *"Isn't it true that you've followed in your mother's footsteps and you've either deceived Alexander Valentine into giving you that rock you're wearing there, or he's paying for your services. Either way, the apple doesn't fall far from the tree, does it? Like mother, like daughter."*

"Pause it. You get the picture, Spaulding."

She gladly paused the horrid video. Her boss only called her Spaulding when he was angry, which he seldom was. She was his golden girl, or had been. He'd shoved into her office without even knocking, slammed a script down on her desk and ordered her to pull up the humiliating piece of trash and play it. All the while she watched, he stood behind her, his hot breath coming in angry little puffs against the back of her neck, the incriminating images on the laptop seeming way too big for the tight little space.

After a pause long enough for her to wish he'd just kill her and be done with it, he spoke, his voice barely more than a lethal whisper. "It's not so much that I mind you calling someone a whore. Hell, you've called people worse and gotten away with it. It's your job. What I mind is that you let the woman get in the last word. And you did it in front of a kid with an iPhone." The whisper was gone, but the lethal tone remained in spades. "What I mind is that the kid put the whole goddamned fiasco up on YouTube and now Talk About Town has to deal with a shit storm of your making. What I *mind*" — his voice rose another decibel — "is that you confronted the woman without knowing the whole story, like a goddamned first year journalism student." He paced the room in front of her desk like he was a drill sergeant dressing down a private, and the image was very fitting under the circumstances. He'd suspended her show for the day and put up some boring-assed documentary in its place. In the meantime, she had been ordered to wait in her office, which felt pretty much like the brig right now.

"What I mind, Spaulding, is that the woman you called a whore in front of the whole fucking Internet just happens to be the fiancée of Alexander Valentine." His rant fell into rhythm with his stomping back and forth in front of her desk. "What I fucking mind is that after she and her neighbor's snot-nosed kid dressed you down properly, Kelly Blake went to her mother's cabin in the mountains to calm herself, and no one has seen her since."

Gale Ann's heart skipped a beat, and the room was suddenly hot. "I didn't know. I didn't..."

"Of fucking course you didn't know! You're not the one fielding the enraged calls. You're not the one trying to convince sponsors not to pull their advertising, are you?" He leaned over her desk, all but yelling in her face, "Valentine's people are threatening to sue the goddamned station for a shit load of money, and if I were you, Spaulding, I'd be checking in with my lawyer because I guarantee your salary, no matter how damn much we overpay you, won't be nearly enough for damages once Valentine's people get through with you. And if you're a praying woman, you'd better fucking pray that they find Kelly Blake safe and sound without a hair on her head damaged. Because if she's injured or, heaven forbid, she dies, then you may goddamn well be trading in your swank corner office for a prison cell."

He stepped back out of her space, which was just as well, because as that little jewel sunk in, there was a very real possibility she just might just throw up. Dear God, surely the woman wouldn't harm herself? Surely she wouldn't do anything rash. A clammy sweat broke on Gale Ann's forehead and she fumbled for the bottle of water sitting on the corner of her desk, struggling to hear over the flutter of wings in her ears as her boss continued.

"Now, Spaulding," he said her name like it was a dirty word. "If you want to keep your job, here's what you'll do." He shoved the script at her. "You'll go into the studio right now — it's all set up — and you'll read the apology we've written for you. You'll read it verbatim. You'll not deviate from it nor will you add to it in any way. Verbatim!" He barked. "You'll apologize to Ms. Blake and Mr. Valentine, you'll apologize to all of their fans and friends and you'll apologize to all of the good people in the listening area for your gross incompetence. You'll say that you've been unwell, that you've been under a lot of stress and that you're taking a leave of absence in which to recover your health. A month's leave, Spaulding. You're taking a month's leave until you can get your edge back. Then we'll revisit your contract." He nodded down to the script. "Are we clear?"

"We're clear," she said, barely opening her mouth.

"Good. When you're finished, the manager will make a general apology for the station, while we all keep our fingers crossed for Kelly Blake's safety and prompt return to the loving arms of her fiancé, and hopefully we can control the damage before it's too great. Oh, and by the way, Carl Freeman will be taking over your show while you're convalescing." He nodded her toward the door. "Let's get this over with, then. The sooner you apologize, the sooner we can start kissing ass and placating the sponsors."

When she reached for the lipstick and mirror from her bag, he gave an angry jerk of his head toward the door.

"Leave it, Spaulding. No one gives a shit about your fucking makeup today. You've lost your right to play diva. Now get your butt out there before I fire you on the spot."

* * * *

They took two vehicles, and Myrna insisted on riding with Lex. She didn't think he needed to be alone, though he would have preferred it. In truth, he didn't want anyone to see him this vulnerable. But none of that mattered, not really. If it came down to it, he didn't care if they saw him naked on his knees, puking, if it would get Kelly back safe. As the traffic of the city thinned, they rode in silence. He was glad that Myrna didn't mind his taciturn mood. He really didn't want to talk. But as they left the lights of Sandy behind, he found he had to say something. What he said wasn't at all what he expected. "I love her."

Myrna's response was even less what he expected. "I know. But then again, how could you not?"

"Why did she do this? Why didn't she come back to me and let me comfort her? God knows she's comforted me often enough."

"Her mother was missing for three months before they found her body. Up until that point, there were a dozen false sightings of her alive and well. Kelly lived without closure, in a horrible nightmare of not knowing if her only close relative was alive or dead." Myrna shrugged. "Well, her father's still alive somewhere in Georgia, but they've had no contact since he left them, and he made no effort to get in touch with her after Elizabeth's death. Turn here," she said, as they approached a forest service road leading off toward Mount Hood.

"I didn't know."

"You wouldn't. She doesn't talk about it. She's fairly closed-mouthed where her emotions are concerned, and we've been her family, me and the kids and Terry, even before it happened. She's not alone, Lex, if that's what you're worried about. Make a left here."

It shocked him to realize he wasn't worried about her being alone, but he was incredibly jealous that Myrna and her tribe were Kelly's family, when he wanted to be that for her. He wanted to take her into his own tribe and they would all love her and care for her. Hell, they already did. Most of all, he wanted to be the one she turned to.

They were suddenly bouncing down an access road that was little more than a dirt track, and Lex was glad he'd taken Dillon's Jeep. "You were in on the subterfuge with the press at the gallery," he said. "Why?"

"Because I saw what you put yourself through to be with her, and what she was willing to do to get you out of there. My track record might not be good in the marriage department, but I know love when I see it. I also know it's worth fighting for when it's real. There's the cabin, and there's her car."

Inside, they found her shoulder bag and cell phone lying on the table beside an empty glass that looked like what might have been iced tea. Otherwise, the house was cool and felt unoccupied. A quick walk-through showed no evidence of use of any of the rest of the house except possibly the bathroom sink.

"Christ, where is she? Why isn't she here?" He didn't think he'd ever been closer to true panic. Being phobic was one thing, but this was worse. This was truly horrible. The weather was deteriorating rapidly and heavy rains were predicted. Up this high in the Cascades, that could be fatal if one wasn't prepared for it. He knew that only too well. He absolutely couldn't think about that right now. All that mattered was finding Kelly and getting her back to Mountain View safe and sound.

"There are two trails that lead into the woods around the cottage," Myrna said, handing Lex a flashlight and a whistle, both of which he handed right back.

"Brought my own." He flashed the whistle around his neck, then settled his pack on the floor and pulled out a headlamp and a Maglite. "I'm pretty good in the outdoors. Don't worry. I'm prepared."

"And so am I."

The door to the cabin burst open, and Terry shoved in, followed by Dillon. "Seriously, bro, you didn't think I'd let you search for her without me, did you? I had a helluva time convincing V and Cookie not to don gear and come along, and Duncan, well, he's waiting in the Land Rover."

"When Dillon called, I filled him in," Terry said. "If something has happened to Kelly" — he raised a hand — "and I'm not saying that it has, but the more eyes the better." Then he added, "The woman knows this mountain like the back of her hand, and she knows what to do if something does go wrong, Lex. Believe me, no one is better prepared than she is. But on the chance that she needs help" — he unfolded a geological survey map on the table — "best you know what we're facing."

Within ten minutes, Dillon and Lex were heading down the trail that led to a small nameless stream at the bottom of a narrow canyon, while Terry and Duncan took the trail up the mountain to a meadow above the cabin. Myrna stayed put, keeping a fire burning and manning the phone.

"Kelly! Kelly!" Their voices echoed and bounced back at them as they both called out into the thickening darkness, careful not to blind each other with their headlamps.

The path was a steep descent down a narrow ravine, treacherous with loose rock and overgrown tree roots, which made the going painfully slow and did little to ease the knot of fear that had been tightening in Lex's stomach since Kelly hadn't shown up when expected. If she were in distress, if she were upset, she might not be concentrating on the path. She could have easily fallen. Hell, it would be the easiest thing in the world for anyone to become distracted and take a tumble. The thought had barely crossed his mind before he heard the sharp hiss of Dillon's breath, followed by the sound of shifting rock and a curse swallowed back in a harsh grunt. He turned to find his friend sprawled on his belly on the ground only scant inches from where the path dropped off steeply into the ravine.

"Jesus, Dil! Are you all right?" His heart dropped to his stomach as he glanced down into the dark nothingness below them.

"Just knocked the breath out of me and bruised my ego," Dillon said, shoving his way back to his feet just as the rain began. It started as a sprinkle, but very quickly became a relentless downpour, which to Lex's dismay, slowed progress even further. If that wasn't bad enough, a glance back at Dillon showed the man was visibly limping.

"Fuck, bro! How bad is it?"

"Not bad. It's fine." The man might be a good liar, but Lex knew him too well not to see that he was in pain.

"Bullshit," he yelled above the rise of the storm and the roar of the water below. Then he scrubbed his hand through his drenched hair and said, "Look, according to the map, it's not that much farther down to the stream, and Myrna says there's a cave there that Kelly might hole up in if the weather's bad. You stay put and I'll go on alone. Surely, I'm within yelling distance, or at least I can flash you a signal or blow the whistle if I find her. Thank God there's no fog."

Reluctantly, Dillon agreed and found a protected place beneath the bows of a Douglas fir. "One flash and one burst on the whistle every ten minutes. You got that? We're not taking any chances. If you find her, blow the bloody thing like Gideon's trumpet at the end of the world. But if I don't hear from you every ten minutes," he said, "then I'm bringing back the troops." Neither of them stated the obvious, that if the storm got worse, if it blew in like the weather reports warned, there would be no sending in of any troops until it let up.

Lex continued the painfully slow descent, going as fast as he dared, slipping and sliding as he went. "Kelly! Kelly where are you? Kelly, I'm here." No matter what, he would find her in the darkness, just as she'd found him, and he would bring her back home. "Kelly, it's Lex! Kelly, answer me, please!" The sound was nearly drowned out by the rain-swollen stream, roaring over the rocks below, a sound that made him stop dead still and hold his breath, listening. Dear God, let it be her! Please let it be her. "Kelly?"

The rain let up just for a second, or perhaps it was just that he was in a more protected spot, but it was enough. It was enough for him to hear a moan and the sound of crackling brush just off the trail to his left. Then there was a flash of light and another and a third. Heart leaping in his throat, he turned on his Maglite, stupidly blinding himself, but not before he caught a glimpse of her curled in a fetal position in the shelter of a large boulder, flashing her light back at him. He broke into a run, stumbled and went flying, barely catching himself on a low-hanging branch before careening into the swollen stream. "Kelly! Kelly, hold on, I'm here. I'm here!"

"Lex?" She blinked owl-like into the bright light, and he got his first good look at her, not liking what he saw at all. The air smelled of blood. There was a bruise blooming along her cheekbone and she was soaked to the skin and shivering.

"Jesus, Kelly! What the hell happened?" He fell to his knees by her side, examining her more thoroughly in the beam of the Maglite, to which she responded with a moan and a feeble raise of her hand to shield her eyes. It was then that he saw where the blood was coming from. There was a deep gash dangerously close to her brachial artery. He sat back hard on the rocks, struggling to breathe, struggling not to throw up. A quarter of an inch, just a quarter of an inch, maybe less, and she would have bled out. She would be dead, but she wasn't. She wasn't dead! She would be fine.

Trying to breathe shallowly, he grabbed the first thing he could get, a bandana stuffed in the outer pouch of his rucksack, and wrapped it tightly around the wound. Then he swallowed hard, and did his best to speak conversationally. "I'm here. It's gonna be all right, I'm here now," he said.

267

As promised, he flashed the Maglite on and off manically in the general direction of where he'd left Dillon. "I found her!" he yelled. "I found her!" Then he blew the hell out of the whistle in loud, long bursts. There was an immediate response from above, but he paid no attention. Dillon was well able to take care of himself. They'd had a fair few outdoor adventures together. The man knew his way around the woods. With the storm worsening, Lex's priority was Kelly, but when he turned back to her, dear God in heaven, her teeth were chattering! So hard! Her teeth were chattering! Bile rose in the back of his throat, threatening to choke him, and the chill he felt had nothing to do with the icy rain. Had he dragged her into his dreams? Could he do such a thing? But then she spoke between the chatter, and it was her voice that brought him back to himself.

"Lex?"

"I'm here, Kelly. It'll be all right now."

"I fell. It was stupid really. I wasn't paying attention, and after, that I don't remember anything. Then I heard you calling. How did you find me?"

"Myrna and Terry. They're here and so are Dillon and Duncan." He dug in his bag for a space blanket, which he settled around her shoulders before he realized what he'd done, before he noticed the panic tightening his chest.

But even in her state of distress, *she* noticed. "Lex? Are you okay?"

"Fine! I'm fine." And he really was—or he would be. Besides, there were more urgent things to think about at the moment than his discomfort. "Can you walk? We've got to get you somewhere warm and dry."

When her effort to get to her feet ended in a gasp of pain and a terrifying slump into unconsciousness, which, thankfully, only lasted a second, he knew they were in trouble.

"I'm sorry," she managed around the pain in her voice. "I don't think the ankle's broken, but I fell a long way. I might have cracked a rib"—she sucked a harsh breath—"or two."

The rain now pelted down full force, and the temperature had clearly dropped another notch as the wind rose. In the slice of light his headlamp provided, Lex was sure he could see sleet mixed with the rain. Please, dear God, no, he thought. It was already taking all of his focus not to associate the chattering of Kelly's teeth with his dream. "We can't stay here," he yelled over a gust of wind. "How far are we from the cave? Myrna said there was a cave you might try for."

"It's just up the stream, maybe a hundred yards. I was trying to get there when…" Her voice drifted off between chattering teeth. "I must have passed out. The next thing I heard was you." She chuckled softly, then caught her breath with a moan. "I thought I was dreaming."

He didn't tell her that he'd had his own thoughts about it being a dream. This was Kelly. This was real, and her injuries were only life-threatening if he didn't get her out of the weather. This was something he could do, something he had to do. For an awful moment, his vision faded in and out of focus at the realization of what that meant. His mother had died promising him everything would be all right. It wasn't. It was never all right again, but that was over. That was the past. This was the present and this was the woman he loved. This was the woman he loved! The words sank in deep and took root, somehow easing the knot in his stomach. Kelly Blake was the woman he loved and he would not let anything happen to her. That was a promise he could keep.

He took a deep breath, shrugged out of his waterproof and was instantly wet. Ignoring the icy bite of the wind, he handed it over to her. "Put this on." She was trembling too badly to do it, and clearly the movement hurt her, so he found himself easing it around her shoulders, holding it into position so she could manage, cringing each time she cringed in pain, gasping each time she gasped, feeling the agony of her every move as though it were his own. And strangely, concentrating on her pain and distress allowed him to forget about his own. He had her bundled and zipped in before he realized he'd been touching her, feeling her convulsive shivers against his. At some point, he had joined her in a duet of chattering teeth, the chattering teeth of two people very much alive and damn well going to stay that way.

That done, he slipped the rucksack onto his back. It had things in it they'd need if they were going to get through until help could come to them. "Now then," he said, sounding a lot more confident than he felt. "I'm going to get you up. All you have to do is lean on me and point me to the cave. We'll get there together." When she gave him an alarmed look, he added, "Trust me, Kelly. Please. I can do this."

She passed out twice before he got her to her feet. As horrible and heart-stopping as it was to feel her go limp, it kept him focused on her and not his own distress. The cold grip of panic was still there threatening to steal his breath away. Nausea clawed at his insides, forcing him to swallow back bile time and again to keep from throwing up. But Kelly depended on him. If he had to, he could puke his guts out later when she was safe and warm.

"It's all right. It's going to be fine. Really, it will be. You'll be fine, you're doing great. We'll make it. We're almost there." It took him a moment, as they fought their way through the wind and sleet, along the rising stream toward the cave, to realize that it was her voice doing the reassuring. Her concern for him rose above all in spite of her obvious pain and the danger she was in. God, that did something to him. There was no doubt he loved this woman, and when they were out of this mess, he planned to tell her and prove it to her over and over again, if she'd let him.

At last, the bouncing ray of his headlamp caught the dark maw of the cave, and he could have cried with relief.

"Let's hope if we have to share it with any bears, they've already eaten," she said.

"Well, they're not getting the snickerdoodles. Cookie

packed those for you," he managed, as they stumbled into the opening and literally fell onto the ground. When he'd had a second to catch his breath and shine the light around, he could see that the place was really less of a cave than just a deep recess beneath an overhang of rocks, but it was dry and sheltered from the wind. He settled her onto the rocky floor and was busy digging through the pack before he realized he had neither passed out nor thrown up, and the urge to do either was, at least for the moment, tempered by more urgent needs. But the relief was short-lived when he turned to find her curled around herself, deathly still.

"Kelly! Kelly, talk to me!" He grabbed the sleeping bag he'd stuffed in the pack and crawled close. "Kelly!" Throwing caution to the wind again, he took her face in his hands and briskly slapped her cheeks.

"Cut it out," she mumbled, batting his hand away with a limp arm. "Just let me sleep for a few minutes then I'll be fine." Her words were slurred and her eyes unfocused.

"No, Kelly! Absolutely no sleeping. Not yet. Talk to me. I saw the video Lana put up on YouTube of Spaulding making an ass of herself. Those kids are really something."

"They are, aren't they?" Her little chuckle sounded like she was spaced out on some really good drugs. "And so smart. I'm not a fan of most kids, but those two, well, I love them to bits."

"I can understand why you feel that way," he said. "You tore Spaulding a new one, that's for sure. Those two put it all up on YouTube. They're amazing." He began stripping her with surprisingly steady hands.

"That's nice," she said. Her words were muffled as he pulled the tank top off over her head and she all but fell against his chest while he unhooked her bra.

"Tell me about your mother," he said. "She must have been really something." As he stripped her, she told him, in little snippets of partially incoherent sentences, about Elizabeth Katherine Blake, as though Gale Anne Spaulding was no big deal, really, and she wasn't at the end of the day. She was no match for Kelly Blake. As he eased her out of wet boots and socks, careful of the swollen ankle, she told him of learning anatomy along with her mother while she was in med school. Her way of studying it was to teach it to her daughter. Then Kelly began, in a slurred sing-songy voice, to recite the bones in the body, beginning with the skull. And suddenly her teeth were chattering again, a sound that he never thought he'd be thankful to hear, but she was no longer listless. She was fully engaged. There was an occasional sob of pain as he worried her out of her clothes, trying to be careful, but needing to be quick. There were other bruises. Remembering Dillon's close call, his stomach bottomed at the thought of that happening to Kelly. In the illumination of the headlamp, he could see that the bruises were consistent with a hard fall. But he saw them only briefly before he shoved and tucked and maneuvered her into the sleeping bag, as she finished her recitation of the bones in the skull and moved to the cervical vertebrae in the neck.

"Lex? What are you doing?" She stopped her recitation halfway down the spine as he began to strip.

"I'm getting naked to warm you up."

"Oh. Oh! Lex? Are you sure?"

"I promise, I won't throw up on you."

"That's nice. But I can't promise I won't throw up on you," she said. "I think I hit my head when I fell."

"I'll take my chances. Anything for a good anatomy lesson."

That made her chuckle, then she inhaled sharply at the resulting pain.

When he'd stripped completely, tossing his clothes carelessly where they fell, he took a deep breath, braced himself, and wriggled down next to her and, for a terrifying moment, he was pulled back into the dream. She was so cold, so icy cold. Like his mother had been. But then she shivered and moved in close to his body, and, even as his flesh recoiled at the chill and his mind fought back the memory, he took her into a spoon position, curling around her, willing himself to stay calm, willing his warmth to become hers. Willing her to be well. Willing her to be his. Dear God, was that even a possibility? Only a short time ago, he could not even have hoped.

"Are you all right?" she said.

"I am now," he whispered against the top of her head.

"Good. I was worried about you for a little while there." She reached around and laid a hand on his flank, and the sound that came from his throat in response was embarrassingly close to a purr. Then she added, with a little wriggle of her bottom, "We can wait out the storm in luxury here. They'll find us in the morning. Myrna will know exactly where to look."

# Chapter Thirty-One

This time there was no prelude. There were no chattering teeth, no words of reassurance that everything would be all right. It never would be, ever again. He knew that. All around him there was nothing but deadly silence and cold. He couldn't even hear the howl of the wind anymore. Perhaps the snow had completely buried them, muffling all sound. He would die with her in this place, slowly suffocating. He might have wept had he been able to do anything more than fight for the next breath from beneath the terrible weight, the terrible, terrible weight that grew colder with each passing moment. It would crush him soon. Dear God, let it be soon. Let it happen and be over with and end this nightmare for good.

"You weren't supposed to be here. You weren't supposed to be here. You weren't supposed to be here." He always just assumed he was hearing his own thoughts. His mother wasn't supposed to have picked him up. They weren't supposed to go over Mount Hood to the Bend house. It was a special treat, she said. They would go skiing on Mount Bachelor, maybe eat out at the Pine Tavern afterward or maybe Chang's. "You weren't supposed to be here. You weren't supposed to be here. You weren't supposed to be here."

"She could have killed you," the voice said. "The bitch could have killed you."

His mother never said that. His mother was dead and now he was suffocating under the cold, heavy weight... His mother was dead! He'd already known that when they told him in the hospital so many weeks later. He'd known that because he'd felt her die. He'd felt the warmth go out of her body.

"Jesus, no! God, no! Not like this! Not like this, please, not like this!"

"Lex. Lex wake up!" From somewhere far away, he heard someone call to him, then he was lying back in the car beneath the weight again. Beneath the weight of his mother. Feeling the warmth leave her body and go to his until there was nothing left but the cold weight of her, and he couldn't move. He was trapped. He couldn't move. He couldn't move!

From somewhere just beyond the panic, he heard the scrape of metal, felt a rush of snow and cold air on his face, and he was blinded by a bright light. Maybe he was dying at last. Didn't they say people who died went toward the light?

"You weren't supposed to be here, you weren't supposed to be here, you weren't supposed to be here," came the chant, and the burn along his ribs made him cry out at a sharp tug of his body.

In his limited vision, he could see a boot, a winter hiking boot. It came down on her shoulder and shoved her off him, and he was propelled into the icy cold to land on a bank of snow. Then a shadow knelt over him and between a hood and a scarf he could see only eyes, and the muffled voice of a man said, "It'll be all right now. Someone will come soon. It'll be all right. It'll be all right, someone will come."

Then, the man walked away! He just left him there where he lay, and all he could do was follow him with his eyes, always following him so far with his eyes, out into the woods, out into the snow before he lost him, before he could go no farther and was forced back to his body, his broken, dying body. The sky was clear above him now. He could see it through the mist of his breath. The world turned beneath the pole star and there was now no weight at all. He was weightless, following the man back along Highway 26, back through Sandy, back to Mountain View.

"It'll be all right," the man kept saying in a voice that Lex should have recognized. "It'll be all right. They'll find you and bring you home because you weren't supposed to be there. You weren't supposed to go with her. You were supposed to come back home with the chauffeur. You were supposed to come back home where you belong."

Then someone was pounding on his chest and shining a bright light into his face. There were lots of lights, lots of people talking, yelling, clustered about him, then something came down over his mouth and nose, and he gave one last desperate gasp before everything went black.

"Lex! Lex! Lex!" It was a hard shaking of his shoulders that brought him up sharp and gasping from the dream world. He woke trembling and covered in sweat, shoving his way out of the sleeping bag.

"Oh God, Kelly!" He lost his footing and fell back hard on the floor of the cave, bruising his bare ass as he went down. "It was him. He was there! He was the one."

"Lex? Who? What are you talking about?"

"My father! Kelly, he's the one who pulled me out of the wreck, out from under my mother. I wasn't supposed to be there. My mother was leaving him. I understand it all now. She was leaving him and she was taking me with her. I wasn't supposed to be in the car that night. I don't know what he actually did, but the press was right about the sabotage. It wasn't just idle gossip. I wasn't thrown clear of the car, he pulled me out and left me, knowing someone, someone he'd obviously paid off, would find me. I wasn't supposed to be there, and my mother was supposed to die alone on Mount Hood that night. That was the only way he could be sure of hanging on to the Valentine fortune, and he'd certainly lose it if I died."

"Christ, Lex! And he never suspected that you knew?"

"He had no reason to. All these years, I didn't know that I knew. Then when I woke up and was…the way I am, well, even if I did suspect, who would believe a boy who was clearly mentally unstable?"

"Jesus, bro! Cover it up already!" Dillon stuck his head into the cave, then disappeared again. "Myrna, you might want to wait outside until my man can get himself decent." Then he peeked in again. "Morning, Kelly? You okay?"

"A bit bruised and battered, but I'll do," she said.

Lex had barely gotten his trousers on when Myrna burst into the cave and enveloped Kelly in a bear hug that made her gasp and cry out in pain, but she returned the hug nonetheless. The EMTs were right behind.

\* \* \* \*

Lex wheeled Kelly into the house, with her protesting loudly that she didn't need a damned wheelchair, which she didn't, but he was taking no chances. Detective Harrison was already waiting in the kitchen, having coffee with V and enjoying one of Cookie's homemade cinnamon rolls. Myrna and her brood and her ex were already out on the patio also partaking of Cookie's largesse and laughing at Dillon's stories of some of their camping exploits as boys. He was pleased to see Dillon's father was there too, along with his lawyer.

"Are we having a party?" Kelly said. "If I'd known, I'd have put on my party frock before we left the hospital."

"Oh, there'll be a party, all right," he said, bending down to nuzzle her neck, "but first we have some business to attend to. I'd hoped we'd have a little time to ourselves before the crowd descended. Still, it's probably best we get it over with. After that, I figure we'll party into the wee hours, but don't worry, you won't be needing a frock for what I have in mind." Before she could manage more than a wicked chuckle, the twins erupted from the patio and mauled her, and Cookie shoved a cinnamon roll in her hand, speaking in rapid-fire Mandarin, and wiping tears on the edge of her apron.

Detective Harrison and V came to join them. Without thinking, the detective extended his hand, to a collective intake of breath, which was quickly repeated when Lex took it and gave it a hearty shake, the sight of which had Cookie crossing herself and whispering something in what sounded like Dutch.

Duncan took Lane and Lana down to the raspberry canes with a couple of small baskets and a thermos of hot chocolate. Everyone else settled into the drawing room that opened onto the patio, and Cookie gave all cups one last top-off before Lex addressed the gathering. He got right to the point. "I'm certain now that my father did kill my mother. He was there the night of the accident. He pulled me out of the car after my mother was dead. I remember now."

No one seemed particularly surprised at his news. Terry gave Myrna's hand a hard squeeze, Dillon looked like his jaw was set in concrete and Cookie whispered something, no doubt seriously obscene, probably in some obscure dialect of some obscure language, to which V nodded agreement. Other than that, the room was silent.

At last Detective Harrison shifted in his seat. "Certainly your father's been the top suspect all along. Sadly, I have nothing to add that you don't already know, Mr. Valentine, the same information we've known all along. That you were an eyewitness unfortunately comes about twenty-five years too late. The detective who handled the investigation is dead, as you know. I've spoken to the few retired officers involved in the case who are still around. Apparently the general consensus was always that someone was paid off, but no one knows who, if anyone ever knew. As I've also told you, there are ways to rig brakes so that it looks accidental, and with the black ice on the roads that night, no one would have questioned a car spinning out of control. Under the circumstances, there was no real reason for anyone to question. Had your mother been anyone other than Ellen Valentine Vance, no one would have. But, even so, as far as I could tell from the evidence and the newspaper articles, your parents kept their private life private, leaving little fodder for the press."

"They may have done," Zack Matthews spoke up, "but those of us who knew the family pretty well knew that the marriage wasn't a happy one. Alden Vance was a philandering bastard right from the beginning. But he had a good head for business, a good pedigree, good genes." He spoke the words as though they left a bad taste in his mouth. "He was just what Ellen Valentine thought she needed. She wanted someone who could take control of Valentine Industries and leave her free to do her charity work. She also wanted a child, a legitimate heir for the Valentine Fortune. It was a marriage of convenience. She knew what Vance was like before she married him. Vance had the name, but no money and no heir, so the arrangement suited them both. What she wanted—what they both wanted—was never any real secret among their inner circle. There was a prenup, and there was an agreement that the two of them would make a good public show of the marriage, but that what was done in private was no one's business as long as they were discreet."

"I know about the prenup," Lex said. "At least I learned about it much later. If my father breached the contract in any way, if she divorced him for whatever reason, he could continue on to run Valentine Industries, but on a salary comparable to any other CEO in that position. It was a huge amount, mind you. But my father got used to the Valentine open checkbook." He waved a dismissive hand. "I might have been ten when it all happened, but I remember well hearing them argue about some of the extravagant expenses he'd racked up without telling my mother. In particular, I remember a yacht in the South of France. It was damn near the size of the Queen Mary."

"I remember that," Zack said. "She made him sell it right away. Turned a tidy profit, as I recall, but he was furious."

"They tried to keep their arguments from me," Lex said. "Funny how parents think their kids are stupid just because they're young. Sometimes when they had an argument over his new toys, he got drunk, then he didn't much care who heard."

"Jesus," Kelly whispered, giving his hand a reassuring squeeze.

"Maybe in his way he loved her, I don't know," Zack said, with a conciliatory glance at Lex. "What I do know is that it was a horrible situation for a young boy to grow up in, and Lex was way too perceptive not to know that they were living a lie."

"Mr. Valentine." It was his lawyer, Jack Fenton, who spoke now. "There's nothing that can be done at this point, at least not that I can see. Any evidence that might have proven Alden Vance's guilt is long gone, and I don't see how the memories of a ten-year-old boy, especially one who has had the mental history you've had, would be an acceptable argument in a court of law, even if the man weren't already dead."

"I know that," Lex said. He realized that he was probably squeezing Kelly's hand way too hard, and his heart skipped a beat at the fact he was holding her hand at all.

"Surely you don't want to go to the press with this," the lawyer said.

"I don't honestly know what I want. It's just that I wanted all of you, those of you who have stood by me, to know the truth. My mother kept me alive with her own body heat. I felt it go out of her as she died. But I probably would have died anyway if my father hadn't come for me. My... my injuries were such that I couldn't... I couldn't get out from under the weight of her. I couldn't... I couldn't move. He pulled me out, and it hurt. I remember it hurt really badly because of the burns. I might have passed out for a few seconds, and when I came to, the storm had cleared and I was looking up at the sky, and he was kneeling next to me, telling me it would be all right, that someone would be there any minute. He kept saying I shouldn't have been there. Then..." Lex heard Kelly's knuckles pop under the pressure of his hand, but she squeezed back just as tightly.

"Then he left me there. I dreamed… I dreamed about following him into the woods, about grabbing him and asking him why, why he'd left me there. It never entered my mind then that he was responsible for my mother's death, or that if he hadn't discovered I was there, I would have died with her. Of course, I never knew who it was who pulled me out, until the dream in the cave with Kelly."

"I can't see how acknowledging the situation publically will change anything now," the lawyer said, then he added quickly, "Though if it's something you feel compelled to do, I'll do my best to cover all the legal bases. I don't believe your father had any living relatives other you, did he?"

Lex shook his head. "He was the last of the Vances and my mother was the last of the Valentines until I was born."

The lawyer nodded. "In that case, there would be no repercussions from family wanting to sue if you do go to the press. Though Ms. Beasley might make an attempt. The timing of your mother's death could implicate her."

"I won't be doing anything for a while," Lex said. "Maybe never, I just wanted all of you to know. It doesn't matter so much if anyone believes me or not, as you can see." He pulled Kelly's hand to his lips and kissed it. "I believe it to be the truth, and I think it was what the psychologists and doctors were trying to help me uncover all these years. Who knows, maybe I would have never been able to remember if Kelly's situation hadn't mirrored my mother's enough to force the issue. I just don't know."

The lawyer spoke again. "Perhaps you should…seek out someone to talk to again. It can't be an easy thing to discover that your father murdered your mother."

"Thank you, Mr. Fenton. I'll take that into consideration. My father and I were never close. We didn't get along before the accident, much less afterward. I must have put him in a terribly difficult situation, his only child and his only link to the Valentine fortune, knowing he murdered his wife, but not remembering." He shrugged. "It must have actually been quite a relief to him that I came back from the hospital such a mess. Even if I had accused him, it wasn't likely that anyone would have believed me."

V huffed out an irritated breath. "Stupid people. There was never anything wrong with your mental acuity, Alexander, and all anyone ever had to do was be around you for a few minutes to know that."

"That's quite possibly part of the reason he kept you isolated," Zack Matthews added.

"I can do my best to pursue the case further if you want, Mr. Valentine," Detective Harrison said, "but I'm not hopeful."

Lex shook his head. "I know the truth now, and all of you know the truth. That's what matters at the moment. The healing that has come from the knowing, the closure, that's recompense enough right now." He shivered as he recalled the nightmares, the pain, the isolation. Then he pulled Kelly's hand to his lips again, needing the reassurance that it was really over, that he could actually touch the woman he loved, that he could finally touch all the people he cared about, that, at last, he could rejoin the human race.

# Chapter Thirty-Two

It felt like ages before everyone left them alone. Cookie fed them a quick late lunch of kung pao chicken, stuffed them with homemade raspberry sherbet and sent them off to 'rest,' with just a twitch of a smile shared by V and Dillon as they said their goodbyes. Kelly was walking now, albeit with a stick, leaning heavily on Lex, which delighted everyone almost as much as it did him. He didn't bother with taking her to the Meadowlark suite. She could go there later if she really wanted to, but he hoped she wouldn't.

"Would you like to lie down?" he asked after a long pause in which the two did little but glance at each other nervously and shuffle their feet.

"That would be nice," she said.

He settled her onto the bed and helped her off with her shoe. The badly sprained ankle was covered only in a soft wool sock in variegated blue, which Lex suspected Greta had quickly knitted especially for that purpose. Once he'd eased her back onto the pillows, careful of the cracked ribs, he sat for a moment just taking in the fact that Kelly Blake was in his bed. Then he asked, "Can I lie with you?" Christ, he sounded like a real idiot. Strange that he suddenly felt so shy.

"I was hoping you would," she said, patting the mattress next to her. "Besides, it is your bed."

He kicked off his shoes and settled beside her, touching her with his body everywhere that he could, feeling the curve of her hip, the rise and fall of her strapped ribs as she breathed, the touch of her fingers in his hair. "How am I ever going to get used to this feast of the flesh?" he said, smiling down at her from where he had settled on one elbow.

She raised his fingers to her lips and kissed them. Her eyes sparkled in the late-afternoon light. "Well, for starters, I suggest you go exploring. I'll guide you." She kissed his open palm and placed it on her breast, her nipple rising instantly through the thin fabric of her T-shirt. He raked his thumb over it, and she caught her breath in a little gasp and arched up against him. His cock stretched in his trousers, already anxious to play.

"Can I undress you?" he asked, then he chuckled softly. "God, that was a question I never thought to be asking a woman who I wanted to make love to."

"And the answer from the woman who wants you to make love to her is an unequivocal yes," Kelly said.

Careful not to force her to move, he slid the shirt up and helped her lift her shoulders until he could get it off over her head. She wore a pale lace bra that did little to hide the peaking of her nipples, and to his delight, the clasp of it was in the front. She watched as he unhooked it, a smile breaking on her face at his sigh, at his dizzy pleasure as she guided both his palms to cup her.

"Christ, woman, I'm never going to make it long enough to enter you, when it's all I can do to keep from coming just from touching you like this."

"You'll manage," she reassured him. "We'll go slowly, and if you come, we'll rest and start again. Besides, we have all evening and all night, don't we? I can't imagine Cookie would let us starve if we don't make it down for dinner."

"Not much chance of that," he said. "And I did promise you a party."

She pulled his head down so that he could kiss and suck her breasts in turn. In his enthusiasm, he pulled nipple and areola into his mouth as deeply has he could, feeling her moans and sighs vibrating against his lips, feeling her swell to impossible heights against the rake and swirl of his tongue. Knowing that it was all in response to his touch made it even better.

"Are you wet?" he asked, pulling away just enough to speak.

"Why don't you find out?" She guided his hand down to the waistband of her jeans. When he struggled with the button, she opened it for him and helped him with the zipper, then, holding his gaze, she eased his hand inside the elastic of her underwear, down over her soft pubic curls, shifting her hips until her bottom was almost off the bed, until she gave a little cry of pain from the pressure on her ribs.

"Shh! Lie still. Let me do it," he said. With just a slight cupping of his hand and a stretching of his middle and index fingers, he found the swell of her, folds heavy and splayed, all ready for him, and it was his turn to gasp. "You're right, you're nothing like a pear. Jesus Kelly, you're so soft down there, and so warm." He caught his breath again as she arched up onto his fingers. "And so slippery."

"Mmm." Her voice was a little cat purr as she began to rock and grind against his stroking. "Your cock will be very happy for that. I know how big you are, Lex, and I'll need to be good and slippery if I'm going to accommodate you."

Then she gave a little jerk and a gasp, raked her teeth over her bottom lip and sighed. "I see you've just found the Tic Tac."

"That's a big fucking Tic Tac," he said, stroking the round wet pearl with his thumb, thrusting and scissoring, circling and probing, just the way she liked it, thrusting in deeply to bring her moisture up and around the swell of her, making her ready.

"The pear was nice," he said, "but I want to taste the real thing." He eased her jeans and panties down over her hips, peeled them off her legs and tossed them on the floor, all the while she writhed like she couldn't lie still.

"It won't be like the pear, Lex," she said. He thought he could see just a tiny bit of fear in her eyes, fear that he wouldn't like the taste of her, or the smell. He'd read enough about women's attitudes to oral sex to know that for some men it was an acquired taste, but for him it was a no-brainer. It was Kelly, it was the most intimate act of pleasure he could give her. He knew he would love it, even as the seashore scent of her tantalized his nostrils and made his mouth water the way the scent from Cookie's kitchen did when she baked trout. Only this was better, this was messy and slippery and so responsive to his touch as he buried his face in the depths of her. The salty sweetness of her dripped over his tongue and down his chin with his saliva and, she was right, he felt the tremors of her orgasm clench and release as she bucked against him, fingers curled tightly in his hair as he eased away just enough to see, just enough to watch the clench and release, the spasm and jerk of muscles darkened and wet with arousal, arousal that was because of him.

"Oh, dear God, Lex, I'm in heaven. I'm in fucking heaven," she gasped. Then she added around efforts to breathe, "Take your jeans off. I want to see your cock. I want to see your lust for me before you put it in me."

He sat up between her legs and wiped his face on his T-shirt. Then he wriggled out of his jeans in record time, his cock at full attention, saluting Kelly, delighted to be the focus of her desire.

"Come here," she said. "I want to return the favor." When he was at a loss, she motioned him up her body. "Straddle me, that's right. Now come closer, up above my chest so that all I have to do is open my mouth, and you can put your cock right in for me to taste and suck."

"I'm not sure that's a good idea," He gasped, holding his cock protectively.

"It's the best idea ever. Trust me, and if you come, well, don't be so naïve as to think this will be the only orgasm either of us will get tonight. I've had so many fantasies about you, Lex Valentine, and masturbated so many times with the thought of this moment, this time when you could touch me, when we could touch each other. Trust me, the night won't be anywhere near long enough to quench the fire."

So he did as she asked. Her words alone were practically enough to send him over the edge, but he was determined this time, his first time, he would make it good for both of them, and he would come inside her just like he'd dreamed about. That determination wavered sharply, though, the moment she took his cock deep in her throat and cupped his ass to pull him still deeper. It took every bit of control he had not to shoot his wad on the first stroke of her tongue along the underside of his shaft. He bit his lip hard and tasted blood. That was just enough of a distraction, albeit an accident, to give him the second he needed to regain control.

"Christ, Kelly! Holy God in heaven, that's...that's..." He forgot how to string words together in a sentence. He forgot how to speak at all other than the odd gasp, followed by an expletive or two. Then, as the haze of arousal parted just enough for him to take in the fullness of what was happening, he noticed that she was rocking and shifting her hips against the bed.

"You're ready for me, aren't you?" he managed.

"Way ready," she said, pulling away from his cock with a wet slurp. She helped him into a condom he'd fumbled from the bedside table then she curled her fingers in his hair, drew his face up to hers and kissed him. "I've been ready for you since the moment I first saw you, Lex Valentine, so don't keep me waiting any longer."

Careful to hold his weight on his elbows and off her injured ribs, he eased back into position, finding that she had beaten him there, holding herself open with one hand and guiding him home with the other. One small shifting of her hips and a little upward thrust from him, and he was in. Dear God, he was inside Kelly Blake! He was actually making love to her. With a little moan of pain that she dismissed with a shake of her head, she lifted her legs to circle his ribs, then it was all happening at once. They found each other's rhythm. The give of the mattress beneath them aided Kelly in her wounded condition, and it was a delicious stretch of time that couldn't have been more than a minute or two. They were both too close to the edge to linger. But it was the exclamation point at the end of the sentence, the reward waited for, the exquisite pleasure of pleasuring the one he loved. When she cried out, at first he thought he'd hurt her, but then he felt it. He felt the tremor and grip, tremor and grip of her body around his erection. He'd done that to her. Fucking hell! He'd made her come like that! And that was all it took to send him over the edge, as though he had totally succumbed to the seashore of her, drowning in wave after wave, spilling himself into her body. Dear God, he'd waited a lifetime for this, and nothing he'd ever fantasized could have prepared him for it. He came until he thought he'd pass out, but always he felt the tremor and grip of her around him, and he had done that for her, he had made her come with his body.

When at last they collapsed next to each other on the bed, gasping for oxygen that suddenly seemed scarce in the Sunrise suite, it felt like the whole world had shifted on its axis, and he supposed that was exactly what had happened. His life had certainly shifted. Careful not to hurt her, he eased Kelly into his arms, feeling the solid weight of her head against his chest, and the press of her heavy nipples against his ribs. This was the way he wanted to fall asleep and wake up for, oh, possibly the next fifty years or so.

\* \* \* \*

They both must have dozed. Kelly woke with him stroking her hair and the occasional kiss on the top of her head. "Did you sleep?" she asked.

"A bit. You did, I know. I've been watching you, making a list of all the ways I would touch you once you woke up."

She smiled and turned her face enough to kiss his nipple, resulting in a sharp inhalation of breath. "I have a list of my own for how I want to touch you," she said, "so don't go away." She eased herself up off the bed. "I have to pee. I'll be right back."

When she returned, he had pulled himself into a sitting position against the stack of pillows. Clearly, he was deep in thought. For a moment, she stood and just watched him, completely naked and completely at ease in his nakedness, nakedness she could seriously get used to seeing on a regular basis. "Penny for your thoughts," she said, settling herself with a careful grunt on the bed next to him.

He pulled her hand to his lips and kissed her ring finger, just above the sapphire he'd placed there only four days ago. "I was thinking, I like the way this ring looks on your finger, and I like the way you look in my bed. Do you think maybe we could consider fooling the press for a little bit longer?" He offered her a quirk of a smile. "Like maybe, I don't know, fifty years or so." Then a bright blush crawled up his face. "If you're okay with that."

She looked down at the ring and sighed. "Well, I really do like sapphires and I was thinking I'd hate like hell to have to give this little beauty back, and your bed." She gave it a little bounce. "To be honest, it's considerably more comfortable than mine. Then there's Cookie."

He nodded his agreement. "I pride myself on comfortable beds, and well, who wouldn't want to stick around at a place where the head cook moonlights for the Avengers? Of course," he added, "at some point, the press might catch on if we just…you know…stayed engaged for fifty years of so. They might wonder why such a long engagement."

"I see you what you mean," she said with a sage nod.

"We might want to consider, if this plan is to work, and we want to keep the press in the dark…you know…getting married at some point."

"Might do," she said. "I look good in white, or so Myrna tells me."

He felt like his smile would certainly split his face as he pulled her close. "I think we might have a plan then.

Agreed?"

"Agreed," she said. Then she straddled him, and it was much later before they talked about anything else.

* * * *

When she woke again, it was not quite dusk, and Lex was nowhere to be found. With unease rising in her chest, she dressed as quickly as she could under the circumstances, grabbed her stick and headed down the stairs. Dillon was just coming in from the drawing room. He offered her a knowing smile. "Lex is in the studio," he said. "I think Cookie just filled the cookie jar with snickerdoodles."

She thanked him and made her way along the garden path and out to the studio, which glowed with light from every window and the big garage door was open to let in the lovely summer evening.

She heard the chink, chink, chink of chisel against stone long before she entered his workspace. She followed the sound back into the main studio to find a corkboard full of sketches of her in different poses and Lex, stripped to the waist, as he usually was when he worked, chipping away. He smiled up at her when he saw her.

"Are you all right?" she asked.

"Never better," he said. "I had a dream." With the wave of a hand he, dismissed her look of concern. "Not a bad dream, a really good dream, an inspiration for the Cascadia Hospital sculpture. If it's okay, I'll have you do some poses later, but I had to get started. It felt right."

She looked at the rough sketch on the easel in front of him. It was of a woman standing a bit like Da Vinci's Vitruvian Man. One upturned palm held the earth above her head, while the other arm cradled an infant to her chest. "It's beautiful," she whispered. "And it's perfect."

He laid down his tools and slipped into the hoodie. "I suppose it's the future I have to look forward to now that the nightmares are gone, making love to my wife and having inspiring dreams that drive me from our bed to my studio in the middle of the night."

"Art's a harsh taskmaster," she said.

"Speaking of which, Myrna tells me your agent is after you to write some story about a haphephobic artist who's saved by the love of a good woman."

"Myrna told you that?"

"The woman sees all, knows all."

She told him the story that Alexander Valentine had inspired long before she'd actually met and fallen in love with the real Alexander Valentine, and he listened and nodded. "Well, I for one, think you should share Tom and Sharon's story with the world." He gave her a crook of a smile. "If you don't, Gale Ann Spaulding might just be tempted to."

"Ah, but hers would probably be a horror story," Kelly said.

"You two up for dinner or are you just going back to the bedroom?" Dillon appeared in the doorway with a broad smile on his face. "Enquiring minds want to know." Then he shrugged. "Actually, Cookie just wanted to know how many steaks to throw on the grill tonight. I told her, whether you joined us or not, that you two would probably be ravenous enough to eat half a cow."

They both nodded.

"It all depends upon what the future Mrs. Valentine wants to do," Lex said.

After a couple of well-disguised fish gasps that ended in a face-splitting smile, Dillon asked, "And just what exactly does the future Mrs. Valentine want to do?"

She squeezed Lex's hand and returned Dillon's smile with a twitch of mischief. "Well, what the future Mrs. Valentine wants to do will definitely be enhanced by a steak dinner in Cookie's kitchen." Then she narrowed her eyes at him. "What's for dessert?"

"Raspberry pavlova, I'm told."

"We'll be there," both Lex and Kelly said at the same time.

Dinner was not without a sense of celebration, especially once the news was out about their long-term plans to fool the press, though no one actually seemed too surprised by it. Kelly didn't miss the knowing look that passed between V and Dillon. She figured there had been some scheming between those two, but then she figured both she and Lex were pretty used to scheming friends by now, and as she thought of Myrna and Terry and the kids, whom she had broken the news to just before they came down to dinner, she decided she liked that just fine. She took Lex's hand under the table, and he gave her fingers a squeeze, lingering over the sapphire before guiding her palm to rest on his thigh. Sometimes, she decided, when scheming friends had your best interests at heart, the wise decision was just to stay out of the way and let them get on with it.

# More books from
# Totally Bound Publishing

*'No-one would understand that my submission empowered me, that I felt stronger kneeling at Gabriel's feet than I ever had standing at Paul's side.'*

He's determined to master her.
But she's no man's submissive.

SIERRA
CARTWRIGHT
INTERNATIONAL BESTSELLER

IMPULSE

SHOCK
WAVE

"Cartwright's writing binds you from the very beginning and
doesn't release its hold until well after the last page."
- Erin Noelle, USA Today Bestselling Author

*In a battle of wills, dominance, and submission, there can
only be one victor…*

MORE THAN SOMETHING

Something Old

ABIGAIL
GREY

She hasn't looked back to small town
life – or Matt Brannon – until now.

*Claire Wallace left town ten years ago. She hasn't looked back at small town life – or Matt Brannon – until now.*

Infatuation

NIRVANA

The secret she harbors threatens to tear them apart

Anise Storm

*Fate gives Hannah Brinkley a second chance with her one-
time infatuation until the secret she harbors threatens to
tear it all apart.*

# About the Author

K.D. Grace

Voted ETO Best Erotic Author of 2014, and a proud member of The Brit Babes, K D Grace believes Freud was right. In the end, it really IS all about sex, well sex and love. And nobody's happier about that than she is, otherwise, what would she write about?

When she's not writing, K D is veg gardening. When she's not gardening, she's walking. She walks her stories, and she's serious about it. She and her husband have walked Coast to Coast across England, along with several other long-distance routes. For her, inspiration is directly proportionate to how quickly she wears out a pair of walking boots. She also enjoys time at the gym, reading, watching the birds and anything that gets her outdoors. What she likes best, though, is writing a good tale.

K.D. Grace loves to hear from readers. You can find contact information, website details and an author profile page at https://www.totallybound.com/

Home of Erotic Romance